BOOK TWO
OF
THE HUMAN AGE

By

Bo

TH

Bo

MA

MONSTRE GAI

BY

WYNDHAM LEWIS

A Jupiter Book

LONDON
JOHN CALDER

FIRST PUBLISHED IN GREAT BRITAIN BY METHUEN & CO. LTD 1928
PUBLISHED AS A JUPITER BOOK 1965
BY JOHN CALDER (PUBLISHERS) LIMITED
18 BREWER STREET, LONDON, W. 1

SET IN BORGIS BASKERVILLE-ANTIQUA
AND PRINTED IN PÖSSNECK BY
»KARL-MARX-WERK«

CONTENTS

1. THIS IS NOT HEAVEN

I

THE WATERMAN was now only a shadow. At last he had gone behind the moonlight. He had passed through a veil of transparent steel. Out of the smoky grey of the waters he rose, lying outlined through the shining wall of the moon. This deaf one-dimensional nonentity it would not be possible to recall.

They were lonely specks; the blank-gated prodigious city was isolated by its riverine moat, and they had cast themselves away, and were committed to effect an entrance or to die. It was darkening rapidly. This was welcomed by Pullman: let the night come quickly and swallow them up and blot them out. These stairs, which must be twenty feet wide, were of the whitest marble; there was not enough shadow for a mouse to take cover upon this starlit expanse where he and Satters stuck up like a couple of misplaced scarecrows upon a field of virgin corn.

From the camp this had not looked so starkly exposed a place as it was. The fag-master, the master-spirit, had not foreseen that they would be two unhideable figures: it was difficult to discern any details from the other side of the water, but his plan was they should wait, in such concealing shadows as could be found, the arrival of the Bailiff and his cortège, slipping in at the end of the procession. But the Bailiff was behind time.

The coming of night would do very little good, it became obvious, because of the light of the stars. As night fell they became conscious of the dark pit of the lightyears exposed in front of them. They were awed and frightened as they shivered upon the giant stairs, rising to the Gates of the Magnetic City. The stars were larger and colder than on earth, the sky was a chillier and emptier depth. Pullman was terrified by these enormous glaring worlds and constellations, three times the size they were in the earthly night. In another respect they differed markedly. Instead of an attractive glitter, or, if they were small, a pretty twinkle, here they had this deadly glare. It was bluish, lending to Satters a corpselike pallor. Pullman

7

thought of his own less robust complexion with consternation. It must look frightful. It could even have a demoralizing effect upon his squire, who might interpret it as the pallor of fear.

There was something even more disturbing than their conspicuousness, and the inhospitable grandeur of the heavens; something which progressively claimed more and more their exclusive attention. The walls, it seemed, emitted a magnetic influence of some sort, which Pullman found it difficult to define, and which, it slowly dawned on them, held possibilities of a superlatively unpleasant kind.

The colossal mushroom-coloured walls, rising out of the water to almost a thousand feet, contained some repulsive agent. It was not heat, indeed there was no heat at all in the slight hostile vibration that was communicated. It was like a new impalpable film, or new atmosphere, into which they had unwittingly penetrated. It held them as it repelled them, like an existential element, neither cold nor warm, but subtly terrifying. The appalling attraction of the black chasm of the sky and this new insidious element, belonging to the gigantic walls, competed for a while for the mastery of their shrinking spines: but the nearer of these two influences in the end alone remained. Everything else faded out in the foreground.

Satters pressed himself up against Pullman, the large moist hand of the overgrown fag clutching piteously the arm of the elder, the arm of authority. "Pulley," he exploded in a ghastly purr, "I shall *die*, Pully, if I have to stand here much longer. I'm through, I really am. What is the matter with this place! It's not cold, is it, really? It's something worse than cold. It's horrible. I wish we had never left the camp. I'd give anything to be over there instead of here, the other side of the beastly water, with all the other chaps, in that awful foxhole of ours. Don't you wish you were, Pulley? Pulley! I feel I am a thousand miles away, it *is* a thousand miles away I believe." He pressed closer, panicking. "I feel just as if I *were* dead this time. I never felt like this before. Oh I do not wish to go through that gate, Pulley! D'you hear? I say, did you hear what I said?" He began to whimper like a frightened dog. He pressed nearer to Pullman. "I would throw myself into that water, if it were not ... if it were not for ... if it were not for ..."

"Exactly," Pullman said, whose feelings were nearer to Satters' than he would have liked to confess. But what was expected of the prefect successfully banished the sensations unbecoming in a senior. He glanced contemptuously at his quailing companion. "We are probably somewhere between the Pole Star and the Sun," he observed with detachment, not too easily achieved. "My spine feels as though it were going to melt. But I don't expect that it will."

The thought of Pullman melting like a man of wax, and of finding himself thenceforth alone, had so disintegrating an effect upon Satters that he clung desperately to that masterful being at his side. "I don't know what I shall do if your sp . . . sper . . . sper . . . spine . . ."

Pullman shook him off irritably. "Put your mind at rest. You will dissolve before I shall."

Satters' trembling limbs grew steadier, his thoughts began to run in less desperate channels. The sense of indestructibility which Pullman had managed to communicate had the desired effect.

Pullman braced himself, and did his best to remain erect, a model to the wilting Satters. He set his teeth, he clenched his hands. But the atmospheric strangeness which was undermining him, rapidly made it impossible for him to keep up appearances. It was not long before he lowered himself into a sitting position. Satters, he found, had already succumbed: he lay at full length upon one of the huge stairs.

"This is awful," Satters greeted Pullman dully. "I feel like nothing on earth. Do you? I say, where have we got to?"

Pullman said nothing. He sat beside his fag, gazing ahead, his forearms clasped around his knees, his stick at his side. He did not sit for long like this. He too lay down below Satters, feeling colder and colder every minute, but quite unable to get to his feet and stamp about to improve his circulation.

Pullman did not realize he had fallen asleep. His eyes opened, he looked up. To his horrified amazement he found that the Bailiff was gazing down into his face with great geniality.

"Are you able to rise?" the magistrate asked.

It was an immense effort to lift himself up to his feet.

"What is your name?" inquired the Bailiff gently, holding out a hand to steady him.

"Pullman," said he, passing his hand over his face.

"It's very disagreeable out here. You will find it warmer inside," the Bailiff smiled. "I don't know for whose benefit they magnetise these walls I'm sure. Perhaps they have me in mind–I often wonder! However, fall in behind my men, Pullman. See if you can persuade that friend of yours to get to his feet. If he is too weak, I will get somebody to carry him in. You will feel much better, Pullman, as soon as you are inside the Gates." The Bailiff nodded and smiled as he returned to his litter.

Pullman succeeded in getting Satters into a standing position, and like two drunken men they staggered through the Gates. The Gates met again behind them with an impressive noiselessness. They entered a sort of tunnel, extending for a distance of fifty yards. As they were so unsteady in the darkness they were apt to hurtle against those ahead of them, who retaliated with savage blows. The structure beneath which they were passing shook with the heavy vibrations of the massive elevator being operated overhead.

At last they stepped out into the Magnetic City, or, it would be more true to say, rocked and staggered out. Pullman's first reactions were simultaneously physiological and psychical. There was the rushing of blood down his arteries, and a tremendously violent romantic disillusion. The splendours of the imagination crashed! Where was the unearthly spectacle he had expected to see? They found themselves in no fairy scene, such as rises in the "afterworld" section of the cloudy crypts of the imagination. They did not find themselves among the radiant structures of solid gold or beneath the ambrosial foliage of glittering trees of the pipe-dream-world paradise. It was not at all like that. It was indeed the reverse; and as though in additional mockery their bodies jumped and exploded as if a djin had got into them. Underfoot was the slovenly dust of a natural city. Behind them, and above them, the cyclopean battlements rose into the sky. The dimensions of what *enclosed* this place at least were unreal, were enormous. But that was the extent of the departure from the norm. Crawling up those dizzily-mounting walls were iron ladders of the kind used in compliance with the safety requirements, for escape in case of fire. Where they stood, on issuing from the

10

tunnel, was a herbless level earth, of parade-ground type (groups of uniformed men stood near the structure which was built over the tunnel, ascending, in steeply diminishing perspective, to the summit of the battlements). There were other signs of the presence of the military, and there was a military flatness and emptiness. A hundred yards away were the bare sides of modern city blocks, up which zigzagged iron ladders resembling those affixed to the battlements.

Now there was an interval, while the Bailiff's patchwork militia was paraded for the march through the city. The companies were sorting themselves out; ten trumpets and ten drums took up their position at the head of the column. Next to them came the negro band, and after that the hundred-and-fifty-strong company of so-called Gladiators. In the wake of this massive body of men came the Bailiff in his litter, and, after him, about one hundred and fifty haiduks and nubians, as also the executioner and his assistants. These were followed by a miscellaneous body of various composition. Finally, a carefully picked nilotic troop, daintily garmented and heavily armed. As a most inelegant bedraggled appendage came Pullman and Satters.

The military master-at-arms, who was a glorified sergeant-major, moved, fiery-eyed, from section to section of his armament. Reaching the negro band he searched for a blemish in the gleaming instruments, next checked the sparkling silver buttons: he examined the fingernails on the track of dirt, and saw to it that the whiteness of the teeth took full advantage of the blackness of the face. He treated the fierce gladiators as though they had been cut-purses, concealing something in their massive cuffs or hiding spoils in their holsters. Shouting at them all the time, he flung them about, and screamed at any spot he discovered on their tunics, or the webbing employed for small-arms. As to the haiduks, no Turk who had caught one could have kid-gloved him less.

The uses of the various classes of warriors would be plain to anyone who had seen him at work. The Gladiators were the personal bodyguard, never used for policing the appellants nor in executions. The Bailiff's savagery was less apparent when entrusted to savages.

These four or five hundred armed men were exquisitely

11

drilled, and, for the rest, spotless. The parade preened itself in outdated military splendour. Each group had a pennon or standard. The Bailiff's personal standard was the most spectacular.

It was borne before his litter, now held in readiness by two leather-aproned bearers. Practically flat, displayed like a tapestry, it was brilliantly coloured, in pale green and dark cinnamon. There were two main features in the design; on the right was the Mundane Egg–this in dazzling white; a Serpent's head, the neck inflated and shaped like a hood, stood darkly beside it upon the green background; all the design, except for the egg and figures, was in dark cinnamon. Then the body of the serpent was rigid, steeply diagonal, and it carried on its back a diminutive E (EL, one of the ten names of God). In almost imperceptible tracery, upon the silver-white of the Mundane Egg, appeared an orphic inscription. On the opposite side were the letters

$$IX\Theta Y\Sigma$$

meaning fish; "The great Fish" was a manner of referring to Jesus Christ. And these letters were enclosed in an oval, pointed at one end, representing a fish, a small circle for the eye standing not far from the pointed extremity. This symbolic consociation duplicated the forms of the ovoid fish and the cosmogonic Egg. Lastly the number 666 was found near the summit of the banner, between the two groups of symbols.

Strolling forward, mainly to stretch his legs, Pullman's attention was attracted by the banner. The Serpent's head in conjunction with the Egg presented no difficulty, but the significance of 666, though it had a familiar sound, baffled him. He paused a moment, his eyes fixed upon the mysterious number, when he became conscious of someone behind the curtains of the litter. Not without some slight misgiving he realized that the Bailiff was within, the curtains drawn. The magistrate exposed his square-nosed smile, as he thrust a hooked finger of informal summons through the opening of the curtains. Pullman approached, his face unmoved. He said, "I did not see you, sir!"

"Do you like my pretty banner?" The Bailiff's voice was insinuatingly dulcet.

"Very much, sir. It is a beautiful banner. Could you tell me the significance of the number 666? Or is that impertinently inquisitive?"

"Noo ... o ... Oh!" sang the magistrate archly. "I have a note of that somewhere. Come and see me at my residence. Let me write down your name—how could I have forgotten it!"

"James Pullman." Pullman's name was written down, and just then an imperious blast was sounded. Pullman bowed and went back to the position allotted him.

"You left me here!" Satters grumbled, with the face of someone with a toothache which stopped him from feeling anything else as much as otherwise he would.

An even louder blast of the trumpet sounded. The parade already faced at right angles, pointing in the direction of its march: so there were no words of command, except what the master-at-arms now bellowed. "Parade–Parade! "Shun. Quick ... March!" Stamping like the Foot-guards do, the parade got in motion.

Trumpets and drums furiously blown and beaten, the Bailiff aloft in his litter, the negro bandsmen poising the mouths of enormous silver instruments above their heads, and behind these tallboys a succession of tubes of blazing silver, each watched over by a shining ebony face—all the barbaric bombast of the Bailiff's parade headed up a cheerless, twentieth-century side-street, stupefied by the customary torpor of that hour of the day.

The Bailiff with his square nose and his apple for a chin, the trumpeters, all the strutters and swaggerers, passed the carpet-slippers of a seated man, exposed to the evening street, relaxed within a doorway, the white smoke of his pipe curling around the bold white cliffs of his hair; passed a black cat seated upon a window-sill, its eyes fixed in a green trance, the membranes of its ears only recording cat-sounds, and in any case not functioning just then; passed a pressing-and-cleaning outfit, the last pair of trousers of the day going into the steaming press. So the white tobacco-smoke continued to curl against the snowy hair, and the old man's smoky eyes saw nothing, the cat continued immobile and unresponsive as a monument, and the steam issuing from the ultimate pair of trousers put a veil over the window, the other side of which passed the glittering procession.

13

In spite of the lack of response, the blast and percussion continued to assault this quiet, unimportant street. Pullman and Satters, with a rickety swagger, followed in the wake of the haughtily-mincing, bare-footed rear-guard.

Meanwhile, the bodies of both Satters and Pullman were subject to internal disturbances of some violence. Satters' face was twisted into the mask of a baby afflicted with wind, the distended eyes a big angry question-mark. But he goose-stepped crazily along nevertheless–he seemed to have grown physically competent in spite of his grimace. But Pullman was anything but immune. None of his muscular and glandular prickings, the wrenching of his innards, qualified for agonised reportage on his face; but he had put the amazed question to himself, "What for Pete's sake is all this?" Then a sensation, originating in the bladder, gave him a clue: for neither the bladder nor intestines had played any part in his life in the camp. He had not made water since his death on earth. Satters whispered, hoarse and urgent, "I must find a urinal!"

Like the personnel of a circus parading a mediterranean city, the Bailiff's big drums, thudding like artillery, wheeled into a grandiose boulevard.

"Is this Heaven?" Pullman at last blankly inquired of the air. It reminded him of Barcelona. This, like the Rambla, was a tree-lined avenue with huge pavements, across which cafés thrust hundreds of tables and chairs, to the edge of the gutter. Thousands of people overflowed the café terraces. Pullman's reaction to this scene, so unexpectedly the reverse of what the imagination demanded, was an explosion of hysterical mirth.

"It's not a laughing matter!" protested Satters angrily. "I can't hold out much longer. I shall just make use of the nearest tree, like an little dog!"

"I was not laughing at *that*, silly," said Pullman contemptuously.

Several thousand *chapeaux melons* must have been manufactured in a celestial factory, Pullman reasoned; for that number now sat upon as many heads of a massive swarm of café-customers. A mild steady roar came up from this compact collection of nonentities, discharging millions of vocables per minute under their *chapeaux melons*.

As they began to pass the lines of tables nearest the road,

14

faces came into view. They were the faces of nonentities; this humanity was alarmingly sub-normal, all pig-eye or owlish vacuity. Was this a population of idiots–astonishingly well-dressed; as noticeably so as the contemporary English are seedy or "utility" clad? Yet this selective mediocrity laughed abnormally, and its voice was high. And then Pullman saw a freckled face, with its mouth open and its eyes fixed upon him. The man was holding a siphon aloft. He pulled the trigger, and a parabola of soda-water ascended into the air, and fell upon the side of Satters' neck, beneath the ear. It had been at Satters that the siphoneer had been looking. The effervescent liquid rushed down, inside and outside of his shirt collar.

Satters did not regard this as funny, either. His hands tearing at his neck, he stamped up and down, roaring at the siphoneer, "You stupid cad! I'm half a mind to come and wring your bloody neck! If you don't take that grin off your face I'll knock your teeth down your throat for you! Silly fool!"

But the cortège had moved on, and Pullman took his young friend by the arm and led him towards a vacant table at a respectful distance from that of the man with the siphon. About to sit down, Pullman remembered that they had no money.

A man who was seated at the next table, at this juncture rose and raised his hat, addressing Pullman. "I witnessed your arrival, I saw the siphon episode," with a smile. "My name is Mannock," the stranger said. "You have just arrived, I think, from the camp outside the city. May I offer you both a drink. to start with: you must be entirely without money."

But Satters broke in excitedly: "I say, I just can't wait any longer!" He was stamping about, with his hands in his trousers pockets. "I know what is the matter." exclaimed Mr Mannock. "Come along with me."

He led them briskly into the café, up to a door upon which they read the familiar word GENTLEMEN. They followed him in, and found themselves in a sumptuous place of gentlemanly retirement, fortunately empty at the moment. After the more urgent exercises the two newcomers plunged their faces in warm water, next washed their mud-caked hands, and Pullman, with one of the lavatory combs, imparted to his hair the backward wave which most became him. Outside Mannock waited for them. "I should have said," announced Pullman, "that my young friend's name is Satterthwaite, and I am James Pullman."

There was a certain high condescension in James Pullman's manner which did not escape Mannock. That gentleman decided that the clue to it was probably to be found in the beard Pullman wore, but refrained from further speculation for the present.

They returned to the table, where Mannock ordered for them a mysterious drink. It was strangely delicious. It was unlike anything they had ever tasted.

"There is no alcohol here," he told them, "but I assure you you will not need it. They say that New York is stimulating, don't they. Well, this is often ten times more so. A cup of coffee, for instance, causes you to feel quite unnaturally stimulated."

When they had sat there for a short while, Mannock informed them that he lived not far away. "Unless you have a date for dinner with the Bailiff, will you dine with me? You do not have to feel embarrassed here about money, by the way. You are given—it is quite automatic—the wherewithal to live. It is not an equalitarian institution," he smiled. "Except for that fact, you ask for what you want and they give it to you. I mean a man who was a crossing sweep on earth will not get so big a bundle of notes as you will, or as I do."

Pullman accepted with alacrity the invitation to dinner. They shortly left the café and started walking up a street running at right angles to the boulevard, and along the side of the café. Almost at once Pullman turned to Mannock and asked him politely, "Is this Heaven?"

"No, this is not Heaven," was Mannock's toneless rejoinder.

"If it is not Heaven what is it?"

Somewhat embarrassed, after hesitating, Mannock replied. "The usual question! It is not easy to answer that question, and I suggest we wait a little before tackling it."

"I have another question to ask," announced Pullman. "What is the matter with all the people here? Are all the people in that café imbeciles? And if so, why?"

Mannock laughed obstreperously. "Yes, yes, they are all nit-wits—their I.Q. level is so low that it may be said not to exist. But they get through life all right, which is mainly because

16

they all, whether young or old (and most of them were young when they started), receive a pension–adequate to keep them at that café all day. Some of them may have been a little intelligent say thirty years ago–though I doubt it–but thirty years at that café . . ."

"I see . . . or rather I don't see, but it doesn't matter." Pullman showed by his expression that, without being satisfied, he understood that his query had been answered.

"You will soon know all that it is good for you to know," Mannock cryptically remarked.

They met with several specimens of that mankind whose weapon was soda-water, and whose faces were like the silly saints in the iconography of a Swabian half-wit. All proudly wore hats: for they had belonged to a hatless generation when alive, so impoverished by two cataclysms that even the tweed cap had to be foregone. The first figure, open-mouthed, blandly grinning, as though welcoming any nonsense, ambled past in newly-tailored clothes. Next came two figures, beautifully hatted (a maroon-pink), ties like a Japanese battle in a stylistic print: they chattered to one another about the socks in noughts and crosses of the ingenious Henry. They frowned and grinned, their hollow noses wagging, and always the black hole of the mouth. Lastly came three, who had not the vigour to think about a sock. Their mouths hung open beneath stupidly smiling eyes, their skins like vellum, their teeth like a mummy's, they encouraged one another to laugh–for if you cannot think you can always laugh–at the stars. They seemed to believe that these were bubbles of light, and that they might at any moment burst. Pullman would have said that they were showing off for the benefit of the strangers, but they seemed too absorbed in themselves to be doing that: their eyes, also, looked aloof and demented. Something that struck one about all these people was that their faces were youthful. They were such as a young man would get if he had been young for a very long time, until the skin had come to look like parchment. Pullman found it difficult to decide whether these people were young or old. But he supposed it was the former. A curious circumstance was that the face of their cicerone, who seemed a man of fifty, was natural and fresh, though possessing no colour.

"Vacuous as London is," Pullman observed, "it does not manufacture a citizenry so mentally void as you do."

Their guide received this with a laugh so harsh and troubled that Satters was visited with an icy touch of gooseflesh, and Pullman glanced sideways inquiringly. Were these skeletons in somebody's cupboard?—Was Mannock responsible for this lunacy? Mannock's voice was as uneasy as his laugh had been, and all he said was, "We are not all like that."

The street in which Mannock lived was named Habakkuk, and was distant five or was it six city blocks from the boulevard. It was eminently urbane and inviting: it had been built for people of the social tastes and economic competence of the gentleman who was acting as their shepherd. It still looked suave and respectable; but Pullman was unable to rid himself of an unpleasant sensation, as he reflected that most of those three or four ambling figures dotted up and down Habakkuk werde idiotic if not idiots, thought the stars would burst, and had a necktie reproducing the visual excitements of a samurai battle. It did not make him any happier to notice, in the middle of the road, nestling between the cobbles, a cluster of violets peaceably growing. The almost total absence of traffic was somehow not very cheering. The coming and going of commercial life would have been preferable to this stagnation and isolation.

No. 55 had a *porte-cochère*, like so many of the houses in these trafficless streets. Mannock led the way, turned to the right, and, with an unexpected agility, mounted to the first floor. He turned his key in the lock, calling out to his Greek house-boy as he went into the hall; Pullman felt relieved, for what he now designated the normal was manifest. Evidently their guide was *not* as others were in this city. What a valuable friend this was to have made under the circumstances.... He noted, too, that it was a very large and handsome apartment. How did this very superior, sensible Englishman come to be living in such a way, and in such a neighbourhood? This was a normal human being, but hemmed in by what they had seen.

"I have two guests for dinner, Platon." A gritty voice was heard somewhere within, in guttural response. "A young Greek looks after me. He was batman to a friend of mine. Odd, is it not!"

18

Neither Pullman nor Satters said a great deal: they listened, and adjusted themselves, marvelling at what they found. But at last, as they were all seated comfortably in Mannock's rather impressively large living-room, Pullman observed, "Much that is here is very strange, we know; but making allowances for that, life in this city does in fact reproduce life-on-earth as near as damn it; does it not?"

"That," Mannock answered, "is the idea, with several very important modifications."

"Yes, of course," rejoined the attentive Pullman. "Of course."

"Which," Mannock added, "really makes all the difference."

Pullman and Mannock looked at one another, as if hesitating to make the next remark. Then at last the former spoke.

"Are these differences changes for the better?"

"That," Mannock answered, "is a question each man must answer for himself. The central fact is that time does not exist here. Or it exists in a kind of unprogressive way, it halts one at one's earthly self, at some specific date. I have been here twenty years, for instance. But, if I look at myself in the mirror, I am quite unchanged. I have exactly the same number of grey hairs that I had twenty years ago. This is a little disconcerting. I am just as active as I was twenty years ago." He paused. "There is a further circumstance it is necessary to stress. When I died ... on earth ... I was older than I am now."

There was a silence. Then Satters spoke in a hushed, automatic voice. "On earth, when I died, I was ... I was ... well, an old man."

Pullman laughed, a brief, dry laugh. "I seem to recall," he said, "to speak of myself, that I was about sixty-five years old when I died. I felt, remember, about the age I appear to be now. It is very queer, is it not?"

Satters shuddered, then burst into tears.

"No queerer than life," said Mannock. "But no less queer." He and Pullman laughed, but Satters continued sobbing.

They all three sat silent for a while. Pullman was digesting what he had heard. But there were so many other questions which now crowded into his mind that he thought he had better do no more catechising for the moment.

19

"Let me find out about dinner," said Mannock rising, and he left the room.

Satters stretched, then said, leaning over towards his friend, in a confidential voice: "Pulley, this is a rum go, isn't it? I am so glad we are together ... I mean that you are here. It is all so strange." He stopped, massaging his face, as if to make sure of its fleshly reality. He even pulled his heavy loose red lips out a few inches, and released them as if they had been indiarubber. "What is the rummiest thing about this place is that it is so ... so ...."

"So like all other places," Pullman suggested: "you are thinking of the *cabinet de toilette?* I mean the washing and urinating place in the café."

"Yes, Pulley! You feel that too, do you, Pulley?"

"Oh yes. It is much more frigtenning than if it were ... if there had been no lavatory in the café, if people did not function as we function. That *Gentlemen's* in the café was so welcome, so tremendously welcome, that one forgot to say to oneself *'Where am I? What is this doing here?'* "

Satters sprang up, saying in a stage whisper, "I say, do you suppose he has a can here?" He began walking about. Pullman got to his feet, but at that moment Mannock returned. "My young friend would like ..." Pullman began.

"Oh yes. Come along, I'll show you," and Mannock led Satters through a bathroom to a most desirable water-closet.

"Thanks awfully," Satters gushed.

Mannock went back to his other guest with a smile of understanding. "The very old, and the very young, suffer from the same disability ..." he observed.

"Satters was my fag at School," Pullman told him. "And it seems that he remains a fag now."

Mannock nodded. "That is so," he said. "It is his rôle. I fear, to be a schoolboy. If he is still here in a thousand years he will still be a big plump fag, inclined to be incontinent." They laughed. There were heavy steps outside. The door opened, and Satters stamped back into the room, smiling bashfully—with a deliberate, rather dirty bashfulness.

"I was going to say," Mannock explained, "there is plenty to eat, happily."

The guests demonstrated gratitude simultaneously. Satters

with the obstreperousness of hearty youth, Pullman with restraint.

When they sat down at the dinner-table Mannock said grace, which put a damper on Satters who was ravenous, and had answered the call to dinner making no secret of the fact, and exclaiming, "Our first meal for months, what, Pulley?"

The soup was a super minestrone, and a second helping was not declined by Satters. "You can obtain plenty of fresh vegetables I see." Pullman remarked.

"All we want. Most people, to begin with, complain that there is no meat."

"What, no meat!" Consternation was soon replaced in Satters' face by another expression. "Oh I see. You are a vegetarian, sir. Are there many vegetarians here?"

"All are vegetarians, perforce. There is no meat to be had. But unless you are inveterately carnivorous, you will soon forget that."

The next course was *Mushrooms à la Grecque,* combined with auberbines so elaborately flavoured that even Satters was satisfied.

"No, there is no meat, no women, no alcohol, no telephones (except public ones in the street), practically no taxi-cabs, and so on," Mannock went on. "There is a good deal of homosexuality. And, as I have said, the air is like champagne! It might be worse. It might be very much worse."

Satters appeared to have cheered up, and Pullman wore a less preoccupied look. "It sounds like life on the Falkland Islands or in Admiralty Bay, if you added a mirage of Zurich or Barcelona. I shall not complain," he observed smiling, "if I can only get some money."

"You will be in possession of that tomorrow morning. I will accompany you to the bank." Mannock held up a finger. "The profit motive is another absentee. There are those financial restraints, of an absolute kind. None that disturb *me*. But if I were a financial wizard I should be very miserable in this place. I should ask scornfully, 'Is this Heaven?'"

"But it is not Heaven, is it?" Pullman inquired. "I apologise for returning to that point!"

A strange expression came into Mannock's face. "No, as I

said before, this is not Heaven. The set-up here is as follows—and this is to simplify very much indeed: if you think of this as a Sultanate, social life centring in the Palace, and around the person of the Sultan, you would be near the mark. The Sultan is called the Padishah. This, the linchpin of everything, is a splendid human being (we may think of him as that), utterly involved with our spatial and temporal system. He shares our mortality, up to a point. He is supernatural, endowed with magical powers of the most enormous kind. The Padishah does not know how long he has been alive.—'Far too long!' he laughs. Anyway several thousand years. He has the aspect of a young man of thirty. We know nothing for certain, but he is generally assumed, though not divine, to belong to the divine order. He discourages very firmly anything venerational. Only God should be venerated, he tells you. I have heard him say that there is not so much vereration in the world that any can be spared from the service of the Deity."

This account of things greatly surprised Pullman. This supernatural potentate aroused his coriosity. "What an extraordinary being!" he exclaimed. "How do you happen to come to now all this?" he added sillily.

"Oh, if you live long enough in a city, down on earth you know, you find out all about it. It is the same here."

After dinner they moved back into the living-room.

Satters having been put on his road to the watercloset once more (an event which invariably produced the same atmosphere of grown-up geniality), Pullman said, "I am all at sea, and, I must confess, profoundly alarmed."

Mannock smiled with sympathetic condescension, but with a tinge of displeasure, Pullman thought.

"Everything to do with human life, is, was, and always will be a little terrifying," he observed. "But I do not think that there is anything here to alarm anybody, more than he had reason to be alarmed by earthly existence."

"I imagine you have got quite used to finding the streets full of imbeciles. You seem to accept what you cannot alter: I must, I suppose, wait until I know more."

"Yes," Mannock agreed.

At this point there was the sound of feet outside, and a deep voice, followed by the entrance of a tall figure, and, Pullman felt, one apt to instil uneasiness in those about it. This new-comer represented one of the combinations of the rugged and the intellectual which makes other men feel that they must be on guard. Thinning hair, a bulging forehead, a voice organ toned, a large intelligent eye, an obvious indifference to details of toilet, plus six foot and evidence of bones which were raw and large: what but discomfort can come of such a combination?

"This is John Rigate," Pullman was told: and he got ready to be badly bored—noisily, muscularly, aggressively bored. But although as opinionated as a rhinoceros, Rigate did not produce the effect anticipated.

"Pullman has just arrived. We were engaged in discussing Third City. Pullman has confessed to some alarm. We were, as you have seen, in troubled waters."

Rigate gave a frosty, sceptical laugh.

"Let me give you the low-down," he told Pullman. "There is every reason for alarm. You are in a degenerate, chaotic outpost of Heaven. The ostensible ruler, the Padishah, is a supernatural being of great charm, but devoid of the slightest trace of gumption. If some selection were exercised at the camp in passing in the applicants, things might rub along all right. It is very difficult for men to live without working. But the planning of life here is nonsensical from beginning to end. Stupidest of all is *immortality*, or—how can I describe it—the age-business. I can quite see that they do not wish to reproduce here all the mechanism of growing old, of demise, of coffins or cemeteries, and so on. But we none of us stop here terribly long. There is no man in the city who has been here beyond the Tudors. What happens to us after this? Not that anyone much cares. The entire show is one great farce. It is far sillier even than life on earth—for at least that was centred upon the mechanical purpose of perpetuating the species. Someone or something seemed crazily set upon *that* happening. There is no *entêtement* of that kind here. Provided with money by the State, we exist in suspended animation, sexless, vegetarian, and dry, permanently about forty-six. If you can see any sense in it, I can't."

"Do we die?" asked Pullman succinctly.

"No," Rigate shook his head. "No death is admitted in

Third City. No man can die here. But this is one of the most extraordinary things about our life here. If a man is crushed by a lorry, or in some other way practically annihilated, he does not die. He is still, however ambiguously, alive. There are few families who have not one or more mortal remains: some human wreck, incapable of occupying any position in social life, or indeed in physical life of any kind. They keep them in some cupboard or drawer; they feed them on a little bread and milk. Some they can converse with, but mostly these creatures are too lifeless for that. They are the terrible victims of this superstition–leading a bedpan life hidden from men. They often create a stink in some small flat, which is recognised by all visitors."

Pullman, with amazed eyes, gazed at his host, who buried his face in his hands. Not long after this, Pullman discovered that Mannock had a secret drawer of this kind. Aware of this, Rigate cast a blackmailing eye in the direction of Mannock.

"You make an excellent guide, sir, to this evidently controversial existence," Pullman said. "Have you any theory as to how all this has come about? It is too irrational to be deliberate. Was not this city intended to be something else?"

Rigate moved his uncouth body in a spasm of restraint, and did not answer. Mannock replied. "Rigate thinks," he said, "this is an outpost of celestial paradise, in charge of a great angel (the Padishah). A beautiful, ineffectual angel, he would say."

"I see," said Pullman.

"It is," Rigate intervened, "the decay of an at one time more sensible system; that is all I can suppose. Perhaps this was a place where dubious Christians were tried out, and subsequently either handed over to the Fiend, or promoted to a more select place. As it is, what are those other cities? Is City One a city of the saints? But *this* magnetised metropolis has obviously lost its rationale. We still have an enigmatic night-sky with its bogus moon–though what in the first instance was the purpose of this deceit heaven knows, with its harsh light as different as possible from the earthly moon–we still have all that."

There was a considerable silence after this. Pullman felt how unnatural it was for men, for Englishmen, without a pipe or something, to remain silent and relatively immobile. There was something sinister about it.

"What is your view, Mannock?" Pullman almost shouted.

"You won't get anything out of *him*," Rigate laughed, a cold blast. "He is in the confidence of the Padishah."

Pullman looked over towards Mannock, whose face wore an enigmatic smile. It was clear, Pullman reflected, that Mannock tended to encourage the belief that he had access to information denied to ordinary citizens; that he had a pipe-line to the Palace.

"I was at the Bailiff's tonight," Rigate suddenly announced.

Mannock looked up quickly, not very pleased, it was evident. "Again? What on earth for?" he asked.

"Oh, you know why. To get a glass or two of whisky. And I have a piece of news, of supernatural origin too. Lucifer is planning an all-out attack upon this effete institution. At the head of all his flies and vermin, and with the help of a huge fifth column within the Gates. There is a lot of brash bragging from Hades, as usual. The old Devil boasts that he will capture the Padishah, and confine him among the fulgurous mountains of Hell, where he will be crawled over by obscene reptiles and be raped by fearful serpent-women."

There was another rather painful silence, as it seemed to Pullman. In the middle of it there was the sound of porcine snores, ending in an abrupt snort. Satters had fallen asleep shortly after Rigate's entrance. Mannock had given the snorer a kick, and was obviously getting cross, and he now took Rigate to task.

"Why do you repeat these threats, Rigate? They spread these rumours as a matter of routine. Flies do not take cities."

"That is true, but the Master of Hell has enormous insects the size of this house."

"They would be blown away. And," barked Mannock, "if you don't think the best-armed police *I* personally have ever seen is not capable of discouraging our Fifth Column . . .!"

After a pause, Rigate remarked, "I repeated that rumour because it was especially circumstantial, and the devil who told me believed it to be true."

Mannock appeared to have forgotten Pullman's presence.

His face expressed frustration and annoyance, in equal measure. He was sourly scrutinising the countenance of this old friend, as if he had to be reconsidered as an intimate.

"In the event of such an attack as you report to be imminent, upon whose side would *you* be?" he asked Rigate harshly.

"Don't be childish," Rigate barked brightly, "I am of course a great adherent of Old Nick, and long for him to come and turn this dull dump of a camp into a proper Hell. That stands to reason doesn't it?"

"I just thought I would ask you."

"But I," Rigate complained, "am in no one's confidence. I am given no opportunity of enrolling myself in the defence of the city. No one informs me what is the philosophy of the city, in contrast to the well-known tenets of Satan: they have never been stated. Everything is taken for granted. No, we are consulted about nothing. Our co-operation, our participation is not solicited. We are treated like packages."

Mannock yawned. "It is very high-handed of the Padishah not to consult you, Rigate . . ."

Rigate gave an earthquake of a laugh as he rose preparatory to departure. "Mannock and I do not see eye to eye regarding the supernatural autocrat," he told Pullman. "I want too much, I expect. I am a *rentier*. I do not have to work for my living. What more should I want?"

When he had gone, Mannock remarked, "Rigate persists in treating this place as an Anglo-Saxon commonwealth. Also, he listens to the propaganda he hears at the Bailiff's."

"I see." Pullman did not see, but everyone seemed to suppose here that you ought to know if you didn't. But what had interested Pullman was Rigate's theory that they had somehow found their way, posthumously, into a decayed sub-celestial system, on the eve of destruction by infernal agency. What this *meant* he could not imagine. The more he listened to these people the more puzzled he became. He thought of the scene outside the city gates, when he and Satters were alone with the implacable, starry face of these regions of the universe. Here inside, surrounded by man again, their perspective was unreal, was falsely human. These were unearthly regions, and their position a truly fearful one.

Pullman looked over towards his host and smiled. "My ex-fag appears to be exhausted. I am sorry he made that frightful noise."

"Oh that's all right . . ." Mannock seemed a little preoccupied.

"I think we had better both go to bed, for I feel a little tired myself." Pullman stretched and got to his feet. Mannock led him into a large room in which there were two comfortable beds. "Is this all right?" he asked. "I have not two single rooms, I am sorry to say." But Pullman begged him not to think of anything of that sort—that this was far more than adequate and they were very lucky to have chanced upon so hospitable a person as himself.

II

THE ACTUAL HOUR of Pullman's disappearance was ten minutes after they had left the breakfast table. And it was a few minutes later that his host made an extraordinary discovery. He had gone to one of the livingroom windows to open it, when, looking out into the street, he saw Pullman, and an attractive-looking dark young man was approaching him raising his hat. Pullman stopped, and he and the young man stood there talking some minutes. They walked away together. Frowning, Mannock watched them turning the corner, deep in conversation, and move rapidly out of sight. Mr Mannock was not a man who talked to himself, but to frown or to smile when alone he considered allowable; this was not an infringement of the law that only the presence of another human being made it permissible to speak, to gesticulate, to laugh, or to cry. But he was really very angry. This man had evidently been deceiving him, though exactly what was going on, and how Pullman's presence at this address had come to be known in this way, he could not guess. He went back and sat down, beginning a review of recent events, of his encounter yesterday, at the café, with these two obvious newcomers. The longer he pondered on these circumstances, the more mystified he became. And then Satters came into the room, carefully shutting the door, a furtive smirk on his face–Mannock knew where *he* had been.

"Satterthwaite, do you know anything about Pullman's movements?" These words appeared to Satters threatening, as well as impertinent.

"No. Do you?" Satters' face was that of a lower fifth protester and determined resister to rotten caddish authoritarian highhandedness. Seeing the face of this glowering baby, Mannock got up and left the room. He would wait till Pullman's return. It was with him this matter must be sifted.

Pullman was away about twenty or twenty-five minutes. Mannock heard his name called, and with nausea, and that agitation which preludes to action usually produced, he went towards the living-room, attempting to compose his face. Pullman was so calm that it made the other's heart throb. "So you are back?" he almost panted. Pullman smiled indulgently–the politest of his responses to Satters, when that young gentleman was tiresome. He assumed that his touchy host had resented his "slipping away".

"I must apologise," he said easily, "for stealing away for a few minutes. The fact is, I felt an 'urge', as they say in journalistic fiction, to have a lightning tour of the district and check my impressions of the inhabitants."

"I see," Mannock responded, "all by yourself, when your impressions would be unimpaired by a companion's comment."

"That was the idea," Pullman agreed.

"Why in that case did you require to have with you on your lightning tour a youthful friend–in a light-brown coloured suit . . ."

Not a very noisy, but a sharp and arresting laugh cut Mannock short.

"Well, well, well, is *that* it now! You had some slight excuse for hurt feelings at my surreptitious sortie, but you had none, my dear Mannock, as regards the young man–in the light-brown suit! That was an impromptu element of my lightning tour. I have not the least idea who that young gentleman is. Here is his name, a Mister Sentoryen, and his address." Pullman took out of his pocket a card and handed it to Mannock. "This is what he gave me when we parted . . . I have not the remotest idea who this young fellow is. Perhaps you can enlighten me."

Mannock said nothing, he was examining the card. As he did so he was recalling what he had seen out of the window, which tended to confirm Pullman's story. The young man's behaviour was certainly that of a stranger, the lifting of the hat for instance. And then, if Pullman had had an assignation which he had wished not to divulge, he would hardly have arranged a meeting in full view of the windows of the room in which they were sitting. There was something else as well.

"How did this young man address you?" he inquired, in a far less steely tone.

"He addressed me as Mr James Pullman, he appeared to know all about me." Pullman showed no resentment at being cross-examined. He gazed mildly at the other. The older man felt rather like a schoolboy who had been discovered in the act of making a fool of himself, and was being watched sedately by his offensively bland master. He set out to retrieve this position; he would take up the attitude of one who was able to lift the veil, provided the other would come clean.

"Pullman," he said impressively, with a soupçon of authority. "Have you been on very friendly terms with the Bailiff?"

Under examination, the prefect looked amused. "I have only been in contact with him once, for precisely one minute."

Mannock threw himself back in his chair, with the manner of a learned counsel who finds a witness a bit of a handful: but he continued to nurse the card which he had been given a short while before.

"This, the Phanuel Hotel," and he was still impressive, "is the address of a sort of private hotel–very luxurious–of which the Bailiff is the patron." Mannock stood up rather suddenly, handing back the visiting card to Pullman. "I cannot help you. If there is nothing you are holding back . . . there is no explana- tion I can give."

"I have nothing up my sleeve," said Pullman evenly, "and I am not very dishonest."

"My dear fellow, please do not misunderstand me. There has been nothing scurrilous about my questions. You might have some excellent reasons for withholding this or that from me . . . No one discovers *everything*."

Pullman put the card away in his pocket. Then he stroked his beard and looked absentminded.

"You have not told me what you saw." Mannock smiled ingratiatingly.

"Well, I peered into St Katherine, into Saul," Pullman paused to summon back to his memory the next street name; "into Simeon, *and* into St Joseph. The last street before you get to the Boulevard is called Maccabees and then I saw where everybody round about buys their food. The street was full. Rather a different humanity from those we saw yesterday."

"Oh yes, in the Maccabees you would see the servants, who do the marketing. Those who do the hard work of the city are not eccentrics. They were working people in their life on earth. The *other* people . . ."

"The demented 'Youth' . . .?"

"Y-y-yes . . . if you like, are one-time bank clerks or drapers assistants, or waiters or club servants, or booking clerks . . ."

"Exactly." Pullman mused. "I saw them too . . . hundreds of them."

"Well?" Mannock queried. "Have you modified your first impressions?"

"Oh no. But I see more how the city is populated. These are the hysterical child-chorus of the Bailiff's Tribunal. It is pathetic."

"Perhaps fifty per cent of the city is the desiccated remains of youth-propaganda of forty years ago. When you were there the Bailiff's Tribunal had its full-blown youth-chorus?"

"Oh yes," Mannock agreed.

"Well, if you banish altogether the mature, reduce everything to the childish, and keep it on ice for . . . for a . . . for a century, or even for two, three, or four decades . . . it does produce something whose mindlessness verges on the mad."

"But why," Mannock was excited, "why preserve–why *can* this . . . this exclusive immaturity!"

Pullman laughed. "Ah, you are one of the indignant sort," he said. „I am content to observe, though what men do makes me a little sick at times."

"You are an amoralist, I am afraid," Mannock told him.

"Excuse me, sir." A short silence was broken by Satters.

"What do you want, Satters? Anything wrong?" Pullman fixed a surprised eye upon his junior.

"I don't see, Pulley, why, when you aren't here, he should . . ."

"Satters! Please behave yourself."

Satters glared, but was silent.

"I think this is the moment for me to visit that bank you spoke of," Pullman said. "If, Mannock, you are free . . ."

"Certainly, my dear chap, I was thinking the same thing. Let us repair to the Central Bank. It is getting quite late."

And so the serious business of the day began, and in not much more than twenty minutes they were all three standing in the crowded hall of the Central Bank. There were no tiresome intricacies here. The customary atmosphere of a bank was absent: although it was called a bank, it was, quite obviously, something else, though it was a little difficult to define what it was, since it had no analogy in earthly life.

31

The interior walls were of glass, and all the floors were of iron pierced into a grill-work pattern throughout. At the end of every glass-built corridor sat an armed police officer. But this uniformed man, with a large holster attached to his belt, was the only sign of deference that was shown, in this social system, to the substance, money, no longer with any of the attributes of dynamite.

In a small glass room Pullman conversed with a small baldish individual, sitting in front of him on the other side of a small shiny desk. With perfect suavity and remarkable intelligence, this official politely elicited the kind of place Pullman had occupied in earthly society. At the end of a quarter of an hour, during which the answers to the official interrogation had been rapidly noted in a large book, and then added up, as it were, the competent little bureaucrat opened a drawer, and drew out packet after packet of bank-notes. From each of these packets he extracted a certain number. Then he passed over to Pullman a pile of notes.

"These are all in the Roman currency. These are the Roman Aureus, which stand in the same position as the English pound. These are half Aurei. These are the Roman Denarius; that was the principal silver coin. Its value was three to a florin–about ninepence ha'penny. And here are a number of tickets," he handed Pullman a square of tickets, resembling railway tickets–perhaps a thousand.

"A big bundle is it not? We think here in terms of dollars. These," pointing to one of the packets of notes, "are the equivalent of a dollar. You will receive a sum of four hundred dollars a month," the official said smilingly. "If you feel that is not enough, will you come and see me? I do not think, Mr Pullman, that you will find this inadequate."

"What work do I have to do in order to earn this money?"

"Nothing," said the official (No. 1051), again smilingly.

"Nothing?" Pullman said blankly with a rising inflection, not really soliciting an answer.

"Nothing whatever," the official told him, "unless you wish to engage in business, or in any pursuit requiring capital, in which case you would no doubt wish to pay me a visit. We provide, in a quite limited way, financial help in such cases."

"Ah," thoughtfully, and rather dubiously, Pullman ejaculated, as though the other had just furnished him with information the *bona fides* of which he was not prepared to accept. "Supposing I wished to write a book? I mean, to write a book not for profit; a serious book, but one which would involve a small expense. What do I do then?"

"You come and see me, and explain to me your requirements," the official politely smiled.

"Thank you," with great dignity, without smiling, Pullman answered, bowed, turned on his heel, and left the room.

As he walked slowly along the passage Pullman gave himself up to the following caustic reflections—what Rigate had said very much in his mind—"A very strange set-up indeed! Money is provided gratis, it is like water, it is a necessity piped along to you, to be drawn off a tap, free of charge. Not even a water-rate. At the camp we were frankly metaphysical; we spoke and acted as men, but we knew that we were only that, as it were, by courtesy. Upon entering the city you become 'real'—your camp status is confirmed, as it were *solidified*—You are provided with a plausible physiological equipment, you are given guts (all this conferred upon you mysteriously, out of the air); you begin defecating and urinating—physically you are a full-scale man once more. But what *sort* of a man are you? You are given enough money to keep going, to supply yourself with a roof, with a lodging, and with food. But it is all artificial; at bottom just as metaphysical as it was outside in the camp. I do not like it any more than Rigate does."

He caught the eye of the armed guard, sitting at the end of the corridor.

"Do you like it?" he asked the armed guard. But that man did not like being addressed by the clients of the bank; he frowned slightly, and did not answer him.

Downstairs Mannock was waiting, and Pullman rejoined him. "Got the dough?" the former demanded with what Pullman regarded as a disagreeable bonhomie. For this had not been for him an agreeable operation, in which he had secured some "dough," the stuff that all men want. It had been rather as if he had been provided with a glass of water—not of a beautiful, fresh, spring water, but a kind of ersatz liquid, the taste of which was not really at all pleasant. And the jolly-old-dough which the jolly-old-bank gives you attitude of Mannock jarred on him somewhat, and, as had been the case with the official upstairs, Pullman did not respond to his new friend's smile with another smile. He made it clear to him, by the solemnity of his expression, that he did not look upon this as a *joke*, whatever else it might be.

Satters did not seem to regard it as a joke either. Far from looking as if a great big glorious uncle had given him a prodigious tip, he was flushed and was scowling. He was an excessively ruffled school-boy. He had had words with the official in the little glass box of an office where the cross-examination regarding his status had not passed off quite so pleasantly as it had in the case of Pullman. He had objected, at the outset, to the nature of the questions. For instance, to the question "What, roughly, was your annual gross income?" he answered, flushing and stammering, that his people had allowed him, every term, at Charterhouse, at least a fiver ... "They were very decent, I will say that, though they didn't understand how much a fellow really needs."

"No, sir," corrected the official, "I did not mean what you received as pocket-money when you were at Charterhouse. I meant how much, when you were grown up, was your gross income, as ... let me, see Mr Satterthwaite, were you in business, or had you a profession?"

Satters remained huddled in a furious sulk. There was a long pause during which the official watched him, and he continued to boil and to sulk.

"Mr Satterthwaite," at last the official spoke. "I asked you what your job was when you were alive ... Were you an accountant, a master-mariner, a tea-planter, a banker? ..."

Satters did not move. He absolutely refused to visualise himself at any time later than his sixteenth year.

"Mr Satterthwaite, we are not making much progress, are we? I am still waiting to hear what was your job when you were alive."

"My job," erupted the sulky mass. "My job ... I was a stock-jobber. Is that what you want? I was a jobber–that was my job."

"Thank you, Mr Satterthwaite. In an average year, how much did you make–approximately?"

Satters looked at him with hatred. A look of cunning stole into his eye. "What did I make? Ten thousand a year."

"Ten thousand pounds a year, Mr Satterthwaite? That was a large income, was it not?"

"What is the use of my answering your questions if you don't believe what I say?" Satters leaned over pugnaciously towards him.

"I said, Mr Satterthwaite, that ten thousand pounds a year was a large income. I did not express any incredulity, I only remarked that it was a large sum. You lived very comfortably? What sort of car did you have, what make?"

"What has that got to do with it!" Satters blustered. "I had a Rolls-Royce."

"A Rolls-Royce? Nice cars, are they not? Very nice cars. There are no nicer cars. They cost rather a lot, is that not so?"

Satters had begun puffing himself out. The more he thought about his past, the grander it seemed. "Oh, I don't know. Yes, I suppose so."

"Mr Satterthwaite, how many servants did you have? You had, of course, a cook, a butler . . .? How many of them were there?"

Satters had stuck his elbow upon the table, propping his furrowed brow with a forefinger near the top of it, and a thumb supporting his cheek-bone. It was the attitude of Shakespeare's statues. "How many servants did I have? Let me see. They varied in numbers. Sometimes I had . . . oh, ten."

"Ten?"

"Ten or twelve. But I had as few as five or six. They are a great deal of trouble, servants. I got very tired of them sometimes. Once, I remember, I turned them all out. Then, of course, I had none. No servants."

The official sat back and looked at him blandly. "No servants? Well, Mr Satterthwaite, let me ask you one last question. Were you ever a bankrupt?"

Satters looked at him steadily. "What for?"

"That is not the point," the official said. "All I want to know is whether you were a bankrupt or not."

"Often," Satters growled.

The official drew out the bundles of notes, and extracted a few of each, added a large bundle of tickets, and put the paper currency back again, locking the drawer. He informed Satters of the nature and description of the notes, and handed them to him. "Here, Mr Satterthwaite, is your monthly allowance. In one month you will return, and I will furnish you with the same amount again. Do not spend the money recklessly; I suggest you take great care of it. This is a city in which money runs away very quickly. Good day, Mr Satterthwaite."

Satters had got to his feet uncertainly, thrusting the notes into his trousers pocket. He stood looking at the official. He knew that there was something between the official and himself which should not have been there; a certainty gathered force inside him that he was being treated very unfairly, very disgracefully. He felt that one day he and this official would say some very hard words to each other. However, there was nothing to be done at present. He nodded his head, and said in a very beastly way, "Thank you ... er ... *thank* you."

With this he left the room; and when he had arrived downstairs, he walked silently up to Mannock, pulled the notes out of his pocket, and said, "This is my share."

When Mannock had examined the notes he handed them back. "It is not much, is it? You will have to be very careful with your money."

Satters' face had become congested with blood of a dark red colour, and Mannock could see that for two pins this excitable youth would rush upstairs and cause a tremendous disturbance. "I hope you did not misunderstand me, Satterthwaite. It is quite a fair amount of money that you have there. I did not mean that you have anything to complain about."

"No?" He glared at Mannock, all his suppressed indignation turning in the direction of that deceitful friend. "No? I see. You need not say any more, Mr Mannock."

It should be said that the bank was absolutely crawling with that type of citizen which had aroused Pullman's curiosity. Here it was actually possible to watch them attempting to wheedle more money out of a cashier, or wildly recounting their exploits to companions awaiting them in the hall, or, on the other hand, furiously denouncing both the institution and all the tiny moneybugs which it employed. Often fights occurred between the clients and the personnel of the bank. There was one never to be forgotten occasion when a dissatisfied client had seized several bundles of the aureus notes and got as far as the hall before he was overtaken by the Bank-police. To see them all here in the place where the funds originated to maintain them in idleness and idiocy was an almost frightening spectacle of subsidised futility. Was there ever so irresponsible a dole!

As they were descending into an underground station, Mannock a little ahead, Satters, lowering his voice so as to exclude that gentleman, heatedly addressed Pullman. "That bastard up there as good as said I was a liar. He has given me hardly any money. He asked me what my job was. On earth, you know."

"What was it?" Pullman inquired.

"I said I was a jobber."

"Oh, a jobber. Were you a jobber?"

"Of course I was a jobber. But he seemed to think I was lying. He asked me how many servants I had, and a lot of boloney like that. This is all he gave me." Satters pulled the notes out of his trousers pocket, and showed them to Pullman, who saw that they were quite few in number.

"I suppose that he thought that a boy of sixteen–and you will always be a boy of sixteen in this place–I suppose he thought that that was all you would need."

Satters spluttered excitedly. "The dirty swine! Boy of sixteen! I suppose making me a boy of sixteen was a dirty crack, I suppose that's what it was. The dirty swine!"

Pullman looked irritated, and replied, as they hurried after Mannock: "The idea is, of course, that, as you possess the mentality of a boy of sixteen, that is what you must be. You have to accept that."

"Oh, I do, do I? Oh, I see . . . you dirty rotter! I have to be for all the rest of time a boy of sixteen, do I? And have the money that a boy of sixteen would have . . . Eh? Well, let me tell you this, Mister Pullman . . ."

"If you speak to me in that way, I shall not answer you. We need not live together, either, if you cannot behave yourself." Pullman was very cross indeed, and hastened his step until he was at Mannock's side. "Our young friend is being very rude and troublesome," he told Mannock. But just then they reached the ticket-office, and the quarrel did not develop. Satters grew quieter, and when he was next by the side of Pullman, he exclaimed, "I say Pulley, I am most awfully sorry I called you a rotter. I did not mean that you were a rotter, Pulley. I just said that because I was terribly cross with what that beastly official had done."

"All right. Don't call me any names in future when people annoy you. Call *them* names if you like. Not *me*."

III

It was only a ten-minute Metro journey to the station of Tenth Piazza. When they reached the street level once more, it was to find themselves a few yards from an enormous oblong space almost a mile long, and probably a quarter of a mile across. Heavy, regularly-placed paving stones emphasised its size and emptiness; it was quite without ornament, and down its sides ran a spacious, arched arcade. Within the arcade were shops, cafés, the entrances to public buildings, theatres, billiard saloons, bowling-greens, and so forth. It was thick with people moving slowly up and down. Since such a vast number of people in this city had nothing to do, and all the time in the world on their hands, this place served as what was perhaps the most popular shopping centre, and a multitudinous promenade; with exchanges of bouquets, of lipsticks and of witticisms. Every square inch of these arcades was covered–though for some reason not many people used the Piazza itself; a strident hum burst out on the right, grew faint in the middle, and grew vigorous, and then frantic again on the left. The architecture was large and bare, mostly of a light stucco, café-au-lait in colour, but with the milk predominating. The effect was South German, and in summer the austerity of the unbroken paved vista was something all its own, an indescribable, accentless void.

Mannock took them across the paved emptiness, diagonally, for a considerable distance (if the Yahoos were timorous about great spaces, he was not); then they entered the arcade. Satters said that he felt tired, complaining that the stone pavement hurt his feet. Mannock promised that shortly he would have a rest, and a bite of something to eat. But immediately they plunged into the crowd. It was the first contact that Satters had had with this strange humanity, and at last even *he* noticed that there was something extraordinarily unusual about them.

"Pulley, I say, these people give me goose-flesh. I feel I am walking among dead people, Pulley, all of them cracking jokes."

"So you are," Pullman told him. "Can you smell them?"

"Yes, Pulley, it is like rotten vegetation isn't it? Oh yes, and there is a scent."

"It is heliotrope mostly. I saw one then," Pullman whispered, "who was actually a fish, I believe. And there are masses of toads."

"Ugh, ugh, Pulley! How sad they look, don't they. When they make a crack their faces break up into a hundred tiny little wrinkles."

There was a croak in their ear, "You two stop whispering. We don't allow that. All cards on the table."

Pullman half-turned round, and said, "My friend is so young, that is why we whisper. We won't any more."

"I don't mind," shrugged the mask—and it was so terribly like a mask that Pullman felt that that was what in fact it might be. This one had a monocle, and he fluttered his hands. "I am a newcomer myself."

"I don't think you are, buddy," Pullman blew at him through his beard.

"I think you're a horrid old man." There was a nasty look in the eye of the mask. "Go away . . . and have a good wash. You are filthy both of you. You stink."

Pullman drew Satters away, towards one of the shops, and pushed Mannock before him.

A voice was distinctly audible, from the section that was being held up by this shopward avalanche. "That dirty old man" (by this Pullman was intended) "pushed against my new waistcoat. It is ruined I fear." Another one answered, "There is a disgustingly young one too with them, Arthur. He put his clodhopper on my toecap. Little beast."

They were glad when they reached the shops, and it was a considerable distance across a very wide arcade. The first shop was a gentleman's outfitter. A dozen people were glued to the window, gesticulating, hissing, and crying out. These window displays were a revelation, to the newcomers, of the city's civilized resources, or as it sometimes seemed to Pullman, uncivilised resources. Very beautifully suited waxen-faced gentlemen, with expressions of ineffable sweetness, and exuding *bon-ton*, stood in attitudes of impeccable politeness.

They kept close together, Satters leading, as he had now become hysterically absorbed in what the shop windows had

40

to offer: they passed the next six or seven shops in close order, but Pullman outraged at the vulgarity, and Satters pressed against him in front, deeply ecstatic. For Mannock, naturally, there was nothing novel about all this. In shop after shop now were rows of startling pink and green shirts, American neckwear of terrific unrestraint, and dressing-gowns in foulard and velour–of the latter, one in scarlet riveted Satters' attention, but he could only see it fragmentarily for at least twenty people were dancing with rapture in front of it, and very soon the shopman took it away, for such a gem as that did not remain unsold for more than a few minutes. "Oh, Pulley, did you *see* it!" Satters began to dance as well. It was difficult to get him away from this shop.

"What on earth do they want to manufacture all this stuff for here?" Pullman protested. "Surely these garish and ridiculous garments are not in keeping with the severity of the Piazza, or, for that matter, with the whole idea of this place? There is something very odd about all this. I do not understand it."

"Well, these are obviously not very edifying garments," Mannock agreed. "But there are all sorts, and, of course, all ages, in this place; and there are great numbers of young chaps for whom these shops cater. I daresay they should not do so. But nothing is done, officially, to interfere with the tastes of the inhabitants."

"It is a pity, to my mind, that something is not done to curb their vulgar exuberance," Pullman answered disdainfully. "What sense is there in so much laissez-faire?"

Mannock remained silent. But a perfect bellow of rapture came from Satters. "Oh I say, I do like that! I'm damned if I'm not going in to ask the price of that jumper, Pulley. Half a moment, I'm going into this shop."

A Fair Isle pullover of the most seductive sort was in the centre of the window, and, pushing aside three or four people, Satters dived into the shop before anyone had time to restrain him.

"Oh damn that idiotic brat," the exasperated Pullman exclaimed. "Let us walk on ... I do not in the least mind if we lose him. Come along, Mannock. Let him go gathering jumpers-in-May. I have had enough of him for one morning."

Mannock laughed, but pulled his angry friend back by the

arm. "We had better wait for him. Be patient. In such a crowd as this we might very easily lose him for ever."

"I dearly wish we could."

Before very long Satters reappeared, a broad smile upon his rugged, big-baby countenance, the tassel of the shabby football cap still dangling over his eye, but a lovely new Fair Isle pullover embellishing his footballing torso. Beneath his arm was a brown paper parcel, containing his discarded jacket.

"You look a smart young man," Mannock told him. But Pullman had turned away, and they resumed their walk. Pullman noticed, as he had done before, that almost everyone they met was smartly dressed. Of course, if you give people, if the State gives them, all the money they want, they spend most of it on clothes, especially if they cannot spend it on motor-cars, because such things are not for sale, and if they have none of the other usual earthly ways of getting rid of money. He began to understand why the clothes shops were so numerous, and stocked with such enticing garments (an explanation which Mannock had preferred to withhold). But he became conscious, at the same time, of his own shabbiness. He began to glance at the suitings displayed in the shops they were passing, and marked down one or two of those establishments for a visit, in which more sober types of garments were displayed.

There were boisterous cafés, with groups of young men (eternally young, too, Pullman reflected), one of whom threw a kiss to Satters, greatly to that youth's pleased beflustification. "Did you see what that boy did, Pulley? But he looked rather a decent chap, don't you think?" Such incidents gave Satters furiously to think; he fingered the banknotes in his pockets, those that remained, and promised himself a trip down there tomorrow, and he thought he would have a cup of coffee too, at that amusing place they had just passed.

But there were other kinds of shops as well, all were not clothes shops; and now they came to a second-hand bookshop which did not attract the crowd. It was even possible to see most of its stock displayed in the window. It had an entire shelf of volumes devoted to the Tantra Sutras. Pullman stopped, and began a scrutiny of this unexpected culture; but almost immediately Satters developed foot trouble.

"All right," said Mannock. "We will go to that café along

there. It is not far. You shall have a doughnut, and some nice cocoa." Pullman, with a muffled curse, left the books, and went on with the other two. As he was going, he felt a light tap upon his shoulder, and a grinning face at his side shot at him in a hissed whisper, "There isn't anything in the window, but they've got some beauties inside. Extremely dirty. Filthy in fact." He gave this leering face such a pulverising glare that it vanished.

It was only a few yards beyond this that a very tall figure seemed to get in Pullman's way. The crowd was very thick at that point, and, if anyone stopped, everything was apt to stop too. The large actorish face was looking down at Pullman benevolently. There was fur on the collar, and for some reason the overcoat had the appearance of a dressing-gown. The soft felt hat was a little jauntily tilted, and there was a suggestion, although the get-up was entirely smart, of an earlier age.

"You should take that beard off," this giant gruffly purred. "You would really look less old, you know. Albert Edward Prince of Wales wore a beard; but he was a prince. You have to remember that."

"I never thought of Edward the Peacemaker's beard," Pullman answered civilly. "I grew my beard in Paris . . ."

"Ah, Paris. yes. In Rome you do as do the Romans." The immoderately tall man turned about, and moved along beside Pullman, to whom for some reason he seemed attracted. It turned out that it was a didactic itch from which he suffered. Apparently he felt that Pullman was in need of instruction; that if he did not allow the hair to grow on his face he would be more like a young man–if not actually a young man, yet slightly resembling one. Whereas at present he was slightly resembling an old man. There was something about this which worried the giant and so he had turned around in order to walk a little way with this misguided person.

"This has been called the Heaven of the Young," he announced, "and that is what it is. In the reign of Queen Victoria who was life for? Life was for the old. Even the man of forty was *too young*. The summit of life was among the Eternal Snows. At sixty the head is white. That was the privileged age: the theory was that you had lived enough and experienced enough to be wise. But who wants to be wise, in that manner? I have not myself taken the trouble to find out the things that make one wise. I have never read books, never studied. I have not grown grey in researching, I have lived for what Youth gives. Youth gives me all I want. In life on earth one could not give oneself up to Youth. How could one? Money kept one away from that; one had no chance of giving oneself up to Youth. But here it is different. *Here* money is abolished. Because money is no longer a necessity. We all are given an average of fifteen or twenty pounds a week. *And* we are given eternal Youth—those of us who were young when we got here. There are ... oh, nearly a million of us and all are as good as princes. I spend my days dreaming, I have no cares, I can buy all I fancy, and I am *young:* I am twenty-one. Merely to be young—to be slender, for one's face to be like a poem, for one's body to smell like fresh-cut flowers, for one to be free because one wants nothing—that is paradise! Who wants to be a rich old man, or a man possessed of *power?* All I want is to be young. To bring my youth to the Tenth Piazza, to be young with other youths on the promenade, for Youth to be shared with other young men, to have one's shoes shone in the lavatories by a redcapped old man—for old age shines shoes, that is the Hell of the withered and moth-eaten. I am in the land of the Young, I am light-hearted. There is only one thing I complain about, that is my ridiculous height. It is *not* an attribute of Youth. But I say to myself it is a revenge of some old and stupid god, because I was given *intelligence* in addition to Youth—so I had to have some blemish!"

Pullman listened in complete silence to this exordium. Now he looked up into the blue-eyed, monumentally ecstatic, amused old actor's face, and said, "How long have you been here, sir?"

The giant kept his head in the clouds, but he turned his eyes down to gaze at his adopted pupil. "When did I come here?" he asked this in a dreamy sing-song.

"That is what I asked you, sir." Pullman fixed his eyes upwards upon the sing-songing giant.

"It does not matter here *when* we arrive, we are given eternal youth."

"You did not answer my question," Pullman insisted.

The expression on the countenance of the very tall promenader suffered no alteration, but his eyes rolled downwards to observe Pullman a little wildly. "Did I not? The time then was one year before the beginning of the Boer War."

Pullman remained silent: and Mannock said in a subdued voice, "I wonder if this gentleman has any more to say?"

Pullman looked up at the too-tall man at his side. "I omitted to ask you your name, sir? If it is not impertinent may I do so now? I should like to know your name, so that I may converse with you again. We have to give a doughnut to this child, whose feet are hurting him. You will understand, sir, that the *very* young suffer from their feet, when they get bored. And they often become very bored. So, before we part, may I again ask you . . ."

"My name? My Christian name—and that is all that matters —is Michael. Michael."

"Mine is James. Good-day, sir." Pullman raised his hat, and turned to Mannock. "Let us now attend to Satterthwaite, Mannock, shall we."

As a café protruded a few seats into the arcade, and one table was just being vacated, Mannock signalled to the abominably disagreeable looking Satters and they all sat down at the vacant table.

Mannock called the waiter and ordered three doughnuts, and a cup of cocoa for Satters, and two drinks of another kind for the two grown-ups. "I often see that very tall man," Mannock told Pullman. "He is usually alone; in fact I do not believe that I have ever seen him with anybody. What nonsense he was talking."

"It was nonsense," Pullman agreed. "But he is no more mad than everybody else. He is just very much taller."

"I suppose so," said Mannock.

"He is intelligent; but he would not have spoken to you, Mannock, he would not even see you. He detected beneath my beard that I was on the borderlands of Youth. So I was not quite dead, you see. I was still capable of understanding." Pullman laughed.

Mannock seemed in rather a hurry. He paid the bill and very soon they left the café, Satters stuffing the last doughnut into his mouth.

Led by Mannock, they forced their way through the crowd

45

until they reached the pavement outside the arcade. The were about midway along the Piazza, and Mannock started to cross it, this time at right angles. "These places are called Piazzas– and really it is rather difficult to know what to call them unless you stretch a point and make use of that term. There are three of them: the Tenth, the Fifth, which is the centre of the city, and the First Piazza, which is on the side where there is a gate in the ramparts from which you can be ferried across to the farmlands. Ahead of us, over there, is Tenth Avenue: and it was in Tenth Avenue that a gentleman fired a siphon at our friend here, and it is in a street five blocks from Tenth Avenue that I live." He smiled amiably at them, as they marched forward, and Pullman said, "That is very clear. What is not clear, is why this place is here, and what the devil we are doing in it."

IV

THAT AFTERNOON PULLMAN occupied majestically the centre of the settee, and Mannock was in the large armchair he favoured, upon the inland side of the mantelpiece. Returned from Tenth Piazza, they had lunched lightly, and afterwards Satters had flung himself like a tired dog upon his bed, greatly to their relief. The mantelpiece clock indicated that it was just after two o'clock; both men sat without speaking, but Mannock was asking himself who this magnate might be, who sat there before him, sought out by the Bailiff, and coming from a world in which he had been Somebody, it would seem.–That rather lofty something about his guest which he had noticed within ten minutes of their first meeting, and which showed no signs of disappearing, what on earth could it be? Erect and silent, Pullman gently stroked his bearded chin. What this aggressive self-confidence might signify, to this Mannock had given very little thought until now. He had not asked Pullman what had been his profession or his trade. Mannock himself had been in business in the East, mainly in China; but he did not feel that this new acquaintance of his had been a businessman. No. Perhaps his calling had been clerical; but there was no clerical collar to indicate such origins; unless he had belonged to one of those sects who dispense with a uniform. A surreptitious glance or two, modification of the central image and he decided against the beard belonging to a preacher.–That out of the way, he gave himself up to a more general analysis. When you began to study him, Pullman had a noticeably impecunious look. He had not the clothes of a gentleman. If any reliance were to be placed upon the rig-out in which people made their appearance in the camp. Pullman had not come out of a top-drawer, but of some intermediate one. However shabby he might be, the man of means would be wearing an expensive suit of clothes, or a pair of shoes made for him. One man, he remembered, had turned up at the Camp in a grey topper and formal suit to match, which, though it was rather soiled, he had no doubt been provided with in order to identify him as an Ascot and Royal Garden-Party guest.–No, Pullman's air of authority had nothing in the way of clothes to sustain it. Obviously it was in no way related to finance.

Having reached this point in his analysis, Mannock could get on without the figure of Pullman as a guide. He marshalled in his mind a number of types with a very high opinion of themselves, but for no visible reason. Well, there was always the Actor. Quite an unsuccessful actor often had an inflated sense of his personal prestige. The fellow would come prancing along towards you, his head in the clouds. His wardrobe might in no way bear out his swagger. Without a bob's worth of coppers to rattle about in his pocket, this fellow was the Prince of Denmark. Mannock smiled; but his expression quickly changed. The *beard*!–whoever saw an actor with a beard? The Actor was a clean-shaven man, and there was no way of fitting his guest into the place reserved for men of that calling.

Then Mannock thought of the Schoolmaster. Yes, that was a possibility. The Schoolmaster often displayed a quite bloated self-esteem: and he might quite well wear a not very graceful or impressive beard. Yes. The more Mannock considered it, the more he thought that he might be in the presence of a Schoolmaster: imposingly familiar with the differential calculus, or terribly good at Greek, but not very affluent. Not a Public-School master, this fellow had not been teaching gentlemen! But there was something quite obvious which Mannock had ignored–something eminently genteel in its associations which he had passed over. It now rose accusingly in his memory. It was quite simply the Fag, evidently of first importance, which had been left out–that English institution of which Satterthwaite was the by no means self-effacing representative. How could he have overlooked the fag?

But the Wykehamist cast a dubious mind's-eye towards the rugger cap worn by Satters. He knew that there were many schools called Public, but ... and a fag wherever a prefect whirled a cane. He would be prepared to find a fag in any institution that was Public enough to boast a House.–Yet who ever saw a bearded prefect? What had happened to Pullman after the fag-owning decade? There were Other Places, he was vaguely aware, outside of those two fairylands with which

Youth terminates in England—the one watered by the Isis, bulging with learning from Jesus to All Souls; the second built upon the Cam, captured by Science, though civilising what has mastered it:—but Mannock's vague awareness had no desire for greater precision. Had he made the effort, in the interest of locating his guest's pigeonhole, he might have found a Place not unknown to learning, where a Chair had once been illustriously occupied by his guest, not at all a bad niche for a rather unusual *Gelehrter*, within earshot of the Hallé Orchestra (to give a hint of where this might be). This would not have caused the Schoolmaster Theory to be quite inapplicable; that had really rather appealed to Mannock. He had amusedly been turning this over in his mind when, with an alarming suddenness, Pullman started to speak:

"On what principle", he inquired, "are people selected for citizenship in the Camp outside the city?"

"Oh I don't know." Mannock was annoyed at his subject speaking, as an artist would be if a cow he had been drawing got up and walked away. "You yourself have been a witness of how they are selected, have you not? The Bailiff is a strange functionary. He *pretends* . . ."

With the utmost suddenness the room became as dark as night. Mannock sprang up.

"Does this often happen?" Pullman, who had not moved from his position in the centre of the settee, inquired. The voice was irritatingly steady.

"Never in my experience." Mannock sounded peevish.

A blast, rather than a flash of lightning, a hundred times brighter and colder than any day, stamped out everything in blinding black and white upon the human retina. Pullman looked clearer and calmer than ever to the exasperated eye of his host. Pullman, too, had the sensation of being unspeakably distinct, but his calmness was, of course, more apparent than real. The switch-off, back to primeval night, was very violent; abruptly the vivid day ticked out. In the absence of all light the eyes ached.

"David Hume observed that, because the sun had never failed to rise every morning since the beginning of the world, that is not to say it will do so tomorrow morning." These unhurried vocables of Pullman's seemed to be uttered in defiance of the blackness, and they had the same effect upon Mannock as if he had personally stage-managed the turning off of the Light. If his thoughts could have acquired a voice, it would have been as a growl that they would have been heard. "What does the fellow think he is doing? Obviously a schoolmaster!"

One stood, the other sat, as if posing for their portraits. Neither liked the quality of the blackness. Pullman felt he could not furnish it with his thoughts, it was impenetrable and alien. Mannock did not recognize it: he was speechless with terror.

But as if the blackness had spoken there was an enormous shock: the house they were in rocked backwards, and then with equal violence it seemed to right itself. This second movement tossed Mannock down on the floor, in front of the mantelpiece. The house then seemed to shake itself, and several of the window-panes crashed, and there was a crashing and banging outside. The door was dashed open, and Satters appeared, flung himself up against Pullman on the settee, his voice blowing into the latter's face, in a breathless scream, "Pulley, wha . . . wha . . . wha . . . wha . . . what!"

Pullman, erect as he still was, was in no position to tell Satters *what*. He had no idea himself. Technically, he suffered from shock, as he would if he had been in a car and it had come into collision with a milk-float. His rigidity was a necessary adoption. Only tensed could he meet the appallingly unexpected.

He began by holding protectively Satters' bloated head, and himself derived a certain comfort from these contact. In the end his fingers got wound round his fag's strong curls. As events developed, he found that he was pulling at a massive lock. In moments of especial stress he nearly pulled out by the roots sections of his young follower's thatch. His hand left the hair, it fastened itself on the nose snorting upon the settee at his side. He noticed his lips framing an apology; his hand released the nose, and Satters, apparently believing, in his shadowy consciousness, that something nightmarish had had hold of his nose, sneezed aggressively.

There were no more shocks; the next development was a world-embracing Hiss. The city and everything in it became a Hiss. If a man is standing on a railway station platform near to a locomotive it is apt to emit a deafening hiss, which causes him to hurry away. Magnified a million times, such a hiss as this resulted with Pullman's fingers sticking in his ears until later they fell down against his sides when his consciousness left him. But actually the Hiss was the last thing he heard. While he sat there, his senses full of a prodigious Hiss, other sounds filled the air. Corked as his ears were, his hearing mechanism, such of it as was not obsessed by the Hiss, dimly attempted to record the chaos but the next blast was final, and it gave up all attempt to hear. Something like a star must have been hurled at the metropolis. Or it was stunned by a rushing world. Or it was smothered by a hostile universe. If anything lived in Third City it lived as a congealed and armoured mechanism as Pullman did, his arms dropped like lead on either side of his body. He sat there bolt upright, but was not a valid witness of the hereafter.

Beneath him Mannock lay trembling on the floor, but it was an automatic rattle of his flesh, not one at which his consciousness assisted. He adhered to the floor like a piece of paper, a gasp stifled and stuck, his mouth as round as a pennypiece. Satters' head adhered to Pullman's body at about the level of the hip, like an unsightly wen of doughy texture. He was quite motionless. It was a stricken group.

During everything that happened subsequent to this, a storm of such force was present, violently rushing into every crevice, that there was not a scrap of glass left in the window, frames, and the pictures, which were hurled to the floor, also lost their glazing. The appearance of the room was entirely changed by the destructive blast, the lighter chairs and cabinets were driven into the corners of the room, the carpet rose into the air, and stopped there, except that it rested upon here a chair and there a projecting corner of the settee. Later on Pullman discovered that he had been blown over on top of Satters, whereas Mannock's hair was almost blown out of his head, and in the end was stretched out to its utmost limit: a fragment of glass was embedded in his neck.

Upon this violent wind missiles of different sizes tore their way into the city; a stone, the size of a sphinx, plunged into the tower of the Central Bank; other large stones visited the citizenry, and splintered glass, like that which had found its way into Mannock's neck, flew everywhere in and out of the houses: the wind was also responsible for transmitting a blistering heat. At times those of the inhabitants who had been practically mummified, as had the group in Habakkuk, were very fortunate, for those few who had not been rendered unconscious reported that they had been grilled alive. They said that they might have been in front of an open furnace, and they expected at every moment to be shrivelled up.

The background to the superhuman uproar, which started with flashes of lightning which were like blows from hard blades of light, the background to this was an orchestral *tutti* as of massed instruments, each straining to its utmost to make more noise than had ever been made before. To supply the simile with an overseer, one might elect as *chef d'orchestre* Satan in person.

A dark cloud had stood over Piazza One, it emptied itself in the form of a spout of malodorous liquid which came down in the centre of the Piazza, and inundated neighbouring streets. Everyone had closed their windows, and held handkerchiefs to their noses. A doctor said if a second cloud behaved in that way, there would be a diphtheria epidemic. This was happening in the poorer quarters of the city about the time Habakkuk was experiencing the first shocks.

The rain of Flies occurred later. The Flies were quite dead when they reached the city; and carpeted everything with a uniform blue-black. With a sound like the cymballing of thin sheets of metal, locusts followed, in lesser mass, the rain of Flies. Pullman by that time had been blown across Satters' body and only a few people in Third City were less of an automaton than he was.

But the Waterspout and the Deluge of Flies were incidental. Mankind practically asphyxiated, what could only be a Battle took place, at once anthropomorphic and supernatural. Its major features were the percussion of great voices, words used as missiles the size of houses, and then what the human soldiers would have recognised as the sound of warfare in the twentieth-century sense, so magnified as to be aurally unmanageable. The apparent slamming of monstrous doors would correspond for those attuned to terrestrial battle, with the detonation of shells and bombs. But the doors which seemed to be slamming must have been shutting out areas as large as the city itself. Taking the sounds literally, beside the hollow roar of the doors a thousand feet high were nests of machine-guns, giving a monster rattle a sky-scraping honeycomb with muzzles for windows. A human listener, in registering such immensities, could not possibly have admitted them to his slender auditory apparatus; he would have somehow translated the gigantic sounds on to a scale more adapted for his sensual possibilities. What would not be familiar to the human soldier would be the three or four mammoth voices on high, crashing out the alphabets of Heaven and of the Pit. The nasal tongues of giant viragos at one time conducted a screaming argument among the clouds, which, if translated, was totally absurd. This terrific contest degenerated into something like a zoological madness. The giant sounds shrank to a hubbub of monkeys, and a psittacine screaming. As abruptly as it had begun this chaotic orgasm ended-like a vast squib it hissed and spluttered, it chattered and squawked to an end, an end at which no one was present, as no one had been fully present at the never-ending encounter. What succeeded it was a silence equally monstrous.

It was in a universal silence that Pullman grew conscious of his surroundings, far more oppressive than any sounds he had ever heard. In every sense his awakening was abnormal. He did not, for instance, become aware of the conditions in which he and the others breathed and had their beings: that was a later and philosophic realisation. What first came was a feeling of a rigid body, as if frozen into an unnatural erectness. It was, as it were, a negative awareness, a cataloguing of things which were *not*. First of all, he could not move. Then he became aware of all the other things which he could not do. And as to the world outside himself, that mainly, to start with, was a list of negations. Everything was upside-down–this was *not* here, or that was *not* there.

When he began to recover his faculties the first sensation was one of such violence that he thought not that he was coming to life, but that he was dying. Nausea weighed him down with a leaden loathing. But that was secondary: his angry liver demanded how its functioning came to be shut down, the urinary system struggled to force two or three pints of liquid, or near-liquid, through the kidneys; most painful of all was the spine. What could it be? Were the meninges involved? If only ice could have been administered. He remembered the treatment he had read about in the case of some spinal ailment. Ice appeared to be essential. He wondered if Mannock possessed a refrigerator, but, even if he had, Pullman realized he was unable to move, so could not have procured any ice from that source. The reactions were so acute at this point that he fainted. When he came to, the spinal column was easier, but in the urinary region the pains were so severe that he again succumbed. When he regained consciousness for the second time the pains had diminished, he just felt sick and completely exhausted: perfectly still, his eyes shut, and his hands pushed beneath his body to secure a little heat, he fell into a profound sleep. When he awakened, the organic disturbances appeared to have subsided. Absolute stillness obtained as before, not a sound was to be heard anywhere; no one seemed to be left alive in the city.

With an analytical mind such as Pullman's, one of the first things to occur to him was the time. But before the bodily ordeal began there had literally been no interval allowing for such speculations. Now he fixed his eyes upon the mantelpiece clock. He stared at it for a very long time, when with difficulty he realised it had stopped. His next reflection was that either (a) the day was drawing in or (b) that henceforth there was going to be less light in the world. It had all been used up! he reflected stupidly. However, what could not be called an increasing *suppleness*, but certainly was a consciousness of a development all over his body of a potential pliability, began to be felt. To look directly at his wrist-watch was of course impossible. Revolving his left arm was painful enough, there was no question of lifting it up. But he found that he was able gently to withdraw his left elbow a couple of inches. Then the wrist-watch was visible. His extravagance had been justified; quietly it ticked on. It was almost five minutes to eight.

He then set about very roughly computing the time occupied by the superhuman disturbance. His guess was that for either two or three hours abnormal conditions had persisted. He checked this later on with many people, and his final conclusion was that what he had allowed at that time was approximately right.

Looking down he was able to see Mannock. His friend was still outstretched upon the floor, before the mantelpiece; the mouth gaped open, his hair stood erect upon his head. He also noticed, for the first time, the piece of glass embedded in his neck. How white he was–how that changed his identity. He stared at the colourless mask. The question as to whether Mannock was alive or dead must be left in abeyance until, as he put it, he himself "came unstuck".

Soon it would be too dark to see: was that delirium to be repeated when the night was there? He shuddered. Would they all be annihilated before they had quite regained their physical competence? Would he die–really be dead this time: and Michael, Sentoryen and a million other "Youths", would they all be wiped out too? He was terrified as he thought of this, yet his fatalism did not desert him. He even allowed his mind to rest upon Michael, that mad giant in his furred overcoat, with his fantastic philosophy. Would he die, or would the Youth-God lift him from his bed and carry him into the Elysian Fields? Someone surely would watch over this *grand halluciné*. –But a cold wind began blowing through the apartment. What was this? Pullman alone in this blasted city . . . everyone else like these two people *dead* . . . alone, with that terrible noise, with this frantic wind? To be alone in such a storm of hatred, a supernatural rage!

His existence was ridiculous–why should he be preserved, in order to be the witness of this horror?–to lie here trembling and gasping, and in the end to be extinguished! He could only guess what was happening in other parts of the city. But he *felt*–and since there were no sounds outside it was perfectly possible–that he was the only man alive. He could not resist the sensation of an unexampled loneliness. Had he heard, all of a sudden, a step outside in the hall, it would not have occurred to him that it was a man's. His heart would freeze, as he wondered what kind of creature this could be. This idea terrified him so much that he revolved his head a little and fastened his eye intenly upon the handle of the door. But there was no movement and at last he forgot about it.

The wind increased to a gale, and the wind was colder than he had ever expected it to be in this city. Had the city not only become derelict, all its inhabitants destroyed, but was it now

55

to be delivered up to the colds of interstellar space? Would those fearful stars, in future, blaze down upon something as cold as themselves? His body grew colder and colder. He began to recover the use of his limbs, the necessity to secure something to cover himself up in appeared to stimulate him to movement.

First he found he could, very slowly and painfully, move his legs, and move his feet up and down. Next came the arms, already limited movement was possible. But section by section he must learn to move his limbs in all directions. The darkness increased: soon the full night would be there. There were of course no lights in the streets, but there were also no stars. In about half an hour he was able to move freely his arms and legs; sit up for a moment, and then subside again. The body was as yet rigid. It was at this point that the door opened.

He sat absolutely without movement, breathing as lightly as possible. He was still facing the fireplace, and the door was behind him. Stiff and motionless, he held his breath, pretending that, like the others, he was dead. A stealthy step crossed the room, then the approaching foot struck something in the dark.

If this was a man, it was a very silent one. Perhaps looters were at large; most of the city was dead, and looters were taking advantage of this fact. Then there were a few diminutive sounds, a sigh, a sharp scratching–a match was being struck.

There, in the brilliant matchlight, was the scared face of Platon. Pullman had never before had occasion to feel so ashamed of himself; he suddenly croaked out a laugh, Platon jumping and the match going out. Another match was produced, and once more they could see one another.

"You are alive." Platon's voice was low and husky. "Good, I thought I was the only live one–in all the city."

"I thought that too," Pullman said truthfully.

Platon burst into a feeble guffaw, and the other joined him in a doleful gasp of mirth.

Pullman sat up, in a rickety and unsteady fashion. Next he rolled over on his side and after a number of unsuccessful attempts managed to stand up. This had occupied four or five minutes; and when he looked down, Platon was kneeling at the side of his master. He had opened Mannock's shirt at the neck, and put his hand sideways upon the latter's chest. He was listening for the sound of the heart. Pullman could see where he was, but not what he was doing.

"His heart beat," Platon said.

"Good." Pullman was now doing loosening-up exercises on the sofa. He found it warmed him too. "Capital!" he said with an attempt at a firmer voice, sitting up and slapping his arms across his chest. Then he said, "We are all alive."

"All," echoed Planton. He slapped his hand upon Satters' chest. "He alive?" he asked indifferently.

"Yes," Pullman said, proceeding with his exercises.

Platon sat down beside the unmoving Mannock.

"Hot drink!" thinly blustered Pullman.

"No gas," was Platon's answer to that.

Pullman, supporting himself on pieces of furniture, reached the electric light switch.

"No electricity," echoed Platon.

Pullman opened the door, and, the palms of his hands pressed against the walls, he reached a hat-rack. Two overcoats hung there: these he unhooked, and shuffled back with them into the living-room. One of them he handed to Platon. "Put this over Mr Mannock," he said. The other he threw around his shoulders. Then he sat down. He must learn to speak again, he told himself. Immediately he began to put words to work, organising things with the houseboy–who, though he was called a *boy*, must have been around twenty-five. The first step was to get a match struck and to look at his watch. Miraculously it still functioned, and the time it alleged was a few minutes past eleven. He showed it to Platon, who philosophically commented "Good! Good!" He felt, no doubt, that eleven was *good* because it might have been worse.

It was best, Pullman laid it down, that Mannock, and likewise his ex-fag, should be left alone, until such time as the gas came on again, and hot drinks could be obtained. "Was it possible," he asked the boy, "to block up the windows to enable them to sleep?" He felt as they were doing this, and reconstructing their life again, item by item, that at any moment they might be overwhelmed like the inhabitants of Herculaneum–or even much more suddenly than that. However–an encouraging sign–the wind abated somewhat. Questions regarding the future presented themselves first. The shops will have no food tomorrow—indeed, there may be no adequate supplies for some time. Had Mr Mannock laid in any reserves? If you have stores, how long would they last?

Sounds in the streets reached them. They both tumbled towards the windows, Pullman falling and again rising to his feet. Two loudspeakers were in neighbouring streets, but what was being broadcast it was impossible to say. But a small motor-vehicle with a very loud mechanical voice burst into Habakkuk. It sternly shouted instructions to the citizens.

"TO ALL CITIZENS. STOP INDOORS UNTIL THE CITY SERVICES HAVE REMOVED THE FLIES FROM THE STREETS. THEY WILL NOT BE LONG. CITIZENS! THE GAS AND ELECTRICITY IS BEING ATTENDED TO. PATIENCE CHILDREN. PATIENCE. IT WILL NOT BE LONG NOW!"

"Children!" grittily expostulated Platon.

"FLIES!" was Pullman's response, in something between a bark and a croak.

Standing inside the windows they stood on glass splinters, and upon some blue-black substance. This had blown in when, as a dark hail, the Flies referred to fell in the city, carpeting it with their blue-black bodies, which had been asphyxiated a thousand feet up.

Then Pullman saw that, to what was left of the windows, the insect blue-black was adhering. Closely packed along that part of the window-frame where the glass fitted into it, and where the wood leaves, as it were, a little shelf, were the flattened bodies of the flies. Distributed among the smaller black-bodied flies were large, pallid locusts. It was these that had made a sound like tin.

Pullman returned shakily to the settee, and Platon resumed his position on the floor beside his master. As Pullman sat down, a kind of complaining wheeze was heard from Satters, and from now Satters gave off more and more evidences of returning life. One of these was to give Pullman a heavy kick on the shin. It was about twenty minutes before Satters opened his eyes. They were two big wondering and alarmed baby-eyes; and then speech began: "Wha... wha... wha... what..."

"Shut up."

"Oh. Per... per... per... I say. Wha... wha... what... Pulley... Pulley..."

Pullman began to feel extremely sick. He had thought all that was more or less over. That of course was not the case. Irritably he grated at his budding responsibility, at his big baby. "How do you feel?"

But he did not wait to listen to the explanations of Satters. He went into the kitchen with Platon. "It will be about a couple of hours I imagine before the electricity and gas fitfully appear. Let us," Pullman said, "plaster up the windows of Mr Mannock's bedroom" (for it was extremely cold). "I suppose nothing is intact, but the curtains may only have been blown down, we could hammer them up. Refix all that: on top of that, spare blankets must be tacked. Tin-tacks."

A bellow came from the living-room.

"As soon as the windows are fixed, I think we should carry Mr Mannock in there, put him on the bed, and cover him up. It is still disagreeably cold."

Pullman now went towards the bellow which had become an indignant roar. When he had first got to his feet, soon after Platon's arrival, his limbs felt as if they were made of paper. When he began to move about, they seemed to have no reality in the way of weight. "Am I," he wondered, "becoming metaphysical again." All his physical reactions led to the formulating of such a question. For, upon entering the city, some supernatural power had endowed Satters and himself with the full metabolism of the human body as known in their life on earth. What had apparently happened during the two terrible hours of inexplicable uproar and attack (and the very atmosphere may have been withdrawn while that was going on) was that these precarious advantages had been lost, and the gut-equipped mannikins had been degutted. The agonies Pullman had suffered were, he supposed, due to their partial re-equipment. But he was far as yet from the normal young man who, with Satters, had first made the acquaintance of Mannock. He was still only a shell, a mere shadow of himself. It was as a shadow that he moved towards the living-room to deal as best he could with another shadow.

But he felt a little uneasy about the shadowy quality of Mr Satterthwaite who, because of his youth, was probably fifty per cent ahead of him in recovery. However, there it was—to his ex-fag he must have appeared as masterfully organising everything. In a second spasm of anxiety, the question as to whether he would be strong enough to deal with Satters presented itself. He would have to lie down on the job, put up the shutters, throw up the sponge, strike, unless this preposterous baby quietened himself down. To make his mind work properly, he found, was nearly as difficult as it had been to gain control of his physical self: and he was not sure which it was, his mind or his body, which now seized the handle of the door, and flung himself inside into the room, looking tremendously tough. He addressed Satters aggressively: "What is all this about? Who told you you could blow off steam like that! Shut up, do you hear! Shut up!"

A howl of despair greeted this. Pullman sat down in the centre of the settee, as usual, his body turned towards Satters.

"Now sir. No nonsense. Your Pulley is not himself. Nobody is his dear old self—*except you*. You are most dreadfully yourself."

An explosion of self-pitying sobs was the response to this statement of the position. Pullman moved along the settee towards Satters and smacked his face. There was enough force in this blow to shake, it administered a shock both to the fat body and to the rudimentary psychology. The former fag put his hand up to his cheek, and there came a sound like a deep *ooo!* The eye above the *ooo* was full of sullen anger.

"I did that to see if you could move your arms. You can. Are your legs equally movable?" He pinched the nearest of the fat legs, a really vicious compression. Satters jumped ostentatiously. "You beastly cad! Pulley, you are a beast to pinch me like that!"

Pullman stood up.

"Can you stand up," he demanded.

He got a grip on Satters—such a grip as you would get on the front of a footballer—and succeeded in pulling him off the sofa. "Now stand up, you lump of dough! Up! On your feet!"

Pullman felt so abominably sick after these exercises, that he moved away in the direction of the door. Satters, collapsed upon the settee, followed him with a big reproachful eye.

"Come with me to the lavatory! Do you want to urinate? Come with me. Quick!"

He left the room, and hurried to the water-closet. As soon

as he reached it he catted: then stood anticipating other spasms—feeling washed-out and empty, but propping himself against the wall, as he gazed down into the pan. Soon there was a heavy blundering step; next the doorway behind him was filled with a glaring, bedraggled, but obviously incontinent, schoolboy.

"I say, Pulley . . .!"

Pullman, the colour of a very green apple, backed away from the pan, and roughly changed places with the other. "Go on. You are more important than I am." He left Satters inside, shutting the door.

That was the end of it as far as Pullman was concerned. He was good for nothing except a bed, he had literally nearly killed himself over the revival of Satters. But Satters had been brought to life and put upon his feet. He had wound up Satters, he was ticking again. Falteringly he made his way to his bedroom, shook the dead flies off his bed, and subsided upon it.

It was three hours later that Platon wakened him. "GAS!" was the word he heard, and at the same time he became conscious of electricity. Subduing extreme fatigue he rose and went to the bathroom. When he had urinated, Platon appeared. The houseboy's face had a different look, it was somehow bellicose, but, that apart, he was utterly jaded, and to say that he was in need of sleep would have been a criminal under-statement. Mannock, he explained, had shifted a good deal, and groaned, but so far he had not opened his eyes.

Pullman went to the kitchen with Platon, where some coffee was being made. As they went, he said shortly, "Mr Satter-thwaite?" The houseboy poked a disrespectful finger in the direction of the living-room. Washed and dressed, he went in where Satters was sleeping upon the settee (a sign of quite extraordinary displeasure on Satters' part to be lying here, preferring the settee to a bed within whispering distance of his master). Pullman gazed down at the snoring fag, but Satters refused to wake up.

"Coffee!" shouted Pullman. "Eats! In Mannock's room." He left him there, and went back to do for Mannock what he had for Satters. Satters, however, had no intention of being out of it. Soon he could be heard evacuating the living-room: and next there he was, sleepily scowling, rubbing his eyes with the back of his hand, and picking his nose. The Masterful One stood gazing down upon the sick man. Ignoring Satters, he went out of the room; in a few minutes he returned with Platon at his side, who placed a tray of coffee near the bed. Platon had painted with iodine the incision where he had removed the piece of glass from Mannock's neck; he had also, with great difficulty, forced the hair to lie down. As Pullman watched, the sleeper's shoulder moved convulsively and the face turned upwards on the pillow.

Pullman again bent over the oldest and by far the most seriously affected of them. "Mannock. Mannock!" he said loudly and emphatically, squeezing his arm and patting it. Within five or ten minutes Mannock was lying with his arms stretched out on either side, and slowly and painfully speaking. "Hallo. Has that terrible noise stopped? I should like to know ..." He stopped, and struggled to piece together several words, in an orderly way. "Is he safe ... Padishah?" Pullman told him (without any justification) that the Padishah luckily had been spared. "S-Stan-field ... all right?"

Pullman had not the least idea who Stanfield was, but he answered firmly, with the ring of truth. "Stanfield is in excellent shape."

His mind put at rest as to the well-being of the Padishah and of Stanfield, Mannock settled himself, closed his eyes, and went to sleep. It was as if he had asked, a look of morbid anxiety in his eyes, "How is His Majesty the King?" and having been assured that His Majesty had never been better, had sunk into a restful sleep. But Pullman wakened him again, and pressed him to drink a cup of coffee. "It tastes like molten lead!" the patient whispered, pushing away the cup. But Pullman insisted that he should go on drinking the molten lead. This ordeal appeared to have made him a little wakeful. Satters, grimacing, was attempting to drink his coffee. Pullman sat down and proceeded to do the same thing. For all of them this was a mysterious and semi-solid liquid. Satters went to the bathroom to vomit. But, in spite of the horrible experience with the coffee, Pullman seemed temporarily even to return to his normal self.

His voice was stern: "Is what we have suffered of frequent occurrence here?" he inquired of Mannock.

Mannock began shaking his head with such emphasis as he could muster. "No, no, no . . . Never before."

Pullman gave his beard a stroke, and emitted a deep, a very deep and dubious "Ah!" Then suddenly he asked, "What does this mean, Mannock?"

Mannock looked frightened. "I do not know. Really I do not know."

"If you do not *know*, Mannock, what do you *suppose*?"

Mannock raised his eyebrows a little piteously. "Nothing at all . . . absolutely . . . I am a spectator . . . like yourself."

"I am sorry you do not feel strong enough to give a guess," Pullman observed, almost disagreeably. "I should have thought that, however rotten you felt, you would have had a dim speculation or two about this awful business."

The invalid seemed about to cry. But instead, making an effort, he remarked fairly audibly, "One thing is clear enough . . . Satan is the culprit . . . Beyond that, I have no idea as to what was going on."

Satters, who had returned, and resumed his seat, lost a few shades of his robust colour. "Satan," he repeated in an awed whisper.

"Yes. The Devil," Pullman barked, "and you will soon find yourself in Hell, and some gluttonous demon will be cooking you in a pot. He will regard you as a tender morsel."

A look of unmitigated terror appeared in Satters' face. "Pull . . . Pull . . . Pull . . ."

Pullman looked at him.

"Per . . . Pulley! Are you serious? Do you really think . . .?"

Pullman stood up, went over to Mannock and patted him gently, saying, "Now you must go to sleep again. I am sure we shall all be alive tomorrow, and possibly the next day. The only one I am anxious about is Satters. He *is* such a great fat tender morsel."

Obtaining some extra blankets from Platon, Pullman and Satters went to their beds. A wind sprang up again, but of a normal type, a little blusterous and with some rain. The glassless windows made it necessary for them to put their heads under the bedclothes. In spite of these conditions, Pullman was asleep almost as soon as he had lain his head upon the pillow. The last thing he was conscious of was the sound of chattering teeth from the bed of the terrified Satters.

IT WAS TEN O'CLOCK in the morning when Platon shook him several times. Pullman had never felt so much at his last gasp as at that moment. It was a strange, at once stiff and limp mechanism which washed a face, and drew trousers over two white, oddly-shaped sticks of flesh.

When his great feats had been performed he had been an entirely different man: the masterful fellow who had brought back Satterthwaite from the dead and even got him upon his feet, the lord of the sick-room who had made Mannock open his eyes, who had put his mind at rest regarding the health of the Padishah, and who had then reawakened him and administered hot coffee–*that* was a man of another clay, a legendary Pullman.

Yes, indeed it was an impossibly ramshackle mechanism which forced the eel-like limbs into the tubes of cloth, and forced the feet into two shoes of iron. The legs took him along the passage, and in the passage there was an impulse in the air, it effected a connection. As he slipped through the front-door he asked himself who it was wanted a *Bulletin?* The apartment door closed behind him and the stairs were a little jolt at every step. He understood better, out in the street, how the atmosphere had altered. It was another mixture, it had stuff in it he did not recognise at all. But it was fresher and also thinner. He sniffed it with pleasure, but it was bad for him, it had no body. It might take some days to thicken enough for him to be able to wind up the clock, but it would be best for them to keep quite quiet until that time. Before he had reached the end of Habakkuk his heart seemed about to chime. It began striking slow and heavy blows. He leaned against the wall of a house. As he stood there, two people were rushing along the other side of the street; one was screaming "No, no, no . . ." as he ran.

The pursuer (for this figure, in expectation of immediately overtaking the other, had his hands stiffened into a claw-like shape) tripped and fell forward on his face, remaining there without any movement. The other, still screaming, shot round the corner. About twenty yards away two men were approaching, as slow as the other two had been the reverse. They were supporting one another—two of the clownish, sad, youthful faces, but now of a deathly pallor.

The heavy sadness all over this city was understandable enough, in view of some of the details of what Mannock had told them by way of elucidation. Some of these mad-looking creatures had been here for several centuries, in spite of what Rigate might say: they might have walked the streets of London at the same time as Dean Swift: they might have been a valet of Bolingbroke's, or something of that kind. Then, having reached this strange city, they must have begun a mode of life quite different from what now obtained; as fashions changed on earth they would change too, at length becoming haggard doctrinaires of Youth, as they were at present. Did they look back? Hardly that, seeing that in order to remain real they must passionately adhere to the fashion. Having heard people speaking differently round them they would always follow suit. It was now, perhaps, nothing but a dream, the life they led when dressed as contemporaries of Gulliver; when first they picked their way down what was now Tenth Avenue, and what then had a different name and aspect. They must sometimes find themselves using expressions which they could not explain, or thinking in a way long discarded, which they could not understand. As he thought about them, Pullman marvelled at this population, living fanatically in a period which was not theirs. This, he reflected, is what would happen on earth if there were no death. Men would be whispering to you of how the Vikings first landed; or would tell you how they had seen Charles the Second, very elegant and smiling graciously, arrive back to take his throne.

He felt a little stronger, his heart beat normally again, so he reacted to the support of the wall and continued his way round the corner. He was now in the street which led to the big café. How hideously deserted it was; how all this peculiar world he had escaped into was getting to look like war-scenery, like blasted cities.

There was what must surely be a bomb-site on the other side of the road; and many of the houses appeared to have acquired cracks in their plaster, or have lost their chimneys. Most windows had no glass.

The question of provisions nagged at his mind—very bad

about provisions. If no provisions could be obtained would these strange creatures eat one another? He could see them in his mind, in all those lines of rooms, tearing their finery off, and devouring their emaciated companions. Was the one in flight just now the weaker "youth"–had he a premonition of a cannibal attack, was he going while the going was good? Ha-ha, the clever little clockwork, scuttling to where he couldn't be eaten.

He gave a start; round a corner had come a man talking to himself. He appeared to be alarmed and puzzled. He did not notice Pullman hastening to escape him. But soon Pullman was alone again, obsessed by the *Bulletin*. Without the *Bulletin* all might be lost; he might be lost, for instance. He thought he would make the *Bulletin* his grail, for if he were not bearing the *Bulletin* he was stuck. He could never come up this street again. But his legs were working, though, if they would continue to do so, that was the problem. Would he ever have the energy to reach the café? Could he drive his body along even a step farther–which had done too much, had been too masterful. Always the master. And now he began to have hallucinations. He thought he was *at* the familiar café: he stood at the side of it and looked into this vast sea of chairs and tables. Perhaps a miserable twenty derelicts were huddled at the side, not very far from him.

But what was this–a figure shot from this little company and sprang through the chairs and tables towards him. Pullman put himself in an attitude of defence, his upper lip rolled back from his theeth, his hands hanging loose and ready at his sides.

The figure came so quickly–and was so small, because he was waiting for a giant, that he could not see him. He heard a voice saying, "Ah, Mr Pullman, how are you, you are still alive, anyhow, that is the main thing. Do you recognize me, Mr Pullman? Sentoryen do you recall?"

Pullman put his lip down over his teeth. What was this speaking? A soothing kind of assailant. And then in a haze he began to see the image of a face that was familiar, a smile that he had seen before. Then came the name Sentoryen.

"Sentoryen," he said. "Oh, yes, of course we met. This is not the best of cafés. I am not quite sensible . . ."

"Oh?" Sentoryen was anxious, very anxious, but still smiled.

66

"I have no strength. That is in addition to having no sense. You understand? Will you come with me to another café, if I can make it . . . It is only a block away."

So they went together (slowly, and sometimes tremulously) to the other café, Sentoryen holding him by the arm, and sometimes by the waist.

"This is less popular, but a far pleasanter place," Pullman informed his guide.

Sentoryen was superhuman: he was affected very little by the storm, and yet everybody in the city was as much exposed as anyone else. Contact with him had acted as a tonic: and Pullman found that he walked with very little difficulty this extra block, conversing an almost normal amount. He would have an escort on the way back to Habakkuk. Sentoryen had his uses.

Pullman found his way to a table, like an actor in a dream. In this quieter place they came upon a man selling the city *Bulletin*. Pullman bought a copy, and Sentoryen looked over his shoulder, laughed with extreme detachment, and lighted a cigarette. The hastily printed message did not set out to be funny, but it appeared so to more people than Sentoryen. It ran as follows:

"A terrible battle is occurring on the earth. What occurred a short time ago was a reflection of it in our atmosphere, only greatly magnified of course. We hope the Citizens were not too much inconvenienced. All householders will be fully compensated for any loss they have sustained."

Pullman looked up, and gave off a haggard laugh. "Is the *Bulletin* always as funny as that?" he inquired.

"Sometimes it is funnier," said Sentoryen.

Truckloads of armed police passed on several occasions.

"This city seems to be well policed," Pullman muttered, as if to himself. But Sentoryen promptly agreed, saying, "It is the only efficient thing about the régime. They have a really terrifyingly efficient police-force. You notice the trucks they are pulling behind. That is to put the corpses in."

"Corpses!" Pullman glanced quickly around him.

"Yes, thousands of people died you know. In the poorer districts the corpses have to be removed to that dreadful subterranean warehouse: the other classes conserve in privacy."

This was a *terrasse,* which was surrounded by a shrubbery planted in boxes, protecting the clients from the street. They had sat down in a corner seat beside the door, and at right angles to them was another table, at which sat a figure, labelled by Pullman a "droop". Suddenly the "droop" addressed them. "I hope we are not going to have any more of yesterday's fearful business. Terrible it was, terrible; I have lived here for forty years, and there has never been anything of that kind. What do you think, sir, of the *Bulletin's* explanation: I am afraid I cannot accept it."

It made Pullman a little dizzy, he found, to listen to this old gentleman. Well, the "droop" had a beautiful forty years to look back on in Third City. Beautiful sedate years, and a quite nice income. There was nothing nearer to paradise than that, for *that* person.

"It does not strike me, sir, as a particularly reliable sheet." Pullman spoke rather thickly.

Their neighbour seemed repelled by Pullman's manner. He had not the energy to supply a superfluous civility. People were speaking excitedly at some of the other tables, and two men were having so violent an altercation that one of them sprang up, gesticulating, and upset his coffee over the other one. This was by accident, but there was a great deal of shouting, and Pullman said, "Those gentlemen must be congratulated, they have a great deal more energy than I have. They are drug-addicts—yes?"

"They seem certainly to be possessed of an unaccountable amount of vitality," the smiling Sentoryen delicately inserted his contribution.

But the neighbourhood of passion was making Pullman feel very sick. He hurriedly paid, and, when they were outside, he realized how unreal that little speck of normality was. It was the world of the streets, this terrible deserted series of streets, which was the ultimate thing. As they were returning to Habakkuk, there were a few figures here and there, but all off them at the last gasp it seemed.

"Was not that café an hallucination," he asked the entirely intact, the sound and smiling young man. And as he looked at him he shivered slightly. "And are you not an hallucination yourself?"

With a great deal of *brio,* intended to chase away the oppressive vision, Sentoryen deprecated: "I hope I am not so improbable as some of the people in that café were!"

They were at the corner of Habakkuk, and bade each other farewell with cordiality. Sentoryen explained that he did not like to knock at the door of the apartment, because he felt that Mr Mannock would not approve. Pullman allowed this remark to go unheeded. He gave Sentoryen a masterful and final handshake, and went indoors. In the precarious apartment once more, he found that, during his brief absence, a very unreal personage had got into it. Mannock had a visitor–Mr Hilary Storr. Their nearest neighbour, this fine gentleman lived in St Catherine, and had dropped around to discover how "Willie" (Mannock) was, and to suggest a trip (by taxi-cab) to Tenth Piazza. This was a male of around the same age as Pullman himself. "How do you do?" he said very patronisingly, his eyelid fluttering, and his eye drifting away over his shoulder, and back to Mannock. It was obvious that Mr Hilary Storr's line of country was in a very different country altogether from that of which this bearded bohemian was a citizen.

"It took me a half an hour, but I telephoned to Charles. He appears to be just alive. He was the opposite of loquacious. When I asked him of he was going down to the Cadogan, he said. "No I am going to Hell," and he recommended *me* to go there too!"

This seemed to bring "Willie" back to life. "I am in complete agreement with Charles!" he cried, creakily, but with a sparkling eye.

"All right," lamented Mr Storr, as he got to his feet, with a kind of jauntiness at half cock, "if anyone tells me to go to Hell, I shall take a cab to the centre of Tenth Piazza, and sit down there till Satan's next attack, I refuse to die in my bed."

Pullman passed into the kitchen, he handed the *Bulletin* to the person on whose behalf he had acquired it. The houseboy read, with more facility than he would have anticipated.

"Do they take us for damfools ah! Their *Bulletin–*their *Bull-ly-teen!*"

Back in "Willie's" bedroom, Pullman said, in so many words. "Your houseboy wishes to see relatives. Give him three hours leave . . . As you have lost Mr Storr, sleep. I shall sleep too."

This was glumly okayed by Platon's master. Very quickly Platon left, and without another word Pullman went to bed. The demonic chaos, above which swam his conscious reason, a lucid speck–the dirtiest recesses beneath–put on a drama of such cathartic excess that he soon awoke, shaking, with obsessional images which survived waking, and continued living and developing upon the black backcloth of his mind. He had recourse to a small flask, containing powders wrapped up in papers. He washed two of these down in a glass of water. In a few minutes he was asleep again, out of reach of black unreason.

VI

M ANNOCK STOOD IN FRONT of the mantelpiece: he stood
a little unsteadily. He said presently, in a tired voice, but in a
dogged way that made Pullman look up, "I don't know what
you're going to do, but I shall get Platon to ring for a taxi-cab
and go down to Tenth Piazza. It might cheer us up, what do
you think? Will you both come along? I want to look in at a
café or two, and hear what the world says. I would have a
brandy-and-soda if I knew where to get it," he added recklessly.

This was Saturday morning. The had all had breakfast together, and were now sitting in the adjoining room. Since the
fetching of the *Bulletin* on Wednesday morning there had
been stagnation; for Pullman had been laid up, at times even
delirious, whereas Mannock had very slowly indeed reached
the point at which he could stand in front of the mantelpiece
and propose a move into the world outside.

Pullman laughed, for he could not refrain from a pointless
analysis of the actual terms of his host's proposal. "I do not
much wish to hear what the world says," Pullman looked
almost as haggard as his host. "I expect its views are very
much the same as my own. But let us by all means get out into
the balmy air of Third City." He turned to Satters. "What are
you going to do, young man? Why don't you lie down and rest
yourself?"

But Satters had no intention of being left behind: and, when
the taxi arrived, they all three went down and found that the
taxi was in fact a large and comfortable automobile. Pullman
and Mannock took up their position inside, and Satters sat with
the driver.

It was half-way down Tenth Avenue, where the houses were
only two or three storeys high, that they ran into the crowd,
collected to inspect and chatter about the flying dragon which
had crashed during the "Blitz" (as it had come to be known).
It was the body of an animal of stupendous girth; its spine was
like a large tree which had been blown down by a storm; one
end of it invaded the shops on the farther side of Tenth
Avenue; the other and somewhat thinner end stuck up over the

71

houses upon which its body lay. Three or four pairs of legs protruded on either side. The back of the beast was not unlike a vast map, printed upon a parchment-coloured oilcloth; it covered three or four houses. Its tail curled over a two-storrey house on the side of Tenth Avenue opposite to the body.

The car in which they arrived was ordered to park on the left-hand side, in an empty back street; and a small street, which was a kind of continuation of this, was perhaps the worst sufferer of all from this tragic end of one of Hell's finest dragons. One of the wings of the dragon was stretched like a tent above it. Its head acted as a hideous arch above the entrance to this little backwater, its eyes staring glassily on one side, its jawbone standing on its teeth at the other side. Its skin was of a greenish white, veined like some marble, but deeply stained beneath the eyes, and where the lips drooped around the teeth. The stench was almost unbearable beneath the bony arch of the face, and where the big sail of the wing tented the little street.

They left the taxi, and Pullman noticed, as Satters got out from beside the chauffeur, that he was bathed in sweat. Taking him aside, he asked him what was the matter.

"I don't know what's the matter with me, Pulley, but I'm trembling all over."

"What are you trembling at? The Dragon? It's dead."

"I feel sick."

"Just be sick, if you feel that way," Pullman told him. But he placed his arm around his shoulder, and, as it were, took him under his protection.

"Come. Keep by me, we will walk along together. This stinking beast would only be alarming if it were alive."

Then, taking Satters by the hand, Pullman and he overtook Mannock, who was walking towards a crowd of people, some of them uniformed officials, others the entire neighbourhood seemingly.

"This is a committee of some kind," Mannock said. "They seem to be discussing the situation."

But their deliberations were held in an atmosphere of such wild disorder that it was surprising that they should consider it possible to continue. The uproar was terrific. This was an Italian quarter, and fully a hundred of the inhabitants of the little street left their card-playing when these uniformed officials arrived, and charged them in a body, shouting at the top of their voices. Not only did they shout, but flourished their fists over the heads of the official party, stamped about all around them in a sort of war-dance, and gesticulated incessantly with all their arms and feet.

Their individual remarks about the personal appearance of each and all of the visiting committee, and the chorus which many of them joined, constituted so multitudinous a libel that it was difficult to see how it could be tolerated under the circumstances. But the nasal provocation would justify anything.

"This is the fourth time," the tenants roared, "the fourth time, you do-nothing imbeciles, that you have brought your carcasses round here, to sniff, at a respectful distance, this fine museum-piece— Do you not understand what you are doing–what you are paid to do, but what you do not do? Do you not realise that we live in the stench of this filthy monster–that morning, noon, and night we have the benefit of the effluvia of this hellbeast! If you do not cart away at once this foul reptile we will throw petrol on it, and set it on fire, even if we burn this part of the city.

You–if we see *you* again, we will take you by the scruff of your necks and rub your snouts against the beautiful body of this stinking beast.–Go! go! go! go! Order the police to bring their trucks, and to cart away this monster in pieces! We will not have it here any more! Do you understand–Sheep's Brains, overpaid nobodies. Worthless servants of the citizenry. Go–Go–Go!"

This and the like continued, in a torrential chorus of scurrility, all day long, or at least as long as these gentlemen remained in the neighbourhood. Mannock and the other two walked beneath the arch of the head, and began to approach the greenish gloom produced by the overshadowing wing. Pullman held Satterthwaite firmly by the arm, but he felt his charge shivering and shaking violently, and then Satters vomited, and, afraid that he might collapse in his arms, Pullman returned with him under the arch, where he vomited again. Mannock caught them up, saying to Pullman, "Phew! I should not much care to be one of the poor devils living in these houses." He began to cough and spit, and Pullman, glancing around at him, saw that his face was of a pallor not unlike that of the dragon's skin.

"How do you feel, Mannock? You look rather rotten."

"I feel as sick as a cat. I heartily agree with the strong expressions used by the people who live here."

A man moving in the same direction as themselves called out that that was nothing to what had occurred elsewhere in the city. "The stink cannot be lived with, and thousands of people have been evacuated to another part of the town; and all the Sanitary Service men wear gas-masks. Even so, some have been taken to hospital. There are twenty of these beasts at one spot, and twice the size as well."

Several members of the party of infuriated tenants turned around and addressed Mannock, overhearing what he and the man were discussing. "These officials," said one, "come here day after day to chat about our dragon. They do nothing. How would you like to have this flying reptile from Hell parked on you indefinitely?"

"Not at all, sir. I should be lying in a hospital bed if I were you. Why don't you go sick?"

"Go sick, go sick! I have two sick little brothers lying inside there, breathing in the stench, oh yes. If this were a proper country, if this were a State . . .!"

The taxi-driver had disappeared; in about ten minutes he returned, saying that the beast must be half full of air to rush about in the sky like that. Mannock assented to the probability of this explanation, adding, "But when they begin sawing him up and release the imprisoned gases, I personally would rather be somewhere else."

They drove as far as the upper end of Tenth Piazza; that is to say the end where the underground station was situated. They got out of the taxi. Gazing around them, they stood at the top of the four massive steps, extending for a great distance, which denied the Piazza to traffic, and from which it looked not unlike an enormous sunken bath.

"Is should not think that there were more than twentyfive per cent of the usual promenaders," Mannock observed.

"There are hardly ten or fifteen per cent, I should say," was Pullman's view.

The shops were open with a few exceptions, and this strange

population moved up and down, looking into them and discussing the quality of their wares, as much as possible as if nothing had happened. For this was their life (if one can speak in this way of people, who, to be quite strict about it, were dead). If they were to be destroyed, and that for ever, the next day, or the next week, why should they behave differently, now, than they always had done, drifting meaninglessly, acting the living without being the living–acting the young without being the young. They looked sadly out of their faces, a little whiter and more pasty-looking than before, a little darker under the eyes, their eyebrows a little more wearily raised; but, without being analytical, with much the same appearance as on Tuesday, when Mannock and his guest first came to Tenth Piazza.

And what they felt everyone must feel, so Pullman reflected –he, and Satters, and everybody else. They were all half alive in a mysterious void; and so long as their hearts ticked and their brains functioned, *tant bien que mal*, and the breath came and went in their nostrils, they must continue to play this game for what it was worth, prepared for a thunderbolt which would blot them out at any moment.

Mannock's thoughts were rather different from this: and now he took them, with a somewhat excited trip to his step, into a coffee house or café which was really a club. It was large and comfortably appointed. You entered it, of course, from the Arcade, through swing doors into a vestibule, and then through curtains into the place itself.

Everyone seemed to know everyone else, and one felt that an intruder would be stared at, and be taught not to treat this place as *public*. Mannock led them to a distant corner where four or five men were engaged in a somewhat violently pessimistic discussion. There was an atmosphere oft the Last Days about this company.

"This is James Pullman and his fag, Satterthwaite," was the way in which Pullman found himself introduced. Everyone laughed. Their conversation was temporarily suspended so as to get used to the newcomers.

"Pullman has only been here since Monday evening. As may be imagined, he does not know what to think of our curious city!" Mannock added, amid general laughter. "He has brought his fag down to give him some exercise."

Satters, who was moment by moment becoming more sure of himself, at this point protested. "I say, sir, if you don't mind my correcting you, I am not Pulley's fag any longer. He does not have to take me for a walk."

There was a roar of delight at this.

"He's been to the Central Bank like all the rest of us!" shouted one of them. "There are no fags where there's a Central Bank."

When this was all over, they returned to the topic which absorbed everyone in the city, except those who were too permanently proletarian to think about anything but being that and so forth. These five typical members of the younger clubman class turned their minds again to unravel the mystery of the shaking of the city, and of the rain of flies.

A man in the middle thirties, with eyeglass and moustache, burst forth: "I was passed into this paradise by the Bailiff, as a perfect specimen of the English Officer-class. The next paradise I have to qualify for I shall demand a prospectus before I apply."

"You are ungrateful," Mannock told him. "The Central Bank gives you a hundred dollars more than it does me because of your military status. I am only an old China hand. My background was the Bund, not Bond Street."

"Still grumbling about your income, Mannock?" a round-faced, round-bellied person remarked. "Give us your opinion, Mannock, of Tuesday's events. I am afraid that things look pretty black to all of us here. Hugh gives us a maximum of twenty days to arrange for the next world, *if* there is any world after this."

A large man, with side-whiskers and heavy eyebrows (this was Hugh), turned to Mannock. "Mind you, twenty days is the utmost limit. Before the middle of next week all that business which burst out on Tuesday will be renewed. I have this from a trustworthy source."

"The Bailiff," Mannock smiled back.

"*Not* the Bailiff. A far more reliable informant. Smile, oh Mannock, but you will see! You have not much time left to write your last Will and Testament. Tuesday was only a trial show."

Satters was showing signs of imminent disintegration. He

whispered to his protector. "I say, Pulley, did he say twen...
twenty days ... or was it years, Pulley?"

"Hush." Pullman frowned at him. "What does it matter, you
damned fool. You have to die some day."

"D'd'd'd'die!" Satters lost such poise as had remained, and
seized one of Pullman's hands in desperation. Pullman looked
at his white face, and expected more vomiting at any moment.

"I am afraid you have knocked out Pullman's fag with your
pessimism," Mannock told the offender. Everyone noisily
relaxed in good-natured guffaws, and Satters' confusion was
complete.

The man sitting next to Mannock said, lowering his voice:
"It is terrible about poor old Quentin isn't it?"

"Quentin!" Mannock's face was dutifully agonised. "What
has happened ..."

"He died during the Blitz. I thought you might not have
heard. There was Bob Slater too; of course he was a bit
elderly ..."

"Elderly! No. Bob Slater was middle-aged, a little senior to
me. I have not seen Bob for a number of years now, but he was
a very decent fellow. I am terribly sorry. But Quentin! I can
understand anyone dying, however. It nearly did for me."

"Willie, you can answer this one. Has a Bishop precedence
over a Baron?"

"Yes, I am afraid he has." Mannock's father had been Bishop
of Coventry, and so he was an authority on matters of that sort.
He had to refrain from showing joy that Bishops should rank
higher than Barons.

He looked smilingly round at Pullman, and said infor-
matively, "My father was a Bishop, and so questions of that
sort come my way."

"Indeed. That is very interesting," and Pullman had the air
of making a mental note.

There was a man rather unfortunately named Charles, and
he leaned over to Mannock, speaking in a pretentious way.
"I say, I could not help hearing you say that you had a bad
time. So did I—in fact I only turned up here a half an hour
ago. And I am told by a man who gets about the city a good
deal that literally hundreds of thousands of people died. And
all of us are sick."

Hugh, who had heard this, joined in. "They say there was some poison discharged into the atmosphere. I felt pretty rotten and I am sure it was not entirely because of the bombardment."

"No. I am positive it wasn't!" shouted Mannock's neighbour. "The atmosphere has been quite different ever since. As I was coming down here today a man fell dead a few yards ahead of me."

"How awful!" Mannock looked distressed.

"Much the same thing happened to me," said Hugh. "I was sitting in a small café near the street I live in yesterday, and a man collapsed in his chair. The police were sent for and announced that he was dead."

"He had probably been doing too much," said another. "It is the heart you know. I fainted yesterday—at home I mean. I just had to come down here today, but I think even now the less one moves about the better."

"I came down in a taxi-cab," said Mannock.

"Very wise," said the other. "But how the devil did you get a taxi-cab?"

"My dear sir," boomed Hugh, "all you have to do is to go out into the street to that public telephone, tell them you are ill, and they will fetch you within a few minutes."

The conversation drifted on, when Hugh returned to his favourite theory, and everyone listened attentively.

"What we all forget when we are discussing this business is the fellow who really has the last word as to the future of Third City, who, if he wants to, can blow it to pieces." Hugh paused and then snapped out, "That man is Satan."

Satters clutched Pullman's hand in such an access of terror that one of his nails left a blood smear at the side of his master's palm. Pullman hissed in his ear. "What the hell are you sticking those dirty nails in my hands for!"–"Did you her-her-her ... Pulley, did you her-her ..."–"Yes, I heard, why don't you cut your beastly nails!" Pullman was sucking his highly septic wound, quite indifferent to the distinguished company.

Mannock was uncomfortably aware of the unseemly scene being enacted at his side. He said, with a slightly embarrassed laugh, "I am afraid that Hugh's last statement has so terrified

Pullman's fag that we shall have to take him out and let him have a little air, or he will faint."

The others had been hanging on the words of Hugh, but, like all true Englishmen, welcoming the comic relief, they once more roared their applause at the matchless fag. So Mannock and his two peculiar acquaintances filed out, since it was impossible, where Satters was, to talk in the way Hugh was talking. There was this other point, that Mannock did not very much like to have the Devil brought into a discussion.

Keeping very close to Pullman, Satters got out of the café as quickly as possible, whispering as he did so, "Pulley, do let's get away from that man!" For he had begun to attribute to Hugh some of the horrifying qualities of Satan. Once in the Arcade, Mannock stood aside from the passers-by, obviously wrestling with some problem. Pullman stopped too, keeping one eye upon his host's face, meanwhile wrapping a handkerchief around the lower part of his hand. At length Mannock spoke. "It seems to me, Satterthwaite," he said coaxingly, "that you would enjoy strolling round the shops better than coming to the place where we are to pay our next visit. If you walk along here," and he indicated the Arcade running at right angles to where they were standing, "you will find yourself at the upper end of the line of shops where we were walking the other day. Where you bought that jumper. You are a strong healthy boy, and a nice walk would do you good. If you would make a tour of the whole of that side of the Piazza, and back, I think you would find plenty to interest you. There is a little café there, exactly in the corner, called the 'Golden Fig'. See it? We will meet you there in just over half an hour. Don't hurry, Satterthwaite. We will wait for you. I will give you some doughnuts when we arrive."

Satters looked extremely dejected, and cast appealing glances at Pullman. Mannock drew a piece of paper out of his pocket and hurriedly wrote on it where he lived. Handing it to Satters he said, "You will not need this, Satterthwaite, but keep it in your pocket. It is my address, and anyone would tell you how to get there. You will not get lost—there is no chance of that. We shall meet at the 'Golden Fig'. This is just *in case*."

"Oh, Pulley, I do not like leaving you, Pulley." There was a deep dog-like entreaty in Satters' voice.

"Nonsense, nonsense. You get under way!" Pullman pointed in the direction of the "Golden Fig". "If you don't hurry up you will not get that beautiful doughnut that Mannock promised you. Be off, now, you silly little coward. Are you an English boy? You don't behave like one, you little cissy."

They at last succeeded in getting him off their hands: after which Mannock headed for a stately looking building not very far from the café they had just left. "This is the Cadogan Club," he told Pullman. They went up several steps, and found themselves in the imposing entrance of what was apparently a Pall Mall Club. To one of the three uniformed men inside an office near the top of the steps, Mannock said, "Is Sir Charles up there?" "Yes, sir, Sir Charles is up there, sir", the man replied. "With Mr Fortescue, sir."

They ascended a wide and sumptuously carpeted stairway, which, half-way up, turned round at right angles and took them up another half a dozen stairs. They soon found themselves in a very large room with a number of very large armchairs. In these sat, here and there, twenty or more gentlemen. Near an over-large chimneypiece several massive armchairs were collected together, and several gentlemen sat in them in conversation. It was towards these that Mannock directed his steps, Pullman following. A few minutes afterwards James Pullman found himself installed in an enormous chair, listening to three or four sahibs discussing the recent "outrage", as they described it. "What next will he do?" inquired one.

By "he", Pullman divined, the Fiend was understood. The attitude seemed to be that "he" had acted with unprecedented impudence. Did this presage some unspeakable action-to-come? Must they regard themselves as being upon the eve of something which was tantamount to . . . well, to the winding-up of a system which had endured for . . .! Heavy indignation–deep alarm–profound alarm, was certainly the order of the day in the leather-upholstered Cadogan.

"You think, Charles, that 'he' will dare . . .? After all, 'he' has challenged the Great Architect of the Universe before."

"Yes, Willie. I do believe that 'he' will. After what they now call the 'Blitz' I believe him capable of anything. He gave me a very bad shaking."

"I am black and blue. He gave me a lot to think about," observed a very perfect clubman, whom Pullman intuitively knew to be Mr Fortescue. There was nothing, thought he, that would make these faded old satraps understand what the world was like. They were persuaded that they were the rulers of this city (or as good as); and here they were, discussing the present "crisis" as if they had been members of the Government (or as good as) in a replica of the clubesque sanctuary where they and their ancestors had sat discussing such things for hundreds of years. "He" (the Devil, of course) was, for them, like Louis XIV, or like Bonaparte, or like Hitler, only in "his" case it was a *supernatural* enemy. The danger was very great, certainly. But they felt absolutely secure, in their enormous leather chairs, whatever they might say.

Pullman listened to the kind of conversation which he had just heard at the other club (or café).

Mannock's at once startled and scandalised face poised itself for a moment, and then he burst out. "You don't mean to say, Charles, that anything has happened to *Fosters* . . ."

"I am afraid so; he died in the Blitz. You know how we were all put to sleep, weren't we. Well, Fosters never woke up."

"How *dreadful*." Mannock sat for some minutes looking so genuinely shocked that Pullman wondered how he really felt on these occasions. He must think that out later on.

It was Fortescue this time who spoke. "You have heard, Willie, haven't you, about poor Peter Mainwaring?"

"Peter Mainwaring?"

"Yes, it is really quite appalling. He died yesterday. I was with him actually. He was unable to recover from the ordeal of the Blitz (excuse me for saying Blitz)–how is one to refer to that ghastly performance of Satan's?"

Pullman felt that one more revelation of members of this circle struck down as a result of the Blitz and Mannock would have an apoplectic fit; this time he appeared to be speechless, actually he said nothing.

But Sir Charles followed Fortescue with a third demise. "Of course this is the first time that I have seen you, Willie, since the Thing. I'm damned if I will say 'Blitz'. Well, I am afraid there is more bad news. Poor Bill . . ."

"Not Bill Sandiman!" Mannock's anguish burst in, by this time his face was quite haggard.

"Indeed, yes. I am sorry to have to say that Bill died—it was *here*, the day before yesterday. Actually in the chair in which you are sitting."

This seemed to have a peculiar effect upon Mannock. It was as if he felt that he was sitting where Bill Sandiman ought to be sitting—or rather, that no one should sit in this chair . . . oh, for at least a month. He was not a Tory, but a sentimental Whig: to hear of the deaths of these three people, and all pillars of Third City Clubland—and what other ones were there about whom he had not yet been informed?—affected him a great deal. Of course they would not die in the earthly sense; but was it not perhaps *worse*? Pullman would not have been at all surprised had Mannock expired at the same spot where Bill Sandiman's demise had occurred. He held his breath, in fact, for a moment or two. Then he leant over and said something to him. Mannock rose (glad to be out of the chair, Pullman said to himself), and stood looking down at his friends. "What you have told me is ghastly. I had no idea that anything of this kind had happened. I have to leave you, I fear. This gentleman's fag is awaiting us at a neighbouring café. He is a very nervous boy, and I am afraid we must go to him at once."

They redescended the splendid stairway, and at the bottom, as they passed the porter's office, the same man inquired, "Did you find Sir Charles, sir?"

"Yes, thank you, Harris," Mannock replied. And he asked if it was possible to get a taxi. "I feel dreadfully tired," he told the man, who answered, "I expect you do, sir," and disappeared, making his way to a public telephone.

When the taxi arrived, Mannock asked to be taken, in the first place, to the "Golden Fig". There was Satters, awaiting them with hysterical anxiety. They hustled him away into the taxi, first purchasing a bag full of doughnuts. "Now you see," Mannock told him, "there was no need for alarm, was there?" But Satters did not at all agree that his panic was merely idle and boyish.

As the taxi hurtled along, Mannock apologised to Pullman for such a strange set of friends. "Such stuffy circles have their uses. I keep in touch with those people because they often get hold of information possessed by nobody else. One of them, Fordington his name is, is particularly good for the official lowdown. Charles is an old darling. I am very fond of him: and the Padishah confides in him a great deal."

Pullman marvelled, as he was saying this, at the sublime conceit of this Carlton Club type of Briton and how Mannock, in talking to an "intellectual" like himself, should wish to dissociate himself from his friends. He did not quite unterstand what Mannock's "intellectual" claims were.

VII

MANNOCK HAD NOT ONLY been shocked by the news he had received at the Cadogan Club and at the kind of "Café-Club" which had been their first place of call, but he felt very exhausted when they got back to the apartment, and he at once took to his bed. It was not only the mortality among his friends at the time of the Blitz that was depressing, but the account of death from delayed shock, which made it obvious that care should still be taken by people who were no longer young. He had a horror of the drawers or of the cupboard which was greater than any sensation he had ever experienced. Pullman strongly advised him to rest up for a day or two, and to see a doctor before resuming social life. Next day was Sunday, and Pullman was only too glad to rest himself for a little longer. Satters was a problem; but he arranged that that greedy boy should be given so large a lunch that he could be relied on to sleep at least till teatime. When Monday morning came, Satters could be restrained no longer. He vanished immediately after breakfast, and did not put in an appearance again until his compulsory return when a police van brought him back that night. Pullman himself felt rather restless, and very much better as a result of his spell of inactivity on Sunday. He had a conversation with his host on the subject of his temporarily installing himself in some hotel in the neighbourhood.

"You see," he said, "the uncertainty here is so great at the moment that I cannot see myself renting a flat or anything like that. In a few weeks it may have been agreed to forget the Blitz, we may all be in blinkers and 'back to normal'. But, for the moment, I can contemplate nothing more permanent than a hotel. Do you know of a good one not far from here?"

Mannock would not hear of this. "Of course you must not dream of house-hunting just now. Why not lodge with me for the time being? Allow a few weeks to pass, and then reconsider the matter."

Mannock had some letters to write.

"I think," said Pullman, "I will go to Tenth Piazza and acquire a wardrobe. It is really high time. I noticed what looked like a suitable tailor during our walk. I did not see any shop where I could get myself something to put my stuff in, a suitcase I suppose."

Mannock explained: the point at which, on that first day, they had decided to come home, after having administered a doughnut to the fag–it was beyond *that* point that he would find two shops, both much the same, where anything from a suitcase to a cabin-trunk could be obtained.

Pullman started off at once. No sooner had he stepped out into the street than, like a djin, Sentoryen stood before him.

"Good morning, Mr Pullman, I am so glad to see you up and about again. Do you feel all right now?"

"I must say that you do not seem subject to the lapses from the norm from which we suffer."

"No?" The young man's face was so richly and healthily toned with a kind of even asiatic bloom that it was impossible to imagine him ill. "For the last few days I made so bold as to call on you at your apartment, and the houseboy was very polite and friendly. What he reported was slightly alarming. But when I saw you and your friends getting into the taxi on Saturday, it was obvious that you had recovered. Now can I be of any use today?"

Pullman did not wish to take Sentoryen with him to buy clothes, and another thing was that he had been looking forward to being by himself. So he declined his offer of assistance, but suggested that they walk as far as the underground station together. On the way they had a pleasant chat, and he was bound to say that Sentoryen was a very sensible kind of djin. But *why* he presented himself in this way, with unbreakable punctuality, he preferred not to investigate for the present. At the Metro, the smiling escort was dismissed.

On the way down to Tenth Piazza he gave himself up to speculative musing. He talked gently to himself upon the following lines, attempting to sort a few things out while he was by himself, and had time to do so. It was a rule with him never to use up time allotted for sleep by cudgelling his brains. He felt that if once one made a habit of *thinking* in bed one would very soon never do any sleeping there. And he greatly prized his ability to sleep.

In any case, he liked thinking things over while he was on the move–or on the wing; while in flight across Europe he had once planned out something which could not have been better planned, though it was himself said it, to be sure. And it was proverbial how the morning bog was an ideal occasion to work out crosswords, or think up the title of a film. What a place he had got into . . . was there any way out of it? That was number one question. Dear me. You would have to be a bit of a genius to get to the bottom of that. But, first of all, had anyone ever got out of it? *Yes.* He thought they *had.* He did not believe that this place was devised to stop in. No. The man, or the god, who was responsible for Third City, did not build it as a permanent residence. It was intended to be *provisional.* It was now practically a permanent place of drooling residence. Hence the delay–or one of the hences. Now, one of the two all-important things to find out was whether a scholarship were still obtainable for a better place–for he doubted whether anyone got shot down to Hell from here. He did not see how a person could demonstrate his wickedness; on the other hand, was there much scope for advertising one's goodness? Not in the circles he had moved in up till now.–There were other circles. There were the Catholics. More than fifty per cent of the city probably was Catholic. The enormous cathedral (he heard it was) near Fifth Piazza must have some influence. These might be idle thoughts. He had in very early days been brought up by the Jesuits, yes, in Ireland. And his family had been Catholic from the beginning. He was not saying that he ought to remember these compromising facts, oh dear me no. All he could tentatively uphold was that, in a very nasty fix (and God knows it was that and all), there was absolutely nothing in the universe that should be overlooked. He could see himself figuring as a saint–an Irish saint if the dice fell that way. And even such an idiotic chance as that had to be examined. Such an inquiry might lead to something else. It might lead quite in the other direction. What had to be discovered was where the true power was to be found. Whatever his private feelings might be, the point of maximum power had to be located, and those possessed of this maximum were the only safe circles to have any truck with. It was a good thing now that he had met Mannock in the way he had. That hat been very enlightening. Anything that Mannock supported was certain to fail.

He was now at the top of the stairs leading to the street, and, as he stepped out on to the pavement, Tenth Piazza lay before him, in all its peculiar attractiveness. The number of people promenading was much the same as two days before: even apart from the numbers, there was no elation, no shopping elation, among the people he passed in the arcades. They were all gathered round the shop windows as before, but in some cases they were completely silent. He walked across the Piazza to about the point at which Mannock had entered the arcades when first he conducted them there, and strolled along taking note of the various objects and shops which it was his intention to visit. His first purchase, of course, must be the suitcase, and so he continued until he reached the first of the two stores mentioned by Mannock. He saw the trunks and suitcases on display in the window, and, after a glance or two at these, he went inside. It did not take him long to select a fairly large, strong, good-looking suitcase. His next visit was to the outfitter's: so, carrying the suitcase, he returned to the shop he had picked as the best for his purpose. There he bought two suits, one for everyday wear, one for ceremonious occasions. And, since he had continued turning over in his mind the problems of evasion as he had strolled along the main arcades, he said to the shopman, who was measuring him for his first suit, "Is there any recognised means, sir, of escaping from Third City? I would gladly take a chance ... risk my neck, I mean, in order to leave this place."

The man, who had the tape just between Pullman's legs, looked up at him quickly.

"I have not often met a man who wished to leave Third City," the tailor said ... "except to die. But there was a time when I felt that a change was desirable myself. There is, I believe, a little town about thirty miles away, over there beyond the Camp."

Pullman pricked his ears up at this. "What is it like? Did you go there? Have you ever met anyone who has lived there?"

The shopman shook his head. "No, sir. It is not a very nice town, I believe. You are hanged if you show any signs of believing in anything."

"That would not suit me," Pullman said. "I never have been able to get rid of my beliefs."

The shopman laughed. "The man who rules the roost there is mad. He thinks he is God."

"That settles it, I shall not go there."

"Do you believe in God, sir?"

"I believe it is necessary to have a God, to keep out men like the fellow who rules in that town you speak of."

The man was standing with the tape in his hand. He looked at Pullman. "That," he said, "is perhaps why the fellow we are speaking about pushed himself forward. Perhaps he thought it was necessary not to have people like himself pushing themselves forward."

Pullman laughed. Next door was a hatter's, into which he moved. There he bought a hat with a rather wide brim, such as is worn in Paris. He looked at himself in the glass, and noticed his disgustingly dirty tie.

The tie. How was he ever to buy a tie in this city which was not as great an insult to man's intelligence as a surrealist picture. He had gazed in so many tie-shops, and he had not seen a tie that a sane man would wear.

Turning to the hatter, he said, "Excuse me, sir, you are not as mad as a hatter is generally supposed to be: you have sold me a very sensible hat. Can you tell me where I can buy a sensible tie?"

The hatter laughed. "Oddly enough, sir, I can answer you what is an incredibly difficult question. If you go along here, as far as a shop called 'Picolo', and say you come from me, the shopman will show you a few ties he keeps in a drawer in a corner of the shop."

"Thank you very much, sir, for that extremely valuable piece of information."

Pullman took up his case, and, following the man's instructions, walked down the arcade. He entered the little shop called "Piccolo", passing, in two windows on either side of the door, a mass of the most scandalous ties he had ever seen, which, indeed, the maddest American would shrink from. He went up to the man in the shop, and said, in a low voice, that he had come from a certain hatter, who had told him that he might obtain a type of tie there which had never been worn in that city. The man took him silently into a corner of the shop, opened a drawer, and there were a variety of ties of the kind you would only buy in Bond Street. He picked out two, and the man wrapped them up. He had carefully selected two of the more gaudy ones. A handy shoe-shop provided him with shoes, slippers and socks (the indecent bravura of the socks would remain hidden, to some extent, beneath the trousers). Since, with the footwear, the outfit was complete, the next problem was to get all these purchases back to Habakkuk. He turned to the shopman.

"When the bank gives you your first packet of money," he said, "does it realize that you will have to spend most of that on setting yourself up with wearing apparel?"

"No, sir," the shopman answered. "But if you go there, sir, and ask for another two or three hundred dollars, they will give it to you. They will give you all you want, or almost all. Do not hesitate on this account, to buy three or four more pairs of shoes. If you have not enough money left, we will give you credit. As much as you like."

"How can I get a taxi-cab?"

"That is quite easy, sir. Outside there is the public telephone. I will order you a taxi-cab." When he had returned to the shop, the man said again: "They do not like us to use taxi-cabs except when it is necessary. Cabs are not allowed to ply for hire. Almost half the people in this city do no work. If taxi-cabs were not severely restricted, and if it were not somewhat a matter of honour not to telephone for a taxi, except in such a case as yours, with the uncomfortably heavy bag requiring transport, there would be an enormous traffic problem, people would drive all day in all directions. Scores of thousands more police would be required; roads would have continually to be repaired; there would be great numbers of accidents. You notice there are no omnibuses? That is an expression of the same determination to keep the streets clear. The taxi companies do not allow people to use their cabs without some legitimate excuse; if you went to that public telephone and asked them to send you a taxi-cab, they would inquire what you wanted it for. I, for instance, when I telephoned just now, explained your predicament, *and they know me.*"

He looked hard at Pullman, as if to say that he was *someone* in this city, and that Pullman should have been flattered at being shown the ropes by such a man.

The taxi-cab arrived, and, as Pullman left the shop, he raised his new black hat. He said nothing. Silence, he felt, would be more impressive.

An hour later Pullman was sitting down to lunch, so changed a man that Mannock burst out laughing. However, it was a good-natured laugh, and Pullman said, "It is too easy. The man who sold me this frightfully elegant pair of shoes said that, if I was refraining from purchasing half a dozen more pairs, there was no need whatever to do that. He would be delighted to give me credit. All I had to do was to go to the bank and ask for another two or three hundred dollars. 'This time,' he added, 'you will be better dressed than you were last time. The man at the bank will be very much impressed. You should have taken the precaution to come here and get yourself tidied up before you paid your first visit.'"

Laughing gently at the lighter and happier side of life in Third City, Mannock agreed with the shop-keeper. "The shop-keepers," he pointed out, "are the self-respecting part of the population, and usually the more intelligent; I know Simpkins very well . . . it was to Simpkins you went, was it not? He is a man of considerable understanding. I may say that we have been in prison together," he laughed. "At the time of the troubles you know."

After lunch, Pullman was invited to come down to Fifth Piazza. "About three o'clock," Mannock told him, "there is to be a deputation from Hades. They are sending a little party of diabolical diplomats."

"Is this quite usual?" asked Pullman.

Mannock sighed. "Most unusual," he protested. "In fact I should not have said that it was possible for such a deputation to come here at all, certainly not at such short notice. However, there it is. A delegation from the enemy who was responsible for that frightful rumpus last week are to meet the home team in a display of open diplomacy. It is, I think, rather a good sign."

They travelled by underground, and eventually came to the surface at one end of Fifth Piazza, a very large open space, only smaller than Tenth Piazza. Like the latter it was paved and arcaded. It had the same bare impressiveness; the houses, of not more than three storeys, were coloured a uniform café-au-lait. The crowd was dense; half of it knew why it was important to be there, and this was the Catholic half; the other half had not the vaguest idea what this spectacle might mean. The centre of the Piazza was roped off, and along the inner side was a continuous line of armed police. Pullman noticed several truck-loads of civil guards stationed near the corner of the Piazza (for the underground was happily not far from the area where the meeting was to take place). The excitement of the non-Catholic half was not less intense because of their complete lack of interest in what was at stake. As this was the vocal half, where Pullman and Mannock were it seemed a solid thronging of idiots. "What *is* Hell, Bert?" and "Does the old Devil smoke cigarettes?" Pullman heard one man say to another. "I've been 'ere a hundred year and never saw a devil, have you, Ernest?" The other said, "Are you *that* old, Arthur?"

There was a loud explosion. The crowd received this with a gasp, pressing tightly up against the ropes, with a deeply drawn "Oh!" The infernal contingent advanced with a dancing step along the Piazza to the appointed meeting-place. That was exactly in front of where Mannock and Pullman were standing; they edged their way to the front, but had their toes trodden on and found themselves in unsavoury proximity with a stunted rabble, determined to see, and resenting the toffishness of Mannock. Straight in front of them, and not distant more than a couple of dozen paces, was the home team: it was beautifully blond and clean, two lines of uniformed men, carefully chosen from the police for their blue eyes and flaxen hair. One was almost white, he was so fair. Standing in front of these picked men was one of the hundred personal companions of the Padishah–angels like himself. He was a very tall and muscular young man, and looked extremely angry. The eyes of the beauty chorus behind him were fixed upon the horrible throng advancing against them, and did not look better pleased than their chief.

As the diabolical contingent drew near, exclamations of horror arose all the way down the line. "Are they yewman?" asked a spectator standing between Pullman's legs. "I'm buggered if I know," the man stationed between Mannock's legs expressed his ignorance. Mannock bristled. "How shameful! I know I shall be sick in a minute," came from him. Pullman trembled; he was silent.

To a roar of fear, of disgust, of half-human cries, snorts, and gasps, advanced pirouetting the double line of demons hoofed and horned, frisking and cavorting, ogling and grimacing, and, not by any means least, emitting the most revolting stench. This assailed the noses of all the spectators, however far away, the moment they made their appearance. As they advanced, with every step they stank more, and the smell developed intolerably.

"What a ghastly sight!" Pullman muttered to his companion; "and oh my god, what a smell! Nothing human stinks like that."

Their leader was a man. He was large and powerful, extremely dark, his face appearing to be discoloured, and, stepping very quickly, he strode up to his opposite number, until their faces were a foot apart. A very elegant summer suit and brown shoes seemed to constitute him a man born of woman, though his countenance was so charged with evil that if he had walked along a city street in London or New York he would have been arrested at sight. He appeared to spit some words towards the face of the angel, and the other shook from head to foot with rage, but glared without spitting.

The crowd everywhere had recoiled a few feet, but the armed police stood their ground.

The infernal contingent eyed, sideways and slit-faced, the onlookers as they passed them; these monstrous, sideways, half-men were throughout naked–except that you would not call them that, any more than you would use such a word regarding an elephant, or a kangaroo, or an ape. Not that they belonged to an unmixed type; they had the smile of an inexpressibly loathsome man, but they stamped upon a hoof which was purely animal. Purely animal were their powerful, oily and hairy legs. Their arms and hands were disagreeably human;

except that the top of the arm, like the breast, was covered in thick hair; the head was a mystery–the face was that of a very large goat, but it had many human attributes.

Most enigmatic of all were the messages which darted from and smouldered in the elongated eyes.

Nearest to the spectators was a hoofed creature, with a human face, goatish and leering. His penis and his tail had the appearance of being a continuous organ, the tail growing out of the body at the rear exactly opposite the place where the penis issued from the body in front, arching downwards as did the tail. The nipples hung from the breasts, like corkscrews, and two short horns sprouted out from the scaly forehead. This man of hoofs kept sliding his eyes around at the spectators, and suddenly he thrust out a hooked tongue, which protruded almost a foot from his face.

"Oo, did you see what the bastard did?"

"Ere, 'Arry, did you see 'im boy!" A head shot about looking for Harry.

In the second rank of the infernal animals was one with so goatish a countenance that his curving nose constituted almost all of the profile of his face.

All the twenty, prancing, shuffling, swaying backwards and forwards, chattering, starting, laughing, snarling, grimacing incarnations of evil, were never at rest for a moment. One of them lifted his tail and excreted. Another urinated.

As they drew up behind their leader, in two tumultuous lines, one or two of them protruded their tongues at the line of blonds in front of them. One turned his back and farted. Several of the beauty chorus held handkerchiefs to their noses, which provoked hilarity in the infernal ranks.

Pullman was fascinated by the abnormal brooding and violent expression of the man detailed to command these monsters at his back. He watched him as he stood there, wondering if he would deliver his message verbally or in writing. He did not have to wait long for the answer. Both Mannock and himself could hear every word with perfect distinctness. What, using a byronic formula, one might call, respectively, His Darkness and His Lightness, gazed into each other's eyes with such an infinity of hatred on both sides that Pulmann wondered how they could stand so still. The hatred that came from Hell

93

was a steady, withering stream of fire, wheras the angelic rejoinder was disposed to flash indignantly.

The first words came from the darker of the two.

"You know what I am here for, Goody-two-shoes!" he hissed in the other's face.

At these words the large blond countenance erupted. A furious response burst out of it on the instant, the big red lips shooting out the vocables in a disgusting moist expulsion: "Potboy for boiling the damned in tar, what should you come for? Travelling for your dung-shop, is that it?"

He from Hell affected dignity. "I am a bearer of an order from my chief. You—all of you—are to leave this place immediately. We order you to get out of this place without delay, and go back where you came from. Silly little songbirds of Jesus. This city is of no use to you. What do you do with it? Nothing that anyone can see. You pray all day, and leave it to the Bailiff to manage. We can make better use of it than you, so hand it over, or rather vacate it, the whole hundred of you. If you do not, we shall come here in very great force, and make an end of you."

"Is that all you have to say? And is it as an advertisement for your perfumes that you bring with you those foul animals?"

The devil's envoy leered back, a long obscene leer. "No, I brought those to shock your sensibilities. Disgusting, isn't it?"

"You should have come like that yourself, instead of dressing up as you have. It was out of respect for me I suppose. Have you anything else to say?"

"There are many things I could say ... about your blond beauty chorus for instance ... I could say a lot about them."

The big blond face in front of the demonic leader was again convulsed, subject apparently to sudden rages. His voice flew up into the highest register.

"We far prefer to be the opposite of what you like, Beelzebub's bottle-washer ... you little fetch-and-carrier for that Smell in Hell ... sucker-up-to-of-Satan."

"You ... You choir-boy of that Humbug in Heaven, you tuneful appendage of that pompous old egomaniac ... the Almightly Sod—beg pardon, God."

What these two figures were saying to one another could be heard a long way away, and in any case all over the Piazza it was obvious that a "row" was beginning. Everyone began to rush towards the centre of disturbance, and an avalanche descended upon Mannock and Pullman.

"I am glad you are here! I shall be able to shelter behind you." Shouting into Mannock's ear, Pullman grimaced.

"I don't advise you to, I am not a very solid wall." A genuine alarm was visible in Mannock's face, mingled with a snobbish distaste for ending his days beneath the feet of a proletarian horde. He began to look round indignantly for police protection. "Where *are* the Police Officers?"

As their pugnacity developed, to the amazement of everybody these two six-footers grew to be seven-footers, and the seven-footers grew to be eight-footers, and so on. The spectacle of these two carnival figures roaring at one another, standing so high above the surrounding people that nobody now looked anywhere except at these two miraculously growing men, had turned the meeting into something even more stupefying; and Pullman noticed that there was something in the nature of a hush at their end of the Piazza. What was going on in people's minds? Obviously the advent of that fear which must accompany a miracle.

A roar of such volume came from the Blond Giant as to strike terror in the crowd, many of whom began to edge away. The huge words crashed out in the air like a supernatural demonstration.

"Demon!" it began, and had a terrible echo. "Demon, I will crush you like a fly! Impudent black bug! I will annihilate you on the spot–Hell-bird, you will regret the day you brought your filthy troop to this city."

Hell's Envoy struck the other on the face, and the blow was a climax of alarm. There was a smothered "ooo" among the spectators: the police who lined the square made ready their arms. Quite half the people near Mannock and Pullman had disappeared, and the others stood with white awe-struck faces.

"If they begin fighting–and *growing*." Pullman whispered to Mannock, "we shall all be trampled under foot."

The blond giant returned the blow, and both the escort of demons, and the blond followers of the Padishah's sprouting Envoy, scuttled to the rear to avoid being trodden on. But the giants were now firmly fastened together, rocking about from

95

side to side. Such panted remarks as "T-t-take your claws away from my throat", or "Blast you, I will tear your eyes out," could be heard, in the midst of enormous breathing and threatening grunts.

Pullman had noticed long before this that both giants had kicked off their shoes, which lay, very minute footwear, not far from where their feet were moving. Their clothes had everywhere burst asunder. But it was at this moment that, with enormous splutters and gasps, they suddenly levitated. With the little garments of a mere six-footer, none of them intact, hanging from them in loops and wisps, two vast nudities rose into the air and disappeared over the roofs. But they made their exit buttocks uppermost. Hell was on top, as they rose out of the Piazza. Hell's messenger protruded against the azure sky an anchovy-coloured balloon. But this was immediately succeeded by an upsurge of pink limbs, of enormous size, climbing up on top of the darker element; and that is how they actually vanished behind the roofs, a picture in pink, wine-brown, and azure, the last things seen being three or four violently agitated feet, pink feet and brown feet, the stiff tumbling spikes of twenty toes signalling the agitation beneath. For those who still watched, with great excitement, the vanishing of the aerial combatants, there was a sequel in a very few minutes. Seemingly a considerable distance beyond where the agonised feet had vanished, the two figures, grown enormously in size, reappeared, locked together in a mad embrace, and aimed upwards towards the sun, the moon, and the stars. The light figure had now, springing out of its shoulders, prodigious wings, stretched to their utmost length, and dazzling white, whereas the dark figure protruded wings of a smaller size, dark and bristling. Blood dripped from both, and splashed down among the markets near First Piazza, so it was learned later on. But there was a third figure, of the white persuasion—an enormous full-sized angel, rising into the sky beyond the moat.

It was obvious at once that the diabolic intruder had seen this third figure, because an intensive struggle began occurring in the midst of the two original antagonists; the dark one was tearing himself away from the embrace of the white one. Almost at once the severance was effected, and a huge black figure dashed away over the roofs, coming down, it was reported later on, in Tenth Piazza; grown smaller already, he made a crash-landing near the centre of the Piazza, rolling over and over like a parachutist reaching the earth at the end of a drop of considerable depth. Then he was seen to spring into the air, and land upon a balcony above the long arcade. There he crouched, getting smaller and smaller as the people watched him, and then there was a loud report, and he was covered in what was described as a little cloud, like that caused by many forms of explosion. When the smoke cleared away, this combatant, the dark one, had disappeared. Above the Piazza the two white angels had flown circling round above the crouching black figure; when their enemy had evaporated, they turned and flew in a wide circle over the city, and were last seen circling down towards the enormous barracks, at the moat-side, where the hundred angels had their post. The wounded one was still bleeding as he flew. And that was the last that was seen or heard of this supernatural combat.

Pullman stood back exhaling noisily. "Almost thou persuadest me to be a Christian," he said, as if to himself. Mannock was about to reply when he seemed to change his mind. He continued to gaze up into the sky, apparently displeased. The crowd stood uncertainly as if in a dream. Everyone began looking at everyone else, some with a smile. But a new event took the place of the old. There was a fresh roar from the crowd, as two of the animals had sprung upon one of the blonds in front of them, and had dragged him over beneath their hoofs. Then they proceeded to tear him to pieces, rolling him over and over, and both of them scratching his face and neck. The blond was screaming, and, at the sight of the blood, the neighbouring crowd began a violent demonstration. However, several of his fellow-blonds had rushed in to rescue him. This they had partly succeeded in doing, but with the result that the entire body of goatish-men and beautiful young policemen were at each other's throats.

It was the lorryful of troops which was parked immediately above the station-entrance, who saw in detail what was happening first. Pullman was nearly thrown to the ground by an onrush of armed men. Jumping over spectators lying in their path, the troops swarmed through the police-barrier, and at once the sounds of rifle-fire mingled with the screams and groans of the combatants. But quite half of the animals had withdrawn from the struggling mass. They huddled together, showing every sign of alarm and anxiety. They chattered together, casting fearful glances over their shoulders, and moving a little towards the centre of the Piazza. Two police blasts sounded, and on the other side of the Piazza they advanced from where they were standing in front of the onlookers. About a dozen, with rifles drawn at the ready, bore down upon the uncertain group of animals, and helped them to make up their minds which way to go, and also determined for them what speed they should adopt for their withdrawal.

Meanwhile the confused battle proceeded where a few more aggressive animals were leading the attack on the blonds; but now the troops were attempting to pick off as many of their infernal visitors as possible. "Crack-Crack. Crack-Crack" went the rifles, and with a howl of unearthly pain an animal fell to the ground. The blond casualties who had been pulled out of the mêlée by the police were in an awful condition. Pullman noticed in one case, that the young man had had his trousers forced open, and his sex had been literally torn from his body. Then, as though obeying a signal, with great abruptness the animals broke off where they were fighting, attempting to disengage themselves. Quite suddenly they appeared very anxious that the battle should terminate. Dragging their casualties after them, they began gliding away, in some cases clutching up the wounded, carrying them in their arms like an enormous baby.

The Civil Guards who had been engaged, though merely as snipers, in the mêlée, at once stepped back, allowing the animals to join their main body without molestation. As to the blonds, more bitterly and totally engaged with their demonic opposites, as if by magic relieved of the necessity of fighting they stepped back too, all more or less seriously wounded. Like a number of big schoolboys, they walked or hobbled back to where their lines had been, comparing notes, showing one another bitten fingers, scratched faces, and, in one case, Pullman noticed, a quite severe eye-injury had been sustained. Some looked back towards the casualties, who lay in a neat row, being given first-aid by the police. Pullman heard one say: "The filthy bastards nearly did in old Albert."

The attention of Mannock and Pullman had, up to now, been

fully occupied. They looked at one another simultaneously, smiling as they did so.

"What was the meaning of that remark of yours . . ."

"About being a Christian?" Pullman interrupted him.

Mannock nodded his head, saying, "Yes. I see you remember."

"Mannock, we have witnessed a miracle! People in this city disappear into the sky, two or three times their normal size . . . and I see live devils in front of me, not many yards away." And he crossed himself.

"A most confirmed disbeliever would publicly beg our pardon," Mannock agreed.

"That is what I must do," Pullman sighed. "But I must do so to a priest."

"Do you know where the Catholic Cathedral is to be found? It is just at the farther end of this Piazza."

"Thank you," Pullman said.

The hostility of the crowd increased, which seemed to entertain the demons. With girlish giggles, and splutters of laughter, some of the demonic creatures were chattering together, evidently saying the equivalent of "What a game! What shall we do next?" But the majority were more serious, visibly uneasy. They all were moving about without ceasing in a kind of St Vitus's dance. At the sound of revolver shots fired over their heads by two officers of the police, several of them sprang up for nearly the height of their bodies. It was in a less orderly group-with shrill noises, and stamping and scuffling, frisking and pirouetting, some of them ogling the crowd as they passed, that they reached the spot where they had first alighted. Then there came a kind of crack, like the sound of an enormous whip, and next moment that part of the Piazza was filled with a dense bituminous smoke. When it had cleared, the fiends, both casualtied and intact, were no longer there. Everyone was choking and spitting where they were near enough to be affected by the smoke added to the bodily stench of the animals. The police had begun clearing the square, and driving the remainder of the crowd before them into the sidestreets. Pullman and Mannock themselves took the way of the underground, Pullman muttering, "Yes, let us get home. I have a great deal to think about."

VIII

PULLMAN AND MANNOCK had not said very much to one another on the return journey. Back in the living-room they appeared somewhat taciturn also. Very soon Platon brought tea, and, after they were refreshed, Mannock spoke.

"I really do not know what is happening here. The man we saw disappear into the sky–I mean the blond one–I have met and talked to a dozen times. He was a very pleasant fellow; not much to say for himself, but as gentle as a lamb. To watch him growing in size until he towered over the Piazza, to hear him roaring out words which a kitchen scullion might envy, and this speech so magnified in volume that it shook the whole of the principal square, and lastly to see him, practically naked, disappearing into the sky, locked in the arms of an enormous demon from Hell, is not the kind of thing I ever expected to see in this city. What would we have said in our former life in London, say, if we saw the Queen growing larger and larger until she was as tall as Buckingham Palace; if we saw her take flight shouting curses at her Chamberlain, or perhaps at the Prime Minister–who also started to become unnaturally large, until his head appeared above the houses in Downing Street. What would our sensations be?"

"We should be justifiably amazed," Pullman declared. "But it is a thing which could never happen, because we are mere mortals, the Queen as much as ourselves. Now, here it is a different matter. You must allow me to say that you have made a mistake. These are supernatural personages, our rulers here. You have tended, I feel, to treat them too much as if they were the King and Queen. All the time that you were talking to that Immortal (whom we have just seen in his proper rôle) you should have expected him to fly out of the window or up into the sky."

Mannock threw himself back in the chair where he was sitting, his face a battlefield of very disturbed emotions. Looking at Pullman with displeasure, he answered him in the following way.

"Thank you for your lecture. I am most obliged to you for pointing out my shortcomings. But I am a very simple man who takes things and people as he finds them, and is not gifted with second sight."

Pullman saw at once that he had made a bad mistake, and that with so conventional a man as Mannock a much milder and duller attitude was essential. He had been very much excited by the spectacle in Fifth Piazza. But so had Mannock, as was shown by his own imaginary picture of a gigantic Queen. Yes, but because Mannock had been betrayed into swollen and fantastic imagery, the temptation to talk big in reply should have been resisted.

"Ah well," and Pullman laughed, as he moved freely about upon the settee. "I am afraid I have been rather intoxicated by what I have seen. The scent of Hell is an aroma which does not suit me. The way I look at this afternoon's events is quite different from you. I am stupefied by the miraculous. All my life I was a sceptic. And now I see that I was very short-sighted. The miraculous here is the most common or garden of things: for men (whom we are able to meet socially) are literally walking miracles. I should not be in the least aston-ished if tomorrow Jesus Christ appeared in Third City; I should merely bow my head. If I heard the voice of God, I should not be surprised."

There was a pause during which Pullman observed all the anger had left Mannock's face, and he was considering what his friend had said to him. His face was so mobile, and ex-pressed his thoughts in such a stylish way, that it might be described as a very charming factor in the make-up of this very simple man. After a little Mannock began to speak in a voice that was completely changed.

"You know, Pullman, I am, I am afraid, a very worldly fool. You have opened my eyes to what I should have seen, instead of the quite dull things which I did see. I can't tell you how grateful I am, I might never have realized this if we had not been together in Fifth Piazza, and if we had not had this conversation afterwards."

His eyes were misted with tears as he looked over at the bearded figure, who, in a few words, had shown him the vast importance of what had occurred. They both sat in silence for some time, Mannock eagerly conning over the backgrounds of this revelation. Of God, he had always been mystically aware ... that is, when he was in a beautiful church and the organ was playing some terrific piece; but at other times this awareness shrank to something that he found it impossible to think of except as a cold abstraction: but *now* he had seen with his own eyes the great Mazdean Principles of Light and Dark, of the Good and the Bad, locked in a fearful embrace, disappearing into the sky. And what had he been thinking of a short while after that? He had been thinking of the indecorous behaviour of one of the leading figures in the ruling caste of the city—of something that was *not done,* or was *not said.* He felt very humble, but he also felt very elated.

He rose and stretched, saying, "I am not quite up to these revelations. I think I will go and lie down for a little."

"I should if I were you," Pullman told him. "I feel rather shattered myself." He stood up. "I think I will go and have a wash to start with. I may have forty winks."

They smiled at one another, and Mannock went to his room, Pullman to the lavabo.

About an hour later, when Mannock re-entered the sitting-room, Pullman was reading. He put down the book and inspected his friend with approval.

"Mannock, you look a new man, you look ten years younger. You respond to rest wonderfully well, and should have at least an hour of it every day."

"A very good idea," said Mannock. "But there are not many days, as a matter of fact, without my getting about that amount of sleep."

"I did not know that. It is as it should be, then." Pullman flung himself back, and stuck his hands in his jacket pockets. "Ah, what is this?" He drew out of his right-hand pocket a much decorated envelope. "When we came in from Fifth Piazza I found this on the halltable ... I don't know how it got there. It has been in my pocket ever since." He tore open the envelope, and pulled out a large card, brilliantly lettered.

"I was waiting for that," said Mannock. "The Bailiff invites ..."

Pullman handed Mannock the card, which he held between thumb and forefinger.

Mannock shrugged, as he gazed at the card. "Obviously, he considers you a Bailiff's Party man. Of course you must go to this Party and see what it's like. It might be instructive . . . you will see the glamorous throng which collects there. All the rogues in Third City."

Pullman shook his head. He thrust back into his pocket the card which Mannock had returned. "It might be rather embarrassing," Pullman said; "the Bailiff is, to my mind, an embarrassment."

"You had better see for yourself the kind of society by whom this man is surrounded. He is prodigiously rich–he is fabulously powerful. I should have a look, if I were you, Pullman."

They were silent. But a rat-tat-rat-tat at the front door Pullman instinctively felt was for him. He sprang up and hurried out to answer the double rat-tat. As he opened the door a slight scent reached him, an odour he recognized, then the smiling face of Sentoryen appeared through the half-opened door.

"You received the card, did you not? The Bailiff's invitation? You will come, won't you? I am sure you will enjoy yourself."

"Oh, I don't know . . . ought I to come?" Pullman spoke as if to himself, but Sentoryen understood.

"A car is waiting at the door. The Bailiff has sent a car to fetch you."

"I suppose," Pullman said gruffly, "I suppose that settles it. Will you wait for me in the car for a few minutes. I am terribly dirty and untidy. It will only take me a few minutes to make myself ready. You will excuse me if I close the door."

Pullman hastily went back into the flat. He explained to Mannock that a car had arrived to fetch him, with the usual emissary of the Bailiff. "I propose to asume my more formal attire." He hurriedly went to his room, washed and brushed, and then changed into his best suit.

Five minutes later he emerged, dressed for parade, sang good-bye to Mannock, and ran down the stairs, developing the party spirit as he went.

IX

WHEN PULLMAN CAME OUT into the street, he was surprised to find himself in the middle of an expectant group. He found he had stepped out into fairyland; the childish mind of Habakkuk was transforming his departure into a fairy scene. Here were a dozen of the standard faces of the ageless Youth of Third City. The nearest faces were smiling politely with raised (or over-raised) eyebrows, with goggling, questioning, astonished blue eyes, and he heard at once a soft voice, in a half whisper, as if for him alone: "Oh what beauty! Are you not happy? The Bailiff has sent his equipage–and his personal secretary. You are like Cinderella going to the great party at the Palace. My friend and I wish we were going too . . ."

This man followed him up to the door of the car, sniffing at the scent which Sentoryen exuded. His friend was just behind him, with almost exactly the same expression. Pullman sprang inside the automobile, adjusting himself beside the patiently waiting escort. The car gave a tremendous purr and glided away from among the smiling masks of the idiotically juvenile neighbours. Pullman gave a slight jump–he had been pinched immediately beneath the knee.

"A pinch for new clothes!" Sentoryen exclaimed softly. "Congratulations, Mr Pullman. I should not have recognised you if it had not been for the beard."

The chauffeur took full advantage of the absence of traffic, and hurled himself so recklessly forward that Pullman felt somewhat relieved when he reached his destination. Two sentries were placed at both of the giant gates; the car shot into the first gate, and, in a flash, stood before the bronze doors of the Palace, which were thrown wide open, a great number of uniformed men, both military and domestic, crowding within. They alighted, Sentoryen stepping quickly into the hall of the Palace and conducting him to the *vestiaire*, where a dozen men sat in a line to cope with the headgear of the innumerable guests. They now turned to the nearest entrance to the vast gallery where the Party was being held. It was of cathedral-like dimensions, accommodating in the centre a towering jet of water which splashed down into a large square domestic lake. This was artificially cooled, and produced, wherever you stood, a delicious freshness. There were over a thousand guests, all shouting at once, and there must have been far more than a thousand electric lights, of all sizes, heating as well as lighting the vast scene; icy as the water was, it produced coolness but not discomfort.

The over-all decoration was equally cold–there was no colour hotter than metallic black and silver, and all the blacks were cold blacks.

The plants, of which there were a great number, had no flowers: their greens were all of the cactus type, preferring a desertic green, bordering on blue: and geometric designs in white repressenting glittering flowers, at times mixed with steel and nickel, bore out the master idea of the décor. And it became unmistakable that the impulses of a polar background, rather than the multitudinous and sultry, the garish and burning elements of a tropical scene were aimed at, and icily carried out.

Against this universal, basic determination to be cool at all costs, Pullman was subtly assailed by the hectic scent of the man-goats of Hell, which had accompanied the dusky leader of the diabolic embassy in Fifth Piazza, mixed with a few ponderous perfumes of the negro attendants, and that king of stylish stinks, only produced by the smouldering vegetation of Havana.

"Corona-Coronas!" sniffed Pullman, "or my name is Susie Grippington."

"Will you have a cigar, Mr Pullman?" Sentoryen inquired. "Yes?"

Large negroes in shiny lemon jackets and white trousers were moving about, in all directions. Many of these bore in front of them very large brass trays–glasses containing apparently cocktails crowded upon them. Sentoryen clamoured, "Boy. One of you bring cigars–quick."

Pullman picked a glass off the tray.

"Cocktails?" he said.

"You bet," the negro answered.

"Alcohol?" asked Pullman.

"You bet."

Sentoryen laughed. "Alcohol. Tiptop alcohol. Would you like a whisky and splash? White Horse? Black Horse? Club? Any Scotch they can get you?"

Pullman sipped his drink. It was a Manhattan. He put his neck back; in two or three jerks he tossed the liquid down his throat. His eyes watered. He dashed the drops away from his eyes. He was now among the guests. All men, of course. They were moving quickly all around him. He did not like their moving so quickly. He sat down in a quiet little place. The water splashed, the orchestra played. It was however not so quiet as it had seemed at first. Not at all so quiet. He rose into the air ... two negroes were tossing him about.

"Drink this. Quick, or we shall be seen!"

It was Sentoryen's voice. His lip was pulled up, he gulped. Opening his eyes he shuddered, and sat up.

"I had forgotten," said Sentoryen. "You haven't been here long enough. Feel better? That's good." Pullman stood in front of the *vestiaire*. Two attendants brushed his trousers. He was unsteady.

"Where was I?" he asked Sentoryen.

"You went scuttling between the legs of the crowd. You made a bee-line for the fountain. I lost touch with you. Should you have disappeared in the lake–the Bailiff would have killed your Sentoryen. But no, you nestled down against the parapet of the fountain. When I came up with you, you had your eyes closed. You slept, I think."

"I had a syncope I suppose," Pullman said.

"Sin Cup? No, there was nothing in the cup."

When Pullman re-entered the Party, he did so unwillingly. For no reason he began meticulously to study the mass of guests. These men were rather young than old, of an unorthodox character; the hair tended to be long. There was a certain tension about the faces. His general conclusions were much the same as Mannock's–regarding his own personal appearance.

"A dirty crowd, on the whole," he observed. Sentoryen smiled, and withheld his assent. He saw several beards. Pullman noticed two small theatre boxes not far away, a half-dozen steps leading up to their hidden doors. Into one of these

Sentoryen led him. "Let us listen in," he said, and fixed a little instrument into his ear, which was attached to an almost invisible pencil-like, flesh-coloured object, which was looped around his forefinger. At once a loud voice sounded in the ear in which the little instrument was fixed.

"A dragon crashed into my house. The police have sealed it. I am homeless."

"That is what I said."

"A lot of beards. A dirty habit."

"The strings are weak."

"Ever since I've been here. The same bloody thing."

Pullman soon learnt to aim this object, rather like a pen-nib, at individual guests.

He heard, "I went to the bank. They gave me a thousand dollars."

"You see that man in that box, with a red beard. That's Pullman. The man who writes all that pretentious nonsense about the Patristic Age... Oh yes, and that too. I'd like to give him a good kick in the backside, but I suppose . . ."

Pullman looked sideways at Sentoryen. He moved back on to the black beard, who was talking about him.

"He behaved very badly about Jessie Blackstone... yes. He ought to have married her. If I'd been in Henry's place I'd have knocked his bloody head off. No. Pullman's yellow ... Didn't he run away when Plowden denounced him!"

Pullman turned the pen-nib down earthwards. He pondered hotly. There was a swine of a man libelling him all over Third City. Should he go down and slap him in the mouth? He got to his feet.

"You see that *black beard*?" He pointed, and Sentoryen nodded. "I want to speak to him."

As they moved out of the box Sentoryen said peremptorily, "No violence, Mr Pullman!" Pullman stared at him. Who did Sentoryen suppose he was?

The black beard decorated the face of so small a man, when he reached him, that Pullman contented himself with an insulting laugh. Pullman looked down into his eyes. "If you chitter-chatter you will find yourself sent back to the Camp." He held his hand in front of the black beard. "Weren't you at school with me?"

107

"Mr Pullman," began the other, the friend of the black beard.

"Do you want me to knock your teeth down your throat?" inquired Pullman.

"Come with me, Mr Pullman." Sentoryen's voice was accompanied by a pluck at the sleeve. He found it very easy to drift away with Sentoryen.

"They are a waste of time," Sentoryen was speaking softly. "You are still a little weak. Too dreamy. I will put you in touch with one or two Square Men."

They were still in the crowd, but two men were coming up out of the swarm. They were looking sideways at Pullman. He had a strong impression of something like two playing-cards gliding towards him, in which the blacks were of great intensity, the faces misty. The next thing was a shock–he caught his breath. Both were on top of him. He was moving along between two Squares with whom it was no effort to move along, but it was a hot glow.

"Most of this is earth-trash, Mr Pullman. We Squares move through a Party gathering like this. We Squares are nothing. We are Filters. We lean up against you and drain you. That funny *square* way of looking at you–that is getting your range, so to speak. We know we look comic. But we sink into the psychic medium you carry about with you, and purify it. There are very few people in this large Party we should care to touch. After the embrace, we offer our clinical services. We discover a great deal in the course of our drainage."

But Pullman did not avail himself of their services. He gave them a *square* look, and found himself with Sentoryen again.

"I think, now, Mr Pullman, you will be ready to enjoy the exquisite frigidity of the Bailiff's design." The orchestra was now playing Alban Berg's lyric suite.

Pullman began to understand that the Bailiff's idea of a Party was to provide you with the means of escaping from promiscuousness, from the psychological hot-water pipes. You had come, not to be with people–but to enjoy the contact of the lunar influences, and to relish humanity (if at all) in an icebox.

Giving Sentoryen a *square* look, Pullman said, "I feel I have a little more hysteria which should be drawn off me. Here is a décor which St Augustine would have welcomed, which the

108

eunuch in Origen would have been in tune with. Is there any further purification I might undergo?"

Sentoryen shook his head.

"Let us," he said, "drift towards the Bailiff, as you call him. "Those two squares you gave yourself up to are two very particular gentlemen. Oh yes. Those queer men who only like other men and dislike women . . ."

"Homosexuals," Pullman supplied the word.

"Thank you for that nasty word. Well, the Squares refuse to go near them. Oh yes, they are very particular. They do not like the Bailiff any too well."

"Indeed," Pullman said. "They are remarkable fellows. What do they do? They are a sort of masseur. They massage the soul. It is wonderfully nice."

"It is a terrific sensation. They will not do me." Sentoryen smiled, coyly, Pullman thought.

As they pushed forward into the crowd, which seemed to be growing in volume and in raucousness, they were in the centre of screaming voices. One said, "Ricardo died in my arms." Another voice said, "No gas. And we had no gas in our district until ten the next morning." Sentoryen, with a frown, pressed forward. Pullman now heard a familiar crowing voice. Ever since he had first entered the mass of the Party, he had been conscious, through the smoke of the cigarettes, in the distance beyond the towering fountain, of something like a stage. He knew that this was the real centre of the assemblage, and that there the Bailiff was to be found.

"I know the Bailiff wants to see you, Mr Pullman. We are a little late." Sentoryen urged him forward, against shrieking and stammering men, mostly discussing the Blitz. Then, sooner than he had expected, there was the platform straight ahead; and they seemed to come out in a kind of clearing, where the crowd was thinner; and, though he was still really at some distance, the Bailiff hailed him in a welcoming crow.

"Ah ha, welcome Pullman—welcome to Eternity! I am so glad to catch sight of you at last, my dear fellow. Come up here, there are the steps, to your left." He was pointing and dancing forward.

Pullman waved his arm, and moved quickly to the place where the steps were, and rose on them without stumbling.

A number of faces, ingratiating and polite, were looking at him as he approached their host; evidently it was an inner circle who never left the neighbourhood of the Bailiff and who participated in all the phases of his hospitality. It was as if Pullman had been entering a family reunion; a large, subservient group of familiars, all with their "kind," permanently amused, watchful eyes, in courtly tension.

As to the Bailiff, he was now a very different person from the barbaric, theatrical figure of the Camp. He was dressed in a dinner-jacket, with a soft white shirt, the wide scarlet ribbon of some order appearing above his waistcoat and crossing his stomach, while in his hand he held a large Havana cigar.

It was at once obvious to Pullman that his magistracy at the Camp was an act. It even seemed to him that he not only dressed up as an actor, but would, for his part, use pads and disfiguring accessories. He could not at once check the position of these. But he felt sure that the hump he made such good use of at the Tribunal was exaggerated. Certainly the Bailiff was bowed, but there was no sign of a dorsal distortion. There were other things as well; in short, he was now a more normal person. He remained an unusual figure; his square nose, his Punchesque chin, his rubicund complexion alone, would be identification assets anywhere. Equally distinguishing was his powerful voice, with its unforgettable nasal richness. Nevertheless, Pullman felt that he was in the presence of a less abnormal personality. Without former acquaintance with him one would have said that he was a prominent businessman, with a great deal of social talent; perhaps an ambassador or statesman, in any case a great (and pungent) personality. There was always the irrepressible malignity of his geniality–when at his most urbane that never quite disappeared.

When Pullman reached him, he had his hand grasped with a great muscular display of friendliness. "I am so glad to see you. During these last days I have felt the greatest anxiety about you. Sentoryen here is a highly trusted secretary of mine; at my instructions he lay in wait for you every day, outside your house (I instructed him not, except where absolutely necessary, to call for you at Mr Mannock's apartment). I would have come there myself if nothing else availed. But I heard from Sentoryen that you were well looked after, and the slight indisposition from which you suffered after what they call the 'Blitz' was quickly overcome. That is good, that is good. Has Sentoryen been a good boy?"

"He has been a very discreet, attentive, and sensible young man. I am most grateful to you for taking so much trouble about my welfare and," said Pullman, turning towards Sentoryen, "for choosing so charming and intelligent a messenger to guard over me and to guide me."

After this speech they all laughed, and everyone was in the best of humours. Sentoryen was dismissed, retiring into the crowd again, and the Bailiff took Pullman by the arm, and led him a little aside.

"I am afraid that you will have received a perfectly diabolic impression of Third City," said the Magistrate, "but let me assure you that it is not always as bad as that. In fact, it has much to be said for it; it is quite a charming city. I built a good deal of it myself."

"Ah," was Pullman's comment. The Bailiff threw him a roguish glance.

"First and last, you must have formed a low opinion of our paradise. Suspend your judgement. You are not properly housed, you know nothing of the avantages of the city, and there was that frightful brawl the other day. I am still black and blue myself," he pointed to his ribs and made a grimace of pain. "I shall not forget that for a long time. But *you*–within a few hours of your arrival to be subjected to something worse than an earthquake, to have the life blasted out of your body, you must have thought this peculiar paradise was about to disintegrate."

"I certainly was rather surprised," Pullman told him sedately. "It was not quite how I had imagined these celestial regions."

The Bailiff laughed heartily.

"I should not suppose you had. But let me explain a little, my dear Pullman, for you have every right both to an explanation and an apology. What it is my duty to tell you is fantastic to the last degree."

The Bailiff stopped abruptly, for a uniformed man was standing in front of him, holding in his hand a salver upon which lay an envelope. He snatched this up and opened it, and read the message in silence. Then, taking the salver from the man, he wrote a few words upon the back of the torn envelope.

"Take this back," he said to the man, "and say I shall be here for the next couple of hours."

The Bailiff wheeled round and faced Pullman again, his eyes a little distracted. He visibly dragged his mind away from something, and began almost violently.

"I was saying," he said with a half-shout, "before the modern age, yes, back in the Age of Faith, there was a Heaven and there was a Hell. There was a Heaven of dazzling white, and there was a good coal-black Hell. Now, to arrange, somewhere in space, a convenient site for these institutions was not too easy in those days." He held up a finger to make certain that Pullman was attending. "This is the essential point. Hell and Heaven are much too near together geographically, and the same applies to Third City–that is much too near to Hell." He pointed through the window. "Hell is just over there. Things have progressed as they have down on earth. These opposites are far too near together for modern conditions." He stopped and tapped Pullman upon the shoulder and lowered his voice. "Another thing of critical importance. Heaven is no longer immaculate–is it?" The Bailiff gave one of his crowing laughs. "You don't know it yet! Wait till you do, my boy! Next–and just as important, Hell is not the place it once was in the days of our old friend Dante Alighieri." Something in Pullman's expression pulled him up. "You saw perhaps that performance down on Fifth Piazza this afternoon? They were a terrible crew weren't they? But that was a beauty chorus Lucifer keeps for such occasions to frighten the bourgeoisie. It is a little family or two of genuine, old-time devils, who live in the wilds of Hades, just as the elk lives up in the Bush, as far from man as possible. These demons are rounded up when they are required."

He took breath. "Well, let us get back to the great changes which have taken place. As we all know, and can see for ourselves, the *Good* and the *Bad* are blurred, are they not, in the modern age? We no longer see things in stark black and white. We know that all men are much the same. An amoralist . . . such is the modern man. And in the same way in these

112

supernatural regions. It is a terrible come-down all round. What was once the Devil (to whom one 'sold one's soul' and so forth) well today, he is a very unconvinced *devil,* and our Padishah, as we call him, he is a very unconvinced Angel. I know *both,* so I know what I am talking about."

The Bailiff had had a growing audience. They were now completely surrounded: there was, first of all, a queue which had collected, while they had been talking, of persons desirous of exchanging a word or two with the host, and, secondly, there was the crowd which had gradually grown at the sound of a typical harangue in progress.

The Bailiff looked out over the crowd, and, spotting what he was looking for, called softly, "Dureepah! Dureepah!"

A dark and smiling, distinctly handsome young man stepped out of the crowd. He was dressed in a short black vest, with silver buttons; with Turkish-type trousers, and shoes with tilted tips.

"Now, here you are, here is an inhabitant of what is popularly called Hell. He is, in short, a devil."

The young man beamed and bowed, and everyone laughed.

"Are you not a devil, Dureepah?"

"A perfect devil," the young man answered, and there was a shout of laughter.

"This young man arrived this morning from Hell. He is a clerk in the office of Lucifer, who runs an office just as does the Padishah, concocting all sorts of mischief; just as our Eminence is busy in *his* offices–with a thousand clerks, if you please–is busy disseminating virtue!" Then he turned more especially to Pullman. "The inhabitants of Hell buy their shirts and ties down in First Piazza, or Fifth Piazza. Why not. But *by law* they are not supposed to enter the City. Why? Are we too good, here? Shall we perhaps be defiled!"

At this point the Bailiff raised his voice, saying again in tones which could reach the back of the crowd. "Shall we be polluted, gentlemen? Shall we issue from the contact stained and sullied?–Gentlemen, it appears to me that it might work the other way round, and some innocent little devil return to Hell, his innocence undermined."

There was a burst of laughter mingled with applause.

"Well," and the Bailiff turned again to Pullman. "*That* is

what the quarrel is about. You had a taste of that disagreement the other day. Lucifer is a proud man; he is bored with the never-ceasing, and, as he thinks, absurd ostracism. How did that ostracism come about, gentlemen. It is as well to remember that God, we are told, created Adam. A great feat–Adam was a chap like us, he was a *man*. It seemed, of course, to Lucifer, a very inferior creation of the Almighty God. Lucifer was a splendidly handsome archangel, second only to God in power and rank. In his maudlin ecstasy God commanded Lucifer should abase himself and pay homage to Adam. Is it at all wonderful that Lucifer refused to do anything of the sort? There was a terrific row. Lucifer went off in high dudgeon– saying to God that he no longer wished to be associated with a Creator who had forgotten how to create. Half the hosts of Heaven followed him, millions of angels and archangels. Their idea was to establish themselves in the cloudlands above the earth. It would have been wonderful had they succeeded; but it was found impracticable to build anything solid there. Many of the angels made their way to the earth and cast in their lot with man. But Lucifer went far afield, and hoped to create for himself a paradise out of a rather wild district which had always been despised. That is where he has been ever since. The story about the Hole, about the Pit, is just an old wives' tale. There is a not very sanitary region there, which is very damp and sometimes very hot, which is low-lying and precipitous, and which lends itself to these ridic-ulous tales about what we call Hell. All that is nonsense of course. Lucifer has always lived in a quite handsome little city, in a very magnificent palace. But he is an artist. He is not a schemer, not a practical man, not powerhungry and vainglorious. Like some people I could mention."

Suddenly there was a loud voice from among the crowd. It shouted furiously, "That is a lie. I have been there–I know what it is like. And it is not like that! What he has been saying is a pack of lies. Satan ... Satan was expelled from Heaven. He ..."

Armed men had rushed in; one had bludgeoned the inter-rupter and the others laid him out on the floor. There had been a great uproar, naturally; some had been violently angry, and one had struck the mouth from which the big, discordant

114

voice was coming. It was just after that the truncheon had descended.

Everyone in the neighbourhood of the Bailiff was speaking at the same time. The Bailiff parted the crowd wihch blocked the way to the prisoner, who was being placed upon a stretcher. The magistrate, when he reached the end of the stretcher, leaned forward and gazed at the face. Then he moved back abruptly, and an official was awaiting him.

"Shall we hand him over to the police?" the official inquired.

"No. I will interrogate him myself. When you have taken him to the guardroom, chloroform him if necessary and search him from head to foot. Remove all his clothes–shoes, socks, *everything*. Give him something else to wear! Let me know when all this is done."

He returned now immediately to Pullman, without answering those in the crowd through which he passed, or stopping for a moment to speak to them.

In an undertone, the Bailiff said quickly to Pullman, "That man belongs to one of the sects with which this city in infested. He may be a Hyperidean: he may be a Salvationist. I don't know what he is, but I soon shall. A lot of lies are told to people like that, and they believe them with an incredible fixity. That man has been taught that God expelled Lucifer and a great number of other 'rebel' angels-that is the orthodox teaching, and he thinks it must be true. However." He did not seem at all excited, and he returned at once to what had been the subject of his discourse when the shouting man put a stop to it. "Well, then, Pullman, that is how what we call 'Hell' came to be. Lucifer is a perfectly normal man, like anyone in this room. The fact that he is 'immortal' makes no difference whatever as regards his character. Now it seems to me that there should be normal intercourse between, in a world like ours, cities such as Third City and cities such as what we persist in calling 'Hell'. Why not? If all the people here were ardent believers, things might be different. Or if 'Hell' were like it was, a half a millennium ago, there might be some reason to keep these two citizenries apart. But Lucifer and his subjects are tremendously 'liberalised', as it is called. They have pictures from Hollywood in their cinemas, and the Devil sometimes smokes a pipe. Yet these gentlemen here (our masters) continue to treat everything

115

in the neighbouring city as if we were contemporaries of Dante, and they were all horned monsters over there."

The Bailiff's voice had been rising, and he was now on a subject of the most urgent topical interest to everybody. He was no longer looking at Pullman but was addressing the audience around him.

"Now all that was happening the other day was that Lucifer was proposing to come over–socially. You all know what the Padishah thought of that. He bickers away like a fishwife, when he is driven to mount his hobby-horse. Poor old Padishah. Poor old, two-thousand-year-old gentleman!"

The whole of this huge reception-room seemed to be rocking with laugther as the Bailiff finished.

"I wonder how all that strikes you?" exclaimed the Bailiff, turning again to Pullman, in a paternal manner, and lowering his voice as he did so. "I trust I have not blasted your illusions?"

"No, sir," Pullman answered. "No. I am amazed. I was somewhat surprised to find myself in Heaven. But it seems that, after all, I shall end up in Hell!"

To indicate to the crowd at large that he was performing no more for the present, the Bailiff turned his back upon it. In a quiet conversational voice, he asked Pullman whether he was in difficulties about finding an apartment. "I should be very glad, Pullman, to help you find a residence. You are temporarily at the apartment of Mr Mannock. That was the address the bank gave me."

Pullman described his meeting with Mannock at the Universal Café, and said he was for the present lodging there. All the Bailiff said, as regards that, was, "Mannock! not the most amusing person to have met! He is a dreadful old reactionary, is Mannock. What did he say when you told him you were coming to my Red Party?"

"He said I should go, sir. He is reactionary, but he is not a fool."

"To be a reactionary is to be a fool." A negro passed with cigarettes upon a tray. "Here, have one of these," Pullman was enjoined, "a rarity in Third City. There is a bootleg store near Fifth Piazza. You can get alcohol there as well. Give him the address," he told a secretary, and Pullman was handed a slip of paper with the address.

"Milligan," Pullman read from the slip of paper. "An enterprising Irishman; I shall pay him a visit."

"Mannock, of course, has not the slightest idea who you are? No, of course he has not. If someone told him that you were the greatest writer of your time, Pullman, he would not believe them." The Bailiff beamed in Pullman's face, the latter with a bored expression stroking his beard. "Ah, Pullman, you did not know I had your secret! I think I shall see that some friend of mine passes on this information to the stuffy and obtuse Mr Mannock!"

"Please do not," Pullman said negligently. He then took the Bailiff by the hand. "I am most obliged to you, sir, for your information . . . and your *bon acceuil*."

"Don't say that, my dear boy. It will be an honour for me to do anything I can to help you. I have my weekends to myself: it would give me the greatest pleasure if you would come round and have a talk. All this herd of people would not be here, we should be by ourselves."

Saying that he would certainly try and get hold of him some week-end, Pullman returned to the body of the crowd, and as he was just about to be swallowed up by it, the Bailiff called after him, "At Mannock's you will soon be receiving a visit from a sparrow!"

All those near Pullman laughed. They knew what the sparrow meant, but Pullman was extremely mystified. The next moment he found himself confronted by Rigate. That gentleman winked at him. "I am sure that you do not understand what the sparrow means. Well, the Padishah sends out all his invitations by sparrows."

"I see," Pullman replied. "I had forgotten that you were fond of the Bailiff's parties."

"I cannot afford to buy much whisky of my own." He moved away beside Pullman. "I could not help overhearing the Bailiff speaking to you just now about Mannock. At the same time I learned of your celebrity. I agree with the Bailiff that Mannock has not the haziest idea as to the quality of the guest he is entertaining. I think I shall tell him . . ."

As he moved along, Pullman again became conscious of that fœtid odour which had nearly caused him to vomit that afternoon.

"Dureepah," he reflected, "is not, I think, the only citizen of Hades in this assembly." And just then the face, slightly of Red-Indian colour, leered in his face as if reading his thoughts. Pullman aggressively jutted his chin, and, in a certain prim firmness of his mouth, seemed to be reproducing the response of virtue to vice. Yes, I see you, it seemed to say, go your way. But prepare for the wrath to come. There was another leer, slightly different in quality, an ingratiating leer, and a voice which began, "I say, you had a jolly nice talk with the old Bailey! He's a jolly good old sort ... I remember meeting you across the water about two weeks ago," said the sugary voice. "The old Bailey gives one a jolly good cocktail, don't you think?"

As Pullman raised his eyes, just for a moment he had the illusion that he was speaking to one of the diabolical visitors seen in the Piazza earlier that day. There certainly was something which provoked this recollection. The leering, goatish countenance was enough. But the hair was thick and beautifully brushed, and Pullman at once perceived that it was a man who had persisted in talking to him over at the Camp, and whom it had been extremely difficult to shake off. Now he was very neatly dressed—obviously he had been to the bank.

"You have got here quickly," Pullman responded, with the coldest politeness of which he was capable.

"So did *you!*" cried the other, with a gleeful goatish grin.

"Certainly I did not take long. I followed the Bailiff in at the Gates."

This appeared a tremendously sporting thing to have done to the young fellow, so prodigal of grins. With a congratulatory guffaw (and his mode of address was almost exclusively exclamatory), "Oh good for you! Did the old Bailiff see you?"

Even more loftily Pullman answered, "Yes. He invited me to follow him in."

This produced a new explosion of enthusiasm about their host. "He is a jolly decent old sort, the old Bailey, isn't he!"

Pullman wished that he did not have to say "the old Bailey", whenever he referred to the gentleman in question—that he were not so virulent a sucker-up, that he were not so ingratiatingly toothy, that he did not show so much of his gums. He

118

moved almost violently away, holding his head high, his back sternly turned towards this matey and vulgar individual.

Sentoryen had been observing this encounter, greatly relishing the lofty technique of Pullman. And now he said, lowering his voice a little, "Not one of your favourites, Mr Pullman."

Pullman was less discreet, and his voice was pitched rather higher than usual. "That living grin gets in my hair."

Sentoryen moved a little closer. "Mister Pullman, there is no hurry at all, but the car awaits you at the door. It is at your disposal whenever you are ready."

What forced itself in upon him now was the memory of what he had been through at this mysterious gathering. Sentoryen had been almost a supernatural escort, and he did not know, in retrospect, whether he liked it or not. Fatalistically he followed him into the waiting automobile, and rushed with him through the night, as if they were flying through the air, not understanding but submissive. At Mannock's door he thanked him, as he had formed the habit of doing, and, as he ascended the stairs, he heard the purr and then the roar of the automobile bearing Sentoryen away.

MANNOCK WAS IN THE SITTING-ROOM, apparently waiting. Actually, he had been watching out of the window Pullman's descent from the automobile, Sentoryen at his heels. Now he said, "Back from your party! Well, was it very grand?"

Pullman took up his usual position upon the settee. "I saw Rigate," he said. "He was taking in his supply of whisky."

"Rigate is an addict–I mean a Bailiff-addict."

"I think you exaggerate the insidiousness of our Bailiff," with calm indifference Pullman said.

There was a pause for Mannock to digest his displeasure, and to say to himself that Pullman, after all, was like Rigate in many ways. Then he said, "Your fag has returned."

Pullman looked up quickly and asked where he was. Mannock thereupon explained that the police had brought Satters back.

"The police!" Satters' mentor said.

"Yes," Mannock explained, "the police . . . in a police van, in which they carry criminals."

He proceeded to recount the violent scene which had ensued; Satters was drunk, he struck one of the two policemen in the face, and the other gave Satters a massacring blow with his truncheon. They were very obliging fellows and carried the juvenile delinquent into the bedroom and laid him on the bed. Before leaving they explained that he had joined one of the large juvenile gangs and was caught breaking into a shop. There were about six of them, but Satters gave more trouble than the other five. "Wo do not take these young ruffians into a magistrate's court," the sergeant said, "unless they half-murder somebody. The courts cannot be cluttered up with their rascalities, because there are half a dozen of these large boy-gangs, and they are misbehaving themselves all the time. We just try to find out where they come from originally, and, if we are successful, we take them back there in a van. You have your hands full, Mister. He is a tough boy!"

Pullman was very alarmed and perplexed at this development.

"How am I going to rid myself of this abominable black-guard of a fag! Is he going to carry my address about in his pocket, and every time he commits a delinquency, is he going to be brought back to me, as if it were a case of lost property? I *must* rid myself of this murderous parasite, this legacy from my schooldays."

Pullman sprang up and walked quickly towards the door: but Mannock stopped him with a shout. "Hi! not so quick. Let sleeping dogs lie. You do not know what he is like. He is very drunk . . . we are no match for him while he is half-mad with liquor. Let him sleep it off, and then you will be able to explain to him what your views are regarding his future."

Pullman returned from the door, and flung himself in a chair. "I must apologise for my frightful fag. I shall separate at once from this ignoble Caliban." They sat there for some time in silence. Mannock then reverted to the thing uppermost in his mind.

"The Bailiff and I," he told Pullman, "first met in a police-cell, at the time of the trouble about Hyperides."

"Oh." Pullman was surprised to hear the name of Hyperides in this connection.

"Yes. I have lived here a long while," Mannock insisted. "You are finding out very quickly what it took me years to find out. But you have a good deal to learn. Let me give you the low-down on the Bailiff, anyway: I have made a study of him. He is really an obnoxious individual."

Pulling the shutters down over his eyes, pursing his mouth sedately, Pullman politely listened.

"To begin with, he is entirely responsible for the degraded type of mannikin which swarms in this city. When you first arrived–I daresay you do not remember–you asked me what was the matter with those people in the Universal Café. What struck you at once was the near-imbecility of those collected there. Has that been borne in upon you since? Do you encounter the humanity frequenting the Universal Café elsewhere in the city–in fact everywhere?"

"Yes, I certainly do," Pullman agreed, gently stroking the back of his head. "The majority of those one sees at the cafés, on the street, or in the underground, are of that extraordinary vacuous type; sixty per cent of the inhabitants of this quarter,

I should say. Not the police, not the shop-keepers–at least not those I have seen; not your friends in the coffee-house or in the club. But practically everybody else. I find it uncomfortable to be in the company of this moronic majority. They are a very odd product indeed. How did they get like that?"

Mannock looked excited. He seemed very pleased at what his guest had said. "Well now," he continued. "What would you say was the philosophy of this place? And of course it is *contrived,* is it not–it is not natural for it to be like this. Is it an institution for the preservation and glorification of mediocrity? What he preaches, outside there, in the Camp, is that it is the *typical* that is valuable. The Bailiff has kept out of this place anyone of the slightest intelligence or character, anyone out of the ordinary. He has very thoroughly sifted the humanity presented to him at that Tribunal. Then there are these gangs of youths to which your fag has immediately joined himself. That is the Bailiff's doing. He is a great glorifier of 'Youth', of the immature, even of the childish. If you and Satterthwaite had gone up before him, our young hooligan lying on the bed in there would have been passed in, you would have been rejected. He does not, of course, say openly: 'I will pass in to the city the most perfect specimens of human nothingness I can find.' He has a lot of fancy talk about uniqueness. But what actually ensues from the deliveries of his magistracy may very well be examined in the Universal Café. And he deliberately wills it to be like that; that is what he aims at, and that is what he secures."

"The Baliff, one would say–don't you think–was justifying the existence of this city. It is almost as if he said 'there are very good men, and there are very bad men; Heaven is provided for the former, Hell for the latter; but is it a crime just to be the human average? Let us keep this city for Mr Everyman. Let *him* have a Heaven too. Let us sift those who come here, until we obtain a quintessence of the average.' And it would seem that, through this insistence upon an ideal of averageness, he has produced a horrible nullity."

"That is wonderfully interesting. You really expressed that beautifully," exclaimed Mannock. "But, if you don't mind my saying so, that would be entirely to misread the motives of this man. He is not seeking after some perfection, and reaching

122

nullity by mistake. Oh no. He has attained to nothingness on purpose."

Pullman smiled. "That may be, of course. Men often arrive at very unpleasant results by pursuing the loftiest aims. But I have not analysed our Bailiff. I was merely throwing out a suggestion."

"Quite. I understand that."

"What is perhaps more interesting," Pullman said quickly, "is the question of why he is here at all. To whom is he responsible?"

Mannock hesitated, and almost scowled.–This was an issue which was exceedingly distasteful to him, but which he knew was always hovering in the background. "That," he said, "is a quite separate question–and very irrelevant, in any discussion of the Bailiff's motives. There he is, and one has to consider him apart from any question of how he got there."

"I hardly think it is so simple as that," Pullman absent-mindedly shook his head.

A memory bursting up into his face, at the same time as it rushed into his mind, Mannock tore his sleeve up from his wrist, and, intoning "I must fly!", rose and hurried out of the room, saying as he went, "I am afraid I shall be keeping Charles waiting." A few minutes later he put his head in at the door saying, "Let that young brute sleep off his drink," and vanished.

Left, as it were, becalmed by this tempestuous exit, Pullman remained where he was, inhaling tobacco smoke, and comparing the Bailiff with "Charles". What a friend to have, Sir Charles whatever-his-name-was! A really old baronetcy . . . fifteenth century.–Tut-tut–a museum piece, no more! The Bailiff might be still more historical . . . "The old Bailey" and himself would certainly find it difficult to agree upon many matters. But they were matters which need never be mentioned by either of them . . . Pullman's mind returned to his present host. What a little Sahib it was! He foresaw the time when it would be looked upon as a betrayal for him to go and have a chat with the Bailiff, in his residence scented with the sweat of Hell! he coughed judiciously and primly. He did not take seriously either the Bailiff or Mannock or Charles: but they balanced one another–although he was afraid that the Bailiff weighed so much more than all the rest of them put together.

XI

"YOU WERE VERY DRUNK LAST NIGHT, sir, were you not?" Pullman fixed a dead eye upon Satterthwaite.

"I am most frightfully sorry, Pulley, those boys gave me ever so much to drink. I was fool enough to drink it. I have never had anything to drink before. I had a most dreadful black-out. I did not know what I was doing for hours and hours and hours. Pulley, I do hope you believe me." Satters, with his forefinger, made the gesture of cutting his throat, "If what I tell you isn't true, Pulley, may I drop down dead."

Pullman yawned, and took a cigarette. "You broke into a shop," he remarked.

"Did they say that, the dirty cads! Those boys in the police don't mind what they say! That is a dirty lie! Oh Pulley . . ."

"They brought you here in a van. You hit one of them. The other clubbed you. They described you to Mannock as a pretty tough customer. Congratulations, Satters. Congratulations. You are making your mark already in this city. Soon you will be the leader of a gang . . . They will call you 'Gorgeous Satters'. You will rise as high as a young man can in this city. Provided you do not murder somebody, you will be a very eminent young thug." Pullman sat up suddenly. "Satters, that is all right for you, but you must not go round with my address in your pocket, and be brought back here by the police every time you commit some outrage."

"Pulley, it's a lie, it's a damned lie, I never did anything at all, I swear on my dying oath, Pulley . . ."

"Satters! Be quiet! Understand I do not want you back here any more. I will not allow the police to dump you here. I shall write to them and tell them to deposit you somewhere else. When I have a place of my own you may come and see me. *But not here.* Now be off with you."

There were many more explosions on the part of Satters, there were even tears. But at last Pullman put on his hat and left the building. When he returned an hour or two later,

Satters had gone. So, presumably, Satters was disposed of for the time being. Pullman did not want never to see Satters again, but he did not wish to be disturbed every time his ex-fag committed a crime.

Mannock, who had been down at the bank, came in about twelve-thirty and took Pullman out to lunch. As they sat, side by side, in the taxi, Pullman warned him that he was over-doing it. "You should take things easy for another week or two. You were in pretty bad shape subsequent to the 'Blitz'." Mannock gratefully promised to follow this counsel.

The restaurant was in Tenth Piazza; it was very "fashionable", one of the best in the entire city. They sat at a large table with half a dozen of Mannock's buddies. This was not a repetition of their visit to the café club, if for no other reason because of the presence of Henry Stanfield, Mannock's friend No. 1. This man was "county" to start with, and he took that origin very seriously. He was also Harrow and Magdalen. These facts entailed the appropriate graces and tricks which Mannock was almost morbidly aware of. What kind of man Stanfield was, shorn of these cultivated gadgets, it was difficult to say, and perhaps irrelevant. He was no doubt a cold, dull, and deeply unintelligent being—all of which was necessary, even, to keep the social varnish intact.

They mourned their dead. There was Dick, and there was Jonathan, who had succumbed to the "Blitz". Of this younger and less pompous circle, Stanfield was almost the equivalent of Charles; but he rather laughed at Charles. He rather laughed at Mannock's, "Charles says", which did not stop Mannock from constantly quoting the oracle of the Cadogan. On this occasion he quoted Hugh and his sinister predictions. "Hugh," said Stanfield, "derives some of his most blood-curdling prophetics from sources close to the Bailiff." There was much laughter over Hugh's secret inspirer. One of them said, "If I went to the Bailiff's Monday Party—though there is no danger of my doing that, I prefer to buy a bottle of bootleg whisky myself—I should not be amazed to see Hugh, slightly disguised, perhaps."

„Pullman here was at the Bailiff's party last night," Mannock informed them. "Did you see Hugh there?"

Pullman pondered. "There *was* a man, now I come to think

of it, who looked like an inebriated gas inspector, who might have been the man you are inquiring about." There was again a lot of merriment—for Hugh did not appear to be a very popular figure. Stanfield asserted that, until the Bailiff was put on trial for treason, Third City would continue to be like a Dr Barnardo's Home for pansy bank clerks. One of them asked Pullman what he thought of the Bailiff, to which he answered, "He is rather like a city boss in the United States, and if you are in such a city you have to be very careful not to displease him—especially if your stay in that city is to be prolonged." To which the questioner responded, "I see."

After lunch they returned to the apartment. Mannock had been saying that they must get out of the city into the farmlands one of these days, and when they entered the living-room he walked towards the window, in the course of giving his guest some elementary instruction in the topography of the city. They were standing there, Mannock tracing routes and directions rather unnecessarily upon the window-pane. His finger mounted higher, until it began to cover the sky with traceries.

Pullman, who made no attempt to follow these directions of Mannock's, was the first to notice that a martial sparrow was performing a passerine goose-step outside the window. Before he had time to speak to Mannock about it, the other caught sight of it, and hurriedly threw up the sash. The bird stood to attention, and Mannock took something from its beak. A harsh and brassy adieu broke from it, it revolved, and the next moment it was in undeviating, and militarily unerring flight.

Meanwhile, Mannock had spread out on the table a small piece of paper which he had taken from the bird's beak. There was a message,

"Please bring your two friends—at the usual time this evening."

Pullman took up the piece of paper. He frowned a little as he read. Then he replaced it on the table.

"What an amazing fellow. He uses the birds as his messengers."

Mannock laughed.

"He writes English as if he were English," Pullman continued.

"English is a lingua-franca here, as it is in New York, for instance."

The parting words of the Bailiff, "You will be visited by a sparrow," suddenly returned to Pullman. "A childish substitution for a telephone!" he mentally agreed with the Bailiff's implied sneer. But what he did immediately afterwards was to imagine the Bailiff using the birds as messengers. This he recognised at once as utterly impossible. Although St Francis was not his favourite Saint, he preferred a world in which St Francis would feel at home because of the presence of winged creatures, to a Bailiff-world of pragmatic exclusiveness. He knew there would be no wings in a Bailiff-world except left-wings: in the view of the "good old Bailey", he was sure, the sparrow parasitically infested the air–of no food value, and inclined to give elderly persons of the female sex something to live for! The use of sparrows in this way for air-mail purposes gave him an insight into the mind of the celestial personage they were to visit. With his sparrows instead of telephones, he was evidently of a gentle, whimsical disposition. As to his being a match for the infernal overlord, that was something he felt very dubious about.

It took some time to reach the Padishah's palace–over an hour. In a not very large square stood the white block of offices, the entrance guarded by police, rifles slung over their shoulders. Mannock gave a password that sounded like "Brish brash", which gained them admittance to the court. The entrance hall, as in the case of the Bailiff's residence, was full of armed men. Here a more searching scrutiny occurred. An official had a list of guests. Mannock was asked for his name. The name was found in the list. Then Pullman's name was demanded, and it too was identified. The official addressed to Mannock a few questions such as the number of times he had visited the Padishah. At last they were admitted, passed through a wicket, and descended a wide marble staircase. At the foot of this they effected a passage of two more doors, this time green baize, and descended another staircase, wooden for a change. On pushing a pair of swingdoors they found themselves in an underground court. On the farther side was the subterranean palace of the Padishah, before which sentries paraded up and down. Officials approached, and once more the password was

127

demanded. Then the list of visitors was produced, and their names checked. After that they entered the palace. A horde of attendants and guards swarmed around them. Then, without any further holdup, they entered the chamber in which the Governor was in the habit of receiving people. It was of a puritanic simplicity, not very large. Even the guests, perhaps fifteen in number, seemed muted, their heads inclined as if in prayer. The Padishah himself, seemingly of thirty-seven or thirty-eight years old, was of as tall and of as athletic an appearance as were all the angels in Third City. His face was of a perfect handsomeness, the mat, even pallor of the skin and large grey eyes giving him a statuesque beauty. Pullman remembered the opinion of Rigate, that this was some great angel, sent to Third City as a pro-consul. He was dressed in a long, closely-fitting white coat, such as is worn in India.

Pullman observed very closely the face of the Padishah; he noticed that it was extremely mobile. His eyebrows were frequently raised, when his forehead was furrowed up. The expressions that seemed to find their way most often into his face were ones of weariness and pain. He had the air of having put aside things weighing heavily on his mind, to spend a short while with some inconsequential visitors. No smile lighted his face, though once or twice his eyes seemed to be softening.—A very severe young man indeed, Pullman told himself: but not weak, and capable of great sternness. To everybody he said a few words and with Mannock stood talking for some minutes. Mannock had got the thing entirely wrong, and persisted in treating him as a great prince rather than a holy man.

Pullman overheard him inquire of a secretary which was "Mr Pull-man". The secretary's powers of identification were miraculous, and, after a moment's consultation with him, the Padishah advanced towards Pullman, and said, "I am glad to meet you, Mr Pullman. Your fame has reached me here, you know." Pullman adopted a devout attitude, which a one-time seminarist must find instinctive. He answered, with his eyes lowered, "Thank you, sir. Please do not speak of my fame, there are very different matters which occupy me here."

Next the Padishah made inquiries as to whether he had found comfortable quarters in the city. He at once replied that, by good chance, he was for the time staying with Mr Mannock.

"I am so glad", said the Padishah, with an amiable glance towards Mannock. "You should get him to show you the beauties of the city." Then with an expression of despair, throwing his head up, exclaimed, "You should get him to take you into the farmlands over there. They are fresh and beautiful."

After a little more talk the Padishah, with a nervous half-smile which was like a sneer, passed on to other duties. Three men, rather like central European peasants, had entered the chamber, and fallen on their knees near the door. At this moment one of them emitted a longdrawn penetrating scream, which seemed to get shriller as it proceeded. One of the Padishah's secretaries hurried over to him. He had seen a vision, it seemed, in which a demon was standing behind the Padishah with a raised arm about to plunge a knife into his back.

The secretary, an impassible, rather Jewish-looking young man, consoled him. He returned to the Padishah, and said something under his breath, at which his master rolled up his eyes with infinite distress, but did not look towards the still kneeling man.

It is hardly necessary to add that the cocktails contained no alcohol, but were merely pleasant drinks, and, when he and Mannock withdrew, Pullman cast a glance backward at the Padishah, about whom he experienced the intensest curiosity. He attempted to penetrate the veil of this immortal, who passed his days in isolation, since there was no one good enough, or supernatural enough, for him to communicate with. What dreams had he at night? Perhaps he flew, with great wings, through the golden skies of Heaven; or imagined the arrival of an angelic visitor, to whom he might unburden himself.

The emotion which appeared to sweep across him incessantly, and which obviously originated in wells of unfathomable boredom, to be found somewhere at the centre of his being, produced the facial expression which remained, above all else, in Pullman's memory. He was a very profoundly bored angelic creature, who, Pullman felt, would have died long ago, if the supernatural had not been incapable of death. Yet with what a heartrending expression he made his last remark of the day to Mannock, or heard of the melodramatic apparition which had appeared to the kneeling visitor. Clearly everything to do with Man filled him with an immense fatigue, a passionate lack of interest. He pitied this winged animal of the Heavens, and thought of the cruelty of God who was to blame in every way for His angel's misery.

How did he lie down at night–was he determined to dream of all that he was denied, of what he was intended for but was odiously prevented from doing? Or was he so exhausted that he sought his bed with thankfulness as a place of utter rest, a blankness without attribute, a void of soundless peace into which to glide. The classic profile, the calm beauty remained in spite of everything. He governed this city as a god would govern a stinking swamp, or as a man would govern a cemetery full of illfavoured spectres.

When Mannock and Pullman were once more outside, in the small cold square, with no people to be seen except a policeman or two, they hurried towards the underground. Pullman was surprised at not being congratulated upon the special favour shown him by the Padishah. As it was, Mannock appeared absorbed, turning over in his mind the very secret information which he persuaded himself the Padishah had communicated to him.

However, Pullman contributed one or two acceptable remarks, such as that in which he observed "What a lovely head" was that of the Padishah. To this Mannock replied with a curt nod, and the answer. "Yes, isn't it." It was plain that Mannock considered it rather offensive to refer to the shape of the Governor's head. Objective beauty. It was like meeting a great general for the first time and saying afterwards what a nice pair of ears he had.

6. PULLMAN ON THIRD CITY

XII

MANNOCK WAS SLEEPING a little late, and it was Platon who handed–manifestly impressed by the ornate official envelope–a letter from the office of the Bailiff. Inside was the briefest note, unsigned. "We hope that you will, at your earliest convenience, visit the Central Bank, where the clerk in Room 301 is anxious to see you."

Pullman did not mention to his host the receipt of this official document, but after breakfast he made his way to the bank. The smile of the diminutive official in the small plate-glass office was cordial, as it had been before. "I fear, Mr Pullman I have been guilty of a grave miscalculation. But our information was ridiculously incomplete. I shall remedy this immediately. From today we ask you to accept the honorarium of a thousand dollars a month." He handed Pullman an envelope. "In this you will find six thousand dollars. There are many expenses which you necessarily incur to start with here. The extra five thousand dollars will of course be inadequate. You will inform us what you need, however, and we will be most happy to accommodate you. I do not know, Mr Pullman, whether you have found what you want in the matter oft an apartment. Should you have failed to find, up till now, the kind of place you are looking for, may I make a suggestion? There is a large, extremely up-to-date apartment hotel, whith a really superb restaurant. I have enclosed a card with the address of same. If you will allow me to say so, almost all the most intelligent of our clients reside in the Phanuel Hotel. It is not far from the Bailiff's residence; it is quite easy to find. Once more allow me to emphasise, this is not a city dominated by those possessed of money; do not hesitate to come and ask for another five, or another ten thousand dollars. We know you would only use it in the highest interest of everybody. You understand, don't you, Mr Pullman?"

It was on that night that Pullman's report on Third City was delivered (or rather administered) to Mannock. This did not happen officially. Mannock was not aware, indeed, that any-thing of this kind was occurring; and when it was over–when a report had been delivered and he was in possession of it, he was quite unaware that anything especial had come to pass. The whole thing appeared entirely accidental. Certainly he had a long talk with Pullman, but that was all.

That day both had felt increasingly exhausted and depres-sed, a sort of delayed shock; of an even more extended type than that of which Mannock had heard in the Cadogan club, experienced by many people in the city. There were many cases of hysteria, and hysterical ailments. The hospitals were crammed; the doctors and orderlies, sick themselves, were in no shape to cope with this mass of ailing people. Pullman, after his visit to the bank, had passed much of the day sleeping. About four o'clock he had gone to a small coffee house he had noticed in a side-street on the way to the Universal Café. There he sat, for an hour or two, listening to the gossip of the Germans and Swiss who frequented this place. It was strange how the mental malady and utter degeneration of much of the more or less Anglo-Saxon citizens did not seem to touch this group. Their mouths were not open, their eyes were not full of an idiot vacuity. Their clothes were reasonably modest. Later he watched a game of chess. After that he in-dulged in some iced coffee, and twisted sticks of pastry, var-nished with sugar. Some mechanical music finally drove him out. Back at the apartment, Greek voices competed for the title of Producer of Maximum of Human Noise. The Greek of midtwen-tieth-century Athens kept the service section of the apartment in an uproar, and blasted away in Platon's bedroom until late into the night. The Hellenic verbosity had been released by the inhuman racket of what Pullman called Black Tuesday. But, lying on his bed, Pullman was grateful for this evidence of life, and of agitated life. He was able to commune with himself, and examine once more what it was best for him to do: for it was clear that he and his fag would be able hence-forth to dispense with one another's society, and neither Man-nock nor he would wish to dwell together any longer than was necessary. Though Mannock had insisted upon his stopping where he was for the present, he thought it would be better to follow up the bank's suggestion to start with. He felt that he had been rapt into some bursting dream of the Apocalypse of Baruch or of the Secrets of Enoch, he must avoid becoming engulfed, he must secure a foothold, however tenuous.

For dinner Platon brought in a wonderful plate of *smorgassen*. This was so delightful that Pullman's appetite awoke, and he began to make a very hearty meal. When Platon came in to remove a macedoine of fruit, which Pullman had greatly enjoyed, and was about to inquire whether he should give him some coffee, he was considerably startled by Pullman exclaiming "Quickly", throwing himself into the attitude of a twentieth-century Athenian, and vociferating. "Ti nostima phrouta!"

Platon's face burst into indecorous affabilitiy and he replied at once, "Ne endaxi ine kala phrouta alla dhen ine opos ta dhika mas tis Evropis."

No attempt was made on Pullman's part to maintain a conversation in Greek: but having shattered Platon's shell of reserve, he now began with a leading question, in the English language: "What do you and your Greek friends think about the terrible disturbance the other day?"

Platon leapt into uninhibited speech. "What do we think? We would like to know what part the human plays in this comedy. My brother says he does not want to live any more."

"And you?" asked Pullman.

"Not very much. I think we should be told where we are, and what this comedy means. The stupid lies they print in the *Bulletin* must end!"

Guest and cook looked at one another across the table. Then Pullman said harshly, "Yes. The *Bulletin* is an insult."

"An insult ... you are damn right! I ask your pardon. An insult. An insult. I shall snatch it from the newsboy and shall crush it in my hand." He whirled his clenched hand up, furiously glaring. He hurled an imaginary *Bulletin* upon the floor. "We are poor miserable half-men, yes. But we are not *idiots*!" His eyes blazed with intelligent indignation.

"Bravo!" shouted Pullman, enthusiastically. So this was what was being said in the kitchen–so much more dignified than the persistent kow-tow to authority in the master's quarters. These men would stand no nonsense from God. If God thought ...!

"Let us boycott the *Bulletin*!" roared Platon. "Let us put it in the lavatory!"

Pullman banged the table. "The water-closet is not the place, but the trash bin!"

The door opened and Mannock entered. He smiled wanly. "A heated discussion," he observed. Pullman laughed with a welcoming expansiveness.

Platon said, "*Crème tomate,* sir? There is a *Pointes d'Asperges Omelette* ..."

Mannock shook his head. "No dinner, thank you, Platon," he answered. "I have had all I want. Give me some black coffee please." As soon as Platon had left the room, Mannock sat down in front of his guest, with a smile which would not materialise.

"So you and Platon found something to talk about?" he remarked.

"My dear Mannock, if you had heard what we found to talk about, you would have ... you would have turned in your grave!"

Pullman delivered himself of a ringing tenor laugh.

"I am glad you manage to amuse yourself in my absence."

Mannock was annoyed at finding his hellenic scullion bellowing in his *salle-à-manger,* and his guest shouting too. It amounted to an unseemly scene. He had arrived in time to hear Pullman vociferating something about the water-closet. Suppose he had brought Charles home; it would not have looked very well to have surprised the Greek cook and his however distinguished bohemian guest, whom he had picked up in the street with his preposterous fag, excitedly conversing.

Pullman read these thoughts without difficulty. He thought the situation must not be allowed to degenerate. "Are you having no dinner, Mannock," he inquired. "Has your stomach not recovered?"

"I should be sick if I ate anything," Mannock answered, at which Pullman showed solicitude, saying. "You were worse, much worse, than I was."

"My age," Mannock answered. "If that happens again I shall not survive, I am sure. Thousands of people died that afternoon."

Pullman had a gesture of impatience. "Do you think they are going on with this nonsense?"

"I cannot say." Mannock had become dignified. Pullman rose abruptly. "Why do we not go into the next room, if you are not going to eat? Platon will bring my coffee in there."

Mannock left the table with him.

"I must go to bed. I will come in for a minute or two."

"It will do you more good to sit up and have a talk."

"I don't think so."

"Well, try stimulating the brain." Pullman spoke earnestly, with an air of mild compulsion, as if he were speaking to a child or to a junior. "There is something you ought to think about a little," he asserted. "The time has come for you to analyse the landscape. Earthquake and seismic shocks make it desirable to take a look at the mountains by which you are surrounded."

"I am not surrounded by mountains," Mannock objected.

"Certainly you are, human hills." And now Pullman began an unrelenting exposition. He battered away, without stopping, at his host, laying out before him in rapid succession all the parts of the complex upon which life in this place was built. Mannock did not particularly want to go away; he was glad to have something to do, he found. Yet he actively disagreed with everything the other said; or certainly did so at the beginning. But the didactic voice was determined to hammer the thruth into him, and not to stop until he was completely enlightened. "Third City is an extremely deceptive place," Pullman spat emphatically. "There is first the question of *scale*. The physical scale of the inhabitants, the citizens, the humans. They are the size they appear to be. But there are some figures here, less innocent than they look. Take him you like to call the 'Padishah'. The Padishah is not what he seems. He is probable an archangel. A martial angel. The hundred men who are associated with him here in ruling the city are undoubtedly angels too: martial like himself, the 'troops', you know, of God. –Now, the height of an angel is variously computed. In the apocryphal books we find angels described as 'tall as a cedar'. In Dante's Inferno, Lucifer is a very great giant, down whose torso he and Virgil slide, and up whose legs they swarm. Galileo put the height of angels at one mile and a quarter. And

135

he was a man of science. In any case, angels were very great giants; the inhabitants of Heaven were Titans; God is a Titan, Lucifer and his rebellious army were all Titans. And, quite certainly, the 'Padishah' is a very great warrior Titan. When we were in Fifth Piazza the other day, and witnessed the meeting between the envoy of Satan and the Padishah's representative, they were both enormous monsters, shrunken to human size in order to adapt their stature to the scale of a human city. When their voices began to roar, they began visibly to grow in size, until they stood head and shoulders over everyone else in the Piazza, and were still growing."

Pullman shook his finger at his listener. "It is distressing, no doubt, but it is quite necessary to recall that the Padishah is not only (in contrast to us) immortal, but also a winged giant of enormous size. He is accustomed to fly wing to wing with Michael and Gabriel, through the enormous heavens in the sight of Almighty God; of God whose countenance is simply too *hot*, to go no farther, to be gazed upon by the puny eyes of man; he could no more face that living cliff of fire than man could maintain himself near any mass of metal emitting giant sparks; and God's eyes are described as like two great, insupportable, blazing suns."

"You have a very physical conception of the Deity," Mannock murmured.

"Is not an angel a highly material animal? And do we not all see an angel when we go to one of the Padishah's parties? One material thing invokes another does it not? I have seen, I have said 'how-do-you-do' to an angel. That obliged me to accept ... with or without piety ... the incandescent face of God." Pullman bowed his head as he paused.

"But what am I saying?" he asked, letting himself slump down, to show himself overcome with his futility. "For is there not another compulsion too? For is it possible to speak, in such a case, of acting *without piety*. You cannot choose to be impious in an existence dominated by an angelic personality, deriving his authority directly from God."

"I am glad that is your conclusion," Mannock interjected.

"But there is another compulsion, too. It is impossible to dispense with piety. There is no such thing as *without piety* in an existence dominated by a visible archangel."

136

"No."

"A demon, or a devil, now, is only a fallen angel—a black angel. After his expulsion from Heaven he grew darker, and he grew coarser and thicker. You will see no great, sad-eyed blond, like the Padishah, in Hell. All the inhabitants of Hell are grimy and swarthy."

"You certainly know a great deal more than I do about the supernatural. But then I am a very ignorant person. I am afraid you must despise me."

"Let me proceed with my contemporary supernatural history. It appears to me that. Hell is astir. I suppose that the position is that ... for some purpose, and quite a long time ago, a warlike archangel, and under his command a hundred warrior angels, were dispatched to this centre, and established here in a military command. Here they still are. But the world has changed. Earth has changed. And Hell has changed. Even the angel garrison here has changed. So we arrive at last at the gigantic disturbance which shook this city, and deafened everybody on that Tuesday. What was responsible for that? Obviously it was the enormous creatures having a row—the hundred fighting winged giants, of more orthodox angelic colour, who are in charge of this city, and Heaven knows how many darker winged giants, of the fallen and diabolic kind, who do not live so very far away, were in conflict. Did Lucifer himself put in an appearance, with a powerful escort, to try and frighten this outpost of Heaven? Was it the thunder of their voices, the whirling of their wings, which we heard? And was this only the preface to a subsequent attack of the army of Hell? What is the purpose of Satan? Is he envious of this relatively polite city? Are a hundred or so of God's winged soldiers, however valiant, of any use, if seriously challenged by the host of Hell? Those are first questions which suggest themselves to us.

"Meanwhile there is *us*, small, mortal, defenceless; naturally on the side of the angels, hating naturally the Devil and all his works: our position is a fearful one. If the foregoing is the true account of what happened and what is brewing, our ultimate ability to die is what we have to be most grateful for."

At this point a break of a few minutes occurred. Pullman

discontinued his harangue, but Mannock showed no intention of disturbing his monologue by speech, nor did he even move. In spite of his exhaustion, Mannock was taking in (so to speak *absorbing*) his friend's discourse, but he had not the energy to respond. Pullman drew up quite near to his seemingly entranced audience, and in a low, as it were intimate voice he resumed.

"This is a position in which we have, of course, never been placed before, Mannock. I mean that *men* have never been in such a situation as this; in your life and in my life we were never in a position like this. The supernatural and the immortal overshadows us—we can see it and touch it, we go to a party at its house. It is fantastic. You have to go a long way back for men to have been in such a position, back to the times of the Greek dramatists (and then only upon a stage)—the plays of Euripides and of Aeschylus for instance. With us it is far more dramatic than in Attic tragedy; it is as if actually the King or Queen of the Greek city-state, put upon the stage, were a god or goddess.—You might add to this that it is as though the city-state were only half material ... We have, Mannock, to use our imagination, such as it is, and to do our best to realise what we look like to the non-human immortals with whom we come in contact. Instinctively we think of the Padishah as another man. But he is not *another man.* He is only pretending to be that, and is pretending to be six feet high in order to be able to treat with men. Well, this giant, magically reduced to our dimensions, still looks upon us as very tiny people. That is the first thing. Then all immortals must look upon mortals, that is, those condemned to die (and that is what happens to the regular man and we, after all, are merely dead men), the undying must look upon the dying as very silly little creatures. It is just impossible for them to take us seriously. They would find it very hard even to think of us as possessing immortal souls, and destined (in some form not a grandiose one like theirs) to browse around in the pleasant valleys of Heaven—even that would not be easy; and if they could regard us as potential little immortals they would not be very impressed. As to the inhabitants of this city, the angel does not discriminate, as we do, between the moronic majority and the minority possessing more character and intelligence. No. To him we all look as the inhabitants, of the Universal Café did to me when I first saw them."

Pullman drew up even nearer to Mannock.

"Just for one moment attempt to imagine yourself as an archangel like our friend the Padishah. What would it feel like to be that? If you were a young Catholic as I was once, before my English public school, your Thomist instructor would inform you that angels were spiritual intellectual substances. Their purity is equal to that of God, only it is limited of course. But we do not inhabit a world of artifice and even verbal icing. For *me* the archangel nicknamed by you and your friends 'Padishah', for me he is an athletic, perfectly ignorant, entirely unphilosophic young man. He is a big baby, who does not know the ABC of life. If he were willing to have a free conversation (such as you are ready to have with me), he would turn out to be naif to an unbelievable degree, a mass of little conventional clichés, and with a basic incapacity to think. Our everyday world is full of such cases as the angel. The cowboy, the aristocrat, the great athlete, the ace airman; each in his way is a perfect being, but completely stupid. For instance, the aristocrat means the average, unreal gentleman with faultless and beautiful manners, bred to be noble and beautiful like the swan. A Bolingbroke or a Chesterfield is exceedingly intelligent; they are able to *see through* themselves and so are no longer perfections: their intelligence makes their aristocratism less pure. They become actors, whereas the aristocrat is never theatrical. Anyone in whom you detect *consciousness of self*–capable of objective understanding of himself–shrinks in your estimation. The moment you read in the eyes of a queen that she was *outside* herself (was capable of looking at herself critically) then she would not be a queen. The essence of the queen, or the essence of the swan, is that they possess no critical objective intelligence. They have to be perfectly stupid." Pullman took in a deep breath. "Now to be a real angel, and, just on the same principle, to be God, you must be entirely stupid. We are compelled deeply to admire such perfections. And it is in no way to take away from the splendid pre-eminence of God–in no way to diminish one's awe of His might–if one said one did not desire to *be* God, or to be an angel. There is the famous saying of an Indian poet,

139

'I like sugar, but I do not want to *be* sugar. . . .' I do not wish to be a humbug. So I will admit that only what is intelligent really interests me. Perfection repels me: it is (it must be) so colossally stupid. Here–in Third City–we are frail, puny, short-lived, ridiculous, *but* we are superior, preferable to the Immortals with whom we come in contact."

Pullman drew himself up and stroked his beard as he smiled at the helpless but dimly attentive Mannock.

"All I would suggest is that we ought to realise the terms on which we live with these *substances*. Some intelligent slave who was on terms of social intercourse with the Emperor Marcus Aurelius should never forget to analyse the personality–with an objective and ruthless acuity–of this 'liberal' Emperor . . . That Roman slave would be behaving blamelessly if he preserved, in some secret recess of his mind, an album of untouched photos of all the men and women he knew.

"I am at present in the position of a slave: I find myself saying quietly and privately, not for quotation: 'I esteem *knowing* immeasurably more than I do *being*.'–The slave is always ideally situated, because everything makes it easy for him to arrive at that supreme truth."

Pullman paused again, lest his audience should become mesmerised by his too incessant voice.

"Let me compress what I have been saying in the following manner. We–the human kind–here consist of a horde of idiots. In addition to this degraded caricature of man, there are perhaps a few dozen–perhaps a few hundred–men of intelligence. This more intelligent, this more sensitive handful, they are all we need to consider. This knot of real living, thinking, men are all that counts, either as mortal or immortal. There are no intelligent immortals; intelligence is a compensation for our weakness, towered over–and tormented by–a number of huge, stupid immortals, who have no more intelligence than bulldogs, or police constables. We are helpless, powerless mites of intelligence. I hear you saying, 'What is the use of all this abstract analysis?' At this point, I will put your doubts at rest. To begin with, there is this deplorable, this senseless city. In your view, the person who is entirely to blame for the rotten condition in which this city finds itself is the Bailiff. It is he and he alone, who is the guilty party. But when one inquires of

140

you how it has come to pass that this little square-nose is in position to do such terrific harm, by whose authority, in short, he is Bailiff (whatever that may signify)—one receives no answer; that is to be taken for granted . . . But the answer, as you know as well as I do, is neither more nor less than the character of the Padishah. You analysed for me very competently, up to a point, the wicked Bailiff. Now I have analysed for you (by way of thanks—for one good turn deserves another), I have provided you with an anylysis of the Padishah—of *the handsome, stupid Padishah.* For the *wicked Bailiff* could not exist without the *stupid Padishah.* They are complementary figures. One exists, as a corollary of the other. The one follows from the other. The number of knaves who are bred out from one big fool is amazing.

"Now look here, Mannock: the problem is as simple as engaging a housekeeper or a secretary. The face, the gestures of a man, and what he says of course, are what people have to go by in many walks of life. The personality is a certificate—it is decisive in a promotion to sergeant, to skipper, to overseer, or to manager, and in much higher commands. If you are an explorer you look very hard at the face of an applicant to accompany you to the summit of Everest, or among the mountains of Antarctica." He paused for a few moments, keeping his eye fixed upon his involuntary listener. "Now, the personality, and especially the face, of the ruler of Third City can really be studied with advantage. For he has authority over the strangest collection of celibate mankind, not easy to manage or to know what to do with. Suppose you were looking at this Padishah for the first time, and suppose it was your task to report upon him, what kind of man would you be looking at? Well, he is a very good man; but is a saint the best man to put in charge of a complex, turbulent community? Then the Padishah is a very graceful, gentle creature. Lastly, he is very lofty and aloof. The main attributes of this personality are there for you to study; he is not a complex or secretive man." He paused again for a few moments, and then continued. "Allow me to give you my reading of your Padishah. Without a moment's hesitation I should say that he is the last person to be given the position of ruler of Third City. The first and most important thing about him, from this point of view, is that he has absolutely no interest in men: what is even more, disgust and contempt are the sensations which come most naturally to him where men are concerned. Personally his boredom is spectacular. Always he seems on the verge of collapsing from boredom. What one has to remember about him is that he is first and foremost a soldier. It will sound to you an absurd comparison, but he seems to me in the position of a big, brave, splendidly reliable, British officer appointed as military Governor to a large island inhabited by a tribe of ugly, stunted, bloodthirsty, corrupt, secretive, thievish 'natives'. Politicians explain to him that the 'natives' are children, who at some distant date will grow up. This appears to the soldier irrelevant, for what, in the end, may happen to these nasty little creatures he finds it impossible to take an interest in.–Now what, in the first instance, was this poor arch-angel entrusted with: for in the early days the population cannot have numbered more than five or ten thousand, whereas now it is a million or more. The idea may have been to give man another chance of salvation, by trying him out under modified conditions. Whatever the idea was, it cannot have been very carefully thought out, or very firmly planned. At some time or other a functionary known as the Bailiff must have had no difficulty in substituting an ingenious plan of his own for the one with which he had been presented. The Padishah would not be interested enough to examine and to modify, or to reject altogether this substitute plan. He would allow this clever official to interpret the original orders in his own way; for the Padishah himself would be quite at sea in such matters. So the resident angel remains the military authority; some resourceful official, of human or of semi-human origin, provides the city with its intellectual structure, and decides who shall be admitted and who rejected." He threw his arms out in a deprecating fashion as he began to come to the end of his discourse. "This is simply a theory; but since there is *no other* theory which takes everything into account, it is perhaps worthwhile to give it a hearing. That is all I have to say, Mannock. It is no more than an hypothesis." With this Pullman rose, and with a demonic and satyric mask of Rabelaisian mischief, whirled his hand above the prostrate Mannock, delivering a slap on the shoulder of some force.

Instead of reviving the sick man, this blow almost liquidated him. Suddenly becoming very pale, Mannock sat staring glassily in front of him. It was some minutes before he showed any signs of life at all, even so much as the movement of an eyelid or of a finger. "This man is obviously a case of a syphilo-aortic. Considerable incompetence of the valves. I should have guessed that from certain signs." Pullman realised that he had only just escaped committing manslaughter.

"Your heart is not so good as it should be, is it?" Pullman put his hand down and felt for Mannock's pulse. "I am not often hearty like that. Must cut it out altogether. I feel very ashamed of myself, Mannock. Take it easy, and then I will help you into the bedroom."

Mannock looked up gently, and smiled a very sickly smile. "My ticker's all right, I think. I am just frigthfully tired."

"I know you are, I should not have kept you up, talking your head off. Come, bed is the best place for you." He held his arm out, and told the other to get hold of it. "You can ease yourself up that way."

Accepting a little help, Mannock got gingerly to his feet. "I think I will go straight to my bed," he said. Then he stopped, half sat on the edge of a table, and gave his helper a whimsical smile–to preface what he was going to say by the slightest touch of banter. "I have only just learned that I have been entertaining an angel unawares. So you are a great celebrity! I must have been a considerable source of amusement to you, haven't I?"

Pullman's face became expressionless, except for a shade of displeasure. "Why has he been saying all that? I think I know. If people could only keep their tongues from wagging . . ."

With almost a touch of heartiness, Mannock laughed as he took his arm. "For you to reproach others with excessive talking . . .! Now I will avail myself of your strong right arm."

XIII

THE PERIOD OF PULLMAN'S STAY in Habakkuk was drawing to a close. For the next morning Sentoryen lay in wait
for him, as usual, in the street outside, and seeing him leave
the house unaccompanied, he came up eagerly. He was the
bearer of news, and of a proposal. To this Pullman felt he
should immediately attend; Sentoryen's news was to the effect
that an apartment had been reserved for him by the Bailiff in
the Phanuel Hotel, and the latter would be glad if he could
find time to visit it. It consisted of a sitting-room–a large one–a
bedroom, a shower and bath; meals in the apartment if he so
desired, also a private table in the restaurant.

All this had been arranged by the Bailiff in person. Pullman
had had in mind a visit to the Tenth Piazza bookshops: but
instead he went with Sentoryen to the address he indicated,
namely the Phanuel Apartment Hotel; they changed at Tenth
Piazza, the next station on the new line being, in fact, the
Bailiff's Palace. They alighted, and found themselves in a little
wood composed of the heroic plane and the city tree, the modest
birch.

"How remarkable," said Pullman. "A forest."

"Not really," Sentoryen corrected him. "It is for the benefit
of the guests of the Phanuel Hotel, to shroud them from the
vulgar. There," pointing towards the gleam through the trees,
"is the Bailiff's residence."

"Ah."

"The name of the station is Phanuel."

They plunged into the wood, and in a few minutes were in
front of a magnificent building, its many windows hooded in
green canvas bonnets, and, down on the entrance floor, a far
larger green awning, where the restaurant projected, allowing
two lines of tables all fresco. There was a light blue-coated,
silver-buttoned, blue-capped and silver-braided commissionaire, who saluted Sentoryen almost with abasement. Other
uniformed persons either smiled or saluted. An elevator took

them to the fourth floor. They walked to the end of a corridor, and entered a door numbered 400.

"A corner apartment is always the best," commented Sentoryen. "There is a through-draught, and then, out of the windows, one is provided with a more extended outlook."

Pullman saw, with amazement which he was far from showing, rooms which were not only of *le dernier luxe* but, considered as places to live in, wonderfully attractive. In the very large sitting-room or living-room, which included everything a human being can want, either for sitting or for living, were brand-new copies of two of Pullman's best-known books. Pullman felt sure that the Bailiff had sent a special messenger to Earth for them. It amused him to visualise the celestial messenger, brightly uniformed in the Bailiff's livery, entering Bumpuses, or Hatchards. There were, however, hundreds of books, from Lautréamont to Lucretius. ("The hundred best books," was Pullman's private comment.) On a table in his dressing-room was a photograph of his wife.

Pullman did not utter a word. At length, sinking into the silken billows of a sumptuous settee, he spoke.

"This is authentic! This, beyond the shadow of a peradventure, is Heaven."

Sentoryen laughed with discreet gusto, if one may say that, for he was never indiscreet, but he saw Apartment 400 had triumphed, and that he could announce to the Bailiff that it was to have a new tenant.

"Tomorrow morning," Pullman asserted, "I shall go to Tenth Piazza, and buy myself one of those portmanteaux which command the respect of a commissionaire, and then I shall move in here."

"Good," smiled Sentoryen. "I am sure you will be comfortable."

"A man who was not comfortable, my dear Sentoryen, in these cushions, upon these springs, would have so unreceptive an anatomy that Heaven, for him, would have nothing to do with animal comfort."

Pullman made no inquiry regarding the rent. He was offered unlimited money at the bank. It did not matter what it cost—it was in fact a gift. This was Heaven. The Bailiff understood Heaven better than most people here, who insisted on treating this place as a kind of life on Earth. Among the English, the privileges and delights were reserved for those vulgarly honoured upon the earth because their families had been rich a long time.

He was not for the Right wing, he was for the Left wing, there was nothing to influence him in one direction rather than the other. But about one thing there was no question whatever: for a writer of his experimental sort it was to the Left wing that he must look, for sympathy, interest, and patronage. It had been like that in his earthly life: and in his unearthly life it was apparently just the same, only more so. As unattached as the "lone wolf" man, of the fierce modern "genius" type, believing not in God, in class, in party, but solely in himself, it was all one to him who it was supporting Pullman; anyone who did so was a good man. He was not, of course, so utterly faithful to the god Pullman as that suggested. Solipsistic he was in principle, but no man is so watertightly an ego as all that. He had started life a devout Catholic, for instance: and that first self haunted him to some extent. There were other selves, or half-selves, too. He possessed prejudices, distinct from the official Pullman. In the present case, to go no farther, the Bailiff was not his favourite type of man. He did not like square-nosed men, for intstance. An ethnic, ancestral self was responsible for that. But that *merely* ethnic self was not indulged. The interests of a literary god, James Pullman by name, were paramount. And most of his *real* prejudices were alien to all the philosophic attitudes of the Bailiff. Nevertheless, all his career-life he had been supported by persons identical with the Bailiff, and he had always lived with, been buzzed around and been rubbed against by, ideas which were the Bailiff's ideas (and many of them were *his own*, contradicting mere prejudice); so his present supernatural life was pre-ordained. It was the literary god, Pullman, whose sacred text had been placed by the Bailiff in the shelves of the sitting-room of Apartment 400, who was established as most honoured guest in the Bailiff's private hotel—built by the Bailiff next door to this palace, owned and directed by him. And, finally, Pullman claimed full independence: would be quite capable of critiising this all-powerful magistrate, and would take sides with him under no circumstances. His tenancy of 400 would in no way change that. When, a short while before, he was considering the necessity of escape from Third City, what first suggested itself to him was to build himself up as a saint. This place might still be serviceable as a testing-out place for Heaven. Indeed, that might be the only avenue of escape. This was in no way inconsistent, the literary god might have to be forgotten—and when he had entered the city with Satters it was not with any idea of surviving in that capacity, of anyone's recalling the literary god. He went back to his schooldays, in a sense, in the company of his fag.

Friday, the day of his installation in the Phanuel Apartment Hotel, was spent very quietly. Sentoryen was in attendance. Some of the windows of the hotel on the opposite side to No. 400 had a view of the barracks at the back of the Bailiff's palace. A thousand men were garrisoned there. There were extensive parade grounds, adequate, in fact, to parade and to exercise the entire garrison. At the rear of this were the living quarters of the men. There was a huge quadrangle, and the buildings could esaily accommodate five or six thousand troops. There must have been, in embryo, a force of this number; for every evening volunteers were being drilled, and once a month these men were paraded, and at week-ends there were route-marches, and all the time small batches of them were marched to the Camp, in appropriate uniform, either as haiduks or as gladiators. The explanation of the training of so great a number of men was the creation of a force to be used as a reserve or as replacements.

Sentoryen's apartment was one of those from which this military background of the Bailiff's official life might be observed. At Sentoryen's suggestion Pullman came up to his apartment, and watched the incessant exercising of troops not on duty at the Camp. In the quadrangle, artillery of small calibre appeared, and groups of men received instruction.

Incidentally the secretary pointed out, with a smile, the severity of his small apartment. "No soft pillows for me!" he commented.

That evening Pullman had dinner in his sitting-room. He took down a copy of the *Odyssey*. "What more appropriate for the supernatural wanderer?" In the psychological region of Calypso he sank into the pneumatic wonders of his bed; soon, before he had extinguished his light, he had fallen asleep, he was dreaming of treacherous magicians, of smoke, and of unknown skies.

The following morning at about twelve o'clock Pullman was in his room. The house telephone rang. It was the office of the hotel; the Bailiff wished to know, the voice asked, if Mr Pullman would lunch with him?

Pullman hesitated for a moment, then he said that he would be delighted to have lunch with the Bailiff. The voice thereupon informed him that the Bailiff would be in the restaurant of the hotel at one o'clock.

Pullman put down the silver horn into which he had been speaking, and returned to the armchair, frowning heavily. He began to examine his position. He was, he said to himself, like a canary, in a beautifully upholstered cage. At one o'clock he must show up in parade order, and be put through his paces, he must sing cheep-cheep for his master. How soon would his master tire of him? What would happen then? Apartment No. 400 would be wanted for somebody else. He would be moved into a far less resplendent apartment. At length, he might find himself in an austere little suite like Sentoryen's. He would meet the Bailiff somewhere, and the old square nose, slyly smiling, would exclaim, "Ah, Pullman, I must apologise for having put you in such uncomfortable living quarters. But No. 400, I realized afterwards, was much too Ritzy for you. For a man of severity of mind, it was quite absurdly unsuitable!" Then his treatment by the bank would change deeply. He would be back at his original modest allowance. How vile it was to be so utterly at the mercy of a capricious autocrat of this type. Ought he not just now to have declined the honour, when the invitation to lunch was telephoned up? *He* should be the first to break the honeymoon spell. He must not jump through the hoops, one after the other, and allow himself to be made a sport of.–How Mannock's lot was to be envied! It was of course true that Mannock would never have been of any interest to the Bailiff. But how awkward a privilege was this of his.

At one o'clock he went down to lunch, his mind made up to tolerate no oily cozenage. The "great man", entrapped by his conceit into unwariness, into being deluded into the belief that he was in Heaven–that was a situation that he must beware of. There must be no blindman's-buff, with himself as the blindfolded one.

But the Bailiff seemed quite aware of the kind of suspicions that his extreme benevolence might awaken. He was determined, it seemed, to forestall anything of this kind. One thing he said, for instance, was that Pullman was to look upon No. 400 as his own, so long as he wanted to keep it. The hotel would let it to him for a period of five years. Again, he said that Pullman must not feel himself under any obligation. He would be presented with quite a stiff bill at the end of the month. He, the Bailiff, he assured him, was an excellent business man!

In the restaurant the diners enjoyed the utmost privacy, for this was not a terrace table: Pullman and the Bailiff sat facing the vast window, shut in at their back by a high screen rather more than semi-circular. All around them were similar screened diners. Murmurs and laughter could be heard, but not conversations. They had a carafe of excellent wine, a bird, something like a pheasant, a *Coupe Phanuel,* iced of course.

The overtures of the Bailiff were at first met with an impassible calm on Pullman's part, which hid an implacable refusal to be deceived. When his patron mentioned the five-years lease of No. 400, for instance, in his surly interior Pullman snarled. "What is the use, old fox, if the money offered by the bank is not forthcoming (the bank having received a note from the Bailiff that he had been misinformed, and that I was very small beer after all)." Evidence was forthcoming that the Bailiff had read several of his books with understanding, that he valued literature very highly, and that he was discriminating; there was for the Bailiff something about Pullman's utterances which had the authentic stamp of *je ne sais quoi*–all this got beneath the guard of the literary god Pullman. The Bailiff detected a softening light in his guest's eye: and he thought the better of the literary god, for a crabbed little god impervious to his unsurpassed skilfulness was, in the end, not of much use to him. They parted on very good terms, all the more so because a few glasses of *fine* were produced.

Shortly after Pullman had returned to his apartment, something very startling occurred. He was sitting in his unbelievably

149

comfortable armchair, near one of the front windows, and a tuneful bird was disseminating optimism in one of the trees of the wood outside his window, when, with an awful suddenness, it became night. Pullman sprang up and switched on the electric light. With an unexpected normality the electric bulbs dispelled the blackness. He returned to his chair, but as he sat down the light went out. Simultaneously there was a frantic knocking and ringing at his apartment door.

He sprang up again, passed quickly into his miniature hall, and flung the door open. It was Sentoryen, of course; he thrust a small bottle into Pullman's hand. He said all in one breath, "Sickening isn't it? Here, take one of the tablets in the bottle, they help the body resist the shocks–lie down at once–at once!" Sentoryen was closing the door as he was speaking; the door closed, Pullman swallowed a pill, and stepped quickly back into the sitting-room, closing the inner door behind him. He took a step in the direction of the settee, and, with great violence, he was hurled to the floor, his nose embedded in the nap of the carpet.

The bottle he had been holding in his hand whizzed away, and, in the total blackness of the room, it might as well have flown out of the window. He lay where he was, half-stunned. There was a series of deafening reports–like blows upon a gigantic gong, accompanied by explosions of light similar to a photographer's flash bomb, and then a crack so loud that Pullman could hear no more for some time. For about five minutes he did not move, and then he began crawling towards the settee, dazed but still conscious.

As, painfully, he had reached a point half-way to his destination, he looked up and saw in the sky a fiery cross. It exactly bisected one of the large panes of the window. It was a blood-red, and quivered upon the blue-black of the sky. He worked himself round sideways to the settee; then, with an immense effort, he pulled himself up, perspiring and panting, and just managed to raise first one leg, then the other, upon the edge of the new and resistant upholstery. He lay motionless for a short while, recovering from the great effort he had made, then a shock, as elemental as that of an earthquake, picked him up and hurled him through the air. His face struck the sharp edge of a chest, and he rolled over limp and unconscious.

It was almost an hour before he opened his eyes. He blinked, for it was daylight again. A bugle sounded, and more faintly a bugle answered some distance away. The Bailiff's militia, of course. He became aware of the blood on his face, the blow against the sharp edge of the chest had left an open wound above his left eye; the socket had received some of the hæmorrhage, which had dried.

Feeling sick and dejected, as his dim mind groped around to adjust itself to the new spell of daylight, which would last for a period long or short (no one could say if they would have a breather of one month, or of one day, or of one hour), he allowed his black thoughts to chase one another, around the same vacant centre. But then he felt a little firmer. Hope, that proverbial liar, made its disreputable appearance. The light however continued. Hope, with less shame, began to make itself at home. He rolled over, and there was no sign of an injury so far.

As a result of the pill he had swallowed, no doubt, he was able to move his arms and legs; slowly, but still he could move them. To rise to his feet was not an easy matter. Once he was up, he was obliged to support himself upon the furniture, and his progress was like that of a post-operational case. First he went to the telephone. He was informed that the lines were all functioning again. Whether Mr Sentoryen was well enough to do so or not, Pullman sleepily observed, he, of course, did not know; but is he was in circulation, he would be glad if he would come and see him. The office answered briskly, "Very well, Mr Pullman." He then took up his position upon a chair near the centrance and waited. Hardly had he lowered himself into the chair when the door-bell rang. Very painfully he made his way to admit his amanuensis. Sentoryen looked a little pale; he had called twice, he said, but had received no answer. He was about to ask the office to have the door opened.

"What is that?" He pointed to the cut above Pullman's eye, which had started bleeding again.

Pullman explained; he asked if a band-aid could be secured, and "is there penicillin in Heaven . . . or should I say Hell?"

And then James Pullman announced that he was going to bed. He had been tossed about a bit, and thought he would have a spell in the pneumatic paradise in the next room.

151

When asked how *he* had fared, Sentoryen shrugged his shoulders. "Oh me. Somewhat like you, I fell out of bed. But I did not fall on my head . . . I am all right. But how much of this I can take I do not know."

"The same thought has visited me," Pullman told him, "I mean as regards myself. I suppose I could put up with it once a week. But if it occurred once a day . . .!"

"Exactly."

"I shall soon have to wear a padded jacket, and put on a crash helmet when it starts." Pullman rose and tottered towards the bedroom.

"Are you able to undress yourself?" his attendant inquired.

But Pullman answered that he felt equal to that, and Sentoryen left to go to the nearest chemist.

When he was in bed, Pullman stared at the ceiling. Was this going on all the time? What would be the end of it? The exquisitely soft bed had lost its attractiveness. He would have preferred a less expensive bed. The spongy and plush apartment was becoming a mockery, if . . . he writhed dismally in his celestial make-believe. What would happen before long was that he would be finally destroyed in his sumptuous living quarters. Each inordinately supple spring and piece of divine upholstery was fundamentally sinister.

XIV

Pullman had to confess as he slowly mounted the stairs at No. 55 Habakkuk, on Monday morning, that that kind of house was much to be preferred to the newly equipped Phanuel Hotel–stinking of new money, of wads of welfare state banknotes, and nothing human about it. Platon looked furious, and Mannock was in bed. Pullman entered the bedroom woefully, and Mannock looked at him with a different kind of woefulness.

"Well, I do not have to ask you why you are in bed. All day yesterday I was in bed. This morning I refused to stop there any more–I am aching all over, but I can see that this is what we shall have to expect all the time now, so . . ."

"It is all very well for you, but you were allotted an age better able to withstand shock than the age I was given. I ache in every bone."

Pullman sat down laughing. "If you were inside my skin you would not feel so youthful and resistant, in spite of the fact that I am three years on the right side of forty. The day before yesterday I was flung down twice with great violence. The second time I was gashed here," he pointed above his eye.

Mannock had an expression of shocked alarm, (one with which Pullman was by this time quite familiar); this was no doubt a precious legacy from his father the Bishop, guaranteed to put a face in mourning with a magnificent promptitude. To belong to a great clerical family–for Mannock's great-grand-father had been an Archbishop of Canterbury–certainly supplied one with a face which would be overworked during an epidemic.

"I am sorry. Are you badly hurt?" the face asked, with a hushed organ-note of grave commiseration.

Pullman liked everything about this English gentleman, on this particular morning.

"Did *you* have a bad time, Mannock? But of course you did!" He took a small bottle out of his pocket and handed it to him. "Take one of these the moment the uproar begins. It really does help. I cannot say what they are, but I took one, and it acted–did me good."

Mannock was as apt at depicting gratitude as he was at making grief visible. "I say, it is *awfully* kind of you! I am glad to have these, Pulley–do you mind if I call you Pulley? I am so used to hearing you called that. But you have some yourself, haven't you?"

"They come from the Bailiff . . . naturally! I shall send for another bottle as soon as I get back."

"If you are *sure* . . ." Mannock's face gave a good imitation of a man who is a martyr to his imagination–at a moment, say, when a dear friend is in acute danger (in battle, or upon the operating table). Mannock was, however, performing much more than usual, and his visitor felt that it must have something to do with reports of the great deference shown him by the Bailiff. But Pullman could never have believed that he would regret the days when he and Satters were guests in this house, as now he was doing, nor how jolly it was to be called "Pulley".

"That there are no private telephones here is the last straw!" he exclaimed. It was arranged that Mannock should come to lunch on the next day, Tuesday–if he felt well enough. Still feeling a little groggy himself, Pullman decided to go to Tenth Piazza. This was his second attempt within a week to visit the Piazza, on the last occasion having been deflected by Sentoryen.

As he stepped out into the street, automatically he looked around for Sentoryen, so much did he associate, in his mind, leaving this house with being met by that tireless young man. Indeed, he felt that something was missing. And then the usual denizens of hereabouts were at their gloomiest that morning, and the underground journey was funereal.

Upon the universal pasty face, with staring Pagliaccio-ish eyes, and mouth open to simulate the delightful privileged vacuity of youth, upon this face, as he saw masses of it in the underground carriages, a new look was being painted, namely a look of suppressed fright and authentic pathos. If you clapped your hand behind them they would almost jump out of their skin. If you touched them on the sleeve, they would shrink from you with a look of terror; if you sat in front of them in an underground carriage wtih hair all over your chin and upper lip, they would look at you with great uneasiness as if they wondered whether you were a man, and, if not, whether

154

you were dangerous. No longer were they to be seen sporting with one another, à la Youth. They scarcely spoke at all.

Pullman winked at one of them, while sitting immediately in front of him, their knees almost touching. This shrivelled exponent of Youth became immobile, and fixed his fearful and attentive gaze upon the eye of the Bearded One. When nothing further happened he relaxed. And then he winked himself (to himself), again and again. Pullman supposed he was testing his own ability to wink his eye–although this explanation did not satisfy him.

When Pullman reached Tenth Piazza, he found scarcely any promenaders, and those who were there scuttled miserably along. Few shops were open, and he could not even find the position of the bookseller he had intended to visit. It was a very hot day, and this lent a strange emphasis to the deserted arcades and the few frightened habitués, hurrying away from their dereliction–faster and faster, in horror that they were the only people there.

He returned to the underground feeling very depressed. There was no reason for him to feel any different from the cosmetically–masked Youth dreamers–terrified but still dreaming. He went immediately into the restaurant when he reached the Phanuel Hotel. The Menu was more luxurious than ever. The meat items were in French, *Boeuf à la Mode d'Autrefois,* or *Cottelette des Neiges d'Antan.* Among the drinks a feature was the mysterious *Consommation Rouge en Surprise.* There was a *Consommation Blanche* also. The word *fine* occurred near the bottom of the list. Pullman consumed a "Red", and two *fines.* As he was finishing his second *fine,* a very dark man who was passing his table stopped an smiled. Much more expansive than he had felt upon entering the restaurant, Pullman smiled back. "Do you ride the Centaur?" the man asked him softly.

"Ought I to do that?" Pullman queried.

"There is no better mount." The man passed behind a screen.

Pullman asked for a cigar, and soon was sitting mellowing in the delectation of a Corona. Before he left the table he bought a packet of twenty cigarettes. He mounted to his apartment, feeling that the thing to do was to live for the day–and to drink a carafe or two of red wine for lunch and for dinner; and he

155

wondered whether there was any bootleg *Weib* to be had in Third City, as well.

He had not been more than a minute or two in No. 400, which looked a great deal pleasanter than the last time he saw it, when Sentoryen presented himself. That young man was not long in discovering that Pullman was unlike his usual self. Indeed, he recognised the effects of *Consommation Rouge*.

Pullman was seated in a corner of the settee. Sentoryen accommodated himself at the opposite end (which Pullman regarded as an unaccustomed freshness).

"I want you to put me right about something," Sentoryen said with an earnest expression, as if he were about to inquire as to the specific weight of the moon, or something extremely remote, and distinctly cold, of that sort.

"I am very much at your service, O Sentoryen," Pullman said, containing his effervescence.

"It involves your lending me your hand, for a ... oh, a minute, no more."

Pullman intoned, "Here is my hand, for better or worse," but looking with a rather bleary surliness at the man who had asked for his hand.

Laughing, Sentoryen gently took possession of Pullman's hand, who surrendered it not with bad grace, but rather with no grace at all.

It was with the ceremony of a conjurer that the hand was conducted to its objective, namely, a portion of the torso of the young amanuensis. "Now," he enjoined, "lie quite still, and keep your eyes closed; for just two or three minutes. Yes, that's lovely." He dragged up his shirt at the side, until a considerable area of golden, almost Samoan flesh was visible.

"For Pete's sake, what are you doing with my hand," Pullman cried, and the hand began to return to its master.

Not attempting to retain the hand–even giving it a little push, Sentoryen sang, "Okay, your hand has played its part. Now, had you not known I was a man, but thought I was a girl, would you have had the same sensations as if you had been caressing a woman? Was it soft, was it warm? Was it ...?"

"Anything you like," Pullman interrupted gruffly. "What is

it you want me to tell you?" His face was quite non-committal, but the sort of shadow it seemed to be in was ominous.

"You must feel uncomfortable in this place without a woman. Don't you?" Sentoryen did not look seductive when he said this, but coldly matter-of-fact.

"I have not been here long, you forget. The time may come, the time may come."

"You are very detached, aren't you? I have been here a long, long time, and I confess . . . I have those feelings. I also experience love . . . oh yes, far more truly than I could in the generally accepted way." Pullman noticed that the other's voice was becoming sligthly thick and guttural. "My master . . . how ingenious, how delightful it would be if we found ourselves in bed together. I would pretend I am a little girl."

Attempting to rid himself of the effects of *Consommation Rouge,* Pullman glared drearily at Sentoryen, "My imagination is defective," he replied. "It would be no use trying to believe that you were a glamorous Screen star. Apart from the question of certain outstanding anatomical details, you have not the necessary lovely husky voice."

The young man sprang up and began pacing up and down.

"Very well, very well. You will go to seed sexually! Just because I have not got . . . oh fou-ee! . . . a great apparatus teeming with germs, chock full of dangers . . . of which a somewhat milder form of leprosy is not the worst–just because I have not got the famous female stink, you scorn my proposal!" He flung himself into a bandy-legged attitude, with a trans-formation of his face into the mask of a repulsive zany, by developing a sparkling squint and pouting his lips out in an obscene smile–snatching a cyclamen form a vase within easy reach, and sticking it in his thick hair, the stalk finding a foothold behind his ear, acquired the flowery symbol of the female.

"Like that, would you love . . . me more!" he cried.

Pullman continued to stare at this performance–hostilely however.

"Can you find nothing disgusting to do," he jeered, "to provide yourself with the authentic female whiff?"

"Very well, Mr Pullman! To pay you out for having got caught in the venustic mousetrap, how many illegitimate brats of yours trot up and down the cities of the earth, advertising their tenth-rate apology for talent by plastering it with your name ('I am a bastard of the great Pullman's, oh yes, oh yes!'). That is something that is worse than the pox."

"Are you an offspring of mine, you glib-tongued tick?"

Pullman shaded his eyes with his hand, as if seeking to identify an heir-apparent.

But Sentoryen turned his back, raised his jacket and faced Pullman with his bottom.

"My middle-face, Mr Pullman. Do you see a likeness *there*?" He worked his juffs up and down. Then he turned round and again harangued his bearded audience of one.

"Identification is extremely difficult——What are women but street-corner photographers? These always have their cameras with them in their dirty little pockets. 'Your photograph, sir, in three or four minutes,' or 'Come back again in nine months– in only nine months–and your photograph will be alive and kicking!'–And they guarantee 'A LIVING LIKENESS!' But it never looks like you, Mr Pullman: pay what you may–pay a salary for life to an expensive woman–and you will not get a replica of yourself. More than half the time the so-called facsimile of you is, in fact, like the woman. What would you say if you had allowed a photographer to snap you and he presented you with a photograph of *himself*?"

"The arguments to which the unsuccessful pathic resorts!" He had heard all this before. Pullman had lost all the factitious vivacity with which he had entered the apartement. He turned a sour, glum eye upon his would-be bedfellow. "Whose phiz is *yours*, O Centaur? What moronic old grease-pot palmed you off as a real man upon some sucker from Asia Minor?"

Sentoryen came over to the settee and held out his hand with a wry smile. "Soon we shall be becoming discourteous I see. I will leave you, Mr Pullman. But do not forget, I am a good clean man; so when you hunger for some little piece of barley-sugar with short legs and a big head, as you hunger and thirst for this hot little pin-cushion probably teeming with venereal bacilli . . . remember Sentoryen loves you."

For the first time Pullman croaked out a laugh. "I might have known that love would come into it somewhere–in con-nection with the unsavoury mouse-trap of the Man! But I will remember that love–the Centaur's love!–when I yearn for a bit of pneumatic humanity to complete the delights of the extremely pneumatic bed!"

"You are a very cruel person."

Pullman rose from the settee, and shook himself. "I know," he said, "I know. When I was in the restaurant just now, a man asked me, 'Do you ride the Centaur?' I understand that question, now. Are you in love with everyone in this hotel? In English schools I remember, in the Masters' Houses, there were things knows as 'House tarts'. Are you a 'Hotel tart'?"

Sentoryen, who was entering the small hallway, looked over his shoulder, and put out his tongue.

Pullman called out, "Sentoryen, are you still my attendant?"

"I am your forever devoted Sentoryen. I wait on you like a Slave of the Lamp."

"Will you bring another of those bottles, for use during storms?"

"Okay, Mr Pullman. I will bring one up immediately."

The door closed, and Pullman returned to the settee. He drew out the cigarettes bought in the restaurant. It could not be called *thinking*: Pullman carried on privately the sort of tit for tat which had been occurring publicly *à deux*.

So he *thought* (as they loosely say) that it would be no use whatever asking the pansy Centaur to guide him to the *blind pig* where women are bootlegged: obviously in a megalopolis whose whisky is illegally peddled, women were to be found, too–at an absurd price. Did he ride a Centaur! So that was what he was expected to do. (It would be like self-abuse.) What a comedy, the next time the Bailiff and Sentoryen met. One can hear the Centaur saying, "He won't ride. That is final." And the potentate, very displeased, scolding his favourite pansy-agent. "You must be losing your charm *and* your intellect. I will send Besseron instead of you." One can hear the scornful laugh of the Centaur. "That would be founny! Bess has a square nose to start with. You have no idea what the difficulties are with a dirty Irishman, whose imagination has been on fire since his schooldays with Victorian drawers and heavily laced chemises–all of the mystery of Sex at its most scented and inaccessible. The big bottom and the bosomy front –that has held the field for so long, there is nothing to be done.

159

The segregation of the sexes is the worst enemy of the So."
And the Bailiff snuffles and snorts, "That is all very well, but
you broke down Tanner, who had been born among crino-
lines.–You're losing your skill–or else you are beginning to
smell."–The Centaur was so angry he could have let loose a
home truth or two, but all he said was, "No, *I* do not smell–
not the faintest trace, even when I'm hot and perspire. But
Bess, now! he stinks out an entire room."–"That's a lie," says
the Bailiff, "and you know it. Centaur, listen to me! I will
leave you with Pull. If you don't sleep with him within a month,
I am through with you. I don't mind *how* you do it, but your
naked body must be against his, and he must learn to *like* it.
It's up to you."

Poor old Centaur, his job is as good as lost. I think I shall
refuse to allow him to serve me any more.

At about that point the Centaur returned with the bottle:
Pullman looked stern, "Sentoryen, I don't want to see you any
more. I am allergic to homosexuals. All I will do is not to
denounce you. But you must not come here again."

Sentoryen stood at the door, dismayed. "Mr Pullman, I shall
lose my job. It is very hard, terribly hard to dismiss me like
that. I made a bad mistake. Please give me another chance,
Mr Pullman. You can absolutely depend that that subject will
never be mentioned again."

"I am sorry. I do not want you around. You will be of use
to somebody else. For me you are simply a bad smell. Why
should I put up with that!"

Pullman slammed the door in his face. He was not the man
to be upset, in the conventional way, of course, by such an
occurrence. He also could not help being amused by the antics
of the pansy. Yet Pullman was distressed as well as annoyed.
Everything that occurred caused him to value less the very
handsome apartment, the exceptionally fine restaurant, where
wine and cigars could be obtained (and nowhere else in this
city perhaps). For obviously the meaning of Sentoryen was
that the Bailiff assumed that, as a protégé of his, you were a
Sodomite, or ready to be initiated as an inmate of Sodom. That
was elementary, he took unnatural love for granted. The rapture and roses of vice was *de rigueur*: but the Marquis de Sade
provided the kind of vice which provoked the raptures. "If I

kick a man out for 'making proposals' of the most normal kind,
Oh! I am not 'progressive'. I shall find myself shown the door
–or at least be reproved for my bourgeois tastes. I can see the
Bailiff twitting me, 'I am *sorry*, Mr Pullman, that we cannot
find you a tea-rose, some lollypop, some Gretchen of the Rhine-
land, or some blushing Victorian damsel.' And what can I say?
'I want somewhere to live in this outlandish city, that is all.
I do not want Lord Alfred Douglas thrown in!' No, it would
not do to answer in that way.–I have turned up my nose at
one of the delicacies *de la maison*, and I suppose I have not
many more days to live in the lap of luxury. I had better look
out for another apartment."

When, next day, Mannock came to lunch, and filled the
restaurant with reactionary conversation, highhatted the
waiters, and described the food as "dago food" and "preten-
tiously rich" in their hearing (for the wine flushed him and
led him into utterance of a provocative nature, for which he
apologised elaborately afterwards), Pullman expected twenty-
four hours notice. Instead of that, the next morning, Wednesday, there was a note from the Bailiff saying how sorry he was
to learn of the inexcusable behaviour of the young man whom
he had entrusted with the business of looking after him, but
that a new sort of batman would present himself that morning.
He added that, however fantastic Sentoryen's behaviour might
seem to Pullman, that young man was sincerely and passionately in love with him. However much he (the Bailiff) discour-
aged it, in a city in which there were no women, this type of
"cock-eyed" love could not be rooted out, and shamefully flourished. The fault was that of the Padishah, who refused to
allow women in the city, and kept them in a pen *incommuni-
cado*. Sentoryen had served, to start with, as a haiduk officer
and he suspected that those young men, like, the Spartans, all
indulged in sentimental attachments for one another. Sentoryen had certainly never met anyone like him before: he had
been dazzled in the course of his attendance upon so extraordinary an intellect as that of Pullman. He hoped that Pullman would overlook this unfortunate scene, and he felt quite
sure that he would find Bates, his new attendant, a serious man,
as well as very willing. He was one of his force of so-called
gladiators. Bates was being seconded to his service.

When Bates arrived, it was all Pullman could do not to burst out laughing. He was a stocky young man who was phenomenally ugly. His ferocious jaw and glaring eyes would not fail to terrify the enemies of the Bailiff. He was even more alarming when he smiled. However, he did everything swiftly and competently.

The Bailiff decidedly had wit, if in all other respects he was an old reprobate. He had no doubt walked round his camp and picked out the ugliest man. Ha ha ha! Whatever Bates might be, he did not look like a pansy.

Pullman indited the following note, in answer to the Bailiff.

"Your Excellency. Your note was a model of the most delicate courtesy. But I hope my feelings have been a little misunderstood. The city does not have to be womanless for Sodomy to flourish. One of my best friends on earth was a Sod. But gratifying as it is to be loved, it is embarrassing. When I was young, a housemaid was hopelessly in love with me, without any familiarity on my side, and my parents were obliged to dismiss the poor girl. It was the same situation apparently in the case of Sentoryen. I very much regret the whole business."

So, on the surface, all was well. There was not the slightest breath of discord between the Magistrate and himself. But the insanitary layer just beneath the surface had been uncovered rather violently, and the surface would never look the same again. What other surprises were in store for him in this establishment he could not guess, but it was, for him, a very fragile environment.

8. THE POLICE PRESIDENT

XV

THAT MASTERFUL CREATURE, of the Stanley and the Livingstone type, who was Setebos to Caliban, who had secured an entrance to this city in the adventurous style of the man of heroic cast, had been leading the urban life in which these glorious qualities had been, of necessity, folded up and laid aside, like the heroic garments called for by actors taking great parts. But the superficial urbanity of this life was a thing of the past, and accordingly the hero awoke, and he surveyed the days which lay before him with the eye of the man of action. For he had a plan. He, and all the other inmates of this Third City might be destroyed at any moment; on the other hand they might not. He was not going to sit down, or lie and await the *coup de grâce*. He would proceed with his life regardless of these threats. If he wandered around, among this huge collection of men-without-women, he might come upon something which it was worth dying and rising again from the dead to see. It was worth essaying. At once he set out, after explaining to Bates what was expected of him. Fifth Piazza was his starting point. He circled around this vast oblong, moving in and out until he reached the side looking towards Tenth Piazza, for there had been no Mercator here; although the sun rose and set as it did upon the earth, where it rose was not the east and where it set was not the west. If you used such expressions as east and west no one knew what you were talking about. All one could do was to use the place of one's residence as a conventional centre–or the nearest landmark, such as Tenth Piazza. This was no more arbitrary than using Jesus Christ as a conventional division, before which time, two-dimensionally, takes its historic road backwards, and after which it gloriously progresses up to the present moment. If you asked a man where he lived, he would say "Near the Yenery", "Near the First Circle", "Off Tenth Avenue", or "Towards the farmlands".

There was a handsome arterial road, several miles in length, he calculated, connecting Fifth Piazza and Tenth Piazza. Entering a street leading off this, not a hundred yards from the Piazza, he was almost immediately halted by the display in a photographer's window. A life-size photograph of two naked men was the main exhibit. He examined this carefully. In both cases fig leaves occurred, where this screening vegetation is customarily found. A police requirement, Pullman surmised. But there were no restrictions as regards the posing of the couple. And the expressiveness of the human face attracted no censorship, and full advantage was taken of this fact.

Everything was done to advertise the conjugal relationship of this pair, which played the part of the male, and which the female: the mental attitude towards sexual indulgence of each of these people respectively. Actually they each seemed to regard it as a dirty joke, no more. Both were lean; the weaker vessel (the softer nature) was almost emaciated. But in both cases the muscular mouths were pursed into a grimace of frolic, obscene insinuation. They looked into each other's eyes as the discoverers of a salacious technique. In this small district he saw many life-size nude camera studies of an *Ehepaar* of this kind, and they varied greatly. Some were a pair of brooding sad-eyed, owls, some a solemn 'intellectual' couple, and, in such cases, it was clearly a union of minds, in which the Sodomy was incidental, the nude display a mere convention, in which no obscenity was recognised, and the physical factor was secondary. One pair orthodoxly put on view their nudities, but, for the rest, exhibited no emotions, or any consciousness that clothes were not there. It seemed to follow from this that the body signified nothing to them; there were of course many others who were absurdly obscene.

After making the discovery of the large nude group–and there were smaller groups of other couples, but in every case undressed–Pullman began the penetration of this district evidently devoted to the pervert. Moving away from the main road for a distance of three or four blocks, he reached a small circus, or circle, full of shops. On the way he encountered some of the living originals of the life-size photographers' groups. They were grey flannel-suited, with flowing Byron collars, horticultural lapels, a heavy swaying of the hips, and great sweeping gestures of the arm in order to pat the back of the hair, or to maintain a silk sleeve handkerchief in place.

St Anne's Circus had not many promenaders or shoppers; like Tenth Piazza, Pullman supposed, it was deserted, or almost so. Some strolled in pairs, sometimes embracing one another, and one pair were violently quarrelling. Some were alone, drifting up to the shop windows, distractedly quizzing a geometric dressing-gown, in saffron and veridian. One was weeping in front of a photographer's. One of the young men he passed stopped for a moment, and said to Pullman, pointing to the figure in front of the photographer's window, "That poor young man! His boy died in the 'Blitz', and there they are together.–In that great big photograph in the middle of the window. He has been there all day."

Half the shops were shuttered, some had gummed paper stuck on the glass, and some had no glass at all. He noticed that more than half the windows were glassless. It was not the time to visit such a place as this.–A most interesting society of perverts, but *en grand deuil*. It was *not* the time for the bearded stranger to come prowling around, note-book in pocket; but he did draw out the scribbling pad he always took with him, and jotted down a few observations regarding the disconsolate pansy, weeping in front of the enormous photograph–a piece of gigantic intimacy, even the mole above the left nipple was there, and many other little things which the poor weeping pervert knew so well. Resolving a return to this chaste little circle if things ever got better, Pullman hastened away and took the underground back to his starting point, the little wood of Phanuel, and the hotel he had grown to dislike. Having lunched with restraint, he went across to the Bailiff's palace, and was at once shown into a small room where the great Magistrate was finishing his midday meal–which he may or may not have described as a lunch.

"Come in, come in, my dear young man, and what is it so urgent as to cause you to give me the great pleasure of your company?" He called to one of the two white-jacketed boys. "A cup of coffee for Mr Pullman, and a bottle of brandy to push it down."

Pullman came to the point almost brusquely. He wanted an introduction to the Police President, one which would admit the bearer rapidly to this personage.

"The Police President!" the Bailiff exclaimed. "What a person to wish to visit–a social call I suppose. Enlighten me, my dear Pullman."

Pullman said he wished to interview this high official, about nothing in particular. There were certain things in this city which awakened his curiosity; the women, for instance. "Ah now, that is a question of the utmost delicacy. However warmly I introduce you, I doubt if he will want to talk to you about the condition of the women. You see, we all deplore the fate of those miserable creatures. But . . . well, my dear Pullman, it is the Governor . . . the 'Padishah' you know, who is responsible for everything to do with females. That is why it is so difficult to talk about the women."

"I did not know that. I understand."

They conversed, at last drifting away somewhat from the Police President; the Bailiff monologued. The latter ended by saying, "Your guess is as good as mine as to the outcome of this terrible quarrel. It *may* blow over, a few more cyclones. But one thing I can promise you, if the worst comes to the worst, you are safe with me. No harm will come to you. But if the *worst* thing were to happen, it would come with extreme suddenness. There might be only a quarter of an hour in which to act. Just for the present I should not wander very far. Just for the present, Pullman. Please take this to heart. No visit to the farmlands, for instance! If I were you I should remain in or near the hotel. It is as bad as that, Pullman. There might be longer than a quarter of an hour. But not a minute more than that is it safe to reckon on. An all out attack would be very terrible.–But let us hope that someone grows tired of this game–you must come over to me at once, whenever there is anything cyclonic."

"Your Excellency, it is exceedingly kind of you to offer me this protection. I cannot thank you adequately."

"My dear fellow, you must not say such things as that. We are confederates, let me put it like that. I would do anything for you, anything you asked!"

"You know how I feel towards you . . . my confederate!"

166

and Pullman looked very serious. "I wish I could offer you some return."

The Bailiff banged his hand down upon that of his guest, which he pinioned to the table. "My dear chap, you know what the *return* is. I am inexpressibly pleased, as well as honoured, to be able to be of service to you!"

Towards the end of this extremely emotional discourse, Pullman smiled and pointed out that he could never reach the Bailiff in an emergency. "How could I get from the hotel to the palace? I am not able to move a foot in my own room."

The Bailiff sprang up, slapping his forehead dramatically. "Fool that I am! But I will take care of that, Pullman. I will attach someone to you, who would be able to assist you even as I would myself. His name is Vbasti. I will put you under his personal care. He will be answerable to me for your safety. I suggest that you take him everywhere with you–let him be your shadow! Take him to the bath, take him to the lavatory. He is not an adventurous young man like Sentoryen! Trust in him implicitly. Do whatever he tells you."

The Bailiff walked quickly over to the telephone. "I am going to speak to the Police President." It was hardly a minute when the P.P. was there, and the Bailiff indulging in his usual noisy facetiousness.

He wished to recommend to him a dear friend, one whom he greatly valued . . . No, he had committed no crime. He was a great–a very great–writer on Earth . . . Yes, that is it, what in the earthly life women get out of the Lending Libraries . . . Yes, yes, but this you know is what sages read–they have their *own* libraries. It is as if I were sending you, President, Goethe or Tolstoy . . . *What* are they? For shame, President! *What* is Copernicus–what is Shylock! You are a most ignorant policeman."

An appointment was arranged for less than an hour thence. Pullman hoped that the Bailiff had not left any wounds in the vanity of this supreme policeman.

"I will send you in my car. But first, Vbasti." He summoned him at once by telephone. "Will you take Vbasti with you to Police Headquarters? It is wiser." Pullman said yes, of course. "I will install him near you in the hotel."

Pullman was presented with a shadow–he could hardly protest. He was not given twenty-four hours to consider it, nor yet twenty-four minutes. It was a command, as well as a great favour. These things materialised with terrific expedition. There was no breathing space. While it was flitting through his mind that his life was lived for him (if a life it was), the door opened and there was Vbasti.

By good fortune he was not a compromising shadow to have. He was stalwart, with the hint of a square nose, in some lights seeming dark, in others fairish. His expression was watchful and intelligent.

Pullman smiled broadly at Vbasti. "This is an awful job to have. I hope you will not hate me too much before it is over!" he said.

"If I thought that," said Vbasti, a little bumptiously, without smiling, "I should not have agreed to do it."

Pullman understood that Vbasti did not like being treated as if there were no difference between himself and Bates.

The Bailiff burst out laughing. "Are you satisfied with Vbasti's wardrobe?" he asked.

"As you ask me in that blunt way," said Pullman, "let me say that if Vbasti and myself are to be twins, one of two things should happen: either I must acquire a light suit like his, or he should borrow a suit like mine—it is no use, I fear, from what I know of Vbasti, to *offer* him a suit."

The Bailiff looked at Vbasti, who stood like a waxwork, obviously determined not to recognise that it was up to him to make any remark.

"I will send to the tailor's tomorrow," the Bailiff told Pullman, ignoring the waxwork. "Vbasti shall have an outfit like yours."

"Your Excellency need not trouble himself. I have such a suit. I shall wear it." The waxwork spoke, but did not melt.

"That is good, Oh Vbasti," smiled his master.

"Thank you, Vbasti," Pullman added.

"You are to go to the Police President, Vbasti. In about ten minutes."

Vbasti turned towards the door. "I shall be dressed as you wish."

When the man had gone, the Bailiff explained. "Vbasti is a very intelligent fellow. He feels that he is not properly rewarded. That he is deliberately denied a position worthy of his talents. He is a very . . . *touchy* man."

"I shall take great care not to offend him," Pullman quietly responded.

The Bailiff did not welcome this assurance. It was as Pullman had expected: he felt sure that the Bailiff's staff was a mass of favourites and of men who had not understood how to attract favour, or who perhaps had some conceit they were unable to conceal. He was being placed in the hands and at the mercy of a man who resented being selected for such a minor job. Oh well, Pullman hoped that, if ever the great emergency came, he would be in, or very near, the palace.

Pullman and Vbasti sat opposite the Police President, a very large desk between them. The light blue uniform of that official, with the wide flat epaulets of the Russian officers, the wide flat gilt and silver braid elsewhere, the mysterious decorations–that irrelevant costumery distracted attention from the face, which was anything but trustworthy. The blueness where the razor had been, matching the uniform, looked unreal, and the large grey eyes told of a great capacity for evasion. The clipped grey hair had been grey when first Mr Lear entered the city, recommending him for high office. The thin mouth twitched sometimes; it twitched as he looked at Vbasti. He was uneasy about the presence of this employee of the Bailiff's (for the colour of his face and even his expression marked him out as that). And this was a source of satisfaction to Vbasti.

"I have been a Police President for a long time, Mr Pullman; and *never* has anyone asked to interview me. This is not Earth; there are no newspapers here. For what conceivable reason a person should wish to interview me I cannot think. But his Excellency the Bailiff is a great friend of mine. If he asked me to interview the Devil," he glanced sideways at Vbasti, "I should do so–after consulting the Governor. So I am frankly mystified by your visit, but I am at your service."

The Police President sat back, continuing to eye Vbasti with misgiving–which continued to give great enjoyment to Pullman's shadow.

"This, I should perhaps have said, is my shadow," Pullman informed the Police President.

That personage looked more mystified than ever, but all he said was, "Ah, hmn."

"The Women's . . . Reserve interests me very much," Pullman announced, in the most uninhibited way.

"What do you want to know?" the Police President inquired coldly.

"Everything interests me about the life of these women. Is there very much venereal disease?"

"How could there be, Mr Pullman?" The P.P. was colder.

"It would be quite possible, your Excellency. But I have already noticed that homosexuality flourishes among the men in Third City. I wondered if the women had recourse to Lesbian practices?"

It was only the presence of Vbasti, Pullman thought, which prevented the P.P. from expostulating, from saying perhaps, "If you are a doctor, I am not the man you should interview." Instead he said, "Yes, there is a good deal of unnatural vice. We can do very little to stop it."

"Are the women in receipt of State credits as are the men?"

"Yes," the P.P. answered. "They do not receive so much; but the system is the same."

"What is the annual percentage of suicide in the women's part of the city?" Pullman asked.

The Police President gazed at Pullman without speaking, for perhaps a minute. "Mr Pullman, I am unable to answer your questions of that kind." He took up the telephone. "The Bailiff's Office," he said. "And put me through from the next room."

He looked again coldly and blankly at Pullman with his large false grey eyes. "I am going to speak to His Excellency the Bailiff about these questions of yours."

Pullman bowed his head. When they were alone, he turned to Vbasti, and said, "Have my questions, do you think, been calculated to embarrass this official?"

"Yes, I suppose so," Vbasti answered, "but from the start it has been funny . . . oh one of the funniest interviews I have ever been present at."

Pullman looked at Vbasti rather as the Police President

170

looked at his bomb-shell questions. The tendency was for Vbasti, upon the slightest provocation, to become too fresh, he reflected. He might have to decline Vbasti's services. While he was turning this over in his mind the Police President returned, with a thudding of sparkling, black top boots, sat down, and drew the heavy chair forward violently, the silent room outraged by the harsh disturbance.

"All right," he said. "I will answer any question you like."

"Thank you, your Excellency." Pullman bowed. "But first I would suggest that you find some place where Vbasti could wait, as I have one or two rather private matters to discuss." He turned to Vbasti. "You understand, don't you, Vbasti?"

"I understand," Vbasti said under his breath, and with an expression of great bitterness.

The P.P. rang a bell and had Vbasti escorted away somewhere. When the door had closed the Police President looked far more comfortable. "I am glad, Mr Pullman, that we are alone. I can speak more freely."

"That is why I got rid of that clerk of the Bailiff's. He is attached to me in case of emergency, when there might be very little time to whip me out of a cataclysm."

The P.P. laughed more easily than Pullman had supposed him capable of. "I wish His Excellency would provide me with some such guardian angel ... or devil of course!"

After this moment of pleasantry Pullman resumed the "interview".–"Well, Mr President, there was this question of statistics, regarding the annual suicide rate in the female ghetto."

The official leaned forward, his folded forearms supporting his brilliant torso upon the desk; he looked up from beneath raised eyebrows and a furrowed forehead.

"As His Excellency tells me that you are a personal friend of his and has asked me to keep nothing back from you: conditions in the Yenery, as we call it, are nothing short of appalling. As to the suicide rate, not long ago that rose to fifty per cent."

Pullman gasped. "Half the female population!"

"It is horrible, yes!" The P.P. looked as shocked as he could. "Over two hundred thousand women were thrown into the City Incinerator; women, many of them, like my mother, or

171

like your mother, Mr Pullman. It was so terrible that I went to the Governor (you know him, perhaps, as the Padishah) and I offered my resignation. I said. 'Your Holiness, I am a man! The woman who bore me was like one of those. I can no longer assist at the *torture* of those women. I must relinquish my post, and resign altogether from the Police Force.'–'Torture!' he said–and he was horrified too–for he is a truly angelic man. Torture,–the idea of *suffering,* affects him as it would us. But death, you understand, has a very different significance for him than it has for man, like ourselves . . . You understand, Mr Pullman–I think he does not realize that death, here, means extinction."

"Yes, indeed," Pullman replied.

"Most men do not understand. I did not understand at first."

"I am a product of the English public school, but I began life in Ireland. I am a Catholic," Pullman replied.

This seemed to startle the Police President, extremely. "Oh," he said, in a quite altered voice. "I did not know that . . . You know Monsignor O'Shea I imagine?"

Pullman smiled disarmingly. "No I do not. My Catholicism wore thin on earth."

"I see."

But the highest Police Executive was still a shaken man, Pullman observed. Which meant, of course, that association with the Bailiff precluded a membership of that communion. It followed, it was clear enough, that were you in the confidence of Monsignor O'Shea, you would avoid any contact with the Bailiff. What would your attitude be to the Police President? From that official's alarm just now it would seem that the Police President was double-faced. It was probable, Pullman thought, that he was more of the party of the Bailiff than of that of the Church. What he had been saying just now, with reference to his scruples in the matters of the confinement (as in fact it was) of the women, was no doubt sincere. But as Police President his position must be an uneasy one–it had been most incautious to reveal his Catholic origin, Pullman realised.

"Well, as you understand what the situation is, Mr Pullman, that makes it easier for me. The Governor is adamant about the separation of the sexes. He says that there are many holy women–saints who are women. But that is all that women mean to him. In all other ways he regards them as a sinful element, which must be isolated. They must at all costs be shut out from a celestial testing ground, like Third City, originally interded for men whose only sin had been due to their earthly contacts with women. I may say, in the greatest confidence, that it is his opinion that all women should be relegated to the infernal regions. . . .

"So you see, Mr Pullman, there is a great weight of prejudice, in high places, against the women as such. It is as if, for breeding purposes, Man were associated with an animal, one of very dirty habits, incapable of appreciating any ethical precept, whose impulses were always mischievous. While he was engaged in perpetuating the species on the earth, such an associate is, however unfortunate that may be, necessary. But in eternal life, it would be absurd to perpetuate this mischievous and unsavoury adjunct of Man."

"You express that admirably. Were you, by any chance, your Excellency, a priest in your earthly life?"

The exalted interviewee gazed fixedly at the interviewer. Very softly he said at last, "How did you guess that? Yes, I was a Jesuit. You must have second sight!"

"Wonderful, is it not! *And* your name was O'Leary."

Father O'Leary flung himself back in his chair.

"You must be in league with the Devil!" he exclaimed.

"Not a bit of it," Pullman assured him. "Just a capacity for putting two and two together. Now, Father O'Leary . . ."

"Ach now, you mustn't say that!" He gave evidence of considerable alarm.

"You may rely, absolutely, upon my discretion. Though a Jesuit as Police President . . ."

"Mr Pullman, we will confine ourselves to the subject of this interview, will we not."

"Certainly, your Excellency. Tell me, what is this annexe, reserved for women, like? It is clean and tidy?"

"It is filthy!" exclaimed the P.P. "It is disgusting. All the sanitary services are in the hands of women. No men are allowed inside on whatever excuse, except myself. Just as all the dustmen are women, so women are responsible for the

Police Force. Women surgeons only are found in the hospitals, and the sewage service is female. None of these services are very efficiently run. There is a complicating factor. A good deal of the money the women receive from the State is spent in purchasing bootleg whisky. We have found it impossible to check this trade. But the Governor, in the end, told us to waste no more time in trying to stamp out the illicit traffic. I have seen, as night was coming on, a woman street-cleaner in the gutter, her broom in her lap, dead drunk. When the streets are done, they are badly done. On the whole, the women regard themselves as persecuted. They are very violent at times. A great many communists and socialists (women of course) are to be found there now. It is no longer possible to go in there, as formerly. The last time I visited the Yenery, crowds of women followed me about, even stoning my car, vilifying the male sex. It was very uncomfortable indeed. As I was making my getaway they attempted to rush the gate. Several had to be killed. We now have an extremely heavy guard of picked men on the gate. Then, day by day, the position of the Women's Police becomes more difficult; a number of these have been beaten to death ... What is going to happen next I have no idea. It is impossible to foretell the course things will take during the next few weeks."

Pullman contented himself with a grimace of dismay.

"Now, Mr Pullman, consider what the position of a nice–of a well-educated sensitive woman, must be, in the middle of that chaos! Asylums (there are six of them) are packed to overflowing. The noise that they make, especially at night, is terrifying. One of those institutions is near the rampart dividing the two sectors of the city–the Yenery and ours. All the residences and big apartments in that immediate neighbourhood are permanently unlet. It is a kind of desert."

Pullman was becoming more and more disturbed. "So this is no secret," he remarked at last. "What is the opinion of the male population of Third City?"

"As you may imagine, they are horrified. The revolutionary party here–for we, as much as the women, have agitators–make great use of this unspeakable scandal."

"I can see how they might do that," said Pullman. He was silent.

174

"Do you wish to know any more about the Yenery, Mr Pullman?" inquired the Police President. "I have told them not to interrupt me. If you will excuse me I will put through a call, just to check." And he contacted his office. The first information that reached him appeared to startle him considerably. "Gosh!" Then he listened again. "Bring her in here right away, Jennings."

The P.P. turned around rapidly, and spoke as follows. "You are in luck's way, Mr Pullman. The Woman Police Chief in the Yenery has been murdered. There is a female messenger outside, she is being brought in. Please sit where you are."

A large woman, in a dirty uniform, thumped in. Her voice was that of an indignant gorilla, of a kindly disposition, but association with people who had too often taken advantage of this kept her voice in that harshest register.

"Be seated, Corporal Pontero," said the P.P.

The woman sat by the side of Pullman, who felt violently attracted by her–the last woman he had seen was on Earth, in the hospital where he had died. His nurse had rather resembled this policewoman.

"Your chief has been murdered," said the Police President. "Please tell us what happened."

Three Police officials stood at the farther end of the table, glaring down at Theresa Pontero, as though she had committed the crime. The policewoman betrayed no unseemly agitation. She even seemed to smile a little. Her feelings towards the Woman Police Chief had probably lacked that warmth which the sentimental would expect. "Mary"–which was how she referred to her hierarchical chief–"Mary was standin' by the trash bin, lookin' for somethin'—*She* got up close, an' "–Theresa slashed her throat with a flattened paw.

"Who was 'she'?" the P.P. asked. "Who was it killed her?"

"Mary had been tryin' to clean up a noo racket: the gul"–which meant girl–"wuz a lady c'nected with the racket, I guess. We got her in the cellar."

"That is good work," the Police President told her.

Theresa gave Pullman a cavernous leer, her deep-sunken brown eyes sportive as those of an amiable zoo animal.

"You did not ill-treat this lady who killed Mary?" The P.P. adapted himself to Theresa's idiom.

"Alice blacked the two eyes of her and pulled her into the Office by the 'air.—Alice is a gul that would uv murdered her, if it ud not been for the law." The policewoman slid Pullman a second leer.

"But there is always the law," said the P.P. sternly.

"The law's there all the time it is," and Theresa waved her head heavily and slowly from side to side, her mouth open. This was a cryptical use of the head.

"You are the law!" almost shouted the Police President.

"Oh yer," droned the policewoman, hurling a third leer sideways at Pullman, whose beard she found congenial.

The policewoman was dismissed, and removed her tank-like form with a thunder of footwear . . . iron-shod and leather from the knee down.

The Police President made a few notes, looked at the clock, and then turned to Pullman.

"Well, was that edifying?" he inquired. "Mary was fool-hardy. There is going to be a civil war now. We may have to go in with artillery, perhaps." The Police President rose to his feet. "Then I resign!" He held out his hand to Pullman, and rang the bell on his desk.

Vbasti came out of the room which had been set aside for him, with a murderous scowl.

"Vbasti . . .!" Pullman exclaimed, upon catching sight of his face; "you must not feel too much resentment . . ."

As they left the Police President's office together, Vbasti trod hard upon Pullman's toe. Without saying anything, Pullman placed his heel upon Vbasti's with no less force.

XVI

THE NEXT MORNING Pullman reported to the Bailiff. Vbasti he left in a waiting-room, and passed himself, almost without pause, into the presence of the Magistrate. It was a very spacious workroom, like nothing so much as one of the galleries in a present-day museum in Paris. The Bailiff sat at a long desk, beside two white-coated secretaries, two of the gladiatorial troops stood at attention at the end of the table. A small shabby group of citizens stood before him: and that was all that was in the room–except for two vacant chairs, one of which was placed ready for Pullman in front of the Bailiff.

"You have come to see me about Vbasti! Ha ha ha ha!"

"Excellency, you are right! He is unmanageable, he is conceited, he becomes fresh."

The Bailiff tossed about in his chair, his crazy mirth exquisitely paining him.

In an unsteady voice he told Pullman that it was a wicked little joke; that of course he realised what the result would be. "I'm surprised you got so far as the Police President's with him. There is another waiting to take his place–a real one this time, not a living joke."

It struck eleven, and the two infantrymen stamped several times, and then marched towards the rear wall. One of them pressed a button in the wall; two enormous masked doors shot back and displayed–for a fraction of a second–about twenty soldiers, fully armed, sitting at a table before a window. There was an instantaneous thumping of forty feet as they sprang to attention, stamping as the other two had done.

"How ingenious," remarked Pullman.

"I take no chances," replied the Magistrate. "No chances."

"You do not care to be caught by some wandering Jackson."

"Jackson?"

"Trotsky's friend."

"Oh yes, yes, yes." The Bailiff appeared to ponder. "He will be here soon. I have plans for him. He shall be transferred to

Hell, they will know how to deal with him. Hell possesses all the Inquisition machinery, plus a fine variety of Hitlerian gadgets. It is those things which give Hell its bad name: but Lucifer is an angel compared to Hitler, although a fanatical moralist." The Bailiff laughed. "But thank heaven he is getting over that."

"Ah, he is milder, is he?"

"To my taste he is *too* humane."

"You have the news from the Yenery?" Pullman inquired.

"About the Police Chief? Yes, she was asking for that! She was most opinionated. She had often been warned, but she thought she knew best . . . The situation in the Yenery is fast approaching a point at which there will be an explosion of such force . . ."

"So it seemed to me, Excellency. I am glad to hear you think like that."

"Oh about the Yenery! . . . Drop in about six tomorrow, will you, Pullman? I should greatly enjoy a talk with you . . . Oh look at the time!" He picked up the telephone. "Send me Abdul Pan." Turning to Pullman, "We call him Pan. He is a very valuable young man. I would not part with him for anyone but you, Pullman!"

Pan was an athletic young man, in appearance of the Italian student class, though his nose was almost as square as the Bailiff's. His suit was navy blue, he was at least an inch taller than Pullman.

When they had reached the hotel, Pullman stopped.

"I get no exercise," he said. "Pan, what do you say to a walk to the Piazza?"

Pan said he would enjoy a walk. Pullman noticed, not for the first time, a faint exotic accent among the dark-skinned staff-members of the Bailiff.

"Have you been in America?" Pullman said as they started.

"No, I wish I had." The o in "No" was a round-mouthed, innocent, American o. The final "had" had a long singing American cadence, and super-added there was the indelible accent above-mentioned–that, no doubt, of the Square-noses.

As they approached Tenth Avenue they heard drums and shouting crowds. They came out into the Avenue; the drums

178

were strong, and the multitude was very near. It was waving its arms, it gnashed its teeth as it bellowed slogans, it was headed for Tenth Piazza. It obviously had a destination, and it was clear that it was approaching it.

Those forming the core of the procession wore a travesty of Graeco-Roman attire. And there in the centre, borne upon a litter, was a bearded man.

"That looks like Hyperides," said Pan.

"That *is* Hyperides," Pullman told him.

"*He* has no business here at this time of the day!" Pan frowned sligtly. "How did he get in? Over the magnetised wall? Not through the *Gate* I hope. Here," he caught one marcher by the arm. "How did you get in, Bud?"

"Through the Gate!" the other shrieked. "Our men were *inside* the gates!"

Pan turned to Pullman, perfectly cool and unmoved. "They have quite enough men guarding that Gate. Armed, too. A *great many* men must have rushed it! The Bailiff will be ... well, angry would be a poor way of describing his feelings."

"Down with the Bailiff! Death to Square-Nose!" Such cries were frequent, and sometimes they melted into one another, and swelled into a roar.

"I don't know what I ought to do," reflected Pan. "Of course he knows all about it by now. But ..."

"There are at least a thousand partisans marching here," Pullman observed. "Perhaps we ought to go back to the palace."

They retraced their steps, and the Bailiff's palace was full of rushing men, and stiff-lipped military faces, like a kennel of fighting dogs who have seen the arrival of several new-comers, also, of course, fighting dogs. And, after all, the Bailiff's battalions had not much to fight. A face like Bates' (who had now returned to the gladiatorial ranks) was one framed so exclusively for combat that its owner could not make use of him for anything else. He was born to bite somebody. And here was Hyperides, and his pugnacious young philosophers, a gift from heaven for the Bailiff's garrison. Their master would not be slow to see how stimulating it would be for his cohorts. That night six thousand men under arms were collected, in and around the palace grounds. Bugles were blowing all the time until midnight.–The Bailiff had not gone

179

to the camp, and the negro band played stirring tunes from a balcony at the back of the palace.

Pullman did not enter the palace, since so much automatic animal activity did not attract him. As he walked slowly to the hotel, he sighed. Hyperides was a figure who bored him intensely; he only hoped that the police would lock him up as soon as possible.

After lunch he lay down, and, as if in protest against the rushing about in so many places near him, he went to sleep. He was wakened at three o'clock in the afternoon by Pan, whom he rather unwillingly admitted.

"Mr Pullman, it is extraordinary how attached His Excellency is to you! His hands are very full, very full. He has desperate need of every intelligent individual he can command. Yet, in this crisis, in this very great crisis, he says to me: 'Pan, you must return to Mr Pullman at once. And you must never leave his side for a fraction of a second. Understand, Pan, nothing must take you away from Mr Pullman.'"

The certain veneer, which was rather apparent with Pan for about twenty minutes after a first meeting, had almost disappeared. Evidently, he was bitterly disappointed at not being in the centre of the fun, at being snatched away from among the hundreds of other young clerks, and condemned to the society of this bearded stranger.

Pullman was intolerant of vulgar excitement, but he was not unkind. He understood how bored this young man was going to be, how much he was going to feel out of it.

"Pan, do you think that we can be of any assistance to the Bailiff? I am not suggesting that we should snoop, I should not like to do that. But could we be of any use merely by strolling around?"

"We might as well stroll *around.*"

"That is what I thought." Pullman was somewhat puzzled by the fine distinction between strolling around and strolling *around.* He hoped that the latter did not differ from the former in too marked a way.

"I do not see what you mean by our being of use to His Excellency," Pan snorted out a half-sneer.

"You mean," Pullman said quickly, "that he has all the information he needs."

180

"Information?" Pan swelled with scornful pride. "Oh yes, he has enough of that, Mr Pullman. In every group of six sub-sections of every district of the city he has an informant, a whole-time informant. In our office there are forty clerks receiving and filing messages all day long. There is an overseer: if one of the thirty telephonists or one of the filers regards a certain piece of news as *hot*, he goes across to the overseer. If the overseer thinks it is news which the Bailiff should know at once, he rings a bell . . . A messenger is always there, just outside the room. Within a few minutes the Bailiff is in possession of the news."

Pullman smiled. "There is no place for amateurs there. There is not a man who wipes his glasses, or one who buys a flower and sticks it in his buttonhole, but the Bailiff hears about it within a couple of minutes. Astonishing!"

Pan narrowed his eyes but produced a smile. Jokes about the system to which he belonged were not well received. "There is nothing which angers His Excellency so much as having passed in to him news which he calls 'of no consequence'. It is easy to get fired in the Bailiff's service for mistaking the value of news."

"Well, let us go out . . . Where shall we go?"

Pan answered slowly, with a smile, "Let us go to First Piazza."

When three-quarters of an hour later they stepped out of the underground into First Piazza, Pullman sneezed violently. He stood there preparing to sneeze a second time, but with the first sneeze the purgative impulse disappeared, and there was no further spasm. He blew his nose and put his handkerchief back in his pocket.

His new shadow had stood watching him, politely quizzi-cal.

"Is that ended, Mr Pullman?" was Pan's softly-gruff inquiry.

"Beendigt," Pullman said, "Vorbei."

They both gazed down the Piazza. There were no arcades. The place had a far rougher look. In the distance as small market was in progress. The underground was busy, with a constant to and fro of people. Pullman remarked the complete absence of youth, so prevalent in the Tenth district. This was a far more normal part of the city.

"Now, I am wondering what we shall find here?" Pullman said as though to himself. "Are we to interrogate the sons of toil as to their views of the Hyperideans?"

Pan stood looking at him sideways, as if he had a bit of a joke locked up in his nose and was wondering if he should let it out or not. Pullman caught his eye. "Out with it!" he said.

"Oh, I was only thinking that the Headquarters of Hyperides is just around here."

"Around here?"

"Oh, about the second turning along there," Pan said offhandedly.

Pullman said nothing at once. Then he asked, "Do you suggest that we pay our bearded friend a visit?"

Pan shook his head and laughed. "I thought out of curiosity you might like to see where they all congregate."

"Well ...!" Pullman seemed so dubious about this project as to be on the point of declining. "Hyperides does not interest me very much."

There was a long interval, and then Pullman said again, "But if you think it would be a good idea to stroll past his headquarters ..."

"It is as you like," Pan said sulkily.

"Very well." Pullman lighted a cigarette. Putting his feet down deliberately, and in a vaguely protesting manner, he set out in the direction Pan had indicated.

"If you would rather *not*, Mr Pullman ..."

"We had better go where it interests you to go," Pullman said.

Soon they were turning up into the moderately large street where Hyperides was supposed to be found. Others turning in the same direction were speaking excitedly. "The police are on our side."–"Oh yes, begum!" said the second man, "we can rely on them. More than half are Irish and are Catholic to a man. My brother is a sergeant."–"Ay, that is so, they are a good lot. The Police President is someone I do not like. I am not the only one who distrusts him!"

"It is over there we should go," said Pan, in a quiet voice, pointing to a very popular looking street. At least there were plenty of people turning into it, and two figures out of the Athens of Pericles standing face to face on either side of the entrance. As they were passing between these two white-clad guardians, one stepped forward and said to Pan, "You know your way, do you, sir?"

"Yes, thank you," Pan answered gruffly. "What impudence!" he exclaimed, turning to Pullman.

"Excuse me, sir!" The blue-eyed, the Nordic Athenian thrust himself in front of Pan. "Are you quite sure you know the way?"

Two armleted men now stood beside the Greek.

"Is this a private road?" Pan asked hotly.

"No," said the Grecian young man. "We do not want people here who do not know their way."

There were now *three* armleted men beside the obvious Hyperidean.

"This is monstrous!" Pan blustered loftily. "This is a public thoroughfare."

A crowd had begun to gather: "Who are they?" said someone at Pullman's ear. "I don't like the look of the darkie! I wonder what he smells like."

"He's no man, he's a hell-boy. Ah here comes O'Rourke, he'll silence the vermin!"

Pullman was feeling rather dazed. He saw quite well that Pan had led them into something he had not bargained for. He knew what an Irish crowd was like, and there was no chance of rescue. From now on, step by step, he had to go through with this stupid scene, just as if they had been actors upon a stage, until the crowd had been purged, had had their catharsis.

He retired within himself; how much nicer it was to be out with Satters. He began thinking of the time in the camp. He remembered how Time had its traps there; he had got into a scene of two hundred years ago—like turning a cinematograph backwards and holding it rigid. Something had slipped, something was there which ought to have been somewhere else.

He was violently jolted. It was the shoulders of Pan which had struck him, as his shadow was dragged forwards. That no doubt was O'Rourke. Smash his ugly face, the rat!

"Come out here, then," he heard a large man shouting, who had seized Pan at the neck and was making him run forward with his head stuck out like a chicken. Pan was a big fellow but no fighting-man, he was just like a doll in this big Irishman's hands.

A fist went into the downcast face, a sock that is a different sound to a smack, sickening, relatively soft.

Pan tried to fall down. But O'Rourke held him up against the wall and socked him; and then the crowd held him up, for O'Rourke to batter and to blacken.

Ah well, it would be his turn next, Pullman sighed to himself, "Let us hope the crowd holds me up!"

But these words he had spoken aloud to himself, and there was a sudden roar of laughter in his ear. This roar multiplied itself until everybody in the world seemed to be laughing.

"Here, O'Rourke! This one here says he hopes the crowd will hold him up while you sock him!"

The roar of laughter was a new catharsis. The crowd was almost crying with laughter at the thought of its holding a man up—a long series of men—to be socked, and socked, and socked.

An enormous, sweating Irish face was a few inches from his. Pullman knew it was the Minotaur, the O'Rourke.

"Is it *you* want to be held up?"

A large, rough, hot paw—flat, palm-foremost—hit his face with such velocity that Pullman lost his feet, and slapped the earth with a shattering wallop.

He heard the roaring of the crowd like a tumultuous sea breaking over his head. Someone thrust his face down not far from his ear and shouted. "There, my boy, let mother Earth hold you up, me old son!"

A hand tapped him lightly on the cheeck: the roar grew much louder, and then died away.

He was kicked, and a new voice shouted, "Hi, you're wanted in the office!"

They bashed their way through the crowd, the someone who held him so firmly by the arm pushing him along at a stumbling trot. At last they began barging their way up a flight of steps. Tromp tromp tromp upon the soft-seeming bare boards, and he was pushed into a room. His head, where he had fallen, hurt a great deal, he sank into a chair and rested his head upon his hand.

"What is your name?"

This was a sharp, strong voice, but it was clear, and not blurred and weighted with drink, with lack of cultivation, and with silly passion.

"James Pullman," he said.

"Not James Pullman!" the voice rose to a pitch of surprised interest. There was a pause.

"The writer?"

"Yes. I am James Pullman, in a semi-celestial region."

There was another short silence.

Pullman looked up, and saw a strong, lean, tightly drawn ascetic face, about forty. It was the clear-cut, the long-necked, classical face of the age of George Eliot. It was Polemon (so-called). He had listened to him in the camp.

"Well, if you *are* James Pullman, it is your own fault! What are you doing here in this company?"

"I can explain that very easily. I have only been in this city a few weeks. The Bailiff offered me a flat in his hotel. There I have lived for the last week or so. The Bailiff is of opinion that at any moment there may be an attack upon this city. He has attached to me the young man you treated so badly, to be of service in such an event. Lastly, it was not I who had the idea of coming to 'view your headquarters'."

Two other men had come in, and stood listening. As soon as he had finished, one of these said, "So! If you are James Pullman, as you say you are, you understand quite enough to have worked out for yourself by now the kind of man the Bailiff is. You are consorting with the scum of the earth, and you *know what you are doing*. To save your own skin you accept help from an inhuman beast in the form of a man. He is so filthy a creature that we cannot be in the same room with him without being polluted. You cannot fail to see all that, as I say. You are a rat—yes, a far worse rat because you are an *intelligent* rat!"

"I am your prisoner," Pullman said steadily. "I am a prisoner of thugs, and one cannot reason with the likes of you."

"You are *brave,* aren't you, rat, because you think that the personal punishment is over. It is *not*." He slapped Pullman's face so hard on both sides that the back of his head hurt almost intolerably.

Polemon intervened. "You must not do that sort of thing, Michael. You ought to be ashamed of yourself. He is *not* quite what you say he is either."

The face of the man called Michael was so full of violence, so full of appetite for destruction, that Pullman wondered, in a dim brain-wracked way, whether Polemon could restrain him.

"It is only because this dirty rat is a book-writing rat that you defend him!" Michael hissed. "It is *you* who ought to be ashamed of yourself! This is not a man who stands rigidly outside the *mêlée*. As he thinks *above*. No, this selfish and immoral individual accepts favours from a man he knows to be a reptile. He gets good wine at that filthy hotel. He is treated as a 'great man'–oh yes, and he is given, by the Central Bank, money unlimited.–You cannot be a skunk on earth and you cannot be a skunk here! This is no different from the earth in that respect. You are not a spectre. You are still a man. If, Mr Pullman, you behave as a rat and a skunk *here* you must always have stunk–you must always have had your home in a sewer, and have been the first cousin of the mouse!"

"You like hearing yourself talk." Pullman spoke strongly and clearly. "You do not speak well! You would not be so dependent upon *rats* and *mice* if you did. You slap better than you *speak*."

Polemon laughed. "You forgot, Michael, that you were speaking to a man trained in the use of words."

"Yes, like so many people living among words, he has grown demoralized as a man. He has no values left. They have become *words* and have been rotted. You are a *rat*."

"He will think you have that animal on the brain," the man known as Polemon said irritably. "Besides, Pullman has done nothing whatever against us. He has explained that he was lured up here by a clerk of the Bailiff's. You consider that, in accepting any favour from such a person as the Bailiff, Pullman has sold himself to the Devil. But Pullman is a newcomer here and strange to conditions. Pullman is of great reputation. Would it not be more sensible to attempt to win him over to our side?"

"What, ask favours of that double-faced, unscrupulous, egotistic, self-advertising verbal trickster; to flatter that man who sells his name to gild with the patronage of a great literary name the misdeeds of one of the most evil and destructive creatures who has ever breathed–to accept the support of such a slimy old mountebank, that immigrant from Hell"–and Michael Devlin, as he was, shook his accusing forefinger in Pullman's face. "For don't you know where you are going, with the assistance of that trusty servant of the Bailiff? Do you not know where he comes from, the man you go about with? Are you so stupid? Every clerk in the Bailiff's service comes from Hell–they were born there and smuggled into this city. They are not mortal, they are not human; the place you will be taken to, if there is an all-out attack on this place, will be Hell. You know nothing of that, do you, sly-puss? Of course you don't! Poor innocent little Mr. Pullman thinks he will be spirited away into safety, to the Bailiff's private estate! He will save his dirty old skin by hopping ten million miles into Old Nick's sweet little estancia. You will find it stinks like the bodies of those delightful demons who came here in deputation the other day. You had better take a big supply of eau-de-Cologne! Listen, you white-livered old punk of a scribbler for a corrupt society! Why not stand and die? . . . Not that you *would* die, even. We and our leader Hyperides will all be massacred. But when Lucifer enters the city, after having stormed it with his stinking demons, *you* would not be interfered with. But you are *afraid*. And you want to be made a fuss of in Hell . . . Good luck to you, sneak! A happy visit to Hades, with piles of praise and loads of honour, Mr Big Name, which you cart around with you like a certificate. You even impress Polemon here! But you fail to impress *me* very much. I regard you as one of the most contemptible old rats–yes, RATS– that I have ever encountered!" And he spat in Pullman's face.

Pullman sprang up and struck Michael Devlin in the face, but at the same time Devlin was flung forward by the violent opening of the door near which he stood.

"The Bailiff's rats are here!" shouted the intruder.

"Call out the Guard!" Polemon exclaimed. But the sound of rushing men, and joyous Irish voices, rejoicing at the prospect of a fight, was the Guard going into action and Polemon rushed to join them.

"How many are there?" asked Devlin.

"Twenty or thirty in a lorry. They have machine-guns trained on the crowd."

"Here, rat, are your pals!" Devlin said fiercely to Pullman. "They have come to fetch you. They have come to rescue their Great Name. Here, I will hand you back, and tell them how *nice* and how *polite* everyone has been!"

Devlin and the man with him dragged Pullman out into the passage. The hall was full of armleted partisans, all were armed. The front door was opened to enable Devlin to take out his prisoner. When he and Pullman were outside the door, Devlin stopped, holding the Big Name tightly, and bent towards him, pointing to the gladiators: "There are your thugs waiting for you. They are much less guilty than you are, rat!" he hissed in his ear.

At this point Pullman struggled with his captor. Employing a jujitsu device, a memory of the school gymnasium, he threw Devlin into the air, so that he fell at the bottom of the steps. Pullman followed him, flying over the last two steps, and reached the lorry in another bound or two. Then he turned and faced Devlin, who had risen to his feet but found himself covered by a tommygun, and stood without moving, his eye beginning to swell where Pullman had struck him. Pullman kissed his hand, saying, "So bad a temper as yours *needs* the word *rat*. What would you do without it. Polemon was wrong to try and make you drop it!"

Devlin turned his head and began dejectedly ascending the steps.

Pullman was the hero of the day. He climbed with a creditable agility into the lorry and stood there smiling amid the congratulations of the gladiators, howled at by the crowd held at bay by the machine-guns.

"What are we waiting for?" he asked.

"For an ambulance. Pan is badly injured–the devils nearly killed him!"

Pullman tried to look grieved.

Ten minutes later an ambulance arrived, and Pan was borne down the steps on a stretcher, his head a white cocoon of bandages. A roar of applause and laughter rose from the crowd. The ambulance departed with the loud and incessant ringing of its bell, charged the shouting Irish mob, which parted with magical celerity. The lorry followed a few feet behind it, bristling with small-arms and machine-guns, aimed down at the snarling faces by frowning men.

XVII

As THEY SAT DOWN in his small study at the top of the palace, looking down upon the tree-tops of Phanuel's wood, the Bailiff said in an unexpectedly sober voice, "This is more of a crisis than anyone knows. It is a very great crisis indeed."

He fixed Pullman with a mesmeric eye, which was quite in vain owing to the fact that Pullman's eye, as was customary, was thrown down out of reach of the emotional discharges of other people. But he did look quickly up at the next words uttered by the Bailiff.

"Many shattering things have occurred; all at the same time. Here is the first of them. The Police President has been dismissed by the Governor."

"Ah!" Pullman was looking at his host, noting the swollen veins upon his temples and the wildly protruding eyes.

"Oh yes," the Bailiff answered the curious eye. "Oh yes. And what does that mean? The latent hostility between the Governor and myself is coming to a head, out into the open, after centuries, Pullman." The Bailiff paused, looking at the dove upon the wall of the balcony outside the window. "There are several things you really have to know. It was my troops who expelled the Hyperideans, two hundred strong, from this city. The police would not do it. The Police President, Lear, was quite willing to expel them, but the Governor would not allow it. The Civil Guards would refuse to do so as a body, independently of what their Commander said; although he is just as reactionary as they are. *He* will not even speak to me. I should say, in this connection, that the Police and the Civil Guard are quite distinct forces. The Guard are purely military, they perform no ordinary police work."

"I was not clear about that," Pullman said.

"The next point," the Bailiff said, "is the question of force. This is absolutely decisive. I have only five or six thousand men at the outside. But there are fifty thousand police, very well trained, and all carrying arms—rifles, machine-guns, and so forth, and a brigade of artillery. Then there are fifteen thousand Civil Guards. They have artillery. I am only a bandit. I have no authority for this little army of mine, which is, of course, imperfectly equipped. I parade it as a mere circus, so that I can say that it is not serious. But all the *real* troops I could put in the field, if it came to a showdown, would be defeated–annihilated in half an hour by the Guards alone."

The Bailiff stopped.

"I see," Pullman said.

"My whole existence is a pure bluff. This is not officially a palace. It has gradually become so: and no one has had the gumption to tell me to live less ostentatiously, and to disband my militia. I could object that I needed armed men at the camp. A Police President could answer: 'That is my affair'; he could provide me with a half-dozen armed police. That is all that is strictly speaking necessary."

There was another pause, during which the Bailiff took snuff.

"You know the Governor. He is rather shy with men. He does not know how to manage men. Good. Another peculiarity of the Governor is his jealousy (for it can only be that) of the professionals of religion. The Archbishop of Third City, for instance, and even such lesser dignitaries as a Monsignor, he treats very coldly.–The consequences of these oddities of the Governor have been of the first importance to me. I need not enumerate the hundreds of advantages I derive from this coolness between the Envoy of the Almighty and the highest *human* authorities in this city . . . You have taken in what I have been saying, Pullman?"

"Yes, your Excellency, my intelligence is strong enough, I believe, to grasp the implication of these matters which you have been confiding to me." Pullman smiled demurely. "You have been beautifully clear in expounding these various complications."

"Thank you, Pullman, thank you. What I am about to say is the essence of the crisis in my affairs of which I have been speaking. Today the Governor is rattled, as the Americans used to say. He feels very insecure in Third City for the first time since his arrival. Lucifer's fireworks–they have not been more than that–have scared him. For the first time he has turned to ingenious Man. Though I do not believe we possess any

191

engineers and chemists who can deter Lucifer. And he appears to have been seeing a lot of Monsignor O'Shea, who is the live-wire of the Catholic hierarchy. A very dangerous man! Listen carefully to this. The Police President who has taken the place of my friend Lear is named von Blitzkopf, who is a Catholic and a very close friend of Monsignor O'Shea. Von Blitzkopf (as his name suggests) is a terrible reactionary. He was a high officer in the Civil Guards (which speaks for itself) with very little police experience." The Bailiff stopped and looked sharply at his listener. Pullman looked down; he declined to play his part in this dramatic pedagogy. "The human factions to which the Governor is turning are not my friends. I am hated by the Catholics. The Governor himself has no love for me. I am now faced with a hostile coalition. Soon I may find myself stripped of the power which I have so painfully built up for myself. And have so long enjoyed." He stamped and waved his hand around the study. " 'The cloud-capped towers, the gorgeous palaces'. All this may go. But now my last point. At any moment Lucifer may make an all-out attack upon Third City." He bent towards Pullman, and tapped upon the table ... "Pullman, whether he makes that attack or not depends a good deal upon ... me. For instance, I might dissuade him. I have much influence with Lucifer. On one occasion, I once by accident did him a service. Good (or *bad,* depending which way you look at it!). Now!"

He drew his chair a little nearer to Pullman–he was perspiring and Pullman had to confess that the smell was not pleasant. "You know the Governor, Pullman–the Padishah? I do not suggest that *you* go to see the Governor. No. But do you think *someone* could make a point of seeing the Governor privately, and saying that his friend Pullman had been talking to the Bailiff? The latter (that is *me*) had told him that he had ways of preventing the final assault of the diabolic power. That he had means of interceding.–That is all."

The Bailiff sat back, pouring with perspiration; and it was not a peculiarly hot day. It seemed nice and cool up here to Pullman.

"You are thinking of Mannock?" he asked.

"Not necessarily. There is Sir Charles de la Pole-Blessington. There are several possible intermediaries."

A youth dressed in scarlet burst into the room. He was the only living person who was allowed to rush in unannounced. He held out a salver. The Bailiff snatched the envelope from the salver: he tore it open, put it down. "All right," he said to the scarlet messenger.

"The first act of von Blitzkopf," he said. "He has marched into the Yenery with ten thousand police, and mowed down with machine-guns thousands of women. The slaughter has been appalling. My most accurate woman reporter–luckily she has survived–says that fifteen thousand women are dead. There are great mounds of corpses in all the streets. The wounded are innumerable."

"How frightful!" Pullman exclaimed.

The Bailiff picked up the telephone. "You know what has happened in the Yenery," he asked breathlessly. He listened, his eyes advancing half an inch more than usual, his eyebrows making a shadow for the nether furrow. "That is what I think! It is von Blitzkopf's first action . . . No. Not that. I will explain. I am coming down right away . . . yes yes."

He whirled round, obviously his brain had been flung into a new dance of fiery action by these events.

He gazed at Pullman as if he were a ghost–a ghost of what had been there, in the immediate foreground, before von Blitzkopf's enormity had pushed everything else into the shade: mad time had substituted a mound of corpses for the sedate figure of the famous writer: her could literally no longer see Pullman distinctly. He saw the streets of the Yenery piled with corpses; he saw his agents in wild flight. He seized Pullman by the wrists as though to steady himself, as though to hold himself back, if only for a moment, in the past labelled "Before the Yenery".

"Pullman, my dear fellow!" he panted urgently. "Do not fail me in that other matter. See what can be done. I have great interests in the Yenery. You could not touch anything in the Yenery without touching *me*! Billions of aurei are involved. This is terrible! I had no warning of all this! It is the very *last* thing I ever imagined could happen–a coming-together of the Governor, the Catholics, the Police. You have no idea what this means to me!" His square nose seemed a distinct object sticking out into space, in front of his face, his eyes terrified, literally bursting out of his head; his mouth was pulled down at the corners like the mouths of the Japanese warriors. He drove his face down upon his arms, which were locked together in front of his torso upon the table, and there were thumping sobs which hammered his head up and down upon the table.

The scarlet messenger burst into the room again. The Bailiff sprang up and snatched the pink envelope from the salver. He stuck his finger into the envelope and tore it open. A scream like that of a stricken pig tore the air, then he sank into and folded up in his chair. A small voice, piping and wretched, rose from this disinflated form. There was no air left to make it more than a wheeze or a little pipe.

"Flossie has been shot. She is dead." There was a gulp.

"They have got Flossie.

"Shot by a police thug.

"Flossie is dead. Flossie is . . . dead!"

Floss was evidently a key woman. Pullman felt that he must not await a third arrival of the scarlet youth, his third dose of bad news might be so severe that the Bailiff would have a fatal seizure. He went over to him where he was gently stamping, and tearing at the edges of his garments.

"I think your Excellency should go down and take some steps towards the punishment of these thugs."

The Bailiff appeared mildly electrified by this contact. His voice even was firmer. "My dear boy, you're right, I should at once, at once . . .!"

He staggered over to his table, and began collecting some papers. Pullman considered that he was bemused, and must be hustled. He went over to the lift-door—for one stepped out of the lift into this eyrie of the Bailiff's— and pressed the button at the side of the door. He stood there watching the Bailiff: he had sunk forward, his head in his arms, and his stomach on the desk, saying over and over, "Floss is gone. Floss is gone."

Pullman believed that he heard someone speak, and turned quickly towards the lift. The lift had not arrived, but a large nude statue of some classical Venus, which stood near the entrance to the elevator, had begun revolving. Its back was now turned, and suddenly there was a loud indecorous report. It seemed it was constructed of plastic, or some such light material, within which it was easy to install the necessary clock-work to enable it to speak. A moment later the statue, whose face was now appearing, said with an alarming distinctness, "Oh I beg your pardon!"

Pullman went back to the table, picked up the telephone, and said to whoever was at the other end, "The Bailiff is not very well. Will you please come up."

As he put down the telephone, the scarlet messenger suddenly stepped out of the lift. Pullman crossed to the lift and asked the liftman to take him down. They shot through the air, and he was in the entrance hall, in a second or two, it seemed. No jet fighter could exceed in its downward drop this private elevator. And, thought Pullman, the Venus still slowly turned near the summit of the house; as her buttocks came round in front of the spectator there was a *poop,* and as she reversed, her face appearing, she apologised, in a voice obnoxiously dulcet. Toys of the millionaire! All the Bailiff's toys would insult human dignity: and it did not at all mean that he was libidinous. The Floss that he was mourning over was a business Floss, a female racketeer. Nothing interested him in the Yenery except the money he could make out of the illicit liquor, dope and such things as that.

Pullman hastened to the hotel, where he went into the restaurant immediately. Since he usually dined alone, the waiter had grown talkative. Today there was no response when he essayed conversation. Pullman was very much preoccupied. For this appeared to be the turning point in the Bailiff's career; and it was likewise the moment at which a decision must be arrived at; either gently to separate himself from this old maniac, or to throw in his lot with him, for it would amount to that.

The Bailiff had set forth a clear statement of his position. It hat catastrophic possibilities. But was it, in the first place, true, and secondly, was it not merely one of the panics to which millionaires, great ministers and so on, are subject, from time to time? No doubt much that he had learned must be accepted as fact. By trafficking in dope, and the illegal sale of alcohol, the Bailiff secured the necessary money for the maintenance of a private army, and other things. He could imagine how a good deal of house property in the Yenery was the Bailiff's:

gambling clubs, meeting places for Lesbians. There were thousands of ways in which large sums of money could be made. The Police Chief who had been murdered there a few days before was fighting the rackets.–Probably, an agent of the Bailiff's bumped her off. Suppose that the Police President set out to break the rackets and to cean up the Yenery, he could see how that might have the most serious effect upon such nefarious exploits as the Bailiff's. Also, if women were given protection, the past activities of the Bailiff might come to light, this arch evil-doer denounced. Impeachment might result. If this policy of the new Police President were taken far enough the Bailiff would be ruined: the threat from the Bailiff's standpoint was very real: but all this was no more than a threat.

The danger centring in Hyperides was the one that had meant most to him before the doings in the Yenery. He certainly would not be able to expel Hyperides from the city if the present alliance of the Padishah, the Papacy and the Police held. Who could say wheter the situation which brought it into being would continue: if that situation terminated, would the alliance persist? Probably not. The angelic Governorship had been aloof for so very long from the human authorities, would its present modification of that aloofness last any longer than Lucifer's threat, which caused it?

How quickly he had been manœuvred into the position of a distinguished adherent, and now an agent, of this loathsome individual. He had behaved very injudiciously: he was ashamed of himself. The mistake of mistakes was coming to live in this hotel: he might just as well be living in the palace. The acceptance of so large a sum of money from the Central Bank was a big mistake too. It was of no use to him; its main purpose was to settle the huge bill (as it doubtless would be) for apartment 400 and for this luxurious restaurant.

Of the Bailiff's arts, flattery was the essential one. Pullman had been rapidly built up into an important figure, so that he might be of use, as at the present moment. Meanwhile, the Hyperideans had just burst into the city. Morning, noon, and night they would be vilifying, blackening the Bailiff: and they would denounce anyone associated with the Bailiff. The more prominent he grew (thanks to the boosting by the Bailiff, and because of the service he rendered that monstrous gangster) the more odious he would become. He would be a traitor to the white race, to the Christian community. Merely through living in this hotel, he would be a scab, a renegade, a rat, and so forth.

Was he going to be intimidated by these people? Was he going to be driven out of this hotel in which every single one of the ranting nobodies would be delighted to live? Was he going to order his life according to the orders of this moralizing gang? Was he afraid of them? No. But it was not only the Hyperideans: it was literally everybody who (quite rightly) disapproved of the Bailiff. He had for a patron a person who was no better than Capone.

So far so good. But suppose that he now refused to act as his agent, his "friend", his intermediary, what then?

To begin with, just as he had been able to cause the bank to assign to him large sums of money, it would be equally easy for the Bailiff to inspire the bank with a very *low* opinion of him. He could do him a hundred ill turns. If he allowed the envious busybodies to drive him out of this comfortable niche, no one else would be likely to patronise him. The Catholic Church, Guard's officers, snobbish, illiterate, English circles, and indeed *any other* circle in the city, would turn a very cold eye upon him. His books, which had now got into circulation here, would make a very bad impression. They were on the Index down below, and were read and were understood only by the intellectuals. There were no intellectuals here. He was in a trap. Obviously he must stop where he was, become involved as little as possible, and act as cautiously as possible.

His best step at present was to see Mannock. He would drop around there now in the hope of finding him. In the foyer of the hotel, he was approached by a wizened little man. This was his latest attendant. They went up to his apartment together.

His first question was regarding the health of the Bailiff. His new attendant knew nothing about that. Pullman picked up the house-telephone and asked for the Palace. A secretary replied. The Bailiff was quite well, and had just gone in to dinner.

Next, he examined the little creature who had been allotted him. He possessed a face scratched all over with minute

197

wrinkles. His eyes were mild, dark, and colourless. His name was Jashormit. He would not offer himself as a bedfellow, he could not be adventurous like Pan. The idea, no doubt, was that he was sufficiently advanced in years to be neutral and unobjectionable as a tortoise. How old are you? Pullman asked. The answer was three hundred years. But Pullman thought he was trimming, or "improving", his age. He informed him that he was going out to visit a friend. Jashormit at once asked if he was aware that a car had been put at his disposal–or rather it was a chauffeur (named Fédor), rather than a car, who awaited his pleasure. Fédor would always be at the garage; sometimes he could use one car, sometimes another.

Jashormit inquired might he telephone? Of course he might, and soon Jashormit was conversing with Fédor. The car would be at the door in a few minutes.

Twenty minutes later, driven by Fédor, and Jashormit seated at the chauffeur's side, they were in Habakkuk.

Mannock had just finished his dinner, and was sitting down in his living-room when Pullman knocked. Pullman felt that he was greeted rather coldly. He stiffened; he became a little formal.

"I have come to see you, Mannock, on what I suppose may be called business," he said. "Are you free for the next hour or so?"

"For an hour . . . yes. I have an appointment with Sir Charles de la Pole-Blessington." (Not "Charles" as formerly–oh, he was in the dog house!) "What is the nature of the business?"

"I will tell you. You know that I had a young man waiting outside for me, from the first moment I was here. Eventually that young man informed me that an partment had been reserved for me in a certain apartment hotel, the Phanuel Hotel– I was there shown a flat which very few newcomers to this city would refuse. It is, actually, the Bailiff's hotel, and the young man who danced attendance on me was there in the Bailiff's service.–I remind you of these circumstances for a certain reason."

"I think I divine your reason, Pullman. I may as well say that to my mind you were wrong to establish yourself in those quarters, under the patronage, as it were, of so noxious a person. This morning I heard of your fracas with the Hyperideans. Again, I venture to think that it is not wise to be spying around . . ."

"I was doing nothing of the sort, and I am surprised that you should accept that story without considering whether it tallied with the character of the man who was your guest. I did not know where we were going until I was actually a hundred yards away from the headquarters of those people." Mannock was about to say something but Pullman interrupted him. "No, I do not want to argue about that. Let me come at once to the business, as I described it.—As a result of my position in the hotel, to which circumstance I referred just now, the Bailiff is inclined to confide in me. I do not seek these confidences, but I do not refuse to listen . . . Today he asked me to visit him, and to my great surprise he spoke very frankly to me about his affairs and about the attacks upon the city by Lucifer's . . ."

"The Devil's!" Mannock sternly corrected.

"Very well," Pullman smiled. "That is what *I* should call him: Lucifer is the perhaps more polite expression employed by the Bailiff. Well, the storms, or whatever they are, have altered things a little, he tells me. I know nothing about this city. I am merely repeating what this rather shady, but very prominent person said to me, and what this led to. He believes he has some influence upon the spirit he calls Lucifer, and I call the Devil. He believes that he could prevent the all-out attack upon the city which threatens. Lastly, he wishes the Padishah to know this. He thought that Sir Charles de la Pole-Blessington might transmit this . . . well, statement, to the Governor. I, of course, do not give a damn whether he does or not, except for one small circumstance; I would be very pleased if someone would, and could, put a stop to supernatural bickering and cyclonic storms . . ." Pullman rose. "As you insult me when I come round here now I shall come no more. Only do, in the interest of all of us, pass on that piece of news." He bowed. "Good night." He wheeled and left the room. Mannock was protesting. "I say, I had no intention of insulting . . ." Then the living-room door slammed, a moment later the front door slammed. After a brief interval an automobile was heard in the street outside, getting under way, and moving to the window, Mannock was able to see a Cadillac about to turn the corner.

"Clever devil!" he said to himself. "But he may find that he is too clever by half!"

XVIII

It was pullman's habit to have breakfast in his apartment. As he was about to sit down, the house telephone rang. "Mr Satterthwaite is here, sir."–"Send him up," said Pullman. "Send Mr Satterthwaite up."

The primitive, very untidy, the unpredictable figure from his schooldays, the eternal fag could hardly have chosen a better time. That statement, it is true, must depend upon why he had come. But Pullman was so anxious to have the advantage of this particular association again that he rather turned a blind eye to the disagreeable possibilities. So he rapidly surveyed the prospects offered by the arrival of his first associate since his resurrection, hazy plans in the back of his mind taking tentative shape. Awaiting the appearance of the juvenile ruffian who hit policemen as soon as look at them, he speculated as to whether the plans he was nursing would be blown sky high by the uproarious entrance of the young thug.

Certainly very little time had elapsed since Satters had been an English schoolboy, when they had first encountered Mannock. Nevertheless, it was astonishing how exactly the same he looked as he entered the door and sat down at the table. Perhaps he had had leisure to examine critically his rough handling of the police. At least one would prefer to believe that this fat-faced semi-baby was not as yet a hardened criminal, whatever he might have done.

Offered breakfast, Satters responded hungrily. When it arrived he devoured it in gulps, his eyes red and staring. He wolfed down successively honey, toast melba, porridge, a yellow fish not unlike haddock, then he sat down with a rather guilty look.

"This is swish," he remarked, looking around, seeming to avoid the eye of his friend. "That porter downstairs, Pulley... Oh I say! I hardly had the nerve to pass him without saluting."

But Pullman was not talkative. He watched Satters, and soon noticed the usual signals of distress. "Come with me," he said, and led him to the lavatory. It was only after that was over that he began asking a question or two. "Why are you so hungry?" was the first. The answer to that was that he had

had nothing to eat. To that Pullman inquired why. Satters explained: why no food had come his way was because the bigger and older boys got all that was going. Usually at meal times they were given coffee and pretzels.–When was the last square meal he had had?–The answer involved no hesitation. The last time was at Mister Mannock's.

Next came the question, What did Satters want?–Nothing, was the answer. When did he have to rejoin the boys?–Never. –Why was he not rejoining his gang?–Because they were mostly foreign boys; and they were a dirty lot.–Oh, Pulley, they were ... not like boys but like dirty old men. They had no homes, they never had had. They spent all their money on hooch, then they robbed people. The robbed an old man the other night, and one of them gouged his eyes out. Some boys protested. His eyes were of no use to him, the gang replied. A few of the boys were not bad, but most of them "were a nasty foreign lot." He seemed afraid too. There was one boy, a Wop, who had it in for him. He said he would "get" him when no one was looking.

After more questioning, Pullman asked if he had learned to be a thief. Satters looked alarmed; he said they only robbed when they needed money for food. He *himself* had taken no part in a stick-up. He had been there, but he had not touched anybody. They surrounded a person, and when that person was in the middle of a "clot" of about thirty boys, two or perhaps three of the oldest boys extracted the money (and sometimes stabbed the victim) or did things to him which made him faint. Satters was one of those who helped to form a thick screen of bodies. Then, as a matter of fact, had a newcomer muscled in and started hunting for money, doing what only a few older boys were allowed to do, the latter big tough savage boys would set on him with coshes and with knives, and probably would kill him. Quite often boys were killed.–It was to this that Satters particularly objected. "Roughness" he liked: but it must be *fun*. In these gangs, fun played very little part. The leading boys were really no longer boys. They were not interested in fun. The boy who said he would kill him wanted to sleep with him. That was how it began.

Question. Did these boys know anything about him (Pullman)?–Answer. No. They operated beyond Fifth Piazza. Each gang had a territory, after the manner of the North American Indians. So they literally *could* not come up this way.–He had received Pullmann's address from Mr Mannock, who "was very nasty".

At this point Pullman asked Satters if he would like to resume life with him. Satters appeared overjoyed. "Oh, Pulley, if you knew how, over and over again, I hoped you would take me back."

Pullman's next step was to ring for the hotel barber. When this expert arrived, it was clear that, among other things, he was a pathic. He came mincing in, in a white garment, carrying a lavender-coloured bag, with BARBER printed on it in red capitals.

"First I want to part company with my beard," Pullman announced.

The young barber, with a round-lipped lisp, deprecated this with much gesticulation. "Oh, why?" he asked. "It is so cute! I do think you should wait and not do it at once. Let me trim it: and give it another shape . . ."

Satters joined the barber in an attempt to save the beard. But Pullman insisted. The moved into the spacious bathroom, and there his beard was removed. After that he allowed his hair to be trimmed, and then shampooed.

Having stood for a minute or two beneath the sugared shower of compliments emitted by the hair-man, ("You look like a young Viking . . . you remind me of Pelleas in the Opera" and "Oh for a chin like that! one can see it now–in combination with cool, oh so cool, grey eyes"), he turned the steam off with reluctance; he was bound to admit he especially liked the "cool, oh so cool, grey eyes" . . . though why must the fellow spoil it by getting so much hair-oil in his voice? But, after more of this than he felt was decent, he said, "Now see what you can do with this young gentleman."

The barber did not even look at Satters, he just pushed forward the chair and Satters sat in it.

It was true that the returned fag was not an edifying sight. He looked like a member of an even tougher gang than the one he had picked; he had not removed the cap especially designed for the terroristic children, who had made it feared and loathed.

"We will, I think—if the young gentleman desires a haircut —have the cap of," the young barber said briskly.

Scowling and flushing a little, Satters dragged off his cap, his ears remaining a bright scarlet for some time. The type of friend Pullman seemed to prefer could only be interpreted in one way, especially by young homosexual barbers. He liked as a bedfellow a young, plump, ugly hooligan. But what kind of hair-cut would be appropriate for this juvenile apache? That was a problem, indeed a teaser.

"Stop," said Pullman, appreciating the difficulty. "Let me explain. Less than a month ago this young man and myself entered this city. We were at the same school together in England. He is a young man of very good family. For the fortnight he has been running wild, but is now returning to polite society. Agreed, he has not got much of a face. But please cut his hair as if you were performing on the Duke of Windsor."

The young barber laughed.

"Thank you, I see what you mean," he said. Evidently Mr Pullman liked the *flesh* but not the chevelure of the boy-apache. He gave him a princely hair-cut and drenched him in delicious scent—Satters attempting to beat him off.

These steps taken, Pullman went to the telephone, was put through to Fédor, and ordered the car, and the Russian answered, "*Tout de suite*, Excellence!"

Pullman turned to Satters. "Where exactly do the guardsmen and high officers live? Not in this neighbourhood?"

Satters explained; it was a neighbourhood a mile or two behind the palace—not near the Piazza, that centre would be First Circle. This was the largest of the Circles.—"And are there *shops* there?"—"Oh lord yes. Much more swish than those in Tenth Piazza."

Fédor was perfectly familiar with First Circle; and when they reached it Satters' account of its "swishness" was confirmed. A military band was playing in a bandstand in the centre, fountains were splashing, and absurdly modish young gentlemen, with impassible military faces, strolled to the strains of *La Bohème*. Fédor was directed to find the best hat shop in this select quarter. Compared with Tenth Piazza the streets were very slenderly populated. Everything you did was therefore conspicuous. As automobiles were practically nonexistent the mere presence of a large Cadillac, with a wizened little man seated beside the chauffeur, and an elegant (but hatless) man seated beside a disreputable looking boy, created a considerable sensation. The movements of the car were followed by everyone in sight, and bitterly commented on, for these military circles were no more able than anyone else to purchase a car, or even to hire one.

However, Fédor, in the dazzling uniform of the Bailiff, whenever they stopped at as shop, sprang out, and stood aggressively beside this unobtainable machine, defying the inquisitive officer-class.

The star hat-shop of First Circle was identified; Pullman entered it hatless, and left it in a black hat, less wide in the brim than the one he had lost, of the most perfect felt, and conforming to the style preferred by the best people. He directed Fédor to a shop in a nearby street. He emerged from this military tailor's in a dark suit of the most startling elegance. Satters was taken to a store or two, and they visited a variety of shirt shops, walking-stick shops, and so on. In two hours' time they were back at the hotel, loaded with parcels, which were brought up to the apartment and destributed on chairs.

When they were alone, Pullman turned to his wizened attendant, who had followed them in. Where, he asked, could this young man sleep? At this question the wizened one was tongue-tied. It was obvious he had supposed that this was a dirty joy-boy in process of transmogrification. Receiving no answer Pullman inquired if a bed could be installed in Jashormit's room. Jashormit beamed. Pullman dismissed him, with thanks for not objecting to sharing his room.

All the parcels were now opened, the contents heaped on tables, and sorted out. Satters had a hot shower, after which he began dressing. In a short while he appeared as an extremely smart schoolboy of the officer-class. It was simply a very well-tailored suit of a material woven for strength, of a lightish colour. It fitted him beautifully. So Satters had become something like an offspring of a high-ranking cavalry officer, aged seventeen (for he had to be promoted one year, in view of his mature outlook). Subsequently, he transported to Jashormit's room, in a brand new suitcase, all the shirts, handkerchiefs, change of clothes, black mackintosh, change of shoes, slippers, cascaras and band-aids. "You will be certain to need band-aids," said Pullman. "You have at least two cuts already."

"Let us go down to lunch," he proposed, looking with approval at his squire. Drawing a note-case out of his pocket, he handed to Satters a note to the value of twenty aurei. "You must have some money in your pocket. This is of about the value of twenty pounds. Now, as regards your status. You cannot be my fag. Which will you be, my son, or my young brother?"

"Oh, I don't know, Pulley. I'm not going to be your kid, Pulley. We were at school together. We are brothers aren't we? Let us be brothers, only you've got much older. That's right, you are a much older brother."

"Right. Now let us go down to lunch."

Looking at the menu, Pullman said, "How about a cocktail, followed by ... oh, everything on the Bill-of-Fare." In the sequel Satters gave a fine exhibition of Nordic voracity, devouring the most delicate dishes as if they had been black puddings or sizzling steaks. When Satters had eaten practically everything on the menu, they returned to No. 400.

"A little sleep, do you think?" said Pullman.

Satters was so heavy-eyed that it would have been impossible for him to remain awake for very long; indeed, wherever he sat down Pullman knew that he would be asleep within a few seconds. Preferring to confine his redoubtable snores to the bed-chamber, he led him in there, waving his hand towards the sumptuous bed.

"Lie upon that, O Satters, and take thy fill of sleep."

Pullman himself indulged a little on the sofa. At five he had a "full" tea brought up to his apartment. Satters was soon back in his gluttonous routine.

Satters was very comfortable in the room he shared with Jashormit. On the second morning, when he came down to breakfast, he said, "While I was washing, Pulley, something happened. I had just stepped out of the shower when Jashormit got hold of ... well you know what, and wouldn't let go. I had to sock him. He was still lying there when I came down."

After breakfast they went to Jashormit's apartment but it was empty—Jashormit's miniature suitcase had gone. Later in the day a new attendant arrived. He smiled broadly. "I am

Torg. I hear that Jashormit misbehaved himself. He didn't mean any harm, Mr Pullman, he has old-fashioned ways."

Torg was a broad-minded young man. "You like women? I understand," he said. "Mr Satterthwaite and I can go down and watch the drilling. The band plays and it is very nice. We shall get on very good, sir, Mr Satterthwaite and me."

Torg was a muscular young man, the sort Satters liked, and they got on well. They went down among the Bailiff's troops, and soon Satters was on the best of terms with some of the under age warriors.

One day a battalion of the "Guards" marched down beside the Bailiff's parade ground–band playing, a proper military band, officers on horseback, each man with white kid gloves and white leather beltings, all of them tall, moving proudly and with great precision. The Bailiff's fantastic militia, dressed like performers in a ballet, watched these real troops in silence; afterwards a number of them deserted. They petitioned the Bailiff for regular military uniforms. Their master, naturally, was unable to take them into his confidence.–He could not tell them that if they were dressed like real soldiers he could be ordered to disband them. So he said nothing. And Satters went down into the palace pseudo-military enclosures no more.

"Why does the Bailiff dress these boys up in that silly way, Pulley? If I was one of them I wouldn't stop there long."

Pullman's plans to take Satters under his direction, to associate himself once more with his ex-fag, proved a success. They went out everywhere together, each with his heavy stick, but Pullman's deceptively elegant.

XIX

THE FOURTH DAY after his reunion with Satters, Pullman received a request form the Bailiff to come over for a chat, the time elevenish. He presented himself as requested; luckily the interview took place, on this occasion, not in the more intimate study of the apologetic Venus, but in a small white-washed room downstairs. It was crowded with papers, even on the floor there were piles of them, and there was a sentry at the door.

When Pullman entered, the sentry was dismissed, and one of the Bailiff's secretaries replaced him, sitting upon a chair where before the sentry had stood straddling.

The Bailiff was buoyant and crowing. He greeted his guest with what had all the appearance of delight.

"My dear boy! My dear, dear boy! how elegant... how *young* you look! I cannot believe my eyes that it is the same man that I found grovelling outside the city gates; you have gone back fifteen years... and now you are a perfect Beau Brummell!"

"I thought this get-up might be of use to me," Pullman explained.

"Useful? A beautifully cut suit is one of the most useful things a man can have. How wise you are ... Also Mr Satterthwaite, we welcome him to the fringes of our household. An angry little bodyguard not to be despised. Ha, ha, you are a deep dog."

"He was my fag at school," Pullman told him.

"Ha ha! That is very funny, a splendid little term, I'll be bound. I have hundreds of FAGS, swarms of them ... but we do not *call* them that! Ho ho ho! A word I shall adopt, my dear fellow!"

They looked at one another smiling.

"I wanted to tell you, Pullman. First, I have heard from the Governor. *You* were mentioned. The Governor's Office is interested ... I will inform you, Pullman, of the outcome. Ha ha! Of the outcome or the come in!"

Pullman made no remark, but he smiled a little primly.

"The Yenery trouble is in hand. Probably Blitzkopf will be assassinated."

Pullman looked grave.

"You disapprove?" The Bailiff's face twisted itself into a parody of Pullman's gravity, puritanic lips and all. "*I* am very shocked, I, too, most awfully shocked! But it may happen. The Police Chief in the Yenery lost her life. I was very upset. But there it is. The wild women—the wild, wild women ...! You know the way the song went. A quite sensible, popular ditty, my dear Pullman!" Pullman smiled a little with a correct pursing of the now naked lips, and the Bailiff kept his own mouth as far as he could a replica of Pullman's.

"But I am no Cesare Borgia, my dear fellow. He was a very crude 'Prince'. Powdered glass in his waistcoat pocket and *ever* so wicked, a Gioconda smile. However—why should a man be allowed to blow off his great big lousy beard at me night after night—in Tenth Piazza, my boy. Yes, that boring old beard, drawing recklessly upon his imagination, and showing an inventive turn which is a little surprising; he broadcasts the doings of an imaginary 'Bailiff'—who is so damned wicked that he makes me green with envy. No. I shall go down there to the Piazza tonight ..."

"Tonight?"

"I built that place, you know, I designed it, and I made it so long that two speakers of excessively different opinions could both blow off steam there without coming to blows. I shall take advantage of that tonight, establishing myself at the opposite end to Hyperides, nearly a mile away."

"This is not the camp," Pullman warned him. "It may be a very rough house indeed."

"I shall have a thousand men with me," the Bailiff reassured him. "Or I can easily mobilise three thousand. I had a bright idea while I was making the arrangements for thonight's performance. I wonder if you would care to speak, my dear fellow? After their disgusting treatment of you, the other day, you might like to have a slap at them. Quite a short speech you know ... Just a few words putting these art-student soap-boxers in their place."

Pullman shook his head.

"On the earth I never was a partisan. The oratory of Hyde Park Corner left me cold. And, Excellency, I am a newcomer here. I must not rush in to the politics of the place, hitting out left and right. Or do you think I should?"

"You have nothing to fear from those ruffians, my dear chap; we would protect you in all circumstances. The fact that you are a newcomer is all to the good. Yes, I think you should show those curs that you are not afraid of them."

"But I *am* afraid of them. I should extremely dislike having my head broken. And there would be no sense in getting up and attempting to convince them of something which is not true."

"You don't look like a coward to your uncle," the Bailiff merrily bawled. "It is sheer laziness, I suppose. It would do you good to give your tongue a little exercise."

"All the same I must decline." Pullman looked very firm, and at the same time, yawned.

"How wise you are, my boy, how cautious and sensible!" the Bailiff chanted. "It was wrong of me to ask you. You have a better head than I have."

And so the conversation ended, except that the Bailiff detailed a few of the things he was going to say in reply to Hyperides. Just before he left Pullman said, "I shall be down there tonight, to watch you. But let me give you a final piece of fatherly advice. Give up your idea of answering these people and of going there in person. It is not the right thing to do in the present circumstances."

Now it was eight o'clock in the evening. Pullman knew that a new drama had started, full of roaring words, of fists flourished, all working up to the great showdown—and the Bailiff was in the field of batttle at the head of a thousand men. He was up on his perch, crowing from that iron throat of his, and the bearded accuser was rolling out the prelude of his accusation. These were the first shots. How would it all end—the great clashing of tongues, the towering brains marshalling their ideas and hoping to intoxicate their audience, a sea of armed partisans clustered together? Verbal geysers centred upon drilled lines, heavily armed, with lead in their rifles, with stiff faces, or in the bearded distance chaotically beset with trembling mouths, tired of shouting. What fell out in the Piazza built by the Bailiff depended upon the Po-

lice President. Not a cheerful thought for this little desper-
ado!

Smelling of soap so expensively delicious that Satters sniffed,
mistaking it for straight cent, the hero set forth, accompanied
by Satters, and Torg, disguised in a darker suiting than it was
his square-nosed nature to wear. They were to go on foot to
the Piazza. They stepped out in silence, moving down the dark
street. No mouth-noise need be expected from Satters, and
square-noses only spoke when spoken to.

When they had walked for about a hundred yards, Pullman noticed what he thought at first was something alive
jumping; he then saw that it was small flames, which were
springing about on the ground, a few feet ahead of him.

Pullman walked steadily on, as if nothing unusual had
occurred. The flames continued to frolic around him. As he
moved smartly along he attempted to find a reason for this
phenomenon. Was it escort by fire? For clearly this concerned
him; there were no flames around Satters or Torg. Not so much
as a spark even. They were approaching a telephone. When
they reached it, he commanded a halt. Picking up the receiver
he dialled the Phanuel Palace. It was a personal secretary of
the Bailiff who answered. Pullman referred to the existence of
small flames wherever he moved, but as soon as he started to
describe these inexplicable fires the secretary interrupted, saying, that ought not to occur, but that all he had to do to prevent
that happening was to exclaim in a voice of somewhat harsh
authority "Sack" and the flames would disappear. The voice
sought to set his mind at rest, assuring him that there was
nothing to be alarmed about. Evidently the Bailiff had felt
that he might need protection. "This is an quite powerful spirit
who is in attendance. In case of danger he can guarantee your
safety, for being under the protection of such a spirit is like
having a great husky dog for a friend."

So Pullman said, in a loud and threatening voice, "Sack",
and the flames dried up at once. The confidential secretary had
told him that if, after having shouted "Sack", the flames
vanished, this would not mean that the great spirit would leave
him–at least, not if it could help it. The cause for the appearance of the flames was, as it were, the making of a little ring
around the person to whom this spirit was attached, so as not

211

to lose sight of him. If he were obliged to dispense with the ring of flames, then this protective spirit *might,* in error, be found rushing violently to the defence of Satters, or to some-one else not far away.

In spite of his desire to avail himself of the services of this demon, Pullman felt he could not go about surrounded by flames.

As they drew near to their destination, they passed thousands of police, all fully armed, and lorries packed with guards in battle kit. "Who are these for?" he asked himself. There was only one answer: they were there, because of the military for-ces possessed by the Bailiff. Staff officers in several cars lay in wait just outside the Piazza itself. In the distance, though it had become quite dark, could be seen a fleet of white am-bulances.

Upon the three vast stairs, down which you stepped to reach the Piazza, were a fair number of watchers, passer-by, or elderly persons hesitating to approach any nearer to that un-ruly crowd.

Pullman had not expected the Piazza to be as it was, and he looked down on it for some time, with fascinated attention. Its romantic quality was not new. The crowds lighted by flares, the crowded balconies, the heavy starlight had been done, or as good as, by Desacroix and other French masters. On the walls of French galleries he had seen such things, sinisterly romantic like this. The hero's face grew stern—it was like a place set for a killing, and his disreputable patron was the obvious victim. When he thought of all the thousands of blades and loaded guns that were hidden, or displayed, everywhere in that dark mass, and then when he computed the massed armament of the police, of the guards, and beyond them the number of hospital orderlies, stretcher-bearers, ambulances, and so forth, it seemed quite certain that they were all bent upon massacre, and who in that arena did anyone wish to kill except his notorious little friend.

This hot-headed little dreamer might be killed in a mêlée by Hyperideans, or, in the end, he might be executed there by the police. He should never have allowed things to come to this. It was mad of him to come out now to defy his enemies—this was not the camp. He should have ignored the fulminations

212

of Hyperides. It was childish anger which had brought him out in force—if it came to a battle, what trust was to be placed in a thousand or so trained men? They were not attached to this repulsive old man by anything that cements men together, such as a religious belief, consanguinity, or personal attachment to a magnetic leader. There was only *esprit de corps*. One does not die for *esprit de corps* when the *corps* is a ragtime body like the haiduks. This little man had outraged everyone in this city, when they were in the camp, and he was popular with no one except racketeers. He would be using the technique he employed in the camp, forgetting how different the conditions were. He had pushed his square nose out of doors once too often.

The lighting of the scene was sinister; the blue and yellow flares, the searchlights of the Bailiff, one of them throwing into dazzling prominence a large group above the arcades, and the flames of the flares, in one case reaching the sky, where the enormous stars contradicted all this agitation by their frigid glare, tipping with silvery light the flame-lit faces below.—It was, Pullman felt, a beautiful melodrama.

The hero-rat, stepping delicately, descended the steps and entered the crowd—a small flame or two darting up at his feet as he did so. He and his two assistants edged their way to a position near the centre of this great concourse of people, but somewhat to the farther side, in the direction of the main arcade. He did not know why he had come to the Piazza. He was not interested in collections of people of this kind, nor would he go to a political meeting anywhere for choice. He was not here of his own free will, therefore, and did not know what to do once he had arrived, except that he supposed he would listen to the speakers, and draw his own conclusion from what was said and done regarding the outlook for the Bailiff.

There was a moving about and shouting continually. Of the four speakers he had seen from the steps he was nearest to a small rostrum with a placard announcing *Father Ryan*. The next nearest was Hyperides, who stood well up above the crowd in a sort of pulpit, given as Hellenic a look as possible by the painting of various devices over a board nailed on in front. The Hyperideans had chosen the part of the Piazza nearest to the underground station; and their leader was about one third of the way to the centre, the whole of that part of the Piazza packed with his followers, except for where Father Ryan had attracted a specific Catholic audience. The other half of the square was dominated by the Bailiff and his thousands of troops and followers. But he was on the side where the clubs, cafés, and restaurants, frequented by Mannock, were situated. The Bailiff was thrust up above the crowd like Hyperides; actually he was standing upon so heavy a vehicle that it would be better to call it a truck rather than a lorry. "He likes a framework," thought Pullman, for he appeared in the opening of a curtained stage for one actor. It was the same kind of idea as his Punch and Judy show at the Camp Tribunal. The arcade-tops were crowded all the way round. Sir Charles de la Pole-Blessington and many other members of the Cadogan Club were on a balcony not far behind the Bailiff; and this was a hissing balcony as were also the arcade-top balconies running at right angles. Where these balconies approached within hailing distance of the truck (wich was hedged in all round with haiduks and other troops from the Phanuel Palace), there were heard well-bred clubmanesque cries of "rot" or "tell that to the Marines", or "go back to Hell."

The Communist's name was Vogel, who had his modest stand roughly parallel with the Bailiff, and he had brought a sufficiently large number of adherents to fill the area at the side of the Bailiff's troops. In addition to those attracted by one or other of these four speakers, there were a quantity of sightseers, who had followed the processions starting from different parts of the city, and some local busybodies.

As Father Ryan was the nearest speaker to Pullman, it was to him that he turned first. The organ-note of Hyperides, and the scream of the Bailiff, were deadened by the universal noise, and the Priest's voice was a strong one. Father Ryan was speaking just then of the Hyperideans.–"The difficulty about Fascists, of whatever kind," the Father said, "is their salvationist passion. The provoke a religious zeal in any subject they take up, often very trivial. A messianic zeal characterises them; on that they launch themselves, and that floats them along; they are false Messiahs, therefore, it is necessary to say. – Fascists are great moralists, we see them hunting down and seeking to punish evil-doers. Their enemy is always diabolic,

214

they are experts on the Devil and the forms he takes among politicians, financiers, lawyers, and indeed in whatever direction we look. What may be said to their credit is that what they denounce is usually bad. But the same can be said of the police, and political abuse nowhere goes unchecked. But if what is Wrong is their prey, the Right is also their victim. They have the instincts of watchdogs, but they have as little idea as have watchdogs of absolute value. They are only of use destructively. It is not very difficult to see that a person is a liar and a cheat, born to be dishonest, and the system which he represents is not too difficult to define. Any averagely competent lawyer could do all that they do, exclusive of the tremendous clamour in which they specialise. Now if these hunting-dogs born to bark, are, for the rest, mere automata, and, when they see a priest, bark their heads off, because they feel he is a stranger and must be barked at–if they are as limited as this, then we cannot take them seriously. It is unfortunate that this has to be said, if for no other reason, because Fascism has in its ranks many young Catholics. Then many people, I among them, have listened to the baying of a certain hound, possessed of a magnificent voice, with pleasure. But there it is. –There is a greater voice than that. To go no farther let me mention the organ in our cathedral–when it is playing a Bach voluntary, the baying of our notorious watch-dog pales and fades, and we realize how limited that deep rough voice was and must always be. Fascism says what the State should have said (but was too enfeebled to say, too sick or too demoralised): but it says it for its own petty ends–it has always been for the glorification, ultimately, of Mr Smith or of Mr Jones, or of Mr Hitler. And those of us who are Catholic know that it is only for the greater glory of God that any great action can be undertaken–that is the only glory that we could admit into our consciousness."

The hero-rat bowed his head and turned sadly away: for he knew that that was the only voice, in this place of oratory, to which he had any right to respond, to which he would listen with more than a worldly–an all-too-worldly–tolerance. He himself should have turned his back on the world when he was on the earth, instead of bending himself to attract the gifts of he world, which at last had led him to the diabolic filth of that

215

screaming puppet over there. Something attracted his eye, in a fissure of the fairly dense crowd. It was a small flame, darting up at his feet, from the stone of the Piazza. He looked down frowning, and when he saw it again he stamped on it and crossed his fingers.

He turned to his left and fixed his eyes upon the stately head of he that went by the name of Hyperides. (Why *Hyperides*? Because that gentleman liked the classically romantic sound of it,–not better reason than that.)

"We fight with a rope round our necks," came the deep and thrilling voice. "We are liked by no one, not even by those we protect. It is a crime to defend the State–that is a monopoly. The care for the honour of the State is a monopoly, however small the pains that are taken to see that it is intact. Again, if you see a felon in the act of committing a felony, and you apprehend him, that is a grave offence, wherever you commit it: for there will be somebody whose duty it is to do what you have done–just as the welfare and honour of the State threatened by some reptile in half-human form like that square-snitch over there, oh be careful: under no circumstances show that you notice this, turn away and think of something else. It has been with a rope around my neck that I have taken every step in my power to bring to justice that emperor of racketeers, who has built himself a marble palace, and supports a private army, on the proceeds of his blood-stained rackets. Did you hear that the other day the Police Chief in the Yenery was murdered? Who did that, do you think? It was that man over there," and he reached his arm out and stabbed his fingers towards the Bailiff, "who murdered that poor lady! he had prosecuted his personal agents in the Yenery, and one of his agents came up behind her and cut her throat." There was a great a roar at this from all his followers that it was impossible to continue speaking for some minutes. Then he held his hand up and the storm hushed itself, to some extent. "That, gentlemen, is the latest of his crimes, and certainly one of the vilest; but his whole life has been made up of violence and outrage, performed with impunity. He has made millions of aurei out of those wretched women, by selling them dope and hooch and everything that was illegal but which, owing to their terrible condition, they would have sold their lives for. He owns

216

Lesbian brothels, a hundred gambling dens, and waxes fat (as you see him) upon the heartbreak and the madness which proliferates in that ghastly ghetto." The buzz of heated talk and angry conversation made it again very difficult for the orator's voice to be heard.

Pullman turned about to have a whiff of the Bailiff's oratory. Satters wheeled with him. But at that moment he heard a voice saying, "Square-nose! Take your proboscis elsewhere, hell-boy. You smell like sin. Get out!"

He beckoned Torg. "It would be better for you to return to the palace. A witch-hunt is on, they will never leave you alone." Torg protested that it did not matter to him. But Pullman insisted. Pursued by jeers and threats, Torg wormed his way through the hostile mêlée, and soon was out of sight.

"A beard is not everything. For *me* a beard is a theatrical property, put on by somebody who wishes to pass himself off as someone bigger than he is, it does not matter in the least which you do,–buy it in a shop or grow it on your chin, just the same thing my children."

The Bailiff with great suddenness disappeared. With an equal celerity he shot up again. Now it was a bearded man who faced the audience. "I could not trouble to grow one of these things, I have bought one and here it is, just as good as the one which is grown . . . Now let me think what silly lies I can tell about prominent people, who anyway are coconut shies.–Aunt Sallies for zealous nobodies."

Ever since he had put on the postiche-beard the constant shouting increased to such a pitch that he could be heard no more, nor could the insults yelled at him possibly reach him. A neighbour of Pullman's for instance bellowed, "It is no good putting on a beard; no one, not even a rat would follow a Square-Nose." But his would hardly carry more than five or six yards. Every spectator heard his neighbours insults, but the Bailiff had to take them on trust, kissing his hand all around. The Bailiff did not attempt to speak for a short while, he settled the beard over his ear, with a small comb he worked at it to make it more fluffy. He chatted with the nearest of his followers. When things were a little quieter he bent forward, and a deep voice issued from the beard–sounding so natural a bass that even his followers looked up to see who it was speaking. Pointing at the bearded figure in the middle distance he ponderously intoned, "There is the dirtiest liar I have ever met. He mobilises every morning a pack of dirty lies, he lets them loose upon some unfortunate official and follows them viewhallooing with all his might. This is a spectacle much to the taste of those who love big bearded calumniation of anyone clean-shaven, and clean in other ways, too."

At this point he ceremoniously unhooked his beard and a clean-shaven rascal's face appeared in its place. "Clean," he shrieked, "clean as a hound's tooth."

There was always a great deal of noise but when the Bailiff thought he saw his chance he resumed his address.

"Gentlemen!–I did not suppose that a *second* beard would be tolerated in the Piazza. I knew that, as I was *clean* in other ways, I had to be clean-shaven. This is a pity. I have a little mirror here, and I must say, although the beard is not my favourite disguise, I thought I looked rather cute."

He paused a moment to allow people to get rid of a great deal of extra steam produced by the beard, then he pursued. "But that bogus look, which a beard may be depended on to give–that failed to satisfy the gentleman in question. A false name as well as a false beard seemed necessary. He hunted around until at last he discovered what he regarded as the most unreal, the most postiche piece of nomenclature of any he could find, HYPERIDES. That, he felt, went with the startlingly large whiskers! Yes, 'Hyperides' was quite meaningless, it was linguistically a mouthful, and it was absurdly pretentious."

There was pandemonium. "What is your real name, puppet!" cried one.–"Lucifer would be jealous if you wore a beard in Hades, wouldn't he?" And one bellowed, "Put your dirty breath in a bottle, and sell it as Hellebore to your compatriots." And one near Pullman shrieked, "Bum-face! Here is a roll of toilet paper!" And he flung a roll at his bugaboo, but it fell among the troops drawn up in close order in a *cordon sanitaire* between their master and the infuriated crowd.

Pullman now moved sideways, until he was within earshot of the fourth orator, the Third City Communist. His name was Vogel, and he was a rough-looking individual with the blood-shot eyes of a man whose only diet was Marx and cabbage. At the moment he was rather quietly complaining of the reactionary policy of the Governor, evidenced by the disgraceful inequality where incomes were concerned. How different the incomes allotted to those who had been working people in their earthly life, and to those who had belonged to the professional classes, to the aristocracy or to the bourgeoisie. So privilege was carried over into eternity. "The workman is condemned to fetch and carry for others ever; the gentleman is for all time to–live easy, eat well, enjoy leisure, have servants from the working class, the slave-class. Here he is more rigidly confined to his pen than he was down below. The root of all this is in Heaven, where God is treated as an oriental despot, and the angels are His musical courtiers, who sing His praises from morning till night. Our Governor, before he came here, was such a courtier. So his view of life is that of the court in an absolute monarchy." It was not applause but a roar of furious agreement which greeted these remarks.

Pullman listened for perhaps five minutes longer to Vogel: the Hyperideans appeared to excite Vogel's contempt and anger more even than the Church.

"This band of idle young men, who can find no better use for their time than to affect a fancy-dress. A kind of amateur theatricals it is, and a playing at philosophers. Many of them belong to the working-class, but they give no thought to the misery of the class from which they come."

Pullman took Satters by the arm, and they pushed their way towards the arcades, which with some difficulty they reached. Here they were among insurgent minds who objected to the beauty of their clothes. They had to force their way between men inflamed by Vogel's words, whose nostrils snorted indignantly at the scents of delicious soaps which clung to Pullman's underclothes. The dark arcades were relatively empty. Pullman began walking along them, lost in thought. Satters' silence could be relied on; nothing but hunger or a stomach-ache would cause him to break it.

In the arena out of which they had stepped into the cloistered peace of the arcades (relative peace, for the din rushed in at every arched opening)–in this arena were concentrated all the major disharmonies of the contemporary scene on earth. Father Ryan stood for Tradition in Third City, a theocracy of course. Vogel's was the voice of Social Revolution. Hyperides represented the most recent political phenomenon–hated or disliked by everybody. Here was the Fascist, the arch-critic of contemporary society. On earth this newcomer proposed to supplant the enfeebled Tradition, of whatever variety, no longer able to defend itself. So this enfeebled Power of Tradition, and its deadly enemy, the Marxist Power, joined forces to destroy this violent Middleman (a borrower from both the new and the old). These earthly alliances were repeated undoubtedly here, Pullman reflected. The other Power which could be seen defending itself in this market-place, the Piazza, was gangster-wealth at its most irresponsible, represented by the Bailiff.

This was to look at it purely as a reflection of the world. Altough ix certainly corresponded to those earthly alignments, Pullman saw that either, (1) the earth was more supernaturally controlled than the living believed; or, (2) here the supernatural dominated everything, the city being ruled directly by God's ministers, and the Bailiff acting under direction from Hell itself. Thereby a situation was created in which Good and Evil battled with an almost Mazdaistic duality. Was one deceived on Earth as to the nature of the struggle forever in progress, did what was supernatural in this struggle escape one as a man? In any case, here you found yourself speedily involved upon the one side or the other; upon the side of God or of His Enemy.

With amazement (Pullman told himself) you discovered that the part you had played on Earth pursued you here, and you found yourself continuing the play. It was made clear to you that the rôle which had been yours on earth was essentially diabolic. To your confusion, your faithfulness to your earthly part in this play led you into the strangest supernatural company.

More and more, as his mind laid bare the ultimate truth involved in these four main opposing philosophies–more and more clearly he understood that the point had been reached at which he was called upon to take a final decision. Should he take the emotional road, or the one indicated by common sense. He realised that upon Earth he had decided in favour of common sense, or, to put it in a more complimentary way, the logical and the practical. He had known that there was such a thing as the Right and the Wrong; that there was no such thing, for a man, as "Beyond good and evil". That was merely the self-advertising eccentricity of an intellectual. Christianity apart, these values of Good and of Bad dominated human life, at its deepest level. On Earth, life was usually lived at a superficial level. Fundamental values played very little part in the conduct of life; and that was the reason for the frightful dilemma in which he found himself; because he inherited a superficial habit of mind.

If this had been Heaven, or if this had been Hell, there would have been no difficulty in understanding what course he should take. Or was this one or the other, or both? Perhaps that was the nature of the dilemma.

But no. This was, in the main, a life, or half-life, controlled by earthly values. Or so it had seemed to him—although here was a turning point, at which he was reviewing the assumption. There was no use denying that he was deeply dismayed.

"Let me examine a few of the immediate issues, then. I have been denounced by the Hyperideans as a rat. To them I would unquestionably be classified in that manner. Mister Devlin, who is out there in the Piazza, he accused me; he has said that a man as intelligent as myself understands perfectly well how vile a creature the Bailiff is, yet, simply in order to be as comfortable as possible in Third City, I accept his patronage. I come here from Earth, with a Big Name, and I sell my Big Name to the highest bidder. The values behind that Big Name either were of a trivial kind on Earth, or, if they were real and important values, I now betray them in this spectral life—spectral life—as such I think of it. But there is my big mistake. This is no more a spectral life than the life on Earth.

"Now, as a man on Earth, the various forms of Fascism were the equivalent of Hyperideanism. It had a considerable superficial air of being on the right side; but, as Father Ryan said, when carefully examined its rightness merely consisted in barking at something which was worse than something else; that was all, but it left you in a chaos, and was a deceptive Rightness." As a result of these cogitations Pullman decided that he was a dubious and unfundamental rat—the rat of a sect; a creature of their dogmas. Nothing more.

Pullman stepped out of the shadow to the side of the arcade.

He stared first at one, then at another of the partisans, as though they might have been able to assist him to reach a decision. But of course, the dazzling light and the deafening noise merely made him more confused; so he returned into the pleasant shadow.

Well, he said to himself, there was still the situation. For publishing with a certain publisher, and for associating with men of approximately the same party as himself, he had not been called a rat on earth. On the contrary, he had received the highest honours, and been treated as an extremely progressive mind. But he was now in a much weaker position, because the person who had singled him out as a friend was undoubtedly an unspeakable blackguard, a limb of the devil, an undesirable acquaintance, and so forth.

"What is, in the first instance, responsible for these extraordinary confusions, is the introduction oft he supernatural into the play, as performed in Third City. What here are archangels or disguised demons, were on Earth simply men and women like ourselves. It may be that they were angelic or diabolic. But this was not visible. So, when you were transported to the scene of Third City, these inoffensive persons with whom you had been associated on Earth were suddenly transformed into supernatural beings, with a strong suspicion of diabolic origin. Or, on the other hand, the most prominent figures on your side in the earthly struggle were transformed into archangelic personalities. There were not, of course, equivalencies of this easily recognisable sort; but before very long these equivalencies, however disguised, began to transpire; and suddenly, as in my own case, you would find yourself involved with a powerful demon, whereas on Earth he would merely be dear old so-and-so, a rich patron of the arts, or a go-ahead publisher."

Having reached this point of enlightenment, the question that he, Pullman, must ask himself was: "Am I now to continue in my earthly rôle, wherever it may lead me–and find myself in the end consorting with Lucifer in person; or am I to go to Father Ryan, to fall upon my knees, ask for forgiveness, and inquire what atonement I can make?" This of course would mean that in future all the actions that he undertook would lead him ultimately to God, not to Satan.

Put like that, how absurd it must sound to a human ear, he thought. It would not do so, however, were the Powers for ever in conflict on the earth to be visibly supernatural. If any side you took on Earth were certain to condemn you to take some prearranged rôle in a highly ethical play in a scene in Third City, then all our actions as living men would be indulged in less lightly.

Outside in the Piazza thousands of men were engaged in a dispute, and they were roughly divided, at the moment, into four camps. The speaker of his choice, beyond any question, was the Catholic priest. But on Earth he had abandoned the Catholic religion; was he now to enter once more into that communion? He should have been able to answer that question without hesitation: of the four speakers he had listened to, it was the first heard by him which spoke to his intellect and to his heart. Yet . . . there was a destiny in this, there was a compulsion from the past.

His life on Earth was the real life. This was not a life at all, but something artificial, in which the values of the life-on-Earth were dressed up in a different way, and manifested themselves with clarity in this sterilized medium. He had lived with the Bailiff upon the earth but had not recognized him. He had built all his success upon Bailiff-like rather 'than Padishah-like interests; and now, here, the Bailiff had acted as a magnet: he had been drawn in that direction at once. And anyhow, where else would he be in this collection of men? Would he be a Fascist, mouthing all that stupid, claptrap, moralistic stuff? Would he be attempting to secure a standing in the social life favoured by Mannock? Would he be inflaming himself in favour of equality, under the leadership of Vogel, or playing the part of such a leader himself? No. As he had been instructing Mannock, only some men were intelligent. No other creature, natural or supernatural, could be; and for him human intelligence alone mattered. Yes; the natural–supernatural problem (problem for a man among supernatural creatures) was the essence of things here, it supplanted everything else. Odious and monstrous as the Bailiff was, he was the supernatural element, paradoxical as that might seem, most favourable to man.

Through an archway he saw the splenetic figure of Michael

Devlin, who was now in Hyperides' perch, shaking his fist and spitting out acid words, the Goebbels of this outfit.–Pullman stopped; if he continued in these arcades upon his present course he would end up in the camp of Hyperides. He looked at Satters' stormy baby-face, he took him by the arm once more, turned him about, and said, "Come. We must retrace our steps, circle around behind the Bailiff, and make our exit from this place of tumult at that corner of the Piazza."

And that was what they did, listening, en route, to their hideous patron roaring inside his curtain, and reaching Tenth Avenue with Pullman in a more morose, confused and irritable mood than had been his at any time during his association with the Bailiff.

11. DIE THE MAN

XX

THE FOLLOWING MORNING, as he went struggling to reach the breakfast table in time to escape reproof, Satters noticed from his bedroom window much military activity in the rear of the Bailiff's palace. What's up? thought Satters. Is the old Bailey going to War?

He arrived flushed and foreboding in Pullman's apartment. "The old Bailey's on the warpath, Pulley." Pullman looked up surprised, a glance of reproof hurrying across the surprise, and tapping Satters a little sharply, for this was the third morning on which he had been late for breakfast.

"Lazy boy!" said Pullman, "slothful beast!" Pullman coughed. "Can't you learn to call that dignitary across the road the Bailiff—instead of always saying 'the old Bailey'? Well, what's the matter? Why do you think he is on the warpath?"

"Oo, you go and look for yourself into the drill-yard, *you'll* see what I mean, Pulley. 'A' Batallion isn't half being put through it. Sergeant-major Pearson too!"

Pullman appeared to be turning something over in his mind. In a minute he said, a little gruffly, "Okay. We will have a look after breakfast."

Twenty minutes later, when Pullman and Satters were walking along by the side of the Palace, an extraordinary tumult was heard through a wide-open window belonging to a large hall at the back of the Palace premises. The Bailiff screamed instructions, he outdid himself in fault-finding; piercing as this was, it was almost smothered by a sound like a truck-train going through a tunnel. Very gruff complaints surged and rasped up like the protests of a seal maltreated by its keeper. To put a stop to grumbling, two revolver shots barked loudly, like the voice of an hysterical watchdog, and the Master's Voice jumped into a higher register; "Take that, Rhobinolaw—I told you I would put that in your ugly hide if you went on trying to be funny!" and so stunning a roar succeeded, so massive a howl of reproof, that it blotted out everything else. Bang bang went the Magistrate's revolver, probably discharged at the floor at his side, but sounding as if he were retaliating on the bellow. "If you make a noise like that no one will ever learn their part, pusface, mass of complaining mutton—worst of your troupe!"

Gradually a sort of silence established itself. Then a fresh shrill expostulation burst out from the Bailiff; "Butter-fingers! That is the third time you have dropped that nail, the third time. If I gave you a bar of chocolate you would be able to hold it—here"—obviously there were domestics—"fetch me a bar of chocolate, and saw it down the middle until it is the shape of a large nail."

There was something like a submerged explosive growling.

"They're laughing, Pulley. That's laughing."

"Yes, the supernatural zoo is convulsed." Pullman propped himself up on tiptoe and gazed into the hall. "He looks as if he were talking to himself. Except that there are unexplained shadows everywhere—sort of shadows."

"That's them, Pulley. They're always like that, sometimes thicker though. Pulley, I saw one once, I saw one."

"What did it look like?" Pullman asked.

"I was passing a door. There was something big and black. It moved, and I saw a glittering light which was an *eye*, Pulley, an eye all in tle middle of the black. It gave me an nasty look."

"But what was its *shape*?" Pullman asked impatiently.

"Nothing, there wasn't any shape, Pulley. It was like a great big jelly-fish standing on end or something, there wasn't really any shape—except that it seemed to be taking shape—there were arms, more than one, Pulley. Then I saw its eye."

"What shape was it taking?"

"I don't know, Pulley. It began to look like a crouching man, oh three or four times the size of me—but the legs, where were the legs, if it was a man, Pulley?"

"I see," said Pullman, "but where was its eye?"

Satters began fumbling about on his chest, about level with the nipples. "About here, Pulley. No, a little higher up." Satters ended not far below his chin.

Meanwhile the uproar in the hall grew brisker. The Bailiff was screeching, "Can't you hold a hammer in that paw of yours?" He was addressing some other figure, and his tone, though rough, was less violent. "Ah, here's the chocolate nail. Now, you unspeakable nincompoop of a crocodile, take *this* and do not *eat* it! No! Do not put it in your mouth! It is a nail– a nail–a jolly old nail, to nail something with. Blast you–blast you–it has disappeared down your stinking throat! You are a waste of time, you are not worth your keep, you are nothing but a heartsore and a headache!" The revolver crashed out, time after time, and in a world-engulfing roar the monstrous shadow died and evaporated.

"Take his place, Simorphi." Then came an enormous musical-chairs, and what sounded like a satisfied grunt, probably coming from Simorphi.

"What is he working at?" Pullman turned to go. "Rehearsing something, the horrible old blackguard–putting his team of monsters through a drill."

Pullman and his squire had begun to walk away; a shrill whistle came from behind them, out of the drillhall, followed by a sound like a stampede of elephants.

"That is the climax, I surmise." Pullman spoke rather to himself than to his striding fag. "I wish I knew what my patron was contriving."

They came to a small door in the high wall, the handle of which Satters turned, and invited Pullman to move inside. Pullman now found himself in the midst of a mass of marching and counter-marching men, roared at by a dozen sergeants of the fiercest kind, bristling and bombastic. At that moment a party was given a rest not far from where they stood, and Satters sidled up and had a whispered conversation with a friend, who appeared to be a minor instructor, who kept shaking his head and laughing. In a few minutes Satters slunk back, looking ashamed.

"Well?" inquired Pullman scornfully.

"Can get nothing out of that son of a bitch," Satters muttered. "Don't go away, Pulley. There's someone I know over there– it's old Birdie. Wait till he gets round here, he'll spill the beans, what do you bet?"

Birdie, in fact, *did* begin to draw nearer; but his progress was so slow, as he drove his party, barking more and more hoarsely, around the drill-yard, that it was all Satters could do to keep Pullman from bolting out of the little door through which they had made their entrance. At a moment when Birdie was no more than twelve yards away, his bellowing growing nearer and nearer, Satters was obliged to wind his arms around Pullman's waist and push him up against the shut gate, to keep him in position.

"Don't go, Pulley, oh do stop just a little, old Birdie is nearly on top of us—*that's* old Birdie, Pulley, that fat bounder with the blue-black waxed mounstache. Hear 'im? He has the biggest voice on the parade-ground has old Birdie—he's like one of those big barkers on the Radio when you've put the volume up too high."

Birdie was standing now with his large back only a few feet away from where they were struggling. "Oh Birdie!" Satters hoarsely whispered over his shoulder, continuing to pin his patron against the gate.

"Stand *ut* . . . ease! Stand easy."

While his party stood in relaxed attitudes, Birdie about-turned, and his waxed moustaches were now pricking the air level with Satters' eyes and an expression of masked understanding, a glitter of reminiscent alcoholic mirth, stood in his commanding eye.

"'Allo, Satter boy!" he rattled softly. "'Ow've you bin keepin'?"

"Oh, fine thanks, Birdie old mate," Satters replied in the same rattle of easy precipitation. "What's the shemozzle, Birdie? When's the battle begin?"

Birdie looked woodenly knowing, shooting his waxed moustaches about as if he were signalling to some confederate. He rolled his eyes, gazing down at Satters, attempting to discover how much he knew. Pullman disquieted him a little, but he dicided that there was no need for more discretion than necessary.

"Well . . .," he coughed. "I guess the old organtones is for it this time, what? I shouldn't like to be in 'is shoes this evenin' as ever was!"

"Got the lowdown, Birdie, on when we pull the trigger?"

Birdie's waxed moustaches were stiff and still, his eyes were wise and forebodingly solemn. He lowered his voice almost to a whisper. "Zero hour's for one 'arf-hour after old Bailey 'as took 'is stand."

"Go on!" Satters rounded his eyes. "All-out attack, what! Oh boy! I wish I were a soldier like you, Birdie!"

Birdie puffed out his chest and glared into the distance.

Satters whispered, moving a step nearer to the oracle. "Is it ball cartridges, Bird?" he hissed.

Birdie looked over his shoulder, scowling at one of his men whom he suspected of listening-in. Then facing ahead again, still with the scowl on his face, he caught Pullman's eye. A wave of caution appeared to submerge him. "No, boy, we shall be in blank, as per usual." He solemnly fixed Pullman with his eye. "Now I must prerceed, Satterboy. Be seein' you."

Abruptly the sergeant about-turned, glaring so menacingly at his drooping party that they sprang to attention before he had uttered the word of command.

"Now come along, Satters, we must get out of this beastly place," and Pullman turned the handle of the gate and passed quickly out, followed by his mortified fag.

"If you had waited, Pulley, I'd have got all the dope out of that old Bird. He was cagey because of you, Pulley. He'd have told *me* all right."

Pullman looked depressed, and at the same time in a bad temper. He said nothing, but, in silence, he hurried back to the hotel. As they moved along together Pullman said, "I am afraid that our patron is plotting something very dark indeed. Obviously he proposes to make use of his supernatural allies."

The tone in wihch he spoke alarmed his squire. He looked terrified. "What do you think, Pulley...?"

"I think... I think we shall have to mind our eye."

It was already night at eight o'clock, and throughout the extent of this vast forum the air was full of the roar of voices, when the Bailiff, almost unnoticed, mounted into the lorry from which he delivered his anti-philippics. He stepped softly, and there was a little smirk on his face which he kept down in the shadow cast by the hood and curtained sides of the miniature mock-theatre form which he spoke . He slid in through the curtains, and was at once exposed to at least forty-thousand eyes. It took some minutes for all the assembly from one end of the Piazza to the other to become aware of his presence. The roar of rage and derision rose minute by minute from the Hyperideans. A low, hoarse, muffled cheer was breathed up towards him from the ranks of his paramilitary followers, and with a shrill exultant cry he answered them. Batallion "A" of his Gladiators stood immediately beneath, keyed up to a terrific degree of self-importance. They were fore-experiencing their great act.

Almost immediately the Bailiff drew out of a box, from just beneath the parapet concealing from the crowds the lower part of his body, the beard he had worn the night before. As it settled in around his face he leapt forward, screaming.

"Shout, gentlemen, shout. Blow the stinking wind from your lungs around my head. See if you can blow away this foul assortment of heterogeneous nesting rubbish in which I have nested part of my face like a bird; this sign of inferiority, stuck on around my massive chin so that I should have no merely physical superiority over your leader. He, poor chap, has to wear all that to hide his pin of a chin–the fluff around the pea. But the teeth go well with the beard do they not? And mine flash better than Hyperides' weaker tusks–remember that, when the two beards join in battle. It will be my teeth that close down and dig into the flesh of your master. Yum–yum–yum. He will taste like putrescent fish. (The Bailiff addressed Hyperides personally in a deafening scream.) Listen to me, for a bit, old spout on two legs. You have told more lies about me than you can remember. I bellow back but I do nothing. Now, I am going to act–to act in so dreadful a way that, could you live to see it, your eyes would drop out of your head. "I have had you thrown out of the city. But you come back, more charged with lies than you were before.

If I cannot whirl you from this world,

If I cannot crack your skull,

If I cannot wrench your entrails out and wind them on a
   stout pole,

If I cannot fill what is left over with benzine and put a
   match to it,–

Then I'm unstuck, throttled, and corked up for keeps.

Hyper-any-thing-you-like.

You have only a handful a countable seconds to live.

Ask for forgiveness of your stupendous Nothingness of a

God, you microscopic rat who learnt in Pontypridd how
to blow yourself up into a pestiferous obstruction.

Ask pardon of the poop-faced old Image of yourself
multiplied ten million times.

You have a few seconds in which to receive forgiveness from
the omnipotent Zero.

Shout!—he is deaf.—Blather out your 'pardons' at the top of
your voice.

Ask for Heaven, and p'r'aps h'ell give you an ice-cream.

Goooo-bye-bye-bye-bye-*eeee*.

Libertine, beg forgiveness for those misdeeds,

Coming under the head of libertinage,

Little matters of Kate and of Alice,

Of Jessie and of Maud.

Don't forget that you have been responsible for the murder
of whole Streets—ay, and at least one Avenue,

In the Yenery, in that sink of iniquity, your special preserve,
the Hell of the Women; and put in a prayer for diddling
your landlord, for borrowing money from that poor man;

Then all the misdeeds committed against followers, money
they could not spare—for you are very fond of money.

You live with mistresses, like all the Welsh you are a lecher,
and you make those pay

Who stand in the Piazza, applauding your waffle.

You owe me four pardons for what you said about the
foundations of my palace.

You owe me five pardons for the disgusting libels about the
upkeep of my infantry.

And for your scurvy slanders and your inventions about
my diabolical pacts with the ruffianly Satan.

May you burn to a cinder upon the grills of Dis."

The wildest uproar had broken out among those contemptible thousands who supported the prophet with the
authentically sprouting beard—whose hand was now thrust out,
a denunciatory finger waggling at the end of it, as he hurled
his voice out over the crowds, aiming it at the insulting imitation to which the Bailiff had resorted.

"A rat with a beard is still an unmistakable *rat*."

The Bailiff danced about, protruding his tongue out of the
bought beard. "A little Welsh chemist is still a little Welsh

chemist in spite of the hair he allows to grow around his muzzle."

"Measly little crook, how do you fill your pockets now that the Yenery is full of hostile police?"

The Bailiff leapt in the air with a hyena-yell–"What, Hyperides, have you found no new lies to dish out this evening? Has the source run dry? Can you think of no new slanders?"

There was a rain of cat-calls, and one missile sped through the air and fell with a thud by the side of the Bailiff. The Bailiff squeaked violently into the teeth of the hubbub, "Taffy was a Welshman Taffy was a thief."

"Square-snout, go home and pack your trunks! You won't be here much longer. The Sanitary Services will sweep you out of the city, impudent cockroach!" bawled a Hyeridean over the heads of the Gladiators.

"Sock him one, boys!" the Bailiff commanded–and one of the Gladiators, obeying, swung at the shouting man and brought him to the ground, amid a tempest of protests.

Pullman and his ex-fag, as the Bailiff was taking his first bow, were hurrying into the Piazza, making for the rear of the truck which their patron used as a stage. Pullman saw the smirk upon the Bailiff's face, and thought to himself, "Obstinate little beast, preparing for your pranks. You are doing all the wrong things, you will bring the whole of your little universe down upon your head." He had come through the lines of police, and had felt it in his bones that all these waiting officers, with brooding faces, were darkly impatient with the Bailiff; he seemed determined to keep them waiting, and not to take the false step which would precipitate the show-down.

Pullman was heartily sick of this Piazza, but there was a kind of apricot light, and deep blue shadows, a new coloration, something he had not seen before. The smirk he had seen, that foretold action: Mister Square-Nose Pasha was about to spring a surprise. Since Pullman had come really to understand his position in this place, he had developed a personal resentment about any violence proposed by the Bailiff, in which he now knew that he was involved. This mighty little old egotist smirking his way into a new folly made him so angry that he was half a mind to climb up on to the truck beside him, and order him back to his palace. However, he settled down with Satters, immediately behind the Bailiff, at a distance of less than a hundred yards, to await the issue,—very grim, thought his squire, who also, during the last day or two, had noticed a change by no means for the better in his chief. The fact was that ever since Pullman had accepted the fact, that, for better or for worse, his adherence to the Bailiff was unavoidable, although it involved him in a rat-like status, the more critical he had become of this compromising personality.

Tenth Piazza was even more full of people than on the preceding evening, although on this occasion neither Vogel nor Father Ryan was there. The crowds were much more unruly, and the atmosphere more electric. It was, this time, a duel between two inflated personalities, everything else excluded as the climax approached. There could not have been less than forty thousand people here, almost four-fifths of whom visibly were of the Hyperides ticket.

"The old Bailey . . ." began Satters.

"Oh!" protested Pullman. "You mean the Bailiff I believe."

Satters looked up smiling, half puzzled. "The Bailey's voice," he confided, "sounds different."

"Different?"

"Yes, Pulley. It's trembly. Is the Bailey afraid?"

"That's unlikely. I can hear no tremor in his voice."

"I'm sure it trembles." Satters was obstinate.

Pullman knew that his sixteen-year-old associate imagined things. But just then he thought he heard a tremor himself. No doubt excitement. Or perhaps Hyperides had said something which had made him shiver with anger? Pullman listened to find if any enlightenment was to be received from the raging words.

"Flossie is a name invented by Hperides," he heard. "There is no such name. No such name. As to the letters he is handing round, how easy it is to forge a letter! Not for expert examination—not *that*, but to hand round in a crowd. I will forge one myself, and then hand it round." He began scribbling something on a piece of paper, while ten thousand voices sang, "For he's a jolly good forger, for he's a jolly good forger. For he's a jolly good for-her-ger, and so say all of us!"

The name *Flossie,* Pullman remembered, had produced a

paroxysm of grief, up in the room of the obscene Venus, when the news of her death was brought in by the scarlet messenger. It was obvious that Hyperides was in possession of secret information of so critical a kind that it might quite well have caused the Bailiff to tremble with terror. Would not the next step be the arrest of his patron? It looked as if the jig were up. Meanwhile the distant crowd howled for his blood.

In the rear of the Bailiff's truck was a mass of uniformed or armleted adherents. Pullman noticed two members of the police come round in the free area between this mass of uniformed men and the carcades–they were very smart compared with the militia of the Phanuel Palace. Having consulted a little, they gently and without urgency, pushed their way in among the Bailiffites, and after they had reached a position about twenty feet behind the Bailiff's truck, they stopped.

It was the quietness and discretion of these two members of the police force which attracted Pullman's attention. Incidentally, there were no police in the Piazza. Thousands were stationed just outside, but none had been posted nearer than that.

Once these two stopped, Pullman ceased to observe them: but in about ten minutes there were sudden shouts of alarm. Pullman had been watching several men inside the arcade, engaged in pasting up a notice, but he turned quickly around. The two uniformed police were rushing up the steps placed against the side of the truck. Several haiduks were attempting to hold them back. There was no one upon the truck itself– except the orator, whose attention was fully occupied within the curtained stage arranged for the framing of the speaker.

The second member of the police was being tackled and held halfway up the steps: but the first policesoldier, flourishing his revolver, had mounted the truck, and the Bailiff had faced about, and was retreating from him, screaming something incomprehensible. The policeman now aimed his revolver at him and fired (a very strange thing for anyone belonging to the police to do, it seemed to Pullman).

The Bailiff fell, wrapping the end of the curtain around him, apparently seeking to conceal himself in the heavy cloth. "He is not a policeman!" he skrieked. "Kill him! He is an assassin."

But the first of the men in the police uniform did not seem

able to advance. It was as if he were enveloped by an invisible enemy. He continued to fire his revolver in all directions. One shot found its mark, it seemed, in the terrace above the arcade, and just over where Pullman was standing. There was a shrill scream, and a great deal of stamping about overhead.

At the same time he who had fired the shot, with a cry–again moved by some invisible agency it would seem–soared into the air, his arms outstretched, and fell among the Bailiff's troops. As he did so, the Bailiff left the concealing folds of the curtains, rushed to the back of the truck and screamed down to where his followers were battering the two members of the police force, bogus or otherwise. "Disarm them and manacle, them. Tie them up! Do–not–kill–them! Tie them up!"

The alacrity one would have expected in the haiduks at the time of the attack on the Bailiff had not been forthcoming: this was accounted for probably by the disinclination to join their master as a No. 2 target, and also because of the presence upon the truck of some bulky but invisible bodyguard, sensed by them. Now, with the two would-be assassins to tear to pieces, they were displaying unexceptionable zeal.

Pullman and Satters moved out into the crowd–Satters elated at the thought of getting in a cosh or two. He did in fact vanish for a few minutes into the confusion, then he returned, very pleased, with a police helmet.

"Oh what a beauty!" Pullman approved.

This was one rather like the long superseded *Pickelhauber* of the Prussian infantry. It was a light-weight, light-coloured head-gear, unlike its original, but the spike was there, and in general the shape was the same.

Pullman took possession of this trophy, Satters mumbling protests; he was examining it when he heard the Bailiff's voice, "Pullman, Pullman, keep that! We will find out where he obtained it!"

He still stood, shouting orders. But a doctor was standing beside him with a hypodermic syringe in his hand, while an orderly was stripping off from his shoulder, which was red with blood, the last obstructing strip of shirt.

"I will look after it, yes," Pullman shouted back.

"No more speaking today!" the Bailiff screamed, pointing to his shoulder.

"Bad luck, sir!" roared Pullman.

Catching sight of a familiar goatish countenance–all theeth, nay all gums showing, the eyebrows arched extraordinarily high, the forehead thereby compressed into a half-inch wide of furrowed flesh, immediately afterwards he heard the words that went with the face.

"Very bad luck! I wish I had the pluck of the old Bailey. He is a good old sort, what!"

There are some sights which are worse than smells, to some people. Pullman was one of these in that this ingratiating face made him feel sick.

All the troops in the rear of the Bailiff's truck were rushing to the right. Pullman saw Hyperideans, halfway down the Piazza, streaming into the long arcade. But now two Gladiators, who had been detailed for this purpose, raised their rifles and fired at the oncoming stream. The Hyperideans attacking along the colonnade panicked, and seemed to melt away. There was now a clear space behind the Bailiff's truck, an the two near assassins sprawled out hatless, in the middle of it.

Inquisitive about the outcome of these events, yet caution told Pullman that the Bailiff wounded, and in a desperate situation, would in some mysterious way, act; he and his follower ought not to find themselves too near the centre in the final stages of this imminent uproar.

"It is time for us to push off", he told Satters. "A match is about to be applied to a keg of gunpowder. We will move aside a little. Come."

They hurried towards the nearest way out of the Piazza, at the side opposite to the Hyperideans' attack. They met a police party of about twelve men, come to investigate, no doubt, the two members of their force or the two men dressed in police uniform responsible for the shooting. A number of stretchers were also arriving. They met, as well, a special Gladiator body-guard, hurrying to the rear to surround their wounded Chief.

"They ought to get him out quick," thought Pullman.

Suddenly the entire city was bathed in an orange light, which appeared to centre in a smoke-cloud beyond Tenth Piazza near the ramparts.

The Bailiff had shot back into his curtained rostrum. Picking up a tin megaphone, in a tone of hysterical exultation, he shouted, "Die the man–die the man–die the man." He paused, and then repeated, at the top of his voice, "Die the man– die the man–die the man."

The doctor sprang in beside his puppet-master and seized him by the arm. There was a very heated colloquy, in the middle of which the wounded Bailiff once more snatched up the magaphone, and in an almost despairing voice shrieked, "Die–die–die–the Man!"

Practically unnoticed at first in the dazzling orange light, a small black cloud began to grow in the air around the figure of Hyperides, until, with great speed, it entirely enveloped him. First, the figure of the Leader disappeared; and then, with a miraculous rapidity, the dark black column of smoke surrounding him thickened to a distance of about twelve feet in all directions.

The Gay Monster, in his dark-curtained puppet-stage, danced like a lunatic, shooting out his arms and tearing off his beard. The followers of Hyperides with a roar rushed towards the black pall of smoke within which their Master was now invisible. Then suddenly the black smoke parted, exactly like two long black curtains being pulled aside. Within, and now visible to all, was the figure of Hyperides, his beard sheared off below the chin, an enormous nail driven through his throat, behind entering the thick board against which he had stood; on his head was stuck a white pointed hat tied beneath his chin. FOOL was painted on it.

Michael Devlin, with great presence of mind, took this opportunity of impressing himself on the consciousness of the crowd as the necessary successor to the stricken leader. People were milling around the built-up rostrum from which Hyperides had always spoken; but Devlin propped himself up upon a baulk of timber which had been the basis for this structure, and started an inflammatory harangue.

"How much will you stand for, Hyperideans? What, will you take from that old bag of guts over there–who is dancing, dancing, can't you see? Having first murdered your master, as he has slain so many other poor people in this city, he now exults–murdered him by his filthy magic!–He is performing a dance of death, a jig of dirty triumph. Watch the little beast flinging himself about–insulting you! Are you going to demand

237

an eye for an eye, a tooth for a tooth–eh? I think you are. I know I am. I will drag the heart out of his body. I will nail it with my own hands upon the door of his so-called palace. Have you a nail? Have you a hammer? Give them to me. Come–I will lead you. We will drag that laughing puppet out of his curtained box–we will stamp the life out of him here and now. We will blacken this Piazza with his stinking blood!"

His words were half lost among the howls of rage of the Hyperideans. Then came the rush, like an avalanche, of nearly thirty thousand men; to avenge their leader, to hammer a nail in the throat of the Bailiff, and burn him on a bonfire, which they said they would collect.

Would his bodyguard give way? No. Battalion "A" and, at its side, the trusty "B", had been for some time feverishly anticipating zero-hour, when at last, at least *once* in their life, they would be doing what it is the function of a soldier to do–*shoot*. They were beside themselves, most of these young week-end soldiers; their faces were pale and set, they were about to go into action; they waited for the words *Die the man,* which was the watchword. And already the half-hour was past. Then it came, it rang out above them with hysterical intensity. They lost all trace of sanity, they were just a crowd of boys with loaded rifles, they would have fired at anything no matter what, but what they *must* do was to *shoot*. And, if they were blinded with excitement, so were their young officers, who yelled "*Fire!*"

The roaring crowd in front of them was arrested by the line of pointing rifles; then came the flash from the rifles, the roar of the discharges. No one had dreamt of this. A second volley crashed into the thick crowd, until the front ranks had dozens of men staggering about, and dozens too who were writhing on the ground, and as many more who were as still as dolls, who were the dead and dying. Horror! the Hyperidean crowd only wished to escape, and they clutched at one another to get away; but ahead, these would-be soldiers were mad. A third volley tore into them; dozens who, a second before, had been as amazed as they were terrified, were corpses, lying where until just now their feet had been. But the rows of pale faces were looking through their sights at them, taking aim, waiting for the order. How still they were!

"Back—get back!" barked hysterically a loud strong voice. They asked nothing better—but how could they get back? Thousands who had *not* got back were pressing on them. Some covered their eyes, some were crying.

With an astonishment almost equal to that of the crowd, the police, massed outside the arena, heard the volleys. Now they were rushing down the steps, and some had already engaged the Bailiff's men, and a section of Gladiators had turned their rifles on the forces of the police. Down the steps also were tumbling the stretcherbearers, and the first were now pushing into the crowd and searching for the wounded.

Picked men of his bodyguard, and the doctor, invading his stage, were, with anxious faces, exhorting the Bailiff to get away. He was standing without speaking, feasting his eyes upon the body of Hyperides still nailed to the board, smiling, as if musing, and these intruders found it very difficult to gain his attention. But bullets began to fly, and then he saw the police, in force, preparing to attack his men. He bent over the parapet in front of him and called to a young officer a short distance below him.

"Form A and B in close formation, Captain. Get them off the field as quickly as you can. They must not stand here to meet the attack of forces so far superior. I am leaving—immediately."

Having issued these instructions the Bailiff charged out of his curtains, looked around him as if he were about to dive, muffled himself and seemed to spring forward, watched by the men who had come to procect him, and the doctor, standing in frowning surprise. But as he fell forward he also immediately disappeared—he seemed to fade into the ether. He was no longer there, and the men looked at one another with bewilderment until a sergeant made for the ladder, shouting, "Save yourselves, boys! Look slippy—get away any way you can."

Pullman stood dumbfounded at the extremity of the colonnade; for just as he and his round-eyed fag had been about to pass out of the Piazza the orange light had so magnificently illuminated the entire scene that he had stopped to gaze, and so had become the witness of the forming of the black cloud, and now, silent and terrified, he was the witness of its unfolding. As he saw in the distance he murdered figure of Hyperides, he remembered what they had overheard as they had passed the drill-hall in the Palace that morning. He remembered the stick of chocolate which was used instead of a nail. He remembered the barking of the Bailiff's revolver, and the violent insistence upon those strange supernatural creatures holding a nail straight and hammering it in where it was meant to go. And now—what was about to happen was revealed to him in the most extraordinary way. Before he heard the fire of the Gladiators, and saw the waving swords of the haiduks, he heard and saw just that. And there was the mad Bailiff, dancing on his six-foot-square stage, and his voice screaming out above the indescribable tumult, "Hyperides, Hyperides! You have lost your beard, Hyperides. What a little chin you have, brother. The little chemist might be back in his shop in Pontypridd, might he not! Who are you going to get now, oh Hyperideans, to be your leader!"

Next the shooting began. The orange light had faded out, and it seemed to grow quite dark, and to rain a little. Pullman put up the collar of his jacket, and as he was doing this a hot bullet smacked into Satters' calf, and there was a howl of angry protest at his side. Looking round, he found Satters sitting on the ground, dabbing his calf with his handkerchief.

"Let me have a look." Pullman knelt down in front of the whimpering Satters and examined the wound.

"It was as if I had been pole-axed, Pulley. I thought I was dead."

Rising, Pullman held out his hand. "Here," he said, "catch hold of this. That won't kill you. You must hobble away as quickly as you can. The first thing is to get away from this bloody place."

Satters, protesting lachrymosely, allowed himself to be dragged to his feet. Thanks to the haste exacted by Pullman, they covered the ground at a rapid pace. But one of two Gladiators in violent flight struck Pullman in the small of the back, and he was flung forward, dragging Satters down on top of him. Afterwards he considered this a most fortunate accident; several of the police infantry were potting at the Gladiators, and had he remained on his feet he would have stood an excellent chance of being hit. As it was, his head struck a jagged piece of stone so hard as to knock him out for the time being. He lay quite still; ambulance men who were hurrying along just above him supposed he had been shot. To the stretcher-bearers, who actually thought Pullman a "deader", as they called it, it did not matter very much, since, in Third City, any corpse which could be collected was destined for preservation, and was, in fact, not dead in the earthly sense. As a result he and Satters were collected, placed in an ambulance, and quickly transported to the Phanuel Hotel.

The next thing Pullman knew was that he was in bed, in a strange room, completely white; turning his head, he saw Satters in a bed at his side. Someone was moving at the other end of the room, beneath a blue light. But his head was aching so much, that he turned over and lay quite still. Then he slept.

It was a long time after that, he supposed, when he awoke. It was daylight, and he knew he was in a dormitory, apparently a hospital. There were several white figures moving about behind a screen; not far away he heard a sound reminiscent of a cock crowing, but doing so with unutterable despondency. It was the Bailiff.

Perhaps an hour later Satters and he were luxuriously fed. Upon the wall was a thunderous SILENCE. They smiled at one another, and Pullman winked. Satters had done justice to his food, he sighed and slept. The ambulance had deposited them at the Hotel, as they found later; from there they had been transferred across the road to the Clinic in the rear of the palace.

XXI

ALTHOUGH THE BULLET had passed through Satters'
healthy calf, he did not get over his wound so quickly as might
have been expected. For some weeks he limped, and while still
in Third City encouraged his injury because of the privileges
entailed. But Pullman was, in a few days, fully himself again.

During their stay in the summit of the palace, as the guests
of the Bailiff, he and his patron talked a great deal, mainly
on the subject of his future. The Bailiff was very surprised that
no steps had been taken against him so far. While downstairs
in the Clinic the nursing staff had the strictest orders to warn
the Bailiff of the appearance of any police officers; to wake
him up and assist him to the window. Wounded as he was, he
would not have hesitated to undertake a very long journey
through space, rather than to allow himself to be arrested. But
the days passed by uneventfully; the funeral procession of
Hyperides had been heard in the palace, as it moved slowly
along the main road, the slow rolling of drums echoing for a
long time for the invalid in his private rooftop study. As he
heard the drums he trembled. But the drums moved away,
the air was still once more, and the menacing knocking at the
front door in the courtyard downstairs did not materialise.
What were all these people doing about this sinister act of his?
What made it quite impossible that they would ignore it was
its *supernatural* character. The angelic masters of this place
attributed any resort to magic on the part of a human being to
Satanic complicity, and dealt with it with the limitless rigours
reserved for witchcraft in the Middle Ages.

The Bailiff warned Pullman that it was *quite certain* that
some very radical step would be taken. "They will not continue to allow me to live in the way I do here, after the occur-
rences in Tenth Piazza. My men have used firearms, many
citizens were casualties, the notorious Hyperides was publicly
executed, but in a very mysterious way, some of the police were
killed, when my men resisted arrest. I shall be tried for all

that. Why they are not acting I cannot imagine, but it is quite certain that they will do so."

To this Pullman listened sombrely. "And I, your Excellency, what will happen to me do you suppose? There is no likelihood that they will have overlooked my adherence to your cause, and the fact that I am at present living up here as your guest. What will happen to me?"

"My dear fellow, that is what I am talking to you about. Did you think that I was merely talking about myself?"

"No, sir." Pullman was deferential, though he wondered all the time what the devil he had been doing. He realised to the full what an unholy mess he had got himself into, implicating Satters, in, he told himself, the most heartless manner.

"Now, me dear boy. Your future! As you have said yourself, your destiny is implicated with mine. I regret it, but there it is. Now, Pullman, I have thought a great deal about this, during my enforced immobility, and there is only one solution. I will have to fly; the best thing you can do will be to fly with me."

Pullman looked at him without saying anything. He was quite expressionless. The Bailiff waited for some change in this blank pokert face. As no change occurred, he continued:

"If I thought that they would forgive you your association with me, I should not be saying this. I should allow you, my dear fellow" (very throatily) "to take whatever steps seemed best to you out of this difficulty. But . . . I do not believe that you have any choice. These unexpected circumstances have forced you into a position where the best course to take is to *continue* your association with me, miserable sinner though I am—to go where I go, to exit from this scene in my company. This is the wisest thing to do. You and your young friend, I and my particular secretary, will set out together on a journey I have often taken: you will hardly know that you are travelling in the magical method of transit we shall employ; you will wake up in another supernatural abode, which in some ways is similar to this. I shall look after you. Whereas, if you stop where your are, Heaven knows what they may not do to you."

Pullman continued to gaze at this horrible, gay, attractive, disgustingly-shaped little being, not even as if he were asking himself any questions, but just scrutinising his unlovely fate, which was explaining to him how there was no escape from it.

"You stare at me, my dear fellow, as if I were a figure in a book with which it was necessary to familiarise yourself." The Bailiff crowed, a quiet little querulous crow. "Let me proceed, then, as if you had conceded my plan was the best possible one."

The Bailiff appeared to be taking a breather, and making up his mind what to say next. His cue seemed to present itself almost at once; speaking easily, he recommenced—"Is there anything you would like to ask me, Pullman? Is there any kind of elucidation which would help you to come to a decision? No matter what it is—unburden yourself, my dear fellow."

Without any preliminary movement, Pullman began speaking. "Of course, I am sure you understand what I would like to know. You suggest that we should come with you . . . somewhere. First of all, sir, I am rather interested in the method of transport which you propose. If I am right, we are flying through space to another star. Humanly, that would be impossible. Nothing of the kind has been achieved by men; they cannot even fly to the moon. Then, where is your aeroplane?"

The Bailiff watched Pullman narrowly and with a humorous air; he was quite silent. Now he heaved a sigh and spoke.

"Pullman. I am not a human being. Probably you have gathered that."

"Yes, sir."

"I enjoy certain advantages . . . certain powers, in contrast with human beings. One of these is a terrific skill. I can make myself invisible; and then, I can throw myself off a rock and fly through the air like a . . . like a . . . oh, a little bird. I have organs and aptitudes which make it possible for me to make great journeys just as easily as a man can walk a couple of miles to see a friend . . . There. I need reveal no more."

"Forgive me, sir, you have told me what *you* are capable of doing; but what about me?"

"I have a drug, Pullman, which I can administer to you, which will enable you, in my company, and in close magnetic contact, to make the same journeys as myself—through the ether, to any destination."

Pullman sat quite motionless, looking at the ground, for

about five minutes. Then he lifted his head. The Bailiff was still looking at him, quizzically, patiently.

"I don't see anything for it, sir. I accept what you tell me as accurate. If it isn't, *tant pis.*"

"You are a man endowed with logical faculties–which, experience tells me, is a gift not found very often in men."

"That is a kind of certificate," Pullman said. "Now, sir, will you proceed with your story. What is this place like to which you would take us?"

"Matapolis? Well, first of all, Matapolis is the place where I was born. Let me be frank; Third City, in which we find ourselves at present, it preferable to Matapolis–the city to which I propose to take you: this is much more tidy, and the goods in the shops are far superior on the whole. Third City is magnificently built . . . I was responsible for a great deal of those architectural splendours you admire, such as Tenth Piazza."

"Oh."

"Yes. Yes, it is my work."

"Congratulations," Pullman said.

"Ah yes. This city is in some ways the finest I know. I can claim nothing of this sort for my native place. No. But there is an old-world charm about that sprawling city, half of it is from four to five hundred years old, much of it far older than that. Do not believe anything you may have heard about Matapolis. It is not, I assure you, inhabited by devils, as the people of Third City are inclined to believe. What our friends here, in this city, describe as 'Hell-boys' are no more demons than is a citizen of Alexandria or Istanbul."

At this point Pullman interrupted–when he had heard the Bailiff speak of the "Hell-boys" he had stiffened. Now he said, "Your Excellency, is that old-world city you are describing by any chance Hell?"

"There is no such place as Hell," was the Bailiff's answer. "It is, believe me, a myth. It is very curious how this 'Hell' story came into being. But do let me assure you, Pullman, there is no such place. Hell is a stupid superstition."

Pullman looked very coldly at his patron. "Very well," he said. "We will think of your birthplace as a jolly little seaside town, very quaint and picturesque."

"No, Pullman, it is not like Torquay—I do not say that. Let me think now; actually it is like a very miniature bit of Birmingham painted over to resemble Le Havre. The inhabitants I should describe as a rather handsome people; like myself they have squarish noses, are a little swarthy, of medium build. That kind of squareness about the nose is what, I suppose, identifies them most; every collection of people has its own physical hall-mark." He fixed Pullman with his eye, but could see no insulting glint in the Englishman's orb, and, after a pause, continued. "My own father was a Portuguese empire builder. The Holy Synod suspected him of 'deviationism', as today it would be called. The wretched man, upon his death, was packed off to Hell; there he was closely questioned; his answers were checked by questioning other Portuguese prisoners, and in the end he was declared to be a by no means evil man—merely a victim of malignity on Earth."

"So," Pullman remarked, almost under his breath. "So the city of your birth *is* Hell."

"But what makes you say that, my young friend?"

"That is what you called it yourself, sir." Pullman did not smile. "You referred to it just now as Hell, as the place to which the wicked go when they die."

"Pest," explained the Bailiff. "Pool-man! If you could only see the street in which I live, which is rather like Fitzjohn's Avenue, climbing up the side of a hill—only white, my dear follow, and the houses look rather like cinema palaces."

"I see."

"Yes. Buit if you are determined to think of this rather attractive little residential city as an Inferno . . . well, my dear Pullman, I have no wish to interfere with your perverse imagination. But let me continue to outline my origins. My Portuguese parent remained in this nearby city . . ."

"Nearby what?" Pullman asked.

"Nearby . . . oh, where he first landed; he married a lady of the place—of this homely little city (hence, my dear fellow, the distinct squareness of my nose); he followed the calling of most of the inhabitants . . ."

"Which is what?" Pullman interrupted.

"Oh, nothing much, psychology mostly . . ."

"A city given up to psychology? That is exceptionally unusual, is it not?"

"I have always rather felt that myself, Pullman. But he prospered. The father of the lady of his choice was an official. I was born in a very good position ... very good; we lived in the select quarter of the town—much more select than Fitzjohn's Avenue. I distinguished myself at the University, and when I came to this city I found I knew a great deal more than most of my contemporaries here."

"Are both your parents alive, sir?"

"*Both* my parents? Heavens, no! How long do you think we live? *One* still rots, as you might say, alive."

"I beg your pardon, sir."

"Not at all, my dear chap. Let me continue. Third City is unquestionably a low-brow spot. Terribly philistine! But Matapolis is an intellectual centre compared to this! In the first place conditions there are very different, it is more like life on Earth. You see time exists there. It does not move with the accelerated tempo of time on Earth, but it *moves*. I am older today than I was three hundred years ago."

Pullman sat gazing at the floor. Then he looked up, and said, "So there is Time, and there are Women. Radical differences. The noses mostly stick out a little, and form a square look rather like a match-box. They live by Psychology. Psychology. They smell slightly."

The Bailiff sat up. "I say, Pullman, do I smell slightly?"

"No, sir, quite a lot." Pullman smiled broadly ...

"I do not see how I can retain you in my service." But the Bailiff smiled as amiably as Pullman, for he saw that he had won the day. "If I really offend your nostrils, Pullman, you should buy a little vial of eau-de-Cologne. Every druggist in Matapolis stocks them."

"Thank you, sir, for the tip." Both smiled again.

"If you agree, Pullman, I will spirit you away—should this great emergency suddenly be there, I will take you under my arm and fly away with you (guaranteeing safe travel and a great welcome at the other end). If you find this prospect frightening, or simply unattractive, and decide to stop where you are, I do not disguise the fact that I shall be extremely disappointed. I have taken a fancy to you, my dear fellow.

However, if you prefer to do this, you will be frowned upon I am afraid by the authorities here; also, Pullman, if where I was born is Hell, this is not Heaven. It was founded as a kind of halfway house to Heaven; but is has long ago turned out to be something else. Its only advantage over the place to which I propose to take you is architectural. What perhaps ... is more compelling than anything else is the practical certainty of an all-out attack on Third City, and Lucifer has some very unpleasant weapons, in addition to thousands of warrior giants as compared with the Padishah's hundred."

At this point Pullman held up his hand. Then he spoke as follows. "Thank you, sir. I am much flattered by the unaccountable interest which you take in me. But it is not that. I will take a chance–I have decided upon that. I will fly with you, sir, to this little beauty-spot, if necessity arises."

"As it will, as it will."

The Bailiff had played with the idea that some further approach should be made to the Padishah. Meanwhile, he was inclined to assume that his message had reached the ears of that dignitary; that was the only reasonable explanation of no police action materializing. Either the Governor was taking counsel with others, or privately attempting to reach a decision regarding the proposal emanating from the Bailiff. Hence the remarkable patience displayed by the Bailiff, expecting hourly a communication from the Governor, charging him to begin negotiations with Lucifer, who would call off the storms, and become once more the peaceful neighbour he had always been so far. There had been almost daily storms of some severity; but up to now they had failed to get any results.

When Pullman next found himself alone with Satters he informed him of his conversation with the Bailiff. He had decided, if the worst came to the worst, to do a vanishing trick under the wing of their great patron. He would do nothing to persuade Satters, against his will, to accompany him. "You must think it over, and do what you think best. It is, no doubt, very dangerous; but there is a great deal of danger in stopping behind. Still, there it is; it might be best for you to stop in Third City, and find friends of your own age."

Satters was indignant. "Me stop here, Pulley! You want to get rid of me! You are very unkind, Pulley, but you don't shake me off so easily." Satters became very red. „I'll speak to the old Bailey: I'll jolly well tell him what you're doing..."

"Don't be absurd." Pullman laughed. "All I mean is that you would be quite safe here. They would not bother you. You are so young. Because you are so young and ... oh, stupid you know, they would say that you could not have known what you were doing."

"Rot."

Pullman shrugged his shoulders. "Well, of course, I would like to have you. But you must not listen to that ..."

"Rot, Pulley! Balls, Pulley! I'm coming with you, nothing would stop me from coming along. When are we starting? Oh, Pulley, I do think it's sooper! Shall I go just like this?" He pointed excitedly to his clothes.

"I should think so," Pullman said. "I shall go like *this*."

XXII

THE BAILIFF was administering the "Five O'Clock" to his two English guests, something resembling toasted scones as well as the Chinese herb. The Venus had just said softly, "I beg your pardon." after having made a most unseemly noise. Satters, the hysterical schoolboy, was convulsed at an obscence remark of the Bailiff: during the few days of his stay in the Palace he had learned to appreciate the foul-mouthed monster, and could listen to the Venus for hours on end–her act seemed funnier every time Pullman had begun his second scone, with puerile relish. The lift door flew open, and the scarlet messenger sprang into the room.

"Your Excellency, the palace is surrounded by armed police," he shouted.

"It has come!" said the Bailiff.

Pullman rose, followed by Satters. He moved towards the lift, Satters at his heels.

"Stop!" The Bailiff stood up. "Pullman, it is too late. You cannot go to the hotel. The police would arrest you. Sit down."

His two visitors returned to their seats. Meanwhile he picked up the telephone and howled into it. He was issuing instructions for the palace to be barricaded, and "defended to the last man". Also, his confidential secretary was ordered to come up at once, bringing with him "you know what".

Next, the Bailiff bounced over to the window. "Pullman," he shrieked. "They are there . . . they are all around us. With fixed bayonets." He was glaring through the window, both palms pressed upon the window-panes, his feet moving restlessly about as though he were dancing. "There is a space in front . . . there are no police. What are they playing at . . . what is their game? Why are there no police out there in front?"

Pullman, with exaggerated composure, had finished his tea, and then strolled over to stand beside the Bailiff, looking with a studied indifference into the street. He noted the lines of police, extending as far forward as the front of the Phanuel Hotel. A police tank had been stationed near the hotel entrance. Beyond the hotel he saw more police, apparently on guard around the hotel, their arms held in readiness. As he was looking out, the Bailiff rushed back to the table, opening and shutting drawers violently, squeaking as he did so. But Pullman noticed that it was suddenly growing dark; he turned back and rejoined the other two.

"Is there anything you especially value, my dear fellow?" the Bailiff snapped urgently.

"No, I don't think so." Pullman's composure, in developing, had assumed an airy offensiveness. "Have you anything you want to take with you, Satters? if so, be quick, fetch it from the bedroom. Oh, and bring me some handkerchiefs."

"Hankies, Pulley? the white ones, or the blue and grey?"

"About one dozen white ones, also a shirt . . . it is bluish, Satters! Stuff them into the small leather suitcase along with anything you need."

Satters shot into the bedroom. Pullman caught the Bailiff's eye, and it looked startled.

"Why is it getting so dark, Pullman?" the Bailiff asked almost hysterically, as if, for some reason, Pullman knew all about it.

Pullman shrugged, looking at the window. "It does seem unnecessarily dark." While his eyes remained fixed in the same direction he saw the whole area of the window blotted out, from the outside, by something blue and green. It had curved lines all over it; it looked like glass . . . it appeared to be lighted from within. Then he saw that it was alive.

"Somebody's eye," he remarked. "The eye is kind of large, is it not?" The Bailiff stood as if transfixed, glaring at Pullman.

"Someone," said Pullman, "of enormous size is looking into this room."

With a piercing squeal, the Bailiff rushed across the room to a door which stood beside the musical Venus. He wrenched the door open, and the room, which lay behind the door, was visible. At the same moment, the lift door opened, and his secretary appeared, holding a large attaché-case under his arm, and passed into the farther room.

"Pullman, over here, quick!"

The room became almost entirely dark, as something began forcing its way in. The two French windows had flown open: something was entering the room.

251

Pullman hastened to join the Bailiff. Satters' voice could be heard inquiring whether Pullman would like to take his snuff-box.

"Tell him, Pullman, to come round the other way," the Bailiff exhorted. "Tell him not to come in here, but to join us at the back . . . at *the back*."

What had entered the room was now opposite to them, slowly moving forward. It reached almost from ceiling to floor, and was covered with strong semi-circular liness. It was almost touching Pullman, who drew back into the room beyond the door, where the Bailiff and his secretary were standing. He caught a glimpse of Satters in the farther doorway, who apparently was truck dumb at what he 'saw—at the enormous "something" drawing near to him in the darkness.

"Hallo, Satters. I say, join us round at the back. Go the other way—don't attempt to come in here. Back! Back, you idiot!"

It was perfectly obvious what the "something" was which had invaded the Bailiff's study. It was a finger, but of such vast proportions that it must have belonged to the eye which had looked in at the window. The horny ridge of the nail appeared along the top edge of the body of the finger, which had now all but filled the room. It was quite impossible for the owner of the finger—who was undoubtedly the possessor of the large blue eye—to do more than stick a quarter of one of his nailed digits into the room. But suddenly he began to waggle it about, and a huge wall of exaggerated flesh, with great abruptness, banged Pullman in the face, and threw him back into the room beyond.

The elastic pinkish mass bulged through the door. Recovered, Pullman drew his revolver and, with an oath, fired into it. It vanished with surprising speed.

"You should not have done that, Pullman. Silly boy!" the Bailiff scolded. "He will pull the house down, you see if he doesn't. If he gives it a good kick . . . if he gives it a really good kick it will be like an earthquake. We shall be picked up among the rubble, shan't we?" The Bailiff looked half-frightened, half-amused.

"Who the hell is he?" inquired Pullman with exasperation. "Is it the Governor?"

"No, Pullman, it is one of his angels. He has come round to

help the police. I wish you had put a bullet in his great blue eye, Pullman. At least he would have had a one-eyed bodyguard in that case!"

"Yes, it's a pity. Hallo, Satters." Pullman saw the terrified face of his young friend, standing there, the little suitcase hanging in his right hand.

"I was nearly caught, Pulley. I didn't understand what was moving about in the room. I thought at first it was an *animal* . . . I was scared, believe me, I could hardly move; I felt as if I was screwed to the floor. I was shaking all over."

"Gentlemen, gentlemen, you must stop chatting. Come and say ta-ta to this remarkable city–for we have no time to lose, gent-le-men . . . le-men. It's no more fun for me than it is for you. I am leaving this palace that I built," the Bailiff dropped a tear, and it seemed at first that he was going to have an emotional breakdown. But he lifted his head, and shook it. He crowed, and then he continued. *"Tempi passati,* ah Pullman, Pullman! You understand don't you, what the old fighter and builder feels?" The palace shook. "Ah, you brigand! Kicking an old man's palace! Well, come along, we must begin our magical flight."

The palace shook more violently than before. He drew from his pocket two bottles.

"This is very precious." The Bailiff held up his forefinger. "Without this you cannot fly. Hold this in your hand, gentlemen. Hold it tight!"

He handed one bottle to Pullman, the other to his secretary. "Here," he said, "your young charge must drink that."

They were almost shaken off their feet by a mighty blow the palace had received. "Here, quick." The Bailiff, nervously clutching Pullman, dragged him towards the open window, clasping him in his arms which were surprisingly long for so short a man, and felt like a vice as they closed around the half-resisting British author.

"Now, Pullman, drink what is in that bottle."

"Well, here goes," said Pullman. "It is a case of 'TAKE ME' isn't it?"

It was instantaneous–had Pullman been flung into a furnace the reaction would have been immediate and blindingly similar. There was one second exactly as the liquid in the bottle sank into his body, during which the Bailiff's face became for him a vivid red. Then came utter blackness, as he felt himself hurled through the air. Pullman was getting smaller and smaller as they hurtled with increasing speed. He became just a metaphysical appendage of this great pasha in flight from his shaking palace.